the next
chapter of
luke

jenny o'connell

Praise for
JENNY O'CONNELL

PLAN B

"Plan B, Jenny O'Connell's first young adult novel, is sure to be a hit. . . . It's full of believable characters, interesting plot twists, and great writing." Rating: 10
—Teen Book Review.com

"Plan B gets an 'A' for a clever plot... [Vanessa is] a vulnerable and sympathetic character."
—Curled Up Kids.com

THE BOOK OF LUKE

"This fresh, honest novel is full of amazing characters and excellent writing. Jenny O'Connell is a smart, talented author; I'm really looking forward to seeing what she writes next! This is contemporary fiction at its best; readers will not be disappointed." Rating: 5 Stars
—Teens Read Too.com

"[A] fun and charming book that's worth reading."
—Young Adult Books Central.com

"Emily . . . is smart, funny, easy to relate to, and so is her narration."
—The Yayas, Wordpress.com

Visit Jenny at www.jennyoconnell.com

ISBN-13: 9781717866295

Books by Jenny O'Connell

Plan B
The Book of Luke
The Next Chapter of Luke
When We Were Summer – an Island Summer novel
The Summer Between You and Me – an Island Summer novel
If By Chance
All I Needed to Know About Being a Girl I Learned from Judy Blume (as Jennifer O'Connell)
Bachelorette #1 (as Jennifer O'Connell)
Dress Rehearsal (as Jennifer O'Connell)
Off the Record (as Jennifer O'Connell)
Insider Dating (as Jennifer O'Connell)

For JP, because some stories aren't meant to end.

acknowledgments

There would be no continuation of the story of Emily and Luke without all the readers who emailed me asking what happens next. I had never planned to write a sequel, and then one day I just knew their story went on. And it was all because of you. So, thank you, for your patience and persistence. I hope it was worth the wait.

chapter one

Two months ago, the Heywood Academy gym fell silent as the entire school witnessed a brown spiral notebook turn my life upside down. Back then, the only sound I could hear was the hammering of my heart as it tried to pound its way through my chest, pummeling me from inside as if trying to beat me to the door of the gym and escape.

Today, the polished wood floor once again reflected the light beaming through the gym windows, the banners hanging from the metal rafters still announced our league championships, and the bleachers were extended accordion-style to handle the overflow of people. But there was one big difference.

Today we were graduating.

As the Heywood Academy senior class erupted into a chorus of cheers, I could hear two people above everyone else, their voices so familiar I would recognize them no matter how many people clapped and whistled and celebrated our big day at the top of their lungs. We were seated alphabetically, which put me first in our row and on the aisle, but there was nothing that could keep me from reaching over to hug both of them, not even the eight seniors whose last names, and legs, came between us.

"We made it!" Josie yelled, and Lucy made a loud whooping sound in my ear.

Lucy pumped her fist in the air in triumph, and the three of us fell together into a huddle of caps and gowns. I squeezed my eyes shut and let my face get buried in Josie's hair, my arms tangled with the billowing sleeves of Lucy's gown.

"I can't believe it's over!" Lucy shouted as our headmaster's voice reverberated off the cavernous ceiling and directed us outside for our class photo.

The band stood to play the recessional, signaling it was time for our class to line up and exit down the center aisle, led by yours truly—the only senior whose last named started with an A, and the only student in Heywood history to turn the senior class time capsule into the biggest mistake in her life—Emily Abbott.

We'd finally made it. High school was over, my hellish semester was a distant memory (well, if not exactly distant, at least behind me). And, even if there was a time after my public humiliation when it looked as if I'd ruined everything, I still had my best friends. Maybe that's why I paused before leading my class out of the gym, why I let my eyes fall on the details of the place where I once felt completely alone. I wanted to imprint this moment in my brain—the crisp, clean smell of the recently polished wood floor filling up my lungs, the sounds of horns and drums and stringed instruments mingling together as they waited for me to step into the aisle and take one last walk out of high school, and the feeling of being hugged tight by my two best friends who weren't quite ready to let me go. This was how it felt to be at the exact point of pivoting from a *before* to an *after*, from the end of something familiar to the beginning of unknowns. From having best friends for years to being on the brink of starting over.

Although we wouldn't have to really say good-bye until college scattered us in different directions in a few months, there was a part of me that knew it would never be the same after this, even if we were going to spend the summer together on Cape Cod. Even if we kept telling each other that nothing would change no matter how far apart we were.

The irony of that wasn't lost on me, even though I never actually said it out loud to Josie and Lucy. We'd spent months of our senior year trying to show that people could change, to prove it by having me turn the worst guy in school into the type of guy any girl would want to have as a boyfriend. And now here I was wanting everything and everyone to stay exactly the same.

"Come on, it's time to go." I felt an elbow in my side as someone between *A* and *H* reminded us that our graduation ceremony wasn't quite over yet. We still had one more walk down the makeshift aisle, and then we were free.

I reluctantly pulled away from Lucy and Josie and glanced down the row behind us on my way to reclaim my spot in front of the first folding chair on the aisle. There was one more person, near the end of the alphabet, who I needed to see in that moment. One more person I wanted to glimpse before turning my back on our senior year.

Luke sat two rows behind me and practically at the opposite end of the aisle. I'd kept my eyes straight ahead as we listened to our headmaster's words of wisdom, the valedictorian speech that just six months ago I'd thought would be mine, and the various awarding of accolades for members of our class. We'd practiced our graduation ceremony twice before the big day, so the fact that I couldn't see Luke wasn't a surprise to me, but I still wished I could have them together in my sight one last time—my best friends and my boyfriend.

"Let's go!" Ricky Barnett was waving for me to take my place at the head of our row.

I hesitated, glancing past the jumble of caps and gowns once more before I had to turn around. And then I saw him, and the cheering almost seemed to dim as we silently recognized one another with a smile, his eyes steady on mine even as our classmates celebrated around us, pushing us in different directions.

And then, like that, he was gone, black caps and gowns tumbling between us like curtains closing a performance.

When the band hit the note I'd been instructed to listen for, I led the line of seniors out of the gym. I passed the applause of my parents and TJ, who just nodded at me as I passed by, an acknowledgment that while I may have graduated, he wasn't as grateful for my diploma as he was the fact that he'd no longer have to share the bathroom with me.

I nodded back, and TJ actually cracked a smile. I guess even my brother wasn't completely immune to the pomp and circumstance of a big day. Either that or he was laughing at how I looked with a square of cardboard bobby pinned to my head.

As the person leading the recessional, it was my job to take the snaking line of Heywood Academy seniors out to the front lawn, where our parents and family members would meet us. While I knew my parents would want to hug me and ooze lovely sentiments about how proud they were, all I really wanted to do was find a way to sneak away and meet Luke, just like we'd planned.

But before I could even find Luke in the crowd, our families descended upon us, my mom leading the pack with open arms, my dad still fiddling with the buttons on his new digital camera. TJ lagged far enough behind to demonstrate he wasn't enjoying the confines of his navy-blue blazer and tie.

Even as the throng of ecstatic well-wishers filled the manicured lawn, and while my dad endlessly instructed me to smile into his camera lens, I searched for the one person I wasn't able to find among the bodies.

"Look over here," my dad coached me, as my eyes darted around in search of Luke.

Over the past six months, I'd memorized everything about Luke—the way his hair curled up around his collar, how it reminded me of the swirls of steamed milk the Starbucks baristas created on the surface of a latte, and the perfectly effortless pale highlights against the mop of hair that always seemed to be in need of a cut. I loved the dimple at the base of his left earlobe, so small you wouldn't even notice it if you didn't know to look, and how it created a shape exactly like an upside down heart. I thought I'd recognize Luke in the sea of black caps and yellow tassels, only I couldn't find him as he blended in with the rest of my class.

My father continued to insist on capturing this proud moment in a series of photographs that required my mom, TJ, and me to stand in twelve different positions while he learned how to use the new camera purchased specifically for my graduation. I thought digital cameras were supposed to be easy, and that there was nothing wrong with the camera on his phone, but apparently the hyped-up model my dad selected had so many buttons and dials he practically had the camera in one hand and the instruction manual in the other at all times. For a second, I considered trying to find Josie and asking her to help my dad. Even though Josie had been old-school about her photography, insisting on developing prints in the dark room at school or the one her dad built in their house, she'd decided that from graduation on it was all digital all the time. Leaving her dark room behind when she left for college was part of the reason, the other was that she'd asked for a crazy professional digital camera for graduation. I had no idea what a 70-200 f/2.8 zoom lens with ultrasonic focus and image stabilization could do, but apparently it was going to make Josie an even better photographer, and she was already pretty amazing.

I raised myself onto my tiptoes and tried to catch a glimpse of Josie in the crowd.

"I think I've got it this time," my dad insisted, as his camera let out a series of rapid clicking noises. I assumed that meant he'd just digitally recorded me frowning at a rate of sixty frames per minute.

One of them had to be half okay, right?

"I'll be right back," I finally told my parents, and ducked into the swarm of shimmery black gowns and out of my mom's grasp as she reached for my sleeve in an attempt to hold me in place.

I politely excused myself through the buzzing crowd of congratulations and selfies, and made my way toward the side of the building, the noise fading as I turned the corner and saw him in the courtyard. Luke was there, waiting for me under the apple tree beside the cafeteria doors, just as he'd promised. His head was down as he stared at the diploma in his hands, the tassel from his graduation cap dangling beside his face while he read the calligraphy that formally declared the end of our time at Heywood.

He didn't notice me coming toward him, and so I stopped walking, letting the moment steep in my mind until it was saturated with this memory and impossible to forget. I watched as he ran his finger inside the collar of his shirt, loosening the tie that all graduating guys were required to wear under their gowns. I knew his hands so well by now, was familiar with the soft pillows of skin at the base of each finger, which surprised me the first time he reached for my hand and I'd been expecting to find oval calluses where they rubbed against the metal shaft of his lacrosse. I knew that he cracked his knuckles when he was nervous, and that he didn't believe the old wives' tale that it would make his knuckles grow bigger. Without even trying, my hand always naturally found his, as if our fingertips were magnets that required the other's to complete some law of science. Somehow, over the past months, Luke had become stitched into my life, a thread that seemed to hold all of me together and kept me from unraveling.

I'd fallen in love with him. He knew that. My friends and family knew it, too. But at that instant, watching Luke alone as he waited for me, the sensation that surged through me with the urgency of an electrical current was new and unsettling. Because suddenly I realized that I didn't just love Luke. I needed him.

Luke looked up and noticed me. "So, do you feel any different?" he asked, letting his hand with the diploma drop to his side.

"Why, do you?" I asked, walking toward him.

"Not really, it's just a diploma," he reminded me, and I realized he was talking about graduating, not about us.

"It does make it official, though. As do the four hundred pictures my dad took. I think my retinas are permanently scarred from repeated flash exposure." I leaned in close so he could get a good look. "Can you tell I'm still seeing stars?"

Luke bent down a few inches until we were eye to eye, and we stayed like that for a long minute, our noses practically touching while we gazed silently at one another as if it was just the two of us outside the cafeteria like any other school day, or like the beginning, when it was always just the two of us trying to figure each other out.

The sound of our headmaster calling our class together for an official photograph broke the spell and reminded me that it wasn't just the two of us; it was our entire graduating class and at least two hundred of their closest friends and family nearby.

I pulled away. "This is ridiculous. Enough with the pictures already."

"Come on, one day when we're too old to remember this, we'll look back and be thankful we have a picture of all the people whose names we can't recall."

Luke managed to make me laugh despite myself. "I think I'm all smiled out."

"One more won't kill you," Luke insisted, and I knew he was right, although I suddenly had a new appreciation for those beauty pageant contestants who slicked Vaseline across their teeth to make constant smiling-on-demand more effortless. It sounded disgusting, granted, but effective. And effective was what I could have used right then.

"I'm fine with *one more* picture. Not hundreds," I replied, and then added. "Besides, there are some parts of this year I'd rather *not* remember."

Luke shook his head and a slow grin slid across his lips. "Not me. All I remember is good stuff."

I rolled my eyes, silently letting him know I thought he was crazy, but I couldn't help smiling back. I guess I did have one more smile in me.

Luke gave me a nudge. "Come on, just one more picture. Besides, we better go over there before we're stuck in the back behind Ian."

Ian O'Carroll was six foot six with another four inches added from a headful of bright red curls he grew out during every basketball season in a superstitious ritual that, this year, lasted even after Heywood won the league finals.

Luke reached for my hand and wove our fingers together as we walked toward the sound of our headmaster pleading for a group of rowdy seniors to stand on a grassy hill in some vaguely organized manner.

"Emily!" Josie was waving me over toward her. She pointed to the small open space to her left, where Lucy was doing her best to keep anyone else from slipping between them and into the slot they were saving for me.

Luke started to lead me toward the row where the rest of the seniors from the lacrosse team were standing.

This was always the problem. Choosing. Constantly.

Luke must have felt me hesitate because he stopped walking. "What's wrong?"

I looked over at my friends.

"Really? You're going to spend the entire summer with them. Can't they spare you for one picture?"

Whenever the subject of this summer came up, I knew better than to remind Luke that he had made plans to go away, too. We'd been going back and forth about our plans for weeks now trying to figure out how we were going to spend time together and still do everything else that was pulling us in a million different directions—my summer on Cape Cod with Josie and Lucy, my job at Josie's dad's ice cream stand, Luke's lacrosse camp, his job as a counselor, not to mention the inevitable end of the summer when we left for college. Graduation was one more reminder that deciding between time with Luke and time with Lucy and Josie was just the beginning of the end.

Shitty girlfriend or shitty friend? Lately, those seemed like my only choices.

"Come stand with us." I tugged Luke along behind me and led him through the crowd of parents and relatives, not once looking back at him for fear I'd see that, once again, I was letting someone down.

When we reached Lucy and Josie, they grabbed the sleeve of my graduation gown and pulled me beside them, leaving Luke to find his way behind us to a spot of his own, hovering over my right shoulder.

I didn't have to look back to know he wasn't happy. All I had to do was glance over at his friends, who were laughing at him and shaking their heads. I didn't have to hear what they were saying to know what they were thinking.

I'd won. Luke had chosen and he'd picked me. So why did I feel so bad? Probably because I'd chosen, too, and that's why I was standing between my two best friends. Sure, I wanted to be with them, to have the three of us together in the official school photo that would arrive in the mail over the summer, reminding me that, even after everything we'd gone through, we stuck together until the end. But that wasn't the only reason I hadn't followed Luke as he led me away from Lucy and Josie and toward his teammates. I still couldn't help but feel like I had to make up for what I'd done—to prove that Lucy and Josie hadn't made a mistake when they'd decided to forgive me.

I craned my neck and turned to look back at Luke. "You can go over," I told him. "It's fine."

Luke bit his bottom lip as he tried to figure out if I meant what I was saying or if this was a test to see what he'd do.

But I wasn't testing him. I really did want him to be with his friends, even if partly because I was still trying to repent for what I did to Luke, too. When I started writing the guide for our senior time capsule, I may have wanted to prove I wasn't the nice person everyone expected me to be, but now I almost felt like I had to prove that I *was*. Nice, *and* not psycho, which is what most of the school called me when they found out about the guide.

"Seriously." I grabbed for his hand and squeezed. "Go."

Luke paused for a moment and then squeezed back. "You sure?"

"Yes," I told him, and let go.

Luke bent down and kissed me, his lips lightly brushing against mine, like a feather landing before being blown in another direction. He slipped away before I could pull him in closer and keep his kiss from floating off.

"Okay, everyone, *smile!*" Our headmaster commanded, "One . . ."

As our headmaster counted down for the photographer, I looked over at Luke, hoping for one more glance, a sign, that even though the school year was over and a whole new chapter of our lives was about to begin, nothing would change between us.

I watched him, the broad shoulders of his graduation gown wedged against Owen and Joey as they huddled together for the final photo of our high school careers.

"Two!" I was still looking at Luke when the photographer and our headmaster shouted the number out in unison.

Only *two* wasn't the number worming through my head as I heard voices around me humming *cheese* through gritted teeth. It was the number seventy-eight.

Only seventy-eight more days before we left for college— I'd counted. Eleven weeks of summer. Just over two months. And then Luke and I would be 108 miles apart (I'd calculated that, too).

"Three!" A flash of light lit the space around our senior class as the photographer recorded our graduation day for the school archives.

In a few weeks, when our senior class photograph arrived in a cardboard envelope with a letter from our headmaster wishing me well in my future endeavors, I would remember that moment. How, unlike Lucy and Josie and the rest of my class, I wasn't looking into the camera and grinning on cue with the other ecstatic graduates. Instead I was looking over at Luke, hoping that he would look over at me, waiting for him to give me some sign that our story wouldn't end once summer was over.

Do you feel any different? Luke had asked me as we stood outside the cafeteria. Although I didn't answer him at the time, I knew that the answer was *yes*. Because there was only one word to describe the girl standing beside Lucy and Josie in our class photo. And that word was *scared*.

> **Long-Distance Relationship Tip #3:**
>
> When you're apart, do similar things, such as reading the
> same book, watching the same movies, or listening to
> the same music. This way you'll have something to talk
> about when you run out of things to talk about.
> Which, I guarantee, you will.

chapter two

"They want me in New York for three days before
heading to Chicago," my mom told us over breakfast
the next morning.

She was going on a three-week tour for her latest etiquette
book, and her publicist had been finalizing travel plans for
weeks, which meant that every morning TJ, my dad, and I
heard about flights and airports and local TV talk shows
that would feature Patricia Abbott, etiquette guru, in a two-
minute segment about the dos and don'ts of *webiquette*. That's
what my mom called it, transitioning from referring to her
latest book as the authority on "online behavior" after her
publisher suggested she come up with a catchier word that
would resonate with a population spilling their guts on social
media. In some perverse way, the whole reason she wrote
the book in the first place was because of Josie and Luke.
My best friend and my boyfriend. Who were boyfriend and
girlfriend for a little while until Luke broke up with her in
an email. At the time, my mom wasn't so appalled that Josie
and her boyfriend broke up, just that he would do it in such
an impolite manner.

It took my mother all of two days to pitch the idea for
a new book to her agent and publisher, and a mere three
weeks to fill 178 pages of dos and don'ts about emails, texts,
social media, and anything Internet related. She dedicated

three whole chapters to online dating, which, unbeknownst to me and my brother, meant that while I was finishing up my senior year in high school, my mother was trolling online dating sites, identifying everything that people were doing wrong in their quest for love. I'd had no idea that while I was chronicling my relationship with Luke in a notebook that would eventually result in my public humiliation at a school assembly, my mom was sitting at her laptop typing out her latest best seller.

I buttered my English muffin and barely listened as my mom rattled off the latest itinerary for her tour. New York, Chicago, Los Angeles, Houston, Dallas . . . they all started to run together until I heard her say something that did not end with a first-class seat assignment. My name.

"What about Emily?" I asked.

My mother folded her hands on the table, weaving her fingers together deliberately, as if there was a precise position they had to be in when she spoke. I knew this meant only one thing: my mom was about to suggest something that was not up for debate. "I think you should come with me."

TJ choked a little on his orange juice and tried to cover it up with a cough that sounded about as genuine as the words that came after it. "That sounds like a great idea, doesn't it, Emily?"

TJ loved to mess with people. And he was good at it. Way better than I was, probably because, as the second born child of Polite Patty, he managed to emerge without the expectation that he'd be anything but the opposite of me—mainly I'd be the good one and he'd be the other one.

"Go with you? Like on tour?" I asked, attempting to clarify what she meant (and hoping that I was wrong).

She sat back in her chair, pleased that I understood her brilliant plan. "Exactly."

I looked over at my dad, expecting some help. I mean, he'd practically just moved back in after staying behind in Chicago for four months while his family moved back to Boston. Four long, winter months without his little girl. Lonely stretches of days missing his only daughter who would be heading to college at the end of the summer. Leaving the nest. This was his chance to step up and declare that I should stay home with him instead of playing sidekick to Polite Patty for three weeks.

My dad pushed his coffee mug aside and swept the crumbs from his English muffin into the palm of his hand. "I think that's a great idea."

I should have known better. Since the morning I woke up and discovered that my dad was back at our breakfast table instead of 867 miles away in Chicago, there hasn't been so much as a disagreement about which brand of orange juice to buy (the pulp versus no pulp debate was one that used to occur on a daily basis in our house). I wasn't sure if my dad didn't want to rock the boat now that he was back, or he and my mom had come to some middle-aged meeting of the minds that resulted in a second honeymoon phase and a unified front that left no hope for my divide-and-conquer strategy.

"But I'm supposed to babysit for the Brocks before heading down to the Cape with Josie and Lucy." My appeal was met with patience, but it was obvious my pleas weren't having any impact. "Mr. Holden is holding my job at the Scoop Shack until I get there."

"It's just three weeks," my mom assured me. "And it would be such a great experience for you."

"Following you around for three weeks? What kind of experience is that?"

"I meant the traveling." She frowned at me. "And there are worse things than assisting a best-selling author on her promotional tour to major cities while learning about the publishing industry. You'd think most girls would jump at the chance to go behind the scenes and visit TV and radio studios."

"That's true." My dad shrugged and exchanged a glance with my mom. Some sort of silent baton passing was taking place, and now it was up to him to get me to see how unreasonable I was being. "Come on, Emily. It's a resume builder."

Really? A resume builder? That was his strategy? I was all of one day out of high school and I was supposed to start thinking about building my resume?

No. What I was *supposed* to be doing was sleeping late and hanging out at the beach with my friends before swirling ice cream cones at night for a few hours. I was *supposed* to enjoy spending the next couple of weeks with my boyfriend before he left for lacrosse camp. I'd spent all of high school doing everything right—the right clubs, the right volunteer activities, the right AP courses. Couldn't I just spend the next few months relaxing?

"But Luke and I don't have a lot of time together before we both go away for the summer." It was lame, bringing up the boyfriend, being the girl who couldn't leave the guy. I never wanted to be *that girl*, but things were looking dire, and I was hoping to tug at their heartstrings just a little. After all, they liked Luke. I was their good kid, the reliable one, the child who always did what she was expected to do while TJ got away with just sliding by. TJ hadn't even bothered to look for a summer job yet, and here I was with a babysitting gig until I left for the Cape *and* a job at the Scoop Shack. Granted, asking customers if they wanted a waffle cone or a cake cone didn't exactly qualify as resume-building material, but I had four years of college for that.

"Please don't make me do this." I practically held my hands together in prayer, bowing my head as I asked for their mercy at the altar of my breakfast plate and half-eaten English muffin.

"You know, Emily, there's something I think you're forgetting."

I looked up and found my mom smiling, like she'd just remembered the most excellent thing that would make me rejoice at the idea of living out of a suitcase for three weeks.

"What's that?" I asked, a sliver of hope still alive.

"Think of all the frequent flier miles you'll earn."

The miles? I was supposed to give up three weeks with Luke and my friends so I could take advantage of the benefits of an airline loyalty program?

"I don't want miles, I want to be home," I told her.

"And you will be, I promise. The tour ends the last week of June. You'll be on the Cape before July Fourth as planned."

One week at home, that was my consolation prize?

"I know that right now you want to stay here, but by the time you graduate from college, you might be able to use those miles for a free flight somewhere great, like a trip to Europe or somewhere else really special," my dad said, attempting to make me see the pot of gold at the end of the very distant rainbow.

The decision was obviously made. I was going on a book tour with my mom. And I should be happy about it because one day I might be able to parlay my misery into a trip to Europe.

It didn't sound like a good trade-off at all. And I knew Luke wouldn't think so, either.

* * *

It was a done deal negotiated without me—I was going on tour with my mom. After breakfast, I ran through the time-line in my head and tried to figure out how to make it all work. If there was one thing I'd learned from my mom, in addition to knowing that a dinner roll should be buttered one bite at a time, it was how to plan. The tour was over June twenty-fifth, and I was supposed to start work at the Scoop Shack on Friday, July second. I knew there was no way Josie's dad would let me start any later. July Fourth weekend was the busiest time of the entire summer, which was why, when he agreed to let Lucy and me work there, we had to swear an oath on a banana split that we'd be available. That may be an exaggeration, but it's not far off. He made us sign a contract. It wasn't a legal contract, just a document stating that we'd be there on the date we promised and we'd work until we had to leave for school in August. Mr. Holden thought it would teach us what the real world was like, and he didn't want us thinking that, just because the Holdens owned the Scoop Shack, it was any less of a real job.

Back when Josie asked us if we wanted to spend the summer at her house on the Cape, Lucy and I had jumped at the offer. I mean, who wouldn't want to live in a beach house all summer? If all I had to do was scoop a few sundaes and mix a few milkshakes, I was up for that. Besides, we knew the Scoop Shack's owner and our future boss, so we thought

15

that gave us instant seniority (and preference over shifts). Josie's dad bought his favorite childhood ice cream stand on Cape Cod when he sold his software company for a ton of money, and that made Josie—and, as her best friends, me and Lucy—practically in charge. The whole thing sounded downright cushy. And after the senior year I'd had, it was exactly what I needed—a low-pressure job with some serious side benefits (I didn't care what my mom said; I'll take free ice cream over airline miles any day).

There was another reason I'd jumped at Mr. Holden's job offer, though. Something I couldn't help think about even if I didn't admit it to Lucy and Josie when I'd said yes: it was a way for me to ensure that no matter what happened between me and Luke, I'd be okay. Although, at that point, we'd all put the whole notebook thing behind us, being with Luke still felt new and different. It felt *real*. I wasn't pretending anymore. I wasn't hiding behind a time capsule or trying to prove a point. I was exposed—not because the entire school knew what I'd done to Luke, but because the buffer I thought I'd put in place between us had been worn down and there was nothing left, like a protective scab that finally falls away, leaving only tender pink skin underneath. There was still a small part of me that wondered if Luke would change his mind—if he'd decide I wasn't worth all the trouble I'd caused, or, even worse, that he could never really trust me again.

I'd accepted the job at the Shack and prepared to spend the summer at Josie's Cape house *just in case*. If Luke *did* break up with me, it wouldn't matter. I was prepared. I was covered. I was with my best friends.

When Lucy and I told Mr. Holden yes we'd just been accepted to college, and everything was moving so fast there was no way I could imagine how it would feel now. Which was like I wanted to press pause and hold onto what we had now just a little longer.

No matter how many times I flipped through the calendar on my phone, it didn't change the timing, or what I had a feeling would happen next. Josie and Lucy knew that when my mom made up her mind, she didn't change it, and even if she did, I had already committed to babysit for the Brocks through the end of the month. My mom's tour didn't change our summer plans, even if they'd agree that spending the next three weeks in airport security lines was more punishment than resume builder. I wasn't so optimistic about Luke. He didn't know Polite Patty as well as Lucy and Josie, but he knew I couldn't just refuse to go. What I *could* do, though, was tell Lucy and Josie that I wouldn't arrive on the Cape until after Luke left for lacrosse camp.

My summer job consisted of working in a red wooden barn with a six-foot tall plastic ice cream cone on its roof. I knew that Luke didn't think making sundaes was nearly as vital as coaching a bunch of future lacrosse stars for six weeks. I also knew that Luke accepted the counselor position last summer, when the director asked if he'd like to come back as a coach instead of a player once he graduated. His choice was made way before we were together, before I'd even moved back from Chicago. It would never occur to me to ask him not to go, and I hoped he wouldn't ask me to blow off leaving for the Cape until he went to camp. Not just because it wasn't fair, but also because I didn't want to have to choose.

I decided to text Luke that I was heading over to his house. There was no point in waiting for a reply. It was barely ten o'clock and he was probably still asleep. It was Saturday, after all.

* * *

"Hi Mrs. Preston." Luke's mom was lacing up her sneakers in the kitchen when I knocked on the side door. She ran five miles every day and had been trying to recruit me to join her and experience what she called a *runner's high*. High or not, while I appreciated that Luke got his athleticism from his mom, I wasn't sure I wanted to be on the losing end of a race with a fifty-year-old woman. Thankfully, I'd managed to politely avoid committing to join her any time soon.

Mrs. Preston waved me into the kitchen.

"Emily!" She stood up and came over to hug me.

"Is Luke awake?" I asked.

the next chapter of luke

"He's upstairs, but who knows if he's even opened his eyes yet. Hopefully I'll be back in less than thirty-five minutes." Luke's mom tapped the black digital watch she always wore on her wrist when she ran. "You can go on up."

It was just one of the differences between our families. Luke was not allowed anywhere near my bedroom if my parents weren't home, and when they were, my mom always popped her head in for routine spot inspections, as if Luke and I would be tearing each other's clothes off and going at it in my bed while my parents were downstairs cooking dinner. They may as well have placed yellow crime scene tape around my bed and installed a tripwire to detonate my pillow in a burst of feathers if we so much as laid our heads down together.

I wasn't sure they knew or *didn't* know that Luke and I had slept together before everything blew up, or that under the glow-in-the-dark planets stuck to the ceiling above us in Luke's room, he'd muttered something that sounded an awful lot like *I love you* and I heard myself whispering *me, too*. It wasn't that my parents would be appalled or that I'd have to listen to lectures about being too young to have sex; after all, I'd been nothing if not responsible in my eighteen years. No, it was the horrifying thought of my mom feeling free to share her knowledge of STDs and methods of birth control, and the fear that I would become the subject of a new book on the etiquette of intercourse.

I watched Mrs. Preston sprint out the kitchen door with a wave good-bye, and then headed upstairs to see Luke.

The hallway leading to Luke's room was quiet, and when I reached his door, I turned the knob slowly and silently. He was still in bed, curled up around his pillow with the comforter pushed to the side, exposing his bare legs. The hairs on his leg were already fading to a pale blond from spending every afternoon outside at lacrosse practice, and he had a faint tan line ringing his ankle where his socks stopped. The far window was cracked halfway open, and I could hear the birds singing outside, calling to each other from one tree to the next in a repetitive way that made me imagine their conversation consisted of *you come here, no you come here* over and over again.

18

I could have said Luke's name or made a noise as I stood in the doorway, but instead I just stayed there.

There were times, like this, when it still seemed unreal, the absolute improbability that Luke and I would end up together. We could be doing something completely normal, like driving in the car or sitting together at lunch, and I'd look over at him and be struck by the reality that Luke Preston had fallen in love with me. And even though I'd tried really hard to avoid it, and even harder to deny it, it had been impossible for me not to fall in love with him in return. After months of stringing him along for the sake of my senior time capsule *project*, after he found out the truth, even after he hated me for lying to him, Luke still found a way to love me. And forgive me. I can't say I'd be that understanding under the same circumstances. It made me think that, even with eighteen years of training as Polite Patty's daughter, Luke had actually turned out to be a better person than me. Which was ironic considering the whole plan had been for me to turn a jerk into a good guy, and I ended up turning myself from a good person into a jerk.

I tried to put it behind us, I really did, but I found myself thinking about it more than I'd like to admit. It was as if I realized, for the first time, that I was capable of doing something I didn't think I had in me. And it had been easy. Too easy. So easy that it made me realize that, no matter how nice I thought I was, or how good, I could also be horrible to the people I cared about most. I guess my fear was they'd figured that out, too.

Luke always slept in boxers and a T-shirt. This morning's boxers were blue and red plaid, and his pale blue T-shirt had an elephant on the front. Jumbo the elephant, the Tufts University mascot. Not exactly the most menacing or inspirational team mascot ever created, but I knew that Luke was thrilled to be recruited for their lacrosse team. I'll never forget the day he found out that he'd been accepted and we'd driven to Medford to watch his future teammates practice. It had rained and the ground was muddy and slippery, and it was an all-around sloppy spring day. Still, I barely remembered the cold or the rain. All I remembered was how we'd slipped and fallen in the mud leading to the lacrosse field and, instead of getting up, we'd rolled around until the brown sludge seeped into my ears and I was sure a family of worms had found their way under my shirt. But none of it mattered because Luke's body was warm against me as we laughed and ignored the sound of the coach's whistle in the background.

It was nothing like today, which already felt like summer.

"You're watching me." Luke's lips moved but his eyes remained shut.

"How can you tell?" I asked.

"I can feel your eyes boring into my soul." He opened one eye and glanced over in my direction before rolling over onto his side and patting the comforter next to him. "Come here."

My mom would have freaked, obviously. Still, I walked over and curled up beside him, our bodies fitting together like puzzle pieces that snap into place with little effort. We were spooning, an expression my mother hated. She didn't understand why anyone would want to refer to a utensil when describing a form of physical affection. TJ had once joked that spooning was innocent when compared to forking. She didn't laugh.

I laid my head on the pillow beside Luke's.

"I got your text. What's up?" he asked. "You miss me already?"

"We graduated less than twenty-four hours ago," I reminded him, although the thought of leaving him for three weeks made my throat ache. "I think I can survive."

"And yet here you are." Luke pushed my hair aside and kissed the back of my neck.

The sun poured in through the window and, even with the breeze, it was already making his room too warm. I could feel my arms growing sticky where our skin pressed together. It was actually kind of gross, and was totally undoing the shower-fresh scent I'd gone to great pains to ensure. But I didn't want to move. I just wanted to savor this feeling until I left with my mom, when Hyatt rooms wouldn't be nearly as familiar or pleasant as this one. "You know you should get up. It's gorgeous out."

Luke rolled away from me onto his back and stretched his hands over his head as he groaned at my suggestion. He was only about four inches taller than me, but stretched out like that, his bare feet dangled off the foot of the bed.

"Okay, fine," he finally gave in. "Give me a reason to get up. What do you want to do?"

"I don't know. We could take a ride to Mount Wilder," I suggested.

Luke considered my option. "And what will we do when we get there?"

"We could have a picnic. And then I was thinking, maybe we drive into Boston for the afternoon. And tonight, we could go to that old drive-in movie theater in Duxmont. I checked, and the first show starts at eight," I rattled off the first three items on our summer *To Do* list—a list we'd started making a few weeks ago when we realized only had a few weeks before we both went our separate ways in July.

"It's the first day of summer vacation. At this rate, we'll run out of things to do after our first week." Luke laid his hand on my waist and pulled me closer to him, my back pressing against the warm skin of his exposed stomach. "We can't do everything the first weekend."

I probably should have turned around and faced Luke when I told him my news, but I couldn't. Instead, I stayed nestled against him as I stared at his bedroom wall.

"I'm going away with my mom, on her publicity tour for the book."

"That's cool. When?"

"We leave next Saturday."

Luke's arms went slack around me. "Next Saturday? Like, a week from today?"

I nodded.

"How long will you be gone?" he asked, and then put his hand on my shoulder and tried to get me to turn toward him. "Seriously, can you look at me?"

"Three weeks," I answered, rolling over and turning my head to face him. "Three very long weeks."

"What about everything we were going to do? What about driving to Newport, going to Sachuest beach, and doing the cliff walk?"

"I tried to tell her I didn't want to go, *believe me* I tried. They think it will be a good experience for me, expose me to new stuff, that sort of thing. And, of course, there's the frequent flier miles." I wrinkled up my nose, crossed my eyes, and hoped Luke would laugh at my joke. He didn't.

Instead he pressed his lips together into a thin line while he thought about my news. "Three weeks?"

"Yeah, but we can have an amazing time before I leave, and then when I come back, we have another few days before . . ." I didn't finish my sentence. Before what? I take off for the Cape and he heads to New Hampshire for lacrosse camp? Before we both leave for freshman orientation?

"There's really nothing you can do to get them to change their minds?"

I shook my head, and Luke fixed his eyes on the ceiling, a plain white plaster with nothing interesting to look at except glow-in-the-dark stars and planets he'd already seen a million times. I knew he wasn't looking at anything, and he was just staring there to avoid looking at me. "What about the Cape?"

"What about it?"

Luke was quiet as he let me fill in the blanks to the sentence he knew I didn't want him to say out loud.

"I can't bail on the Cape, Luke. I have a job. They're expecting me, I promised."

Luke inhaled and held his breath so long I wondered if he'd decided to just stop breathing in protest. Or maybe he was just deciding if what he was about to say would make things better or worse. I wasn't sure I wanted to know the answer.

Finally, he exhaled. "It's Josie's dad. Do you really think he'd care if you didn't show up to work until after the Fourth of July weekend? It would at least give us one more week together before I leave."

My body stiffened. "Well, I know that he would care, actually, but that's not exactly the point." And it wasn't. Basically, Luke was asking me to just ditch my job until he left for camp, to tell my friends they took a backseat to my boyfriend.

"Why don't you skip the first week of camp and come down to the Cape for the Fourth?" It wasn't so much an invitation as a challenge—a dare to see if he was willing to do what he was asking me to do, and I wondered if he could tell.

An exasperated puff of air escaped from Luke's lips. "You're kidding, right?"

"You're asking me to change my plans, but you won't consider changing yours? I mean, you already have a spot on the lacrosse team, they recruited you. So what if you show up at some summer camp a week late? It's just teaching some kids how to cradle a ball in a net."

The way Luke's face twisted into complete disbelief, you'd think I'd just described lacrosse in a way that was completely incomprehensible to someone who believed it was the most complex and rewarding thing in the world.

"I'm not saying camp isn't important," I started over. "I just don't get why it's okay for me to show up late for my job, but you never even considered showing up later for yours."

The room fell silent except for the sound of the birds singing their happy morning songs, which only made me realize how unhappy we sounded.

"Look, I'm sorry, I know it's not your fault. It's just that I was really looking forward to having time with you before we both take off for the summer." Luke was saying the right words, but his voice still sounded like he *did* think it was my fault. "We had all these plans. Plans that *you* created."

My fear of leaving things to chance was now being used against me, and I didn't like it. That's the thing about plans: the person breaking them is always at fault, even if she's the one who made them in the first place.

"I know. But there's no reason we can't still do those things. We just have to do them faster."

Luke looked at me, and even though he didn't roll his eyes, the tone in his voice rolled them for him. "A fast walk on the cliffs in Newport?"

"You know what I mean." I let my hand fall beside Luke's and waited to see if he'd take it. "We'll make the best of it."

Luke was quiet as he continued staring at the ceiling, both of our hands grazing my thigh but not actually touching. I hesitated before resting my head lightly on his shoulder, watching Jumbo the elephant rise and fall on Luke's chest.

23

It had almost been easy, or at least *easier*, before April, before we were really a couple, when I could deny that I was falling for him and pretend he was nothing more than a test subject.

I'd never *ever* want to relive the day when the entire school watched the seniors place items in the time capsule—the moment when I saw Luke remove the infamous notebook from behind his back and place it atop the pile of keepsakes that were supposed to commemorate our class for graduates to come. Was it horrifying to have the entire school witness the scene as Luke exposed me, as I realized my best friend had been the one to give him the notebook? More than I could ever explain. But what was worse, what truly made me realize the damage I'd done, was the look of betrayal on Luke's face as his eyes met mine and I saw the hurt settling in, like a blanket smothering the feelings we'd shared.

I never wanted to do that to him again—I never wanted to do that to anyone. The thing was, now that we were together, I realized that the experiment had shielded me from the impact of anything Luke did or said. Admitting that I loved Luke had meant I couldn't hide behind a notebook *or* a plan.

"You know if there was any way I could get out of going on the tour, I would," I explained.

Luke cast his eyes away from the ceiling and looked at me. "I know."

I rested my forehead against his and let my hair fall around our faces until it created a curtain that blocked our view of anything but one another. "Don't hate me," I whispered, which finally made him smile.

"Seriously?" He let out a small laugh and burrowed his head against the pillow we were sharing, which only made his smile wider. "Hate you? I don't hate you, Emily. I—"

"I'm back!" The sound of his mom calling to us from downstairs made me sit up. I may have been allowed in his room, but I wasn't exactly the kind of person who wanted to get caught laying down on her boyfriend's bed while he was in his boxer shorts.

"Okay, you win. We'll do whatever you want today. Let me shower." Luke kissed my forehead and then playfully pushed me toward the edge of the bed. "I'll meet you downstairs."

I rolled over onto the floor, landing with a soft thud. Luke peered over the edge of the bed, his chin resting on his forearms as he assessed my body sprawled out on the carpet below.

"All good down there?" he asked. "That wasn't exactly a graceful dismount."

"Not a good score from the Russian judge?" I joked, and Luke reached a hand down toward me and held it open, waiting for me to grab it and pull myself up.

"Maybe a 6.5, and that's being kind."

I took his hand. "I may not be graceful, but I promise we're going to have a great week together before leave."

"I know."

This time, I wouldn't let him down. I could do this. I could live up to the hype of being Polite Patty's daughter and plan a week that was so memorable, so filled with amazing moments for him to remember while I was gone, there was no way Luke wouldn't be counting down to my return. The next week would be a solid ten, even from the tough Russian judge.

> **Long-Distance Relationship Tip #5:**
>
> Imagining the worst is productive when you're preparing for a natural disaster. But all the bottled water and canned soup in the world won't make you feel better when you're envisioning him frolicking on the beach with a hot lifeguard in your absence. This is not the time to use your imagination.

chapter three

"**S**o what was today's activity?" my mom called out as I passed her office on my way upstairs to my bedroom.

I stopped and stood in the doorway, my hands resting against the white carved molding outlining the entrance to my mom's workspace. It was something I'd learned years ago, to make it seem like I was in the room with her while stopping short of actually entering. Most of the time, she hardly looked up when someone passed by, her fingers tapping away at her keyboard as she frantically tried to keep up with her publisher's deadlines, or the due dates for the columns she wrote for a variety of magazines, newspapers, and websites; my mom was a one-woman cottage industry for the etiquette impaired and manners minded. But once in a while, she'd hear me pass by and I knew that one foot in her office would turn a simple question into a twenty-minute conversation.

"We played miniature golf and then rode the bumper boats," I recited, giving the highlights of my day with Luke so far. My mom knew we were trying to fit a month's worth of plans into the little time I had left before embarking on Polite Patty's publicity tour.

"Sounds fun," she told me, tapping out a few last words before looking up. "Hey, can you come in here a minute?"

I stepped into her office, crossing the point of no return, and sank down in the leather chair facing her desk. I was still hoping this would really only take a minute, which was unlikely. "What do you need?"

"Well, I was telling my publicist that you're joining me on tour and that you were a little sad about leaving your boyfriend and friends behind—"

"Yeah, just a *little*," I interjected. Ever since she'd dropped the bomb on me, I'd been trying to get her to change her mind. I tried guilt. I tried making her feel sorry for me. I tried logic. I tried desperation. So far, I wasn't having any luck. The woman was a rock.

"Okay, I get it. Anyway, she had a great idea that may help you feel better about being away."

"Luke can come with us?" I guessed, a suggestion I'd made a few days ago and which was resoundingly rejected without any further consideration.

My mom ignored me. "She thought that it might be nice if you wrote a little how-to journal—something that could help other young women who are balancing long-distance relationships." My mom removed her glasses and placed them on her desk. "Did you know that more than ten million girls head off to college each year? There have to be at least two million leaving boyfriends—or girlfriends—behind, I'd think."

I almost laughed. For someone who was all about teaching people time-honored rules like how to excuse yourself from the dinner table and writing thank-you notes on crisp white monogrammed stationary, my mother had no problem embracing the idea that girls could have girlfriends. That was the thing about my mom, she could totally surprise you.

Of course, what didn't surprise me was that she'd already spoken with her editor about my situation. I should have known she'd turn my misfortune into a new book idea. My mom believed that every situation brought with it an opportunity to find the bright side. In January, when I'd told her that Luke broke up with Josie in an email, she'd come back to me a few days later and told me that 2.5 billion people used email. And her latest book was born. It wasn't lost on me that Josie's breakup not only resulted in my relationship with Luke, but a publicity tour for the book that was now taking me away from him.

"I think my how-to writing days are over," I said, without reminding her of the problems my first advice-dispensing attempt had created. "Lesson learned."

"It would be a great resume builder. I could show my editor your work. You never know, it might actually turn into something."

Again with the resume building. I was beginning to get the feeling that my parents were either counting the days until I graduated from college and became an independently functioning member of society, or they were deeply concerned that my plan was to move back and permanently install myself on their couch for years to come. I'd heard stories of kids who went off to college and returned home to discover that their parents had turned their bedroom into a scrapbooking room or yoga studio. I was beginning to doubt that my bedroom would survive in its current form for very long.

"Thanks, but I'll take a pass." I stood up. "Is that it?"

My mom slid open a desk drawer and removed a book, which she set down on her desk. "Well, promise me you'll think about it. No one your age has ever done something like this before, so it's a huge opportunity."

"I have to go change. Luke and I are going over to Josie's to swim." I swept my eyes toward the clock on her wall so she'd see I was losing time. "I'm already late."

I thought the late comment would get her. After all, being late for anything was a real no-no for Polite Patty. I actually thought I saw her struggle a little about what to do next—let me dash or let her finish our conversation. Getting in her parting words won that battle.

"Well, before you head off, I bought you a little present." She slid the book across her desk toward me. "In the event that you change your mind."

I reached over to take the book, which, it turned out, wasn't a book at all. It was a leather-bound journal. I cracked the spine and thumbed through the pages, which were all blank.

"You might get inspired during our travels. It's a place for you to write down your ideas."

I took the book, which felt soft and smooth in my hands and had an earthy, sweet leathery smell. The back of the book was branded *Hand Crafted Genuine Leather* and ivory stitching ran around the edges of the cover. A cow died for this book, and some craftsman had probably spent an hour sticking a needle through the tough hide so I could fill one hundred empty pages with my sage advice. Talk about pressure.

I was supposed to meet Luke at Josie's in ten minutes, and I didn't want to invite any more discussion about my resume-building opportunities or the burgeoning population of girls in long-distance relationships.

"Thank you," I told her, and then smiled so she'd know I meant it. "I promise I'll think about it."

As I took the stairs two at a time on my way to my room, I already knew I wouldn't *think about it*. There was nothing to think about, nothing that would make the next three weeks better, and definitely nothing that would make leaving for school at the end of the summer any easier. If there was a book in all of this, it wasn't a how-to with advice. It was more like those sad romance novels where the main character says a tortured good-bye to the love of her life and embarks on a journey by herself, alone, only to look back wistfully at a kinder, gentler time.

Okay, I'd read the book jackets of way too many novels lining the bookshelf of my grandmother's bedroom, so maybe that was a little exaggerated. I knew I was supposed to be that *other* type of heroine—the independent one who wrote a book telling other people how to kick ass in the long-distance relationship department. The girl who laughed in the face of the challenge before her and blazed a trail for others. But right now, I just wanted to get to Josie's pool. Not nearly as profound, but also not nearly as daunting.

* * *

Josie's pool was like something you'd find at a five-star resort. After her dad sold his software company, her parents built a new house, which was nothing like the house they'd lived in before, when we first met in elementary school. Back then, the only water in her backyard came out of a hose, and the only entertainment we had was a Slip 'N Slide. Now, the kidney-shaped pool was fed from a rock formation with tumbling water on one side, and an infinity edge on the other, which made it appear as if the pool dropped off the side of a cliff. A water slide was hidden inside the rock formation, and swirled its way down through the boulders until it dumped you out into the deep end, where two hippopotamus statues waited to greet you.

The thing is, Josie had always been deathly afraid of water, thanks to a bad experience in a Y swim class when she was five. Now, she'll at least dip her toes in and even sit on the steps in the shallow end. That water slide, though? She'd never even tried it.

"When's your flight leave?" Josie asked me, and then went on without waiting for my answer. "Where are you staying? Are you going to have any time to actually do anything fun?"

My mom's head had practically exploded the first time she met Josie and realized she rarely paused to let anyone answer a question before rushing on with a few more. Polite Patty was adamant that a single question should be followed by the opportunity to provide a single answer. I was so used to Josie's stream of consciousness approach by now, I never even started thinking about how to respond until she stopped to catch her breath.

We were splayed out on lounge chairs on the pool deck while Luke and Owen raced each other down the water slide. When I heard Josie finally inhale between the sounds of splashing water, I knew that was my cue.

"Tomorrow at nine o'clock, various hotels, and I seriously doubt it," I told her, my eyes closed as I enjoyed the sun's warmth spreading over my skin and the tropical smell of my coconut suntan lotion. It felt good to be horizontal after a week following the Freedom Trail around Boston, walking almost six miles of cliffs in Newport, and packing a month's worth of activities with Luke into one week while working around my babysitting schedule. If Josie hadn't spoken to me, I could have easily fallen asleep. Luke and I had jammed so much into the last seven days I was not only exhausted from all the *fun*, I was almost looking forward to a five-hour plane ride where I could do nothing but sleep. *Almost.*

"It'll go fast. When you think about it, three weeks is nothing in the grand scheme of things." Lucy set down a tray of lemonades and Doritos—one of the benefits of having a pool house stocked with snacks and drinks within arm's reach.

I took one of the glasses, which was actually plastic. Mr. Holden didn't allow glass anywhere near the pool. "Easy for you to say, you'll be on the Cape in less than two days."

Lucy and Josie clinked their lemonade glasses together in a toast, splashing pale yellow liquid on the flagstone patio as they yelled, "To sun, sand, and summer!"

Those three S's had become their rallying cry in the weeks leading up to the Cape—only they were forgetting one all-important item in their alliteration.

"And scooping," I reminded them. "We still have to work."

Josie shrugged. "It's going to be a blast. I wish you were coming with us now and not waiting until July."

I mirrored Josie's shrug. "Tell that to Patty," I reminded her, as if joining them any earlier had ever been in the plan. I'd committed to babysitting for the Brocks all summer, so when Josie invited us to spend the summer on the Cape with her, I'd still had to get out of that. When I'd asked Mrs. Brock if she could find someone else, she wasn't happy, but she was able to line up someone to replace me, even if she couldn't start until July first. So even though the plan was for us to spend the summer at Josie's house, I was always going to miss the first few weeks. Which, even though I didn't tell them, actually worked out kind of nice for me. It meant I could be with Lucy and Josie this summer, and still spend time with Luke before he went to camp—all without feeling bad about choosing Luke over them. It was what my mom would call a win-win. Of course, all it took was one phone call from mom and Mrs. Brock magically found someone to take my place while I went on a book tour, which felt like a Polite Patty win.

Almost on cue, Luke and Owen cannonballed into the deep end. I watched as the water rained down on the dents they pounded in the surface, their heads popping up to find one another before swimming to the basketball net secured to the side of the pool.

Lucy and Owen had been together since April and were, in my mother's terms, about to also embark on a *long-distance relationship* for the summer. I knew that Josie couldn't wait to meet a whole new group of guys on the Cape, but Lucy and Owen seemed to be working out, and I wasn't sure Lucy was on board with the idea.

I waited for Luke and Owen to start their battle for the hoop, making sure that between the splashing water and their attempts to dunk one another under the surface as they reached for the rim, there was no way Luke could hear me. "What about you and Owen? What's going to happen when you're on the Cape and he's here?"

"Well, actually we decided that nothing will happen." Lucy licked orange Doritos dust off the tips of her fingers. "We broke up."

"You what?" I asked, my voice louder than I intended. I glanced over at Luke and Owen before asking more quietly, "Why didn't you tell us?"

I waited for Josie to react, if not to their breakup than at least to the idea that Lucy hadn't even told us such big news. I waited for her to react. But she stared down at her nails as if they were suddenly the most interesting thing in the world.

"It just happened on our way here. I didn't exactly want to make an announcement." She nodded toward the pool, where Owen was celebrating a basket by high fiving himself with a four-foot long foam noodle.

"Are you okay?" I asked, although Lucy certainly looked okay digging her hand into a mound of artificially nacho'd chips while turning her face to the sun. And Owen certainly wasn't showing any signs of severe anguish.

"I'm fine, we're both fine. We just decided that neither of us wanted to stress out over what we should or shouldn't be doing this summer."

Again, I waited for Josie to react, but she just sipped her lemonade through a pink curly straw.

"I guess I'm surprised," I admitted, as it occurred to me that Josie wasn't. Which meant that Lucy had probably talked to her about breaking it off with Owen before it even happened. And she hadn't talked to me. "It seemed like things were going great with you guys."

"They were, they *are*, but it is what it is. I'll be in North Carolina for school and he's heading up to Vermont. Besides, neither of us really had any expectations. I mean, it's only been a few months." Lucy paused, and even though she was wearing sunglasses, I could tell her eyes had shifted in Josie's direction. "We were never as serious—"

"As you and Luke," Josie finished for her. "I wouldn't worry if I were you. It was a totally different situation."

"I'm not worried," I told them, even though the only real difference between Owen and Lucy and me and Luke was that the beginning of our relationship had come with way more drama and doubt, which would make you think we had a *higher* likelihood of falling apart over the summer, not *lower*.

"That's not what I meant," Josie tried again. "I just meant that . . ." This time, Josie looked to Lucy for help.

"We want us all to have a great time this summer, and we don't want you to be all bummed about Luke not being around, and thinking about what he might be doing without you. That makes sense, right?" Lucy gave me a hopeful smile. "We just want to have fun with you."

"Is that why you didn't tell me you were thinking about breaking up with Owen?" I asked, as much for an answer to my direct question as to find out if she really did tell Josie first. A part of me really hoped she hadn't, that Josie was just immune to the news of their breakup because they were leaving for the Cape in a few days and it really didn't matter what happened between Lucy and her boyfriend.

I held my breath and waited for Lucy to stop hesitating. I should have known the long pause meant all the hoping in the world wouldn't change that Lucy had told Josie first.

"A little," Lucy admitted. "It's so not a big deal. I would have told you both at the same time, but you weren't here yet."

Because I was with Luke. She didn't have to say it, but I knew we were all thinking it.

Josie handed me the Doritos. "Have you and Luke talked about what will happen when you're apart?"

I took the bag from her and shook my head.

"It might be a good idea to talk about it before you leave, just to avoid any issues," Lucy suggested, and I was pretty sure Lucy and Josie were imagining the same thing I was: the nights ahead with us all on the beach, a raging bonfire lighting up the faces of all the new people (and by *people* I meant *guys*) we'd meet this summer. "Like how often you're going to see each other, any ground rules, is he going to visit you, are you going to visit him…that sort of thing."

"I can't visit him, he's working at a lacrosse camp for boys," I reminded her. "He may as well be in lockdown."

"Yeah, I guess I didn't really think about that."

I set the bag of chips down on the table between our lounge chairs. "Now you're starting to freak me out."

"We're not trying to freak you out," Josie assured me. "It's just that this long-distance relationship thing might not be so easy."

"That's why Owen and I decided to end it now, as friends, before the really hard stuff started." Lucy sat up and removed her sunglasses. She looked from me to the deep end of the pool, where Luke and Owen were drying off with the big monogrammed beach towels the Holdens provided to each pool guest. Lucy bit her cheek and slipped her sunglasses back on before I could tell whether she was wondering if she made a mistake by breaking up with Owen, or wondering if I was making a mistake by *not* breaking up with Luke. "Look, you and Luke went through a lot this year. I'm sure you can figure out how to survive being a car ride away from each other."

"You guys sound like my mom. You wouldn't believe what she wants me to do."

Luke appeared next to me, his hair dripping cool beads of water onto my stomach. He wiped his damp hands on his wet bathing suit before reaching for a handful of chips.

"What won't we believe?" he wanted to know.

"My mom and her editor think I should write a how-to book about long-distance relationships. They think there's a huge college-aged market for something like that, but obviously given what happened the last time I did something similar . . . well, there's no way I'm going to do it."

34

Lucy tapped her fingers on her lemonade glass as she pondered my announcement. "It's actually not a bad idea."

I almost spit my drink at her. "You have *got* to be kidding me."

Josie nodded her head in agreement. "Your mom might be on to something."

"Sure, why not?" Owen draped his damp towel across the back of Lucy's lounge chair, reached for the chips, and took them from Luke, who still hadn't said anything.

"What do *you* think?" I asked Luke.

He took my glass of lemonade and washed down a mouthful of Doritos before answering. "I guess I haven't thought about it much."

This was where I should have let it go. Instead, I could feel my pulse quicken—*he hadn't thought about it much?*

"We're going to be apart for most of the summer and then . . ." I didn't really need to remind him that we were going to school two hours apart. "How is that even possible?"

"Um, because he's a guy," Josie answered.

Okay, sure. He was a guy. I got that. But he was also the guy who'd just played a round of miniature golf with a pink ball because it was the only other color left and he knew I wanted the blue ball since blue is my favorite color. This was the guy who let a six-year-old girl bang the crap out of his bumper boat because every time she bounced off of his boat, she dissolved into a fit of giggles.

Luke shrugged. "I guess I didn't think about it because I don't think it's a big deal."

That should have made me feel better. And it did, a little. "I'm not saying it's going to be a *problem*. I'm just saying it's something we should probably plan for, so we both know what to expect."

"I'm spending my summer with a bunch of guys with lacrosse sticks. The only thing you can expect is that I'll be hoping my roommate washes his socks."

Luke was right. He was one of twenty coach counselors at the camp, and he was going to be supervising a group of twelve-year-olds who were more likely to be interested in smacking each other in the head with their sticks than scoping out girls at the sister camp across the lake. (Okay, that was me totally making that up based on clichéd summer camp stereotypes. Luke's camp was at a college in New Hampshire, and I had no idea if there was a lake, let alone a sister camp.)

"It's going to be fine, Emily." Luke laid his hand on my shoulder, his damp, cool skin sending a shiver through me even though it had to be almost ninety degrees on Josie's pool patio.

"I know." I brushed his wrinkly fingers with my chin.

I caught Josie and Lucy shooting each other a glance that could have meant one of two things—either they'd gorged themselves on bean dip and salsa and wanted to throw up, or they weren't so sure Luke and I knew what we were in for once we were apart.

I told my mom I'd be home by four o'clock so I could pack and prepare for our cross-country promotional tour de force. My mom was an impeccable packer who secured her shoes in plastic bags—so they didn't soil her clothes—and pressed everything before placing it in her suitcase just so, which meant stacked according to the date she planned to wear each piece. I can't say I ascribed to her theory that a well-packed bag was truly the start of a well-planned trip (her words), but I knew she'd be hovering over my shoulder driving me nuts if I didn't demonstrate a little pre-travel organization.

"We should go," I announced, and stood up from my lounge chair.

Luke took another handful of chips and reached for his towel.

"So this is it? The next time we see you, we'll be on the Cape!" The force of Josie's hand came close to pushing Lucy off her lounge as she high-fived her. "Let the fun begin!"

Lucy regained her balance and leaned over to give me a hug. "We'll miss you, try to enjoy your trip."

"I'll do my best," I told her. "You, too."

"Oh, we're going to have a great time." Josie stood up and wrapped a towel around her waist. "We'll scope everything out, so when you show up, it will be instant party. You'll be there on the second, right? Because my dad will kill me if you're not there for July Fourth weekend."

"Yep, the second," I confirmed, glancing over at Luke.

"She'll be there," he echoed.

"Sun, sand, and summer!" Josie sang as she hugged me good-bye and pressed her cheek against mine. "We love you."

"Love you, too," I told her, because we'd been best friends forever, and because I really did.

* * *

"Where are you going?" I asked Luke when he missed the left turn toward my house.

His hair was still wet and I could see the waves of wrinkles on the pads of his fingertips as he held the steering wheel. Luke reached for my hand and set it on his leg while he drove.

"We have some time to spare. I thought we'd make a pit stop for old time's sake." He accelerated in the opposite direction. "I'm in the mood for a strawberry Fribble. You in?"

Was I in?

"Absolutely," I told him, and squeezed his thigh.

When we pulled into the Friendly's parking lot, Luke led me inside and ordered for both of us, something I hadn't let him do the first time we came here. I wouldn't even let him share my french fries back then, and he'd given me a confused look but also seemed slightly impressed, not because I was so stingy but because I wasn't afraid to tell him I wanted to eat them all myself. It wasn't some attempt to show Luke I wasn't like other girls who pretend they aren't hungry and then pick at a plate of fries while pushing a salad around with fork. No, I'd wanted those fries, but I'd also wanted something else: to be honest about what I wanted, to not pretend that I was okay with sharing. It was as much a test for me as it was for him—could I say what I really felt, and could Luke let me? We'd both passed the french fry test, and I think that was the first time I realized Luke was different than I'd expected, and his difference allowed me to be myself.

It was hard for me to believe that just a few months ago, when Josie had arranged for us both to meet here again, we'd been sitting in a booth against the wall, staring across the table at one another, not sure what would happen next. I'd truly doubted he'd be able to look at me and believe anything I said after what I'd done. But that day, we'd both ordered strawberry Fribbles, and over extra thick milkshakes, Luke had found a way to forgive me.

While we waited for our Fribbles at the takeout counter, Luke swept his hand in front of the refrigerated display case filled with frosted cakes and gallons of ice cream. "You better get used to this—it's your future!"

"Not my future," I corrected him. "My summer."

"Well, every time you scoop strawberry ice cream, I hope you'll be thinking of me."

And vanilla, and chocolate, and every other flavor, I wanted to tell him.

"You know, this might be our last time here together." I scanned the restaurant, taking in the vinyl booths, the hot fudge–stained floors, even the paper placemats and crayons intended to keep fussy kids busy. It wasn't exactly the most romantic spot, but it still felt like the place where we'd started. And started over.

"Why do you have to be so morbid? Let's just enjoy one last extra-large cup of strawberry goodness." He leaned against the counter and I tried to smile.

Luke was right. I was getting way ahead of myself.

The server handed over our Fribbles in to go cups, and we took them outside with us as we walked across the parking lot to Luke's car.

"How about this? Let's just pick a date now." Luke stopped and turned to face me. "That way we're sure to come back even after we're at school. No excuses."

"How can we do that?" I asked. "We have no idea what'll be going on."

"I know that I have a short break in October. What about you?"

I took out my phone and Googled the academic calendar for the year. "Me, too. Saturday the eleventh through Tuesday the fourteenth."

"Then it's a plan, right here, Saturday the eleventh, exactly this time." Luke glanced at his phone. "Two o'clock. We'll come back and meet here, and then hang out for the long weekend, or we can go back to my dorm, which, now that I think about it, is actually a much better idea."

Now I was smiling—a big, wide grin that I was sure matched his, except for the tiny spots of pink froth clinging to the corners of his lips.

I loved the idea. It was perfect.

I reached over and wiped the spots of strawberry from the corners of his mouth, swiping the ice cream across his lips until it disappeared.

"Deal. Let's shake on it, so it's official. No backing out, no changing plans, no matter what." I held out my hand and waited him to seal the deal.

Luke reached for my hand and pulled me toward him until I was pressed up close against his chest. "A handshake? Really? I can do better than that."

Luke's lips were soft and cold, and as he kissed me, I could almost taste how much he loved me—because as far as I was concerned, Luke's love tasted just like strawberry ice cream. I closed my eyes and inhaled the faint scent of chlorine still clinging to his skin and tasted his warm, sweet tongue.

"There," he said, slipping our lips apart but keeping our faces close together so that the tips of our noses touched, like Eskimo kisses. He held my cheek in his empty hand and rested his forehead against mine so that we were looking straight into each other's eyes, so close I could identify where each individual lash began before fanning out in a blur. "Now it's official. I love you, Emily Abbott."

I closed my eyes again.

"Don't you have anything to say?" he asked.

I opened my eyes and tried to bring Luke into focus, the fringe of his eyelashes sweeping up and down as he blinked.

"You were right," I agreed. "That sure beat a handshake."

Little crinkles formed at the corners of his eyes as he laughed at me. "That's it?"

No, that wasn't it. There was more, so much more. "The Russian judge gives that a 9.9."

"Damn. How can I get the extra point one?" he asked.

"I guess you have to keep practicing," I told him.

Luke feigned exasperation. "Well, if I have to," he lamented, his shoulders sagging in mock defeat. "I should probably start now."

"If you think it will help," I answered, knowing that a perfect ten was about to be achieved right there, standing in the middle of a parking lot, our extra thick milkshakes melting from the heat of the sun.

chapter four

Three weeks. Twelve cities. 11,020 miles added to my frequent flier account. At the end of the day, not nearly enough to get me to Europe. Wish I'd done the math ahead of time.

By the time we arrived home, I never wanted to see my tastefully selected, neutral-colored stack of clothes designed to *mix and match for optimal flexibility* (my mother's words) again. I was so tired of wearing the same rotation of skirts and tops and pants and shorts that it didn't even matter that I hadn't had to do laundry for three weeks thanks to an invisible staff of hotel miracle workers who picked up our bags of dirty laundry and returned them to our room smelling fresh and pressed to perfection. In fact, the whole experience inspired my mother to write a new book on how to bring the fabulous hotel vibe home with you, including how to form origami roses out of toilet paper (my mother explained to me that the toilet paper roses the staff created on the roll in our bathroom not only looked lovely, but also indicated that the room had been cleaned with care). Her new book, *Checking Out Without Checking In: A Guide to Hospitality at Home*, will be available next year.

Unlike my mom, I did not have a book to sell to her editor after three weeks away from Luke, although I did bring the leather-bound journal along on my trip and managed to fill a bunch of pages with ideas that should work in theory. I say

41

theory because even though I thought my tips sounded like they made completely practical sense, I can't say they really helped me when I was sitting alone in an empty air-conditioned hotel room counting the number of shower caps I'd collected on my journey.

When my mom had suggested I wipe down the TV remote control with the sanitizing gel in her bag, and, out of boredom, I'd decided to kill time by Googling the other items in my room I should sanitize...bad idea. Basically, I'd learned that the cleanest place in my room was the desk, so the notes in my new leather-bound journal were really a result of germ avoidance, not an enlightened view of long-distance relationships. I'm not sure I learned much on my trip except that navigating time zones and missed calls with a boyfriend hundreds and, at times, thousands of miles away really sucked (and to use my elbows when hitting the light switch).

My mother's tour mostly consisted of me waiting around while she was interviewed by journalists and TV and radio hosts who asked the same questions over and over again. I'd had no intention of creating another how-to guide, but the journal was in my bag and scribbling some thoughts down on its pages was infinitely more interesting than listening to my mom repeat her top five tips for social media etiquette. The truth was, though, even after three weeks away from Luke, I still had no idea how to stop thinking about the future and what would happen to us, even if I did have a leather-bound book with the beginning of what I thought I *should* do.

Fortunately, our three weeks on the road, or what my mother referred to as my *internship*, went faster than I anticipated, thanks to the mad dashes for the airports, the shuttling between TV and radio stations, the newspaper and magazine interviews conducted over lattes at Starbucks, and my mother's insistence that we experience at least one piece of local culture in each city. This included lunch in a rotating restaurant 500 feet above Seattle, which taught me I am, in fact, not just afraid of heights, but also prone to throwing up a cheeseburger when taking in 360 degree views of my potential plunge to the Earth. There wasn't time to think about everything I was missing at home, although there weren't enough text messages in the world that could make up for not being there in person. It didn't help that Lucy and Josie sent me at least six pictures a day of all the fun they were having on the Cape.

At first, it was nice to feel included, to see what I had waiting for me after sitting in the lobby of a Hyatt for two hours while my mom discussed the importance of maintaining correct grammatical structure when trimming down your thoughts to 280 characters or less. Toward the end of my trip, when I could recite the *dos and don'ts of emojis* in my sleep, the pictures of Lucy and Josie started to include people I didn't even know—new friends they'd made at the Scoop Shack, or at the beach, or in town. I wasn't sure where they were meeting all these new people, but I did know that it looked like they were having a great time without me.

After three weeks of playing *where in the world is Emily Abbott*, I'd become intimately familiar with the proper procedures for takeoff and landing, read the seatback safety card enough times to identify the nearest exit within three seconds of entering an aircraft, and memorized the SkyMall catalog from cover to cover. My personal favorites among the infinitely useless, and sometimes downright disturbing, catalog items were, in no specific order: the Human Slingshot, which involved four people slinging back and forth at one another inside a human-sized rubber band; decorative toilet flush handles for people who want to hold onto an elephant tail as they wash away evidence; and a talking dog collar with remote control, because having a human voice emanate from Fido's throat isn't creepy, right?

But this was my last flight, the final plane ride home. As the Boston skyline came into view, it was all I could do to keep from turning on my phone and calling Luke from the sky. But years of Polite Patty training had ingrained a certain adherence to rules that I couldn't bring myself to disregard. Besides, I had visions of the bars on my phone going up just as the plane started going down, the little device in my hand wreaking havoc with the communications system designed to operate free and clear of mobile phone interruptions. I decided, in the interest of relying on the screens and buttons and satellite navigation systems in the cockpit to deliver me safely to the ground, I'd wait until I heard the squeal of rubber on the runway.

the next chapter of luke

I powered up my phone and texted Luke as soon as the plane's wheels touched down: *Just landed, be over soon.*

It took a few minutes for his reply to appear: *Not home, call me.*

I knew my mom would kill me if I actually dialed his number right then, with two hundred anxious passengers ready to trample over me to get to carousel six and reclaim their luggage. Public phone conversations were one of my mother's pet peeves.

Instead, I texted: *Can't talk. When will you be home?*

And this time, the reply was instantaneous: *Not going home, on Martha's Vineyard. Call you soon.*

If it wasn't for the line of passengers propelling my body down the aisle, I probably would have stayed planted in place, unable to move until the cleanup crew swept me away with the gum wrappers, empty water bottles, and wrinkled SkyMall catalogs.

Martha's Vineyard? Luke was almost two hours away, if you counted the car ride and the ferry. I was finally here, and now he was there? Luke knew I was flying back today, and even knew the exact time I landed and my flight number (in case he wanted to track the plane online, which I thought was a cool idea). We'd been planning to see each other as soon as I got home, which would be in less than one hour, if traffic on the Mass Pike cooperated.

The flight attendant smiled at me as I approached the exit. "Thank you, have a great day!"

"Thank you! You, too," I replied, because that's what you do when you've spent three weeks on the road listening to an etiquette guru dispense her wisdom to the masses. You smile politely and pretend everything is perfect.

As my mom and I made our way to the baggage claim area, I continued to check my phone and waited for the screen to light up with another message from Luke. Instead, it remained dark.

"Glad to be back?" my mother asked as we stood at the carousel watching it go round and round with luggage that wasn't ours.

I nodded.

"I know you can't wait to see Luke." She beamed at me, the daughter who had been such a good trooper for three weeks

44

and who had finally returned home to the welcoming arms of her boyfriend. I almost got the feeling she was expecting Luke to be waiting for me in the baggage area with a hand-painted cardboard sign held over his head: *"Welcome back, Emily!!"* My mom was a big fan of grand gestures like that, even if I couldn't remember one time when anyone had ever met us in an airport arrival area holding anything other than a grudge for having to suffer through traffic on their way to pick us up.

"I bet he's on his way to our house right now to surprise you when we get there," my mom continued, once it became apparent that there was no welcoming committee waiting to greet us.

"I bet he isn't," I mumbled, but my mom didn't hear me because that's when our luggage turned the corner of the carousel and came into view.

"What was that?" she asked, reaching for her bag and lifting it off the rotating belt before it passed us by.

"Nothing." I walked up to my bag and snatched it from the moving conveyor.

There's a saying: If you love someone, set them free, and if they come back, they're yours. If they don't, they never were. Makes sense, right? But what happens when you're the one set free for three weeks and you come back? What if there's nobody to welcome you home or even answer your call and tell you how much you were missed? They never came up with a pithy saying for that, probably because the only lesson you can possibly learn from the experience is that it feels pretty crappy. Well, that and you're stuck carrying your own luggage to the parking lot.

* * *

"Why aren't you home?" I'd been staring at my phone for almost an hour by the time Luke's name finally appeared, a photo of us from graduation lighting up my screen.

"It's a long story," he said, and then added, "I'm glad you're back."

"So am I, but I'd be even more glad if you were here." Even I could tell my voice sounded a little whiney, which wasn't how I wanted to sound at all. "What's going on?" I asked, purposely changing my tone. "Is everything okay?"

"You're not going to believe it."

I threw myself on my bed and propped the pillow up behind my head. "Try me."

"We came over to the island yesterday for the day. My mom wanted to visit her college roommate and I went along because I had nothing else to do and I've known her kids for, like, forever."

Forever was a long time—so long that I wondered why I'd never heard of these very good family friends before.

"And you decided to stay?" I asked, attempting to remove all the disappointment from my voice.

"Long story short, we went bridge jumping. This other kid and I left the railing at the same time ,and I don't know exactly how it happened, but we ended up colliding and the next thing I know I'm being pulled out of the water because my knee is all screwed up, and every time I go to move, it's like an ice pick being jammed into my leg."

"Did you go to the hospital? Is it serious? Did you break something?" I fired off questions one after the other without even doubting if Luke was exaggerating the pain. It had to be bad. There were days he walked off the lacrosse field with scrapes and bruises and crusted blood embedded in cuts, and he never complained, so if he was admitting how bad the pain was, it had to be horrible. "Are you okay?"

"Depends on what you think is okay. I'm on crutches."

"How bad is it?"

"Well, they think it's my medial collateral ligament, my MCL," he told me, as if that meant something to me other than that I should have paid better attention to anatomy in my biology class. "I have to go see an orthopedist tomorrow to find out what grade it is—that's like a measurement of how screwed I am," he explained.

"What's the worst-case scenario?" I asked, although from the sound of Luke's voice, I had a feeling I already knew the answer.

"A grade three means up to eight weeks off my knee and a brace."

"But what about lacrosse camp?"

"Forget camp, Emily. I might not be able to play this season if it doesn't heal. What if I need surgery?" Luke's voice was strained, and I could tell he was getting upset.

"I'm really sorry," I told him, because I was, and because I wasn't sure what else to say. It was obvious any attempt to try and downplay his injury wouldn't help, not unless I suddenly obtained a medical degree.

"Do you know what that would mean?" he asked.

That you'll be around all summer, I thought, and then immediately hated myself. I suddenly envisioned a special place in hell for girlfriends who hear about a potentially lacrosse career–ending injury and the first thing they think is *at least you won't be going to camp in New Hampshire.*

"I'm sure you won't need surgery." I tried to sound convincing, but it's not like my assurance held much credibility.

"Emily, I might not be able to *play,* don't you get it? This is a big deal."

"I get it, of course I do, Luke. But think positive!" I added, and instantly realized I sounded like a bumper sticker. "Before you start thinking the worst, wait until you hear what the doctor has to say."

Luke's silence meant my pep talk wasn't helping. "Is there anything I can do?" I asked, wishing there was some way I could make him feel even a little hopeful.

"No, there's nothing anyone can do. I just have to stay off my knee and see what the doctor says."

"So what happens next?"

"I can barely get around, so I guess I'm here for a while," Luke told me, and then added, "Camp is out of the picture, and you're heading to the Cape anyway. Melanie, my mom's friend, invited me to stay here and hang out until they go back to New York in August. She said I could keep Sam and Charlie company. Charlie's not real psyched about being on the island all summer."

"Charlie?"

"He's going into his senior year. We've known each other since the day he was born, my mom always likes to remind us."

I started to get excited, and then pinched my hand hard to remind myself that this wasn't a good thing for Luke. Even if it was starting to feel like a good thing for us. "So you're going to be on the Vineyard the entire summer? Josie's house

47

in Falmouth is right across the water, so we'll only be a ferry ride away."

"I know. That's a bonus." He attempted to sound happy, but it wasn't working. I tried to not take his lack of enthusiasm personally, because I'd never heard Luke sound so down before. Given the crazy circumstances of our relationship, I'd seen a whole range of reactions from Luke, but this one was new for me.

"Look, you've been running and training, right? You've never hurt your knee before, so it had to be healthy to start with. And even if you can't work at the camp, you have almost two months before pre-season conditioning starts A lot can happen in two months."

"I know, you're probably right." Luke paused, and I heard a rustling sound that made me think he was moving the phone from one ear to the other. "These crutches aren't exactly conducive to ferry travel, though. Which is why Melanie told me to invite you to come here. When can you get a ferry over?"

I wasn't even unpacked from my three-week romp across the United States. I hadn't slept in my own bed in what felt like ages. I'd eaten every meal in a restaurant for more than twenty days, and all I wanted to eat was a homemade peanut butter and jelly sandwich from my own kitchen.

"Really? You're inviting me to come see you?"

"Well, it's actually me, my mom, Melanie, Charlie, and Sam, but yeah. That's exactly what I'm doing. So, can you come?"

In a few days, I was leaving for Josie's house, and I had to imagine my parents wouldn't be too thrilled to hear I was taking off for Martha's Vineyard, especially since my mom just spent the past three weeks telling me how much she was going to miss me when I left for school in August.

"How about Friday?" I suggested. "My mom is taking me to Josie's first thing, and I can drop my stuff at the house and head over to see you."

"You can't come any sooner?" Luke lowered his voice. "I've missed you."

I laid my head back against my pillow and closed my eyes, letting his words wash over me. I'd missed him so much. I missed the way he absentmindedly tapped his fingers on my leg when we watched TV together, as if he was playing keys on a piano. I missed the way he slid his big toe from his right foot into the space between the big toe and second toe on his other foot, hooking them together until I pointed it out, and he'd laugh about how stupid it was and how he didn't even know why he did it. Mostly I just missed being with him because, even though I'd never admit it to Lucy or Josie, after everything we'd been through, Luke had become my best friend.

"I can't. I just got back. We're doing the whole family dinner, group love thing tonight. I have to stick around for a few days. Besides, I have a lot of packing to do for the Cape, and I'll have to drop my stuff off there before I head over to see you."

"Okay." Luke sighed, but I wasn't sure if he was resigning himself to the fact that he'd have to wait a few more days to see me, or if the pain in his knee was getting worse. "Charlie and Sam are waiting for me to head into town, which takes twice as long now that I'm hobbling on crutches. I'll call you later and we can figure it out."

"I can't wait to see you, you know." I pictured Luke spending his summer on crutches while he waited to find out if his dream of playing college lacrosse slipped away. "And Luke? I'm sorry about your knee. Really, I am. I hope it all ends up okay."

"I know you do. That's why I love you."

"It is?"

"Yeah. Well, that and the fact that you're willing to take a ferry to see a guy with a bum leg and insanely sweaty armpits from hopping around on crutches all day."

My mom was wrong. The best reward for giving up three weeks of my summer to go on her publicity tour wasn't frequent flier miles. It was the chance to spend the summer with Lucy, Josie, *and* Luke.

"Are you kidding me," I told Luke. "I wouldn't miss your sweaty armpits for the world."

chapter five

After five days at home without my best friends or boyfriend, I couldn't wait to get in the car and go. I'd made my mom promise we'd be out the door by eight thirty. It was a Friday morning, and the last thing I wanted to do was hit traffic heading over the bridge to Cape Cod.

"Make sure you're always on time for work," my mom reminded me for what felt like the tenth time. "You don't want Mr. Holden to think you're taking advantage of the situation."

"I will," I agreed, even though I knew there was no chance Mr. Holden would let any of us *take advantage of the situation*. Our *contract* may not have been legally enforceable, but Mr. Holden was completely serious when he laid out the rules for our jobs. He'd been willing to let us only work the night shifts because we'd pointed out that it was the busiest time of day, and he needed at least three trusted employees manning the Shack. We also mentioned that parents were more likely to take their kids out for ice cream at night, and they were better tippers than the kids who rode their bikes there during the day (we'd all promised our parents we'd save half of everything we made). We didn't mention that we wanted to sleep late and spend our days at the beach. I don't think Mr. Holden would have found that rationale nearly as convincing.

"And don't forget to send Mrs. Preston's friend a thank-you note after you leave the Vineyard," my mom added. "I put a hostess gift in your bag, along with your stationary."

The stationary had been one of my graduation gifts. In my mother's world, the only thing worse than not sending a thank-you letter was not having monogrammed stationary upon which to declare your appreciation.

"I will," I assured her, the Bourne Bridge coming into view ahead of us. The canal under the bridge was the official dividing line separating the Cape from the rest of Massachusetts, and even though we'd taken family vacations in various Cape towns over the years, a mix of nervousness and excitement started to swell inside me. Sure, I was less than thirty minutes from seeing Josie and Lucy, but I was also about to spend the summer living in a strange room, in a house I'd never seen, in a town I didn't know, working at a job I'd never done. It wasn't as simple as merely transplanting my life into a new place with my best friends. If you didn't count Lucy and Josie, everything else would be new to me. And I was already something of an outsider, arriving weeks after Lucy and Josie had settled in. It felt like I would be trying to learn the steps of a new dance when everyone else had been practicing for weeks.

I knew from the pictures and texts they'd been sending me that Lucy and Josie had a ton of stories to share. When they'd first arrived at Josie's house, I'd received photos of a bedroom with three twin beds covered in matching comforters and pillows, the last one with the caption: *yours*. The pictures kept coming—different rooms of the house, the pool, a hammock that I assumed was strung between two trees in the Holdens' yard, a path of windswept seagrass leading to a stretch of sandy beach. Then there were the videos that followed Josie and Lucy around the Scoop Shack as they showed me each of the flavors in the ice cream case, demonstrated how to use the milkshake machine, and where the extra napkins were kept. Because I was basically starting my job at the Shack on the busiest weekend of the year, they thought it would be helpful if I had some idea what I was getting myself into before I arrived, even if I was sure dipping a soft serve cone into chocolate sprinkles without having the entire tower of ice cream fall off was more difficult than they made it appear.

After the first week, though, the pictures and texts were less about the finer tips of working at an ice cream stand and more about the other people working there, and all the new

51

names and faces were actually more difficult to keep track of
than the skills I'd need at the Shack. At first, it was fun to see
my summer unfold. It was infinitely more amusing to watch
Josie whisper about the guy carrying the garbage out to the
dumpster as she panned her phone's camera on his ass than
it was to listen to my mom explain to yet another journalist
why using all caps in a text is the equivalent of shouting in
someone's ear and should only be used in the case of an
emergency—and if it truly *is* an emergency, then you should
be dialing 911, not texting. But toward the end of the tour,
there were fewer and fewer texts and photos from Lucy and
Josie. I'd convinced myself that the novelty of being on the
Cape had worn off and the realities of working at the Shack
weren't as exciting as those first days. I tried not to dwell on
the other possibility—that they were having so much fun
they forgot to share it with me.

"There it is," my mom said, pointing to the low green
bushes spelling out *Cape Cod* on the bank of the rotary that
connected the bridge to the rest of the Cape.

In twenty minutes, we'd be at Josie's house, and then I'd
be on the ferry on my way to see Luke.

As the car's navigation system directed us through
downtown Falmouth, and we wound our way toward the
Holdens' house, I could barely keep still. My mom gently
placed her hand on my knee in a not-so-subtle hint to stop
bouncing it up and down and annoying her.

"Sorry," I apologized, and she laughed.

"Just don't get out until I stop the car, okay?"

"I won't," I promised, but it was all I could do to keep from
unbuckling my seat belt and preparing to bolt the second the
car pulled into the Holdens' driveway. Suddenly, three weeks
without Josie and Lucy felt like months.

The voice on the GPS informed us that we'd reached our
destination, and my mom pulled into a driveway lined with
crushed shells that popped and crackled as the car slowly made
its way toward the house. But even though the navigation
screen declared we should stop driving, I wasn't convinced
we were in the right place. The house was nothing like I
expected, because what I expected was something huge and
new and befitting a tech mogul. What I discovered when
we reached the front door was a traditional Cape Cod beach

house with sun-faded gray cedar shingles and cornflower blue hydrangea bushes lining the front walkway. It was a decent size, but nothing like the place the Holdens called home in Branford. The house wasn't even directly on the beach, which is what I expected from the photos I'd seen. Sure, the beach was across the street, but it wasn't the same as walking out of your house and digging your toes into the sand.

My mom pulled the car around the circular drive and stopped when we reached the path leading to the front door. "This is really lovely."

She was right, it was, but for some reason, I felt like my vision of the rest of the summer had already shifted, as if I'd set myself up for one thing and was realizing that I didn't really know what I was getting into at all.

I expected the sound of the car's tires crunching along the shell driveway to send Lucy and Josie bounding out the front door to greet me, but as my mom killed the engine, the only noise I could hear was the distant crashing of waves. It was barely past ten o'clock and Lucy and Josie had probably been out late with their summer friends, but still.

"Let's go say hi!" My mom grabbed the smaller of my bags from the backseat and left me to empty the trunk as she headed up the walkway and waited for me to join her.

She had barely tapped the brass pineapple-shaped door knocker when the front door flew open. This was more like it. I closed my eyes and braced myself for the onslaught of hugs and high-pitched shrieks I expected after not seeing my best friends in weeks. What I got was a polite hug and a deep baritone voice.

"Emily! You made it!" Mr. Holden was holding a mug of coffee in one hand and an iPad in the other. "Come on in!"

Mrs. Holden appeared from around the corner, carrying two more steaming mugs toward us. "Patty, come have some coffee with us." She kissed my mom on the cheek, handed her one of the mugs, and then turned to me. "Emily, the girls are still sleeping. They didn't get home until . . . well, I was asleep, so I imagine it was pretty late. Go on up, you're all sharing the first room on the right."

My mom handed me my second bag and followed the Holdens down a hallway that I assumed led to the kitchen.

There was no exuberant greeting, nobody running up to tell me how much they missed me.

It was the opposite of the reaction I'd received when I moved back to Branford and saw Lucy and Josie in the hallway of Heywood Academy for the first time in almost three years. They'd screamed my name, wrapped their arms around me, and assailed me with questions to bridge the gap between the girl they'd been best friends with freshman year and the person returning as a mid-year senior. I'd instantly noticed the differences in my two best friends, the little things that didn't make them who they were, but nevertheless changed who they seemed to be—the new highlights in Josie's hair, or Lucy's once haggardly bitten fingernails that were polished and shaped into perfect half-moons. It was as if in my absence they'd become more complete, like a painting that appears finished until additional details and brushstrokes are layered on top, and you realize that what you'd seen at first was nothing more than a rough sketch.

This time, I'd only been away for three weeks, hardly long enough to make a difference. But as I walked up the stairs to find what would be my bedroom for the rest of the summer, I felt it again, that twisting in my stomach, the uncertainty of what—or who—I'd find when I opened the door.

What I found were three twin beds in a darkened room, the brilliant yellow morning light filtering in around the drawn curtains. A sliver of sunbeam landed across the two beds against the far wall, where Josie and Lucy were passed out under matching seafoam green comforters. The rumpled starfish pattern suggested where I could find their heads.

My bed was opposite theirs, and perfectly made up with a single matching throw pillow. Neither of the bodies in the beds moved. I set my bags down on the hardwood floor more loudly than I had to, and hoped they'd hear me.

The body in the bed nearest the door stirred, exposing a bare foot as the comforter slipped off the side of the mattress.

"What time is it?" Josie's hoarse morning voice asked, right before she poked her head out from under the comforter.

"Almost ten thirty. You guys don't have to get up," I offered, hoping they would. "Your mom said you got home late."

"Anyone who thinks working at an ice cream stand on Cape Cod in the summer is easy has never done it." Lucy's head appeared from under her pillow. "It's nonstop. I swear, if I have to listen to one more kid debate chocolate versus rainbow sprinkles while a line of seventeen people stand there waiting for the verdict, I will poke my eyes out with a waffle cone."

"It's only been four weeks," I said, laughing. "It can't be that bad."

"Bad?" Josie chimed in, perking up a little. "We're working for the ice cream Nazi. I swear, my dad must have harbored a serious grudge against some ice cream worker from his youth, because he acts like we're curing cancer, not serving dessert."

I sat down on my bed, kicked off my flip-flops, and tucked my legs under me. "You guys aren't making it sound that great."

My eyes had adjusted to the darkness and I could finally make out my room for the next seven weeks. Josie's discarded clothes were piled in a heap on the floor next to her bed, probably exactly where she was standing before crawling into bed last night. The shade of the lamp on the nightstand between their twin beds was tilted toward Lucy's bed, as if she'd bumped into it before falling into bed the night before and hadn't bothered to set it straight. (I knew if my mom came upstairs to see my new room, the first thing she'd do was align it into its proper position.) The night table was piled with tokens from their weeks without me—seashells, a crumpled-up paycheck, a bottle of suntan lotion, and what looked like a fish-shaped bottle opener, its gaping mouth ready to pop the cap off whatever Josie and Lucy were enjoying on the beach with their new summer friends.

Lucy flung her blankets off and flipped over so she was on her back facing me. "Oh, you'll find out tonight. We're just warning you."

"You're heading over to see Luke?" Josie asked, and I wondered if she was just confirming my plans or asking if I'd changed my mind. There still wasn't enough light in the room to tell for sure.

"Yeah," I told them. "But I'll be back by five."

"You better be. We need reinforcements." Lucy rubbed her eyes and yawned. "So what do you think of Casa Holden, your new home for the summer?"

Our room wasn't large by any stretch of the imagination. With the three of us living together, and Josie's tendency to prefer piles of clothes to drawers, it was actually going to be pretty cozy (my mom's code word for *small*). The dormered windows and pitched ceiling made me realize the room was actually above the garage, which didn't have room for four cars like Josie's house back in Branford, but just two bays like my house. Our room was almost half the size of Josie's bedroom back home, where she had her own bathroom and a sitting area. Still, from what I could tell, the Holdens' interior designer had lent her expertise to make our room as color-coordinated and comfortable as possible. "I thought this place would be more . . ."

"Obnoxious?" Josie offered. She was always appalled by the house her parents had built back home.

"Bigger?" I tried instead. "It's not as extravagant as I thought it would be."

"Yeah, I actually like it here better. My dad used to pass by this place growing up, and he always thought it was the nicest house he'd ever seen. So when he heard it was for sale, he bought it, fixed it up, and now it's home away from home. I think when he was a kid, it seemed a lot bigger."

Even though the only light in the room glowed around the curtains concealing the windows, I could still see why Josie preferred this place to the house back in Branford. The Holdens had built the other house from the ground up and, years later, it still smelled new, the immaculate paint and floors creating a flawless and pristine space, like a beautifully preserved museum. I could already tell the ceiling in our bedroom was slightly uneven, the blue-green walls freshened up with new paint but highlighted by white crown molding that imperfectly ran the circumference of the room. Much like the outside of the house, with its crushed shell driveway and window boxes overflowing with purple and hot pink petunias, our room felt more relaxed.

"I like it here already," I told them.

Lucy started braiding her hair, wide awake now. "What's not to like? We've met a ton of people. Wait until you meet them tonight."

"And there's a huge party in August before everyone starts going home. It's going to be amazing." Josie stretched her arms over her head and let out a huge yawn. "Are you sure you can't just stay now?"

I could, we all knew that. I had a feeling what she was really asking was, *did I want to?*

"We could give you the lowdown on everything—the beaches, the stores, the hot guys." Josie grinned at Lucy, who laughed under her breath.

"You're missing out on some great stories," Lucy teased, and I could tell she was trying to get me to change my mind.

"I told Luke I'd be on the eleven o'clock ferry over from Woods Hole."

I stared down at my flip-flops and could almost hear the left one telling me to stay with my friends while the right one told me to go be with my boyfriend. But flip-flops don't really talk. They just sit there waiting for you to make up your mind—either let them stay on the floor while you curled up on your new bed and talked to your best friends, or slip your toes into them and leave.

I unfolded my legs out from under me and set my feet on the floor. "I'll be back tonight for work, promise."

"Okay," Lucy conceded. "We'll fill you in later."

Josie burrowed beneath her comforter again, covering her head until she disappeared.

Lucy turned over onto her stomach and pulled her blanket onto her bed so that it hid almost all of her. "If I have one more dream about drowning in a pool of butterscotch topping, I swear I'm quitting," she mumbled into her mattress.

Once again, the room was silent. As I quietly walked to the door, I turned around one last time and saw that they'd both vanished into a sea of seafoam green and white starfish. "See you guys tonight," I whispered.

"See ya," Lucy whispered back.

Whether Josie had already passed out because she was exhausted from their late night, or she couldn't hear me, I didn't know. All I knew was that she didn't answer me, and I had a ferry waiting to take me to Luke.

I closed the bedroom door behind me and headed downstairs.

* * *

It finally felt real, that in less than an hour I'd be with Luke. I found a seat outside on the upper deck of the ferry, where I could see the island in the distance and feel the wind on my face as the boat roared toward Martha's Vineyard. I tried not to think about Josie, although it was hard not to. She was the one who helped get me and Luke back together after he found out about the guide. I knew it couldn't have been easy for her. But I also knew that she did it because I meant more to her than Luke did, and she knew how much Luke meant to me. Josie had moved on—that was obvious from the pictures and texts I'd received since she'd arrived on the Cape—but she never talked about what happened between her and Luke, or her and me. There were times, though, like back in the bedroom, when I couldn't help but feel like it was still there, the lingering hurt and the feeling that I'd betrayed our friendship, or at the very least, somehow made it less important.

When you screw up so monumentally, it's hard to imagine that other people can forgive you, and it's nearly impossible to believe they could forget. Josie, Lucy, and Luke had decided to forgive me, but there were still times when I felt like I had to prove myself, as if I was on probation for a crime I committed instead of being exonerated and given a clean slate. Not that it was anything they did or said. Maybe it was my imagination—or lingering guilt—that made me feel like I was always on the verge of losing them all for good if I made even the slightest mistake.

I watched the seagulls soar beside the ferry railing, dipping up and down with the breeze, keeping pace with the boat as if they were hitchhikers looking for a ride. Soon we were close enough to the island that I could make out the houses lining the water's edge. As the wide mouth to Vineyard Haven harbor opened to greet us, I went to the railing to look for Luke. I had been preparing myself to be away from him for the summer, and now here he was, just across the water, within reach.

As the ferry slowed, a white froth of water surged from the front of the boat until an unexpected bump against the dock jarred me back from the railing. I hadn't spotted Luke, but I had no doubt he was waiting for me.

chapter six

"**H**ere it comes," I told Sam, maneuvering my leg so my foot pressed up against the back of the driver's seat to take some of the pressure off my knee. The leg brace made it practically impossible to get comfortable, even laying across the backseat of the convertible Jeep. I'd left the ice pack at the house. I was supposed to place it on my knee every two hours to keep the swelling down, and I figured we'd be back in time. I still couldn't figure out how to keep the ice pack in place without sitting completely still, and Charlie suggested duct taping it to my knee, which didn't actually sound like a bad idea. I wouldn't start physical therapy for another two weeks, and if that didn't help, Dr. Thomas told me we'd have to think about surgery—which meant I'd still have six weeks before I'd know if I had to call the Tufts lacrosse coach to let him know I couldn't play. Everyone kept telling me to stay positive. I knew they were just trying to keep me from dwelling on the worst-case scenario. It didn't work, even though I pretended it did.

My crutches got to ride shotgun on the way to Vineyard Haven, which meant every time Sam said something, I shouted, *"What?"* from the backseat and tried to understand at least every other word as the wind blew them past me. After four days of riding in the back, I'd given up actually trying to have a coherent conversation in the car and was just thankful Sam and Charlie were willing to chauffeur me around. There was no way I was going to push my luck and ask them to put the Jeep top on just so we could talk.

In the Steamship Authority parking lot, Sam held the car door open and handed me my crutches from the front seat. "I'm going to grab a drink in the ferry terminal. I'll meet you back here."

I probably could have used the help navigating between the cars jockeying in line for the return ferry to Woods Hole or impatiently waiting for passengers to arrive, but I knew the last thing Sam wanted to do was wait for me to find my girlfriend. So instead of asking Sam to stay, I quickly scanned the deck of the boat for Emily and decided that, since I was a slow-moving target, it was probably smarter to make it to the sidewalk before trying to identify Emily among the bodies that were about to begin spilling out of the ferry's side exit.

Fortunately, the combination of my crutches and the black neoprene brace with aircraft-grade aluminum was enough to stop traffic while I hopped over to the sidewalk beside the ferry terminal. I guess that was one upside to having to be on crutches for the next seven weeks—people tended to get out of your way.

After cars started emerging onto the ferry ramp, the first passenger exited. It wasn't Emily. I almost had to laugh, because I could picture her just inside the doorway, letting little kids and families leave ahead of her, Polite Patty's voice in her head telling her to let them go first.

I lifted up my left arm, then my right, to air out my T-shirt. Crutches may be essential when attempting to walk without the use of one leg, but it was obvious that whoever invented the rubber cushions pressing against your armpits all day never had to use them in eighty-seven degrees of humidity.

I watched the stream of people zigzagging down the steel ramp until I finally spotted her. Emily was scanning the parking lot, her head craning from side to side as she searched for me among the waiting crowd. It had been almost four weeks since our last day together, I probably should have waved and drawn her attention, maybe taken off my faded Red Sox hat so she could tell it was me, but there was something nice about watching Emily without her knowing, the way she shielded her eyes against the sun and squinted. Even from the sidewalk, I could see her lips muttering, "Excuse me," as she accidently bumped into people on her way down.

There was a part of me that had thought maybe Lucy and Josie would try to convince Emily to stay in Falmouth with them. It wasn't until Emily texted me a picture from the deck of the ferry that I actually believed she was really coming over for the day. It wasn't something we talked about, what had happened between me and Josie before Emily moved back to Branford, and I was glad, because the last thing I wanted to do was rehash the whole scene at Owen's New Year's Eve party.

At this point, I think all of us—especially Emily—wanted to forget about everything that happened with the time capsule and the Guy's Guide and how it all blew up. And even though it was Josie who helped get me and Emily back together, I knew she did it because she was Emily's best friend, *not* because she'd forgotten what I did to her. I think Josie just decided that it was more important to be Emily's friend than it was to be my enemy.

I didn't cheat on Josie with the sophomore from St. Michael's at Owen's party like everyone thinks. Well, I *did*, but what Josie didn't know was that I wasn't surprised when she walked into the laundry room and found me making out with some random girl from St. Mike's. I knew Josie was looking for me, and that she would eventually look in the laundry room, so I just grabbed the first girl who walked by—who actually had a name, Allison, which I found out later—and started kissing her. And she kissed me back, which probably had something to do with the champagne she'd been guzzling with her friends for the last hour rather than a burning desire to make out with some guy beside an ironing board and a bag of Tide Pods. I'd planned the whole thing. But Josie never knew it was a setup, or that it was easier to let her think she caught me and assume I was trying to hide what I was doing instead of actually making sure she found me.

I'd wanted to break up with Josie but couldn't figure out how to do it, especially with Christmas coming up and Josie's hints about presents she wanted. That's why I emailed her that I wanted to end things—she rarely checks her email, but I knew I could always tell her it was over before she even found me in the laundry room. It wouldn't make what I did all right, but I figured it would take some of the heat off me. Was it a dick move? Sure. But sometimes it's easier to let people think you're an asshole than letting them know you're actually a coward. So I didn't cheat. I wasn't a cheater. That time.

Emily finally spotted me and started waving frantically to get my attention, unaware that I'd been watching her the whole time. When she finally stepped off the passenger ramp, she ran in my direction, her arms flailing in the air, and for a minute I thought she was actually going to knock me over, crutches and all.

"I missed you so much," she gushed, wrapping her arms around my neck and squeezing me so tight I almost had a hard time breathing and staying upright at the same time. Emily started to whisper into my ear, and then pulled back a few inches. "You feel really good, but you don't smell so great."

I laughed into Emily's hair, which *did* smell great. It was one of the reasons I fell for Emily in the first place—her ability to be completely honest and say exactly what she was thinking. It had surprised me at first, how I never had to try to figure out what Emily was *really* saying, or if she meant what she said. In the beginning, it was a little unnerving, how she just spoke what was on her mind instead of making me feel like I had to guess—and hope I guessed right. When I found out about The Book of Luke, I think that's what confused me the most—trying to decide if the girl I fell in love with was the real Emily or someone who was just pretending to be a certain way so she could prove a point.

Josie finally convinced me it wasn't all an act, and even though Josie was the *second* least likely person I should have trusted after what they did, I decided to believe her. If the person who handed me that notebook in the middle of our school assembly thought Emily was worth giving a second chance, I should, too. Even though we'd all moved on, and things with Emily had been great ever since, there was a small part of me that was still hoping Josie wasn't wrong.

"Yeah, sorry about that. These rubber pads are meant to be comfortable, but they're not exactly conducive to underarm ventilation."

Emily grinned at me. "What's with the freckles?" she asked, touching the small spots on my cheeks with the tips of her fingers.

"The sun," I told her. "And they're not freckles."

She laughed. "Whatever they are, they're cute."

Emily went in for another hug, but as she moved toward me, her foot accidentally kicked a crutch out from under me.

"Whoa!" I shifted my weight to her as I attempted to regain my balance.

"Sorry!" Emily stooped under my arm and tried to help me stand upright.

Before either of us could reach for the crutch that had crashed down on the sidewalk, a tanned hand was picking it up and handing it to me.

"Hey, thanks." I slipped the crutch back into place under my arm and took my weight off of Emily. "Emily, this is Sam."

Emily looked from me to Sam and back to me again, her eyebrows slanting together like she'd just been asked to solve a perplexing puzzle and had no idea where to begin.

"You know, the family I'm staying with on the island?" I clarified, but Emily still looked thoroughly confused. "As in *Charlie and Sam.*"

"Actually, it's just Sam. I'm not part of a crime-fighting duo or anything," Sam joked.

Emily laughed, but I knew her well enough to know it wasn't a real laugh. When Emily really found something funny, it was like her whole body was in on the joke. Her face scrunches up and her eyes sort of sparkle with light, like they're laughing, too. This time, her laugh was more like a forced breath being pushed through an equally forced smile. Emily wasn't laughing *with* Sam, she was laughing *for* Sam. It was nothing more than a polite response.

"It's nice to meet you, Sam." Emily pointed to Sam's tank top. "You're a lifeguard?"

"Yeah." Sam frowned at her, or maybe squinted into the sun; I couldn't tell because Sam's eyes were hidden behind blue polarized sunglass that reflected the confused look on Emily's face. "It's my first year and I have to say, it's not as great as I thought it would be. It's actually really boring."

"Charlie doesn't have a job this summer and it's driving Melanie—their mom—nuts," I told Emily. "Sam's actually the one who jumped in and pulled me out of the water after I messed up my knee. Charlie wasn't even watching because he was trying out his latest pick-up line on some girls who were sitting on the rocks. If Sam wasn't there, I probably would have drowned."

"Good thing you were there," Emily agreed, her smile fixed in place.

Emily was saying all the right things, but they were all wrong in a way that was so subtle, I wasn't sure if she was trying to make a good first impression on Sam, or it was just that we hadn't seen each other in almost a month.

"You all set?" Sam nodded at the bag Emily had dropped on the ground next to us.

"I'd take it but . . ." I held up my left crutch and shrugged. "I'm sort of useless these days."

"He is, really," Sam agreed. "The car's over here."

Emily didn't move. "Um, I'm going to run into the terminal for a sec. Be right back."

"You want me to go with you?" I offered.

"No, I'm fine. You guys head to the car, I'll meet you there."

"Okay, it's the red Jeep with the top down." I pointed over to our parking spot.

Emily swung her bag over her shoulder and practically raced up the steps to the terminal. "Be right back!"

Sam waited until Emily was out of earshot to say anything. "So that's Emily."

"Yep, that's Emily."

"She's not exactly what I expected," Sam admitted.

"And what was that?"

"Seriously? Well, based on what you told me, someone a little less . . ." Sam paused and tried to find the right word. "Nice. Normal."

I knew I'd regret it. It was so stupid to tell Sam about Emily and what happened with the notebook.

"Come on, give her a break." I started hobbling back toward the car and Sam followed behind me.

"If you say so," Sam reluctantly agreed, but without even looking at her, I could tell she wasn't very convinced.

chapter seven

S am was a girl.

As we walked toward the car, I tried to think if I'd missed something, some allusion to Sam *not* being a guy. Some comment about how the Sam who rescued Luke from drowning was, in fact, not the unshaven, muscled guy I'd imagined would be capable of pulling my six-foot tall, lacrosse playing boyfriend to shore.

I splashed cold water from the bathroom faucet onto my cheeks. I knew my mom would suggest using water from a public restroom sink probably wasn't the best way to ensure unclogged pores, but I wasn't looking for a dewy glow. I was trying to figure out why Luke hadn't told me that the person he had decided to live with for the summer was a girl. With sun-streaked blond hair and a body that looked perfect in a tank top and torn, faded jean shorts, which meant she probably looked even better in a bathing suit.

I tried to channel the voices of my best friends and their calm reassurances, as ferry passengers shot me dirty looks for blocking their access to the paper towel dispenser.

"Excuse me," I apologized, and moved over against the opposite wall so I could pretend to hear Lucy and Josie's voices while avoiding the wrath of disgruntled ferry passengers with dripping wet hands.

First, I heard Lucy's calm, practical explanation: If Luke was remotely attracted to Sam, he wouldn't have invited me to visit, right? And he wouldn't have had me travel all the way to the island to tell me he'd decided he wanted the hot girl he'd known forever instead of the girl he'd only been with a few months. He didn't bother pointing out that Sam was a girl because it didn't matter. To Luke, she was just a girl he'd known his whole life.

Then I listened to Josie's voice: Get over it.

So that's what I resolved to do. I ripped a paper towel from the dispenser and dried my hands and face. Then I used the damp paper towel to pull open the bathroom door before tossing it into the trash, because, if I learned anything on my mom's book tour, it was that the last thing I needed, in addition to a girl living with my boyfriend for the summer, was a handful of festering bathroom bacteria.

Luke and Sam were waiting for me, the Jeep already idling as a line of cars impatiently waited to take our parking space. Luke was sitting behind Sam, his tan arm draped across the seatback as he twisted around looking for me.

I wove my way through the cars maneuvering for parking spots and tossed my bag onto the back floormat.

"Sorry, I pretty much take up the whole thing." Luke pointed to his outstretched leg laying across both seats. I took that to mean I was supposed to sit up front with Sam.

I slipped into the passenger seat, and before I even reached for my seat belt, Sam was backing out of our spot.

I turned around so I could face Luke, even though that meant the seat belt was cutting very unattractively across my boobs.

"Does it still hurt?" I asked, nodding at Luke's knee.

"Yeah." His voice was raised as he shouted into the wind beating against his face as we drove. "We'll see what happens in seven weeks, right? Hopefully it heals and I won't need surgery."

"Right," I assured him, then turned around to face the road. I thought Sam would try to have a conversation with me, ask a few questions or just make small talk considering we were seated two feet away from one another. But she just mouthed the words to the song playing on the radio and kept her eyes straight ahead.

I couldn't tell if Sam was so perfectly comfortable around Luke that she didn't need to make small talk to fill the silence, or so *uncomfortable* with me that she didn't want to.

Sam was a girl. I still had a hard time wrapping my head around that change in events. Since I returned from my mom's tour, I'd heard about Charlie and Sam every day. Luke didn't elaborate about the family friends he would be staying with all summer, but their names found their way into our conversations and, in my mind, they were always two guys. One of them did not have long, chunky curls that caught the wind as she drove a convertible. And I never pictured Sam as someone so petite I'd feel positively Amazonian in comparison.

Twenty silent minutes later, we were winding our way through the narrow one-way streets of Edgartown until we finally pulled into the short, grassy driveway of a white clapboard house. A wooden plaque next to the front door noted it was built in 1726, and the uneven, sagging steps leading up to the front porch made me think that, unlike Josie's home in Branford, this house hadn't been touched by an interior designer.

Sam barely hesitated long enough to pull the keys out of the ignition before leaving Luke and me in the driveway to fend for ourselves.

"This place is historic?" I asked as I grabbed my tote bag from the back seat, helped Luke out of the Jeep, and handed him his crutches.

"Charlie is convinced it's haunted, but the only noises I hear in the middle of the night are Marvel having dreams about chasing squirrels. There he is now."

A brown, floppy dog galloped down the porch steps toward us. I dropped to my knees and let him sniff me while I ran my hand along his back. "He's a cutie!"

"That's Marvel. He loves me, probably because he's the only one around here who'll fetch a lacrosse ball. Come on, I'll show you around." Luke led me through the front screened door and pointed out the rooms to our left and right as we made our way toward the back of the house.

"They only live here in the summer?" I asked.

"Melanie is a college professor, so she spends her summers here, mostly writing research articles and stuff. Come on, you can meet her."

Luke led me to the entrance of a screened-in porch running along the side of the house. Luke's mom and Melanie, who were eating lunch around a white wicker table, stopped talking when they saw us.

"Emily!" Mrs. Preston stood up and reached her arms out for me. "You made it!"

She hugged me and then turned me to face Melanie. "This is Emily."

"Hi, it's nice to meet you." I reached into my bag and handed Melanie the small box of scented soaps my mom had given me. "It's just a little something for having me here."

"Thank you, that wasn't necessary." Melanie held the box up to her nose and inhaled, closing her eyes and grinning. "Mmm, gardenias, my favorite. I've heard a lot about you, Emily. All good, of course. You two want to join us?"

I hadn't eaten since my mom and I stopped for blueberry muffins on our way to Josie's house. But before I could accept the offer and dig into the pasta salad in a bowl on the table, Luke spoke up.

"I'm going to show Em around," Luke told Melanie. "We'll grab something in a little while."

I hoped *a little while* meant sooner rather than later. I followed Luke outside into the backyard, where Marvel was waiting for us with a saliva-coated lacrosse ball in his mouth.

"Did you bring me a present, too?" Luke asked me.

"It's just soap."

"Soap?"

"Don't ask. Is that a chicken coop over there?" I pointed to the small, fenced-in area toward the left corner of the yard.

"Yeah, Melanie likes fresh eggs. She swears they taste better." Luke bent down and tugged the ball loose from Marvel's clenched jaws. "Gotta be honest with you, though, I can't tell the difference."

Luke threw the ball in a high arc toward the coop, giving Marvel time to follow it with his eyes and then race to retrieve it.

"Usually he just drops the ball into the net of my stick so I can avoid this," he told me, wiping his hand down the side of his shorts.

"What's that?" I asked, pointing toward the opposite corner of the yard. I thought maybe it was a shed for a lawn mower and gardening equipment, but it actually had a window and a real front door.

Luke tipped his head toward the shed, indicating I should follow him. "Come on, I'll show you."

As we got closer, it looked more like a guest house than a shed. The white-painted shingles hadn't weathered the winter so well, and while some paint had blistered up in puffy pockets, in other places, the paint was peeling back like skin after a bad sunburn. The roof was coated in mounds of green moss, but the front door still shone a glossy red, which made it seem too nice for just a shed filled with Weed Wackers and fertilizer.

"This is the boathouse, which isn't really a boathouse at all because, obviously, we're not on the water." Luke pushed open the door and hopped back to give me enough room to enter. "But for some reason, we've always called it that."

"Ping pong?" I asked when I saw the table. Lined up beside the ping pong table, there was also a pool table, a faded pink and blue floral couch pushed against the far wall, and a dart board on the side wall. A wobbly bookcase was stacked with board games in faded, warped cardboard boxes. The *boathouse* was more like a well-worn game room, with scuffed wooden floors and sheer, almost transparent blue checked curtains that had seen better days. There was also barely enough room to navigate around, which meant we had to walk along the perimeter of the boathouse to even get to the sofa.

"Yep, and so far, I've taken Charlie for over fifty bucks."

"You talking about me?" A guy who I assumed was Charlie stood in the open doorway. I could immediately see the resemblance to his sister, which meant he also looked like he stepped out of a J.Crew catalog. "Don't let him fool you, I take it easy on him."

"Yeah, right." Luke shook his head. "Charlie, this is Emily."

Charlie picked up a ping pong paddle and bounced a ball over the net toward me. "You play?"

I caught the ball and held it. "A few times."

"Don't do it," Luke warned me. "We'll never get out of here."

"Just one game," Charlie insisted. "It'll be quick."

I glanced over at Luke, who looked like he was about to continue protesting, but instead he nodded.

"Okay, fine, just one," he reluctantly agreed.

Charlie clapped his paddle against the table. "Cool, you can serve first."

"You sure?" I asked, picking up my paddle and spinning it against the palm of my hand to get a feel for the grip.

Charlie laughed at me. "Yeah, I'm sure."

Luke hopped over to the couch and sat down on the far end so he could rest his leg across the sagging cushions.

"You ready?" I asked when he'd finished settling in.

Luke gave me a thumbs-up. "When you are."

I can play ping pong. Well. Actually, really, *really* well, thanks to an insanely humid and rainy six weeks spent at a summer sleepaway camp with a single air-conditioned activity room—the one with three ping pong tables.

Luke hadn't told me a lot fabout Charlie, other than his aversion to working and ability to drive Sam nuts. I had to admit, after a car ride that made me feel like I'd entered the cone of silence, I'd been hoping for a warmer reception from Charlie than I got from his sister. I was pretty sure kicking his ass in ping pong wouldn't be the surest way to make him like me. I had a choice to make: let him win, make it a close game, or show Charlie I knew how to play.

Honestly, it probably should have been a tougher decision. I tossed the ball in the air, let it bounce once on the table, and smacked it across the net.

Charlie returned my first serve, *barely*, but after that, he had a hard time keeping a volley going. He may have underestimated me, but Charlie was right about one thing—it was a quick game. I won eleven to two.

"Nicely played." Charlie acknowledged my win with an approving nod before turning to Luke. "You didn't tell me your girlfriend was a ringer."

"I didn't know," Luke admitted. "I'm just glad I figured that out before she whipped me."

"Whipped? Really?" Charlie cringed. "I don't know that I'd say she *whipped* me. Do you play on a varsity ping pong team or something?"

I spun the paddle in my hand once and laid it back on the table. "No, just lots of hours indoors avoiding blood-sucking mosquitoes."

"I can acknowledge when I've been outplayed." Charlie put his paddle down. "Just give me a chance to redeem myself before you leave."

"She's only here for the afternoon," Luke told him.

"Well then." Charlie paused and looked around the boathouse like he was trying to decide what to do next. "You play?" he asked me, pointing to the dart board on the wall.

"Okay, enough, I'm starving." Luke reached for his crutches.

Charlie let out an exasperated breath. "Fine, but I want it noted that you owe me a rematch."

"Noted," I agreed.

"I was going to head into town. You guys want a ride?" Charlie offered.

Luke winced as he lifted himself off the couch. "No, I think we'll just grab something here."

I'd really been hoping to be alone with Luke, maybe walk around downtown and see the harbor, but the way he tentatively moved his braced leg to the floor made it clear he wasn't up for going anywhere. The house wasn't very big, and I knew Melanie and Mrs. Preston were still home and Sam was lurking somewhere inside. A ghost wandering the halls of the house, that I could handle. But Sam? At least a ghost would acknowledge my presence.

"Okay, your call." Charlie turned to leave us, but then spun around and faced me, forking two fingers into a sort of peace sign and then pointing them at me as if casting a spell. "Later, you, me," he said, rotating his hand back and forth between my eyes and then his.

It was official. Charlie was definitely my favorite sibling in the house. "You're on."

* * *

Melanie and Mrs. Preston actually weren't inside the house, but they'd left us a note telling us they'd gone grocery shopping. They'd also left us two sandwiches, some pasta salad, and a bowl of grapes they'd put out on the kitchen counter. I grabbed the tray with our lunches, and Luke and I went out to the back patio.

71

"You never told me you could play ping pong," Luke said between bites of pasta salad.

"Luke, I can play ping pong."

"Is that what you did when you lived in Chicago? Hustle people at ping pong?"

"Hardly."

"I have to admit, it was pretty cool watching Charlie's face when he realized he'd underestimated you."

It had never occurred to me that Luke didn't know I was a pretty fierce ping pong player, or that he had no idea I'd gone to summer camp in New Hampshire for a miserable two summers in elementary school. It wasn't Earth shattering stuff—just small details and experiences I rarely ever thought about until it mattered, like today in the boathouse. Still, it was weird to think that there was so much Luke needed to learn about me. Which meant that, even though I felt like I knew Luke almost better than anyone else, there was also probably so much I didn't know about him.

"What other talents are you hiding from me, Emily Abbott?" he asked.

"Hmm, let me think." I took a bite of my sandwich and chewed until I came up with a few more obscure skills to share. "Did you know I can change a flat tire?"

"I did not," Luke admitted. "Go on."

"I can name the twelve major Greek gods," I told him.

"Is one of them named Luke?" he ventured, and then waved his fork at me. "Never mind, continue."

"I can do this." I tossed a grape into the air and caught it in my mouth. "And I can open a Hyatt bathroom doorknob with my elbows."

"That sounds vaguely useful."

"Spoken like someone who didn't spend three weeks living in hotel rooms. Not vaguely useful, *very*. Now what about you? What should I know that I don't?"

"Let's see . . . well, I can recite all the words to the theme song from SpongeBob SquarePants."

"Talk about useful," I agreed.

"We were here visiting Melanie one summer, and there was a SpongeBob marathon on TV. Sam and I basically watched every episode about seventeen times."

I'd wanted Luke to tell me something no one else knew about him, not something Sam had known for years. It made me realize that she probably knew things I'd never find out unless we spent the entire summer playing this game of question and answer.

"Did you come here a lot?" I asked.

"Every summer for as long as I can remember, usually for a week, sometimes just a few days, but always."

"How come you never mentioned Charlie before? Or Sam?"

"How come I didn't know you had such talented elbows?" he replied.

He was trying to get me to laugh, something that was usually so easy. But I didn't feel like laughing. I closed my eyes and took a deep breath, inhaling a combination of damp, salty air and fresh cut grass. "Come on, I'm serious."

When I opened my eyes, Luke was staring at me. "Some new yoga thing you learned on the road with your mom?"

I stared at the mound of elbow pasta on my plate and moved it around with my fork as I carefully chose my words. "This is probably my imagination, but I get the feeling Sam doesn't like me."

I wasn't expecting Luke to tell me Sam thought I was the best thing ever, but I thought at least he'd remind me that Sam didn't even know me. Instead, he was quiet.

"We just met. How could she not like me already?" I didn't even know she existed until a few hours ago, but Sam already knew enough to dislike me?

"Are you saying that once she knows you, at least she'll have a reason?" Luke joked. When I didn't smile, he shrugged. "What's it matter? *I* like you enough for both of us."

His answer should have satisfied me, but it didn't. "Why doesn't she like me?"

"I didn't say she doesn't like you. Look, she hates her job. And she hates that Charlie gets to do nothing all day but sleep late and hang out. She didn't even want to come here this summer. All her friends got internships in the city or something, and she wanted to stay home. If she's not exactly the friendliest person in the world, it's not personal, believe me."

I wanted to believe him, because the only other option was that Sam had decided she didn't like me before she even *met* me, and there was no logical reason why she'd do that. Unless it involved Luke. Because she may not know anything about me, but she obviously had a long history with my boyfriend.

"Okay, if you say so," I conceded.

"Good." He speared what was left of my pasta salad with his fork and took a bite. "Besides, I'm sure once you two spend some time together, she'll love you as much as I do."

"And how much is that?" I asked.

Luke tapped his fork on the table while he thought of an answer. "A 9.5."

"Oh, really? And what about the other point five?"

"The Russian judge is tough."

I pushed my chair away from the table, scraping the legs across the slate patio like nails on a chalkboard. "How about I bring this stuff inside and meet you in the boathouse... without Charlie this time?"

"I think I like where this is going." Luke smiled at me, and I couldn't help but smile back thinking about being alone with him on that faded pink and blue floral couch. "I'll get a head start, since I don't move very fast these days, as you've noticed." He reached for a crutch and used it to pull himself up from the table.

I started piling our plates on the tray, and Luke hopped away in the direction of the boathouse, moving more quickly than he had since I'd arrived. Obviously, he was looking forward to the couch, too.

As soon as I pulled open the kitchen screen door, I saw Sam standing at the counter with her back to me. Maybe Luke was right about her. Maybe we just needed to get to know each other.

"Hi." I set the tray down beside the sink and opened the dishwasher door.

"Hey," she answered.

"So you don't like being a lifeguard?" I asked as I scraped what remained on our plates into the trash can and then placed them in the dishwasher racks. "I always thought it seemed like a fun job."

"You'd think so," she answered, not taking her eyes off the sandwich she was composing with the care of an artist working on a canvas.

"I have a job at the Scoop Shack in Falmouth. I start tonight," I told her. "Have you ever been there?"

"I have some friends in Falmouth for the summer." Sam peeled two slices of Swiss cheese apart and carefully laid them on the two slices of bread laid out on the cutting board in front of her. Either she found me to be the most boring person on the Earth at that moment, or making a turkey sandwich was something that required extreme concentration.

Obviously, we weren't going to bond over summer jobs.

"It's supposed to have some of the best ice cream on the Cape," I added, but Sam was now focused on folding slices of turkey into perfectly portioned pieces.

Luke was wrong. Sam wasn't going to try to get to know me. She was barely going to carry on a conversation with me.

Pickles. Lettuce. Sam just continued to meticulously build her sandwich like she was on a cooking competition show where the precise placement of green flourishes was the difference between being voted off or winning the grand prize. I tried to do what Luke suggested, not take it personally, but that was difficult because it felt awfully personal.

"Well, I'm just going to grab us some drinks." I took two bottles of peach iced tea from the refrigerator and paused to see if Sam would acknowledge anything I'd said. She didn't. "See ya later."

"Luke told me what you did." Sam's voice stopped me as my hand reached out to push open the screen door.

At first, I thought she meant Charlie—that he'd told her about our ping pong match. But she didn't say Charlie. She said Luke.

I turned around and found Sam standing there with her sandwich in one hand and the mustard knife in the other as she chewed her first bite. She still didn't look up at me. "What I did?"

Sam continued chewing and didn't answer me until she'd swallowed. My mother would applaud her manners. "How you got together." Now Sam turned her eyes on me. "Your experiment. *The guide.*"

I stood there silently while Sam consumed her lunch and the meaning behind what she just said sank in.

"I've known Luke for practically my whole life, and he's a good guy. A *really* good guy," she repeated, as if I didn't get her point the first time. "I know he wants us to like each other and be friends and all that, but I think what you did was shitty."

I opened my mouth to respond, attempting to formulate a response to Sam's declaration of war. But nothing came out. After ignoring me in the Jeep and avoiding my attempts at conversation in the kitchen, Sam was finally ready to talk, and that meant she wasn't going to wait for me to defend myself before continuing.

"I mean, who does something like that?" She shook her head at me and turned back toward the counter, placing the knife in the sink before twisting the end of the bread bag and tying it closed.

I was torn between pointing out that what happened between me and Luke was none of her business, and wanting to explain what happened—to have her understand that no matter what she thought, it wasn't that simple.

And that's when it hit me. Luke told Sam. The only way she could know what happened was if Luke told her our story and all of its gory details.

There was no forgiving and forgetting, no putting it behind us and moving on. What happened was part of our brief history, but by telling Sam, Luke had made it part of our present.

Instead of explaining, I turned my back on Sam and let the sound of the screen door smacking closed speak for itself.

* * *

"You told her?" I found Luke in the boathouse, his leg up on the couch as he bounced a ping pong ball against the wall. "You told Sam?"

"Told her about what?" he asked, continuing to bounce the ball against the wall and catching it in his left hand.

About what? Was he kidding me? "*The guide*, Luke. How could you do that?" I demanded.

"She asked how we met."

"We met at school, Luke. That's all you had to say."

This time, Luke didn't catch the ball when it bounced off the wall. He just let it land on the floor and roll under the couch. "First of all, I didn't mean to tell her, and second, I didn't make it sound terrible at all. I just started explaining how you'd just moved back from Chicago and I hadn't seen you since you moved away after freshman year, and the next thing I knew . . ."

"The next thing you knew, you were telling her about the guide?"

"I didn't make a big deal about it, Em. I told her we figured it out, that everything was fine. Better than fine."

"You acted like you didn't know why she was being such a bitch to me, but you knew! And you let me walk into a trap. She just ambushed me in the kitchen, where I was trying to have a nice conversation, and she starts telling me what a horrible person I am."

"Come on, I seriously doubt she did that."

"Now you're defending her?"

"I'm not defending anyone, Emily. Jesus, I don't know what you're getting so bent out of shape about."

"Are you kidding me?"

"Why don't you calm down and give *me* the benefit of the doubt this time."

It felt like a low blow, a backhanded way of reminding me that no matter what he did, what I'd done would always be worse.

"Look, I was telling her about my girlfriend. So when she asked how we got together, I told her. I wasn't going to lie about it."

"I'm not saying you should have lied. I'm just saying you didn't need to tell her everything."

The hollow chime of a church bell echoed in the distance. It was already three thirty. "I should go. And I'm not asking Sam for a ride. I'll take the bus or something."

"Em—" Luke jumped off the couch and reached to stop me, immediately letting out a pained groan as his hand brushed my arm.

"Are you okay?" I asked, lightly touching his elbow as he inhaled deeply and rested his weight on his good leg.

The sound of the bell's last chime faded away. "Em, what's going on? You come here for the day, and now you're pissed at me. Yes, I told Sam, but I had no idea she'd make it into a thing with you. I'll talk to her if you want."

Luke chewed on his lip, his face serious. I noticed his hand rubbing the side of his knee as he waited for me to say something, anything, as long as it would get us back on track now that I'd derailed our day together.

"Here . . ." I led Luke back to the couch and helped him swing his braced leg up onto the cushion. I watched the tight lines across his forehead fade. Then I sat down on the edge of the sofa and faced him. "You don't have to talk to her about it."

"I will if you want me to, like I said—if it matters to you that much."

I laid my hand on his brace, the metal cool against my fingers. I knew that somewhere under the aluminum, black mesh, and Velcro, his skin was warm, the fine hairs pale from hours in the summer sun. "No, it's fine."

"Okay, if you say so."

I moved my hand to his other leg and laid it just below the hem of his shorts, so I could feel his skin. "I can't be late for work, though. I should probably head to the ferry."

Luke moved his hand over mine. "Stay."

"I can't stay, Luke. Mr. Holden will kill me."

"I doubt that. Come on, the rest of the day, just you and me." He patted the sofa and then rubbed his palm in circles against what was supposed to be a hot-pink petunia, but which looked like a pale, threadbare memory of its former self. "It's awfully comfortable here."

I smiled and shook my head.

"Em, I'm sorry. Believe me, if I thought it would upset you this much, I wouldn't have said anything about it to Sam. I had no idea she'd call you out, and if I did I would have stopped her."

"I just don't understand why."

"I told her because we're friends. I told her because she asked and I really didn't think it was that big of a deal because everything is good now. I just told her the truth."

The truth. It was something we promised each other moving forward. No more secrets.

"When we said no more secrets, I meant between us. You can keep secrets from anyone else you like!" I expected Luke to laugh, which was my intention as I tried to lighten the air between us before I had to leave him. I didn't want to end our day like this.

But Luke didn't laugh. I couldn't even get him to smile. Instead, he cast his eyes down at the faded petunia and avoided looking at me.

He just told Sam the truth. Maybe what really bothered me wasn't the fact that he told Sam, but what telling her meant. Luke confided in Sam, let her into our relationship in a way that made it feel less special, less *ours*.

But I believed him. I may not have eighteen years of history with Luke, but I did know him. He wouldn't have told Sam if he knew it would hurt me.

Luke continued to stare at the faded floral pattern between us, his brows knitted together like he was struggling with what to say next.

"Okay," I conceded, and Luke finally looked up at me.

"Please stay?" Luke pulled me toward him and brushed his lips against my neck, his warm breath softly blowing on my damp skin. "It's your job, I get it. But you have the entire summer to prove you're the model employee with the skills to swirl a large cone like nobody's business. I'm just asking for a few more hours."

Josie and Lucy were expecting me. Mr. Holden was expecting me. My mom would probably write an entire chapter in one of her books about being accountable for your responsibilities if she knew I was even thinking about skipping out on my first night of work.

Still, it was hard to believe I was that indispensable to an ice cream stand that had managed to survive the month of June without me.

"Okay, but I have to go back tonight." I wiggled away from Luke and sat up so I could text Josie and Lucy. *Catching the last ferry. See you at home tonight.*

I waited for a reply, but there was none. That was a good sign, right? If they were pissed or the entire place was going to come crashing down in a pile of waffle cones and rainbow sprinkles because I wasn't there to put cherries on top of sundaes, they would have texted back and I would have caught my ferry as planned. But there was none of that. I was good to go.

"Any way we can walk into town and look around?" I asked Luke.

"Only if you're willing to have a five-minute walk take six times longer than it should."

I gently moved Luke's leg over and laid down beside him. The couch wasn't attractive, but it was wide. "That's okay. I think I like my other idea better."

"Which idea was that?" Luke asked, sliding his arm under my neck and rolling me over onto my side so my chin rested against his chest.

No secrets, that's what we'd promised each other.

I ran my fingers along the waist of his shorts and pushed his T-shirt away, exposing the tanned skin of his stomach. "The one where it's just the two of us here alone."

chapter eight

I'd texted Josie and Lucy from the terminal to let them know my ferry would arrive right around the time they got off work. I hadn't planned on it taking me almost twenty minutes to finally find a cab in Woods Hole, which is why when it finally dropped me off at the Holdens', all the windows were dark and the house was silent.

For a minute, I almost wondered if Josie and Lucy had gone out after work, but then I remembered seeing Josie's car was in the driveway. A noise down the hallway made me think they had waited up for me, but as I followed the only light in the house to the kitchen, I didn't find my friends—just a tall figure standing in front of an open refrigerator. "Mr. Holden?"

Josie's dad turned around to face me, a carton of milk in one hand and a bowl of strawberries in the other.

"Emily." It wasn't the most welcoming greeting. He nodded toward the kitchen table, where a box of Mini-Wheats sat beside an empty bowl. "Take a seat."

I did as he asked, even though it was almost midnight and I wasn't exactly in the mood for breakfast. From the look on Mr. Holden's face, I had the feeling he wasn't inviting me to join him for a meal.

"I have to say, I didn't expect this from you of all people." Mr. Holden came over and sat down across from me at the table. "I mean, Josie, sure, Lucy, maybe, but not you, Emily."

"I'm sorry, Mr. Holden. I promise I'll be ready for work tomorrow right on time, even earlier if you want," I offered, hoping he'd see that this was a one-time thing and not an ongoing employment habit.

"You know I like you, Emily, but if I let you slide on this, what message does that send to the rest of the staff?" He held the carton of milk in the air mid-pour, as if pondering the answer to his own question.

"That you're understanding?" I tried, but it was already obvious he had come to his own conclusion.

"I'm sorry, Emily. You know I don't want to do this, but I don't really see any other choice."

"What are you saying?" I asked.

He poured the milk into his bowl before continuing, and I hoped he was just going to cut my hours for a few weeks or make me work the day shifts. "I'm saying you're fired."

"Seriously?" I stammered. "You're firing me?"

"I guess I am, but you know what else I'm doing?" he asked, and all I could think was *ruining my summer, helping me go broke*, and *giving my parents an excuse to make me go home?*

But instead of letting Mr. Holden see that I was on the verge of freaking out, I decided to let him see me as the poised, mature person I wanted him to think was sitting in front of him. Someone worth giving a second chance.

"What's that?" I replied.

"I'm giving you an opportunity to learn from this experience. I know it will be difficult not being with Josie and Lucy at the Shack, but I think we both know you'll be the better for it."

Better? There was no way I would be *better* because I lost my job.

Mr. Holden stood up and pushed his chair back. He picked up the milk and strawberries and walked them back to the refrigerator: then returned to the table and took the bowl of cereal before turning to leave. I wasn't above begging him to change his mind, and I was about to do just that when he stopped and faced me again.

"I'll tell you what, Emily. I've known you a long time, and you've always been a good kid. So I'm willing to give you a break."

I let a huge breath of relief escape and almost wanted to hug the man. "Thank you, Mr. Holden. I really appreciate that."

"I know you do." He smiled at me, and I felt like we were having a moment. "You can borrow one of the bikes in the garage. That should help you get around while you look for a new job."

So much for our moment.

Mr. Holden had to know my parents would kill me for losing my job at the Shack. Not just *losing*, but being *fired*. I was a crappy employee. Irresponsible. Unreliable.

I was my mom's worst nightmare.

As I made my way upstairs to my new bedroom, I could hear Mr. Holden laughing at something on the TV he was watching in the family room, completely unaware that while he was eating a bowl of Mini-Wheats, my entire summer was blowing up.

I couldn't help but wonder if Mr. Holden had told Josie and Lucy he was going to fire me. And if he had, why didn't they warn me?

"Are you guys awake?" I whispered, closing the bedroom door behind me with a soft click. As my eyes adjusted to the darkness, I started to make out two rumpled figures in the beds.

"What happened to you tonight?" a voice asked. I didn't need to see her face to recognize that it was Josie, or that the flat, snipped tone meant she wasn't just awake, she'd been waiting for me. I knew my best friend well enough to know she wasn't asking because she was concerned. She wasn't even asking because I'd promised her dad I'd work tonight. No, Josie had been lying awake in bed, waiting for me to come home and explain why I'd chosen Luke over my friends.

"I decided to stay until the last ferry," I told her, feeling my way toward the bed until my fingertips found the cool, soft comforter, its embroidered starfish guiding me toward the pillow propped up and waiting for me. I kicked off my flip-flops and crawled between the sheets. I could see the shadow of my two unpacked bags sitting on the floor, reminding me that I hadn't even been here twenty-four hours and already things were out of whack.

"We know that." I heard the click of a lamp switch just before the room exploded with light. "What we don't know is why."

Josie was sitting up in bed looking at me. Lucy was in the other bed, on her side, her head resting in her hand as she waited for me to answer.

I wished there was an easy explanation—I missed the ferry, I lost my wallet—anything that wouldn't sound as bad as the truth. *I made a choice.* I couldn't even tell them it had been worth it, only that, at the time, it had seemed like the right choice.

"It's a long story," I told them instead.

"I could go for a good bedtime story," Lucy offered, giving me a weak smile and, at the same time, letting me know she was willing to hear me out. "What happened?"

I could tell Lucy was hoping for a good excuse—something that kept me from looking like the terrible friend I resembled right now. My only real option was to tell them the truth and hope they'd understand.

"I'm sorry, I know I blew it. It's just that, well, remember Sam? The family friend Luke's staying with?"

"Yeah." Lucy yawned, and even though it was late and she was probably tired from working, I couldn't help but think my bedtime story wasn't as interesting as she'd hoped, and she thought my reason for staying on the island with Luke was going to be lame.

"She hates me."

"*She?*" they both repeated in unison.

"Yep. Sam is a girl. And apparently she hates me."

"So?" Josie shrugged. "You decided to blow off your first night of work so you could try to make her like you?"

"Of course not," I told them, even though Josie was sort of right. Hadn't that been what I was trying to do in the kitchen before I realized Sam had no intention of becoming my friend? Josie knew me too well. That's the thing about best friends, there's no bullshitting them, even when you wished you could.

"Then what? I don't get it. Besides, it's just some stupid family friend he never sees anyway. Who cares if she hates you. She doesn't even know you," Josie pointed out, which was so like her, to come to my defense even when she was pissed I ditched them tonight.

But the thing was, *I* cared.

On the ferry back to Woods Hole, I'd kept thinking that if only Sam knew me, everything would be fine again. Only now, watching Josie and Lucy wait for my answer, I knew that Sam not liking me wasn't what really bothered me. Of course I wanted her to like me. I wanted all of Luke's friends to like me. I'd gone out of my way to show all of them that I knew I'd made a mistake and I wouldn't screw Luke over again. But it wasn't *why* Sam hated me that bothered me so much, because she was just looking out for Luke, which is what friends do. I mean, Sam jumped into an ocean and saved Luke from drowning while everyone else sat on the rocks and watched. She didn't do that because Luke was just some guy, even if she *was* a lifeguard. Whatever was between Sam and Luke, it was important.

How could I compete with the eighteen years of summers Sam and Luke already shared? How could Luke ignore what Sam thought about me when she obviously knew more about Luke than I did?

"It's not *that* she hates me so much, it's *why* she hates me. Luke told her about the guide."

"He did?" Josie punched her pillow and positioned it behind her head. "Why would he do that?"

This time, it was my turn to shrug. "He said he didn't do it on purpose. They were just talking."

"Still, that seems weird, don't you think?" Lucy asked. "I mean, he had to know how that made you look."

"I told him that, but he didn't think it was a big deal."

I half expected Lucy and Josie to agree with him, but instead they were quiet. The chirping of crickets crackled through the screens in our bedroom windows, and I pictured a row of nocturnal insects lined up outside listening to our conversation.

"It's weird, isn't it?" I finally asked. "I mean, I thought all that was behind us."

"It doesn't exactly make you look like the greatest girlfriend ever, but I don't know." Lucy turned over onto her back and rubbed her eyes. "Maybe he wanted her to know so she'd understand what you both went through to be together. Maybe he thought she'd like you *more* if she knew."

"If that was what he wanted, then it backfired, because you should see the way she looks at me." I rested my head against my pillow and pictured Sam's face in the kitchen—the air of confidence she filled the room with, her certainty about me, and about her relationship with Luke.

"Well, it doesn't really matter what this Sam thinks, right?" Josie told me, once again on my side. "And obviously her opinion of you doesn't matter that much to Luke, because it sounds like everything is fine between you two. Don't let her get to you."

"I know, you're right."

"Of course I'm right. Forget about Sam. You're here now and our summer is still going to be awesome."

I'd been trying so hard to get Lucy and Josie to understand why I'd stayed on the Vineyard with Luke that I almost forgot Sam was only half of my problem.

"Oh yeah, there's one more thing." I sighed. "Your dad just fired me."

Josie tossed a pillow at the window screen and, for a second, the chirping stopped. "I had a feeling he was going to do that. Now I feel bad. I can talk to him if you want, but I don't think it will do any good. You know how he is."

Yes, I knew. "He told me to look at this as a learning experience."

"Oh, that is *so* my dad." Josie cringed. She plumped up the one remaining pillow on her bed and laid her head down before giving me a weak smile. "It probably doesn't help, but you still have us."

"What are you going to do now?" Lucy asked.

"I guess I have to find another job. It's either that or go home, right?"

Josie shook her head. "No way, you can't do that. You just got here."

"At least there's one good thing in all of this," I told them, my voice hopeful as I tried to find the silver lining in the huge storm cloud hanging over my summer.

"Sam's really ugly?" Josie laughed at herself but when she saw my face crumple, she turned serious. "Oh, wow, that sucks."

My inability to answer must have said it all, because Lucy and Josie climbed out of their beds and came over to sit with me.

"I was kidding. Come on, it can't be that bad." Josie put her arm over my shoulder and hugged me.

Lucy took Josie's cue and wrapped her arm around my waist. "Seriously, tell us, what's the one good thing?"

It was hard to even remember that I'd thought there was a silver lining to this storm cloud. "I was going to say at least your dad said I could borrow a bike."

chapter nine

I had no job. No paycheck to look forward to. No car to get anywhere. No idea where anything was in town and, even if I did, no idea where to go. But I had a bike.

The next morning, I thought Mr. Holden might actually reconsider, but it turns out he's a big believer in sticking to his word. I was going to be the example for all the other Scoop Shack employees. A cautionary tale for anyone else who thought Mr. Holden might be the kind of guy to offer second chances.

So I had two choices: call my parents and tell them to come pick me up, or find a new job. Fast.

If my parents found out I was unemployed, my summer with Josie and Lucy would be over. Not only would I have to listen to lectures about responsibility and good decision making, but they'd make me live out my last summer before college at home, by myself, solo. The only reason they agreed to let me spend the summer at Josie's was because I had a job lined up and Mr. Holden had assured them he wasn't about to let any of us become slackers. It was not my parents' intention to have me lounging around the Holdens' pool all summer working on my tan.

I left Lucy and Josie sleeping in bed and headed out early in search of anyone still looking for summer help. My transportation was in the garage—a metallic purple mountain bike with nubby tires that I hoped would keep me from wiping out on the sand-swept roads I had to navigate on my way into town.

After a few wrong turns, and asking for directions from three people who were out walking their dogs, I finally found the main street. It was exactly what you'd expect to find on a picture-perfect postcard of a quaint Cape Cod town. Green-and-white striped awnings shaded paned picture windows showcasing homemade fudge, pastel-colored flip-flops, and oversized canvas beach bags. Almost every weathered and shingled storefront seemed to have a starfish or shell motif, and American flags swayed in the breeze beside front doors propped open by heavy stones painted with the word *Welcome*. There had to be at least thirty shops and cafés lining the street, not to mention the colonial bed and breakfasts and seafood shanties I'd pedaled past on my way into town. I figured one of them would be grateful to have an able-bodied girl walk through their front door ready to roll up her sleeves and go to work.

But, it turns out, I figured wrong. The gift stores were fully staffed, the ice cream shops had a waiting list of students just like me hoping to score a paycheck, and the restaurants and inns wanted someone with prior experience. I tried to explain that if anyone knew how to properly serve and clean, it was the daughter of Polite Patty Abbott, but they didn't seem impressed. Even though they all said they'd love to have my mom stop by if she ever came to town, and a few even had her bestsellers on their sitting room bookshelves, just being related to Polite Patty didn't make up for my lack of any marketable skills.

By eleven o'clock, I'd walked in and out of every store and responded with a smile and a *thank you* when the managers told me they'd call if something opened up. Defeated, I pushed my bike toward a bench and sat down to figure out my next move.

Even if I could argue that it was partially Luke's fault for even asking me to stay in the first place, I knew I had no one to blame but myself. One bad decision, and why? Because at the time, in the moment, all I could see was the knowing look on Sam's face, equal parts disdain and satisfaction, as she stripped away the person I was trying so hard to prove I was and reminded me that it wasn't that simple. There was something in the way she watched my reaction that made me think she enjoyed my surprise as she laid out how Luke had told her about the notebook, as if she knew he'd shared a secret, something that was meant to just be between Luke and me. She didn't just want to protect Luke; she wanted me to know that he trusted her enough to share the details of our relationship. And she wanted me to know that, given what he'd told her, she didn't trust me at all.

I could stay with Luke an extra hour, or two, or three, but eventually I'd have to leave and Sam would still be there. She'd share the bathroom sink every morning, kill time with games of ping pong and pool on rainy afternoons, and have hours to drift in and out of conversation instead of trying to squeeze it in to a few hours between ferry arrivals and departures.

When I was in the boathouse with Luke, I'd reduced it to a decision about a ferry. It was black and white, a yes or no answer. A or B. Go now or go later. But it was more than that. As Luke and I laid on the couch together, his warm breath in my ear every time the smooth, tanned skin of his stomach rose and fell under my fingertips, the consequences of staying didn't scare me as much as leaving him with Sam.

All I had to do was tell Luke no. To catch the ferry as planned. I'd made the wrong choice, and instead of being able to spend my nights with Lucy and Josie and still spend some days with Luke, I was pushing a bike around Falmouth and on the verge of heatstroke.

I couldn't call Lucy and Josie. I had a feeling I'd used up my allowance of friendly empathy last night. Now I was on my own to figure out how to undo what I'd done.

I hadn't told Luke yet that Mr. Holden fired me. First of all, it was humiliating. I mean, he's my best friend's dad. You'd think if anyone would give me a break, it would be him. Second, I was hoping I'd have another job lined up before I had to tell him, which wouldn't make my firing any less embarrassing, but at least I'd prove I hadn't totally screwed up the summer. I didn't want to have to tell him I was one phone call away from being exiled back to Branford.

"Wow, that sucks," Luke commiserated with me when I finally gave in and called him. "But as long as you don't have to work today, why don't you come over?"

"I can't do that, I just got here." I took a sip of the four-dollar lemonade I'd purchased at the last café that rejected me. Apparently, quaint summer towns knew vacationers wouldn't complain about spending an insanely ridiculous sum on something as simple as lemonade when they were just here for a week. But I was supposed to spend my summer in Falmouth and, at this rate, I'd be out of money by Monday.

"But without a job, you have no reason to hang around there all day," Luke pointed out.

"Actually, not having a job is *exactly* the reason I have to hang around here. I have to find a new one."

"Let's be honest, Em, nobody is hiring anyone on July Fourth weekend."

"It's the busiest weekend of the year. If ever there was a day to ask if anyone is hiring, it's today." I was trying to convince myself as much as convince Luke.

"Fine, but when you finally give up, remember I'm just a ferry ride away."

"I'll remember."

"So what about tomorrow?" he suggested. "Charlie and Sam's friends have a bunch of fireworks."

"Isn't that illegal?" I could practically hear my mom's annual Fourth of July warning about losing fingers, or at the very least an eyebrow.

"Illegal but awesome."

"We'll see," I said, but between yesterday's ferry rides, catching a cab back to Josie's, and the jacked-up price of a lemonade, I'd already burned through half of what little babysitting money I had left. The last thing I needed to do was compound last night's bad decision with another one, no matter how tempting Luke's invitation.

Instead, I said good-bye, hopped on my bike, and decided to ride until I reached a beach, which wasn't a guarantee since I didn't know my way around. I just headed in what seemed like the direction of the water and figured I'd find a stretch of sand when I got there.

After twenty minutes of pedaling, I was grateful to spot a glimpse of water at the end of the road. Unfortunately, there was no sandy beach to dig my sweaty feet into. Instead, I found a small, gray-shingled building sitting at the edge of the water, where rows of docks splayed out into a harbor like fingers. A wooden sign with gold lettering hung over the building's open door—Edgewater Marina. The place was practically deserted, the docks occupied by just a few boats bobbing up and down as the water rolled in and out from Vineyard Sound. It was a Saturday, July third, and it had to be ninety degrees out already. Anyone who owned a boat was probably gone for the day, and as I wiped the beads of sweat from my upper lip with an unattractive swipe of my T-shirt sleeve, I wished I was out there with them instead of about to combust in a puff of dehydration.

I pedaled through the dirt parking lot and set my bike against the side of the building, which was more like a one-room house than a hub of maritime sophistication. Thankfully, I wasn't looking for someone to overhaul my engine or repair a sail. I just wanted a cold, refreshing drink.

"Hello?" I called out, stepping into the Edgewater Marina office. There wasn't much to it—just a varnished wood counter displaying a few boxes of candy bars and bags of chips—but it had exactly what I was looking for in the corner. The refrigerator was stocked with bottled water and sodas, and the freezer lining the wall was labeled with a blue handwritten sign: *ICE*.

I opened the refrigerator's glass door and grabbed a water, placing it against my forehead and letting the cold, moist bottle numb the spot between my eyes. I knew my mom would frown upon what I did next, but I couldn't wait any longer. I twisted off the cap before even paying for my purchase and gulped the entire bottle. When the last wet drop slid down my throat, I just stood there, between the open front door and the open back door directly across from it, catching what little breeze was drifting through the shed. As small as it was, with two doors on opposite walls and a double window against another, the room was filled with sunlight.

The only solid wall was lined with rows of nails tacked into wood planks laid in horizontal rows. A single knotted rope was tied around each nail on the top two rows, every knot different from the one before it, the ropes alternating color—yellow, red, blue, white, and black. The remaining rows were left empty. It almost looked like a piece of artwork, but I figured it was probably something only a boater would understand, like navigating by the stars or charting the tides. I couldn't do either, so instead I listened to the air ruffling the papers pinned to a bulletin board behind the counter and stared out at the water reflecting white slivers of sunlight.

Finally, between the cool water and circulating air, I actually felt like I could move without the skin on my knees sticking together.

"Hello!" I called out, hoping someone was nearby to hear me. I waited. Nothing. "Hello!" I tried again, poking my head out the back door. "Anybody here?"

I spotted a man toward the end of a short dock, his hands holding a fuel nozzle in the hull of a boat as he watched the numbers on a fuel tank tick away. His oil-stained jeans and gray, bushy beard pretty much fit every stereotype of a fisherman, so I figured he was probably the guy I was looking for.

"Excuse me, can I pay for this?" I asked loudly, holding up my empty water bottle for him to see. "Nobody is behind the register."

He glanced over his shoulder at me. "Just leave a dollar on the counter. We're a little short-handed right now."

I went back inside and laid my last dollar on the counter, placing a SNICKERS bar from the display on top of it at the last minute so it wouldn't blow away. Then I went out the back door, walked to the end of a far dock, and sat down, dangling my brown, dust-coated feet over the edge to buy myself a few more minutes before heading home to Josie's jobless.

I could see Martha's Vineyard in the distance, the expanses of beach creating an outline of white rimming the island. It was too far to actually make out anything in particular, but I knew it was sand, and that somewhere over there, Luke was without me. Lucy and Josie were at home, probably finally awake and getting ready for the double shift they were going to work because of the holiday weekend. They were also most likely planning what they were going to do when they got off work tonight.

I sat there on the dock, my feet suspended above the water, and realized this wasn't just what my summer would be like. This is was what every day would be like come September, minus the brown outlines forming a *V* on my feet where my flip-flops kept the dust from settling.

This summer was just a preview—just the beginning of being apart and saying good-bye.

* * *

"I'm screwed," I told Josie and Lucy when I found them upstairs in our room getting dressed for work, both already sporting one of the standard-issue Scoop Shack T-shirts that each employee wore for the summer. "There's nothing out there. Nada. Not one single store was hiring."

Josie bit her lip. "You can't be *that* surprised. It's already July. I mean, you knew this could happen when you didn't show up for work last night."

"I didn't think I'd get *fired*. I thought maybe I'd get some less than desirable task like cleaning the hot fudge machine or something, but I didn't think I'd lose my job."

Lucy gave me a sympathetic half smile. "I'm sorry, Em."

I waited for Josie to tell me she felt bad for me, too. Instead she reached for her deodorant.

"My parents will kill me when they find out." I went over to my bed and flopped down on my back. "*I* want to kill me."

Josie flapped her arms a few times to help her armpits dry. "We better get going. Can't be late."

"Be down in a minute," Lucy told her.

Josie blew into each armpit twice, grabbed her keys, and headed downstairs.

"You both think I brought this on myself, don't you?" I asked Lucy once I heard Josie's footsteps fade away.

She placed her Scoop Shack baseball hat on her head and pulled her braids into place behind her ears. "We don't think that."

"Honestly?" I prodded, looking at Lucy through my thumb and index finger, measuring barely an inch apart. "Not even just a teeny, tiny little bit?"

"Well, maybe just a teeny, tiny little bit." Lucy laughed at me. "But I get it, the whole Sam thing."

"What about Josie?" I wanted to know.

"What about her?" Lucy asked, her voice cautious.

I almost felt bad for even asking her the question. We didn't do that, pit one of us against the other. Maybe it was because there were three of us. Lucy, Josie, and Emily, each one necessary to make our friendship work. We were like a tripod—remove one leg and it topples over, unable to function properly.

When I'd moved to Chicago after freshman year, I'd wondered if they'd replace me, fill the hole I left, to restore the balance of their friendship in my absence. But when I came back in January, it was as if they'd been holding my spot for me, and I easily slipped back into place.

"I'm not asking you to take sides, Luce. I'm just saying it's pretty obvious Josie is pissed I stayed with Luke instead of going to work."

"Look, Em, a lot's happened between you two. I mean, I know we all had to deal with the whole Luke thing and the guide, but it was different for Josie. Luke breaking up with her was what gave us the idea for the guide, and then, well, you know the rest."

"But they weren't even together that long," I reminded her, but she just frowned and shook her head at me, the way a disappointed parent looks at a child trying to get out of admitting they'd done something wrong.

"I'm not trying to make excuses or justify what I did. I just wish she didn't make me feel like I'm an awful friend."

"I don't think she does that, Em." Lucy came over to my side of the room and sat next to me on the bed. "I'm just saying that you need to stop feeling like Josie is watching everything you do to find a reason to be mad. Maybe you should just take it for what it is—she wishes you'd come home last night and gone to work so we could all be at the Shack together like we planned. That's it. No conspiracy. Pretty simple, and not totally unreasonable, right?"

"Right," I admitted.

"Okay, now I have to get out of here or I'll be on the receiving end of Mr. Holden's wrath, and that's the last thing I want."

Lucy stood up, pulled her Scoop Shack T-shirt down so the cherry on top of the sundae wasn't directly over her nipple, and headed toward the door.

"Hey, Luce?" I called out.

She stopped, one of her braids smacking the doorframe with a small thud as she turned to face me. "Yeah?"

"Thanks."

Lucy smiled at me. "Always."

And just like that, I was alone again on the Cape in a strange room that was supposed to feel like home, even though I barely knew where the light switch was located.

Lucy and I had helped decorate Josie's old bedroom, the one she had before the Holdens built their new mega-house. We'd decided that, as seventh graders, it was time to purge Josie's room of the ladybug-shaped rug dotting the middle of her floor, the pink ruffled curtains held over the windows by rods accented with bright yellow daisies, and the watchful brown eyes of Samantha Parkington, the *kind and generous* American Girl doll who was *always ready to make new friends* (according to the book that came with her). She sat on Josie's bookshelf practically *tsk tsking* every time we said or did something that was neither kind nor generous.

Josie had convinced her mom that the three of us could paint the room and redecorate with the money she'd saved from feeding her neighbor's fish. Mrs. Holden had reluctantly agreed, but after finding out Josie had saved all of thirty-two dollars, she'd kicked in another twenty to help our cause. Mrs. Holden drove us to the paint store and told us to pick out a color for Josie's bedroom walls. We couldn't decide between Breathtaking, Tantalizing Teal, or my favorite, a pale yellow called Icy Lemonade. Josie was really pushing for Breathtaking, and since it was her room, I resigned myself to the pale bluish-lavender, but Josie surprised us by handing all three color samples to the man at the counter and telling him we'd take a can of each. "I get two walls, you each get one."

That's how Josie's room ended up looking a little like a colorful circus tent, which didn't make her mom happy when she walked in and saw that we were each painting a wall with our chosen color. But it did make the three of us feel like we shared Josie's bedroom, even if she was the only one to sleep there every night. I didn't find out until our freshman year that Josie had started to wake up with headaches every day, and Mrs. Holden insisted it was the schizophrenic walls and it would be best to cover them with a more subdued and less anxiety-inducing hue. Josie refused.

Two years later, I was living in Chicago and the Holdens moved into their new house. I was sure the new owners of our Breathtaking, Tantalizing Teal, and Icy Lemonade bedroom made new paint a priority as soon as they signed the sales contract. As much as I liked to think those four walls would live on without us, there was also a part of me that knew that, even if the new owners were fans of our color choices, they would never appreciate what they meant to us.

Now the three of us were living in seafoam green for the summer, a color I actually really liked, even if we didn't choose it.

I was picturing our summer bedroom with three different colored walls, and which colors I'd choose, when my phone vibrated. I looked down expecting to see Luke's name, and instead saw a name I was dreading: My mom. *Did you write Mrs. Preston and her friend a thank-you note? Have fun at work!*

I replied with a smiling emoji.

Between getting home late last night and leaving early this morning, I hadn't bothered to unpack anything except my toothbrush and the clothes I was wearing. Now I wondered if I should even bother.

I fished my hand toward the bottom of the monogrammed duffel bag my mom gave me for my sixteenth birthday (because canvas with your initials embroidered on it lasts way longer than a car) and felt the square edge of what I was looking for. Only what I thought was a box of stationary was actually another little gift my mom had decided to pack for me—the leather-bound journal. I stuffed the book back in my duffel bag and pulled out the box of stationary so I could convey my sincerest thanks to Mrs. Preston and Melanie for my visit. Then I placed one of the stamps my mom also provided on each envelope and set them on my bed.

At least I accomplished one thing today. Or, if you counted both Mrs. Preston *and* Melanie, two things. That sounded way more productive.

There was no way I could have 24/7 access to Luke like Sam did, and Mr. Holden had made sure I wouldn't be working with Lucy and Josie, but the least I could do was make sure I didn't have to go back home and spend my summer even farther away from them.

I knew what I had to do. It wasn't my first choice, but after putting on my most employable face and visiting every business in town, there was only one option I could think of that might save our summer. It was a last resort, but I'd run out of options.

My bike was still in the driveway, where I'd left it leaning up against the side of the house. I forced myself up from the comfort of my bed, grabbed the envelopes to drop in a mailbox along the way, and went to pedal to my future.

> **Long-Distance Relationship Tip #17:**
>
> Being good with numbers is an asset in life.
> But now is not the time to use your math
> skills to calculate the miles between you, the hours
> until you see him or the number of times you
> called and he didn't answer.

chapter ten

There are two good things about working at seven o'clock in the morning. It was early enough that I didn't have to worry about getting run down by overly eager Cape beach traffic, and the sun was still about six hours away from sweltering.

Since it was a holiday, I also figured I'd have time to ease into my first day on the job. But as I rode into the marina's dirt parking lot, it was quickly evident that while the rest of Falmouth may have been sleeping in for July Fourth, people who owned boats weren't like everyone else. There had to be at least ten people out on the docks, loading big, insulated coolers and fishing rods onto the decks of boats with idling engines.

I parked my bike beside the marina's office and went inside to get my marching orders for the day.

George, the gray-bearded man in the oil-stained jeans who was now my new boss, wasn't behind the counter, which didn't really surprise me. With all the activity on the docks, I figured he'd be helping some of the boaters tie ropes or check GPS systems or whatever it was someone did when they owned a marina. Instead, I found a guy around my age stooped down in front of the refrigerator, refilling the dwindling rows of bottles and cans.

"Hi, is George here?" I asked him.

He didn't even look up before answering. "Nope, not today."

When the person who supposedly hired you isn't there for your first day of work, it doesn't feel like a great beginning. In fact, I started to wonder if maybe George wasn't in charge at all. Maybe he was just some nice guy who felt sorry for me and decided to say yes when I begged him for a job. Maybe he was actually just a boat owner who happened to be standing on the dock when a sweaty, red-faced girl dropped her bike in the parking lot and swore she'd be the best employee the marina had ever seen.

Or maybe I just got the day wrong. Was I supposed to start on Monday?

"I talked to him yesterday," I started to explain. "I thought he told me I could start work today."

This time, the guy turned around and stood up, closing the refrigerator's glass door with his foot as he folded the empty cardboard cases into small pieces.

"Are you Emily?" he asked, and I nodded. "I'm Nolan. George is my uncle."

"Did I get the day wrong?"

"No, you got it right. George asked me to get you set up. He had to go over to the Vineyard and work on a customer's boat. I'll show you around." He glanced up at the clock on the wall behind the counter. "But you're four minutes late. He told me that if you weren't here on time, I should fire you."

Fired twice in less than two days? Seriously?

I must have looked panicked, because Nolan quickly laughed at me. "I'm kidding. Besides, that clock is five minutes fast, so you're actually a minute early. Come on." He nodded toward the back door. "Follow me out to the recycling bins, and I'll give you the grand tour."

I trailed him out of the shop, letting the screen door slam shut behind me.

"Things sure start early around here," I observed as Nolan waved hello and called out *good morning* to people by name. He led me around the docks, and as we walked along the salt water–stained boards, Nolan pointed out things I should take note of—the fire extinguishers and pedestals with power outlets, the wheelbarrow-like carts marina members could use to carry supplies to and from their boats, the hoses and nozzles used to wash away the salt at the end of a day out on the water. It wasn't terribly daunting, and by the time we made our way back to the marina office, I was feeling like this might not be so bad after all.

"That's the fuel pump," Nolan told me, pointing to the dock where I'd first spotted George. "And the waste pump-out station is over there," he concluded, indicating a wide black hose on another short dock about ten feet to the left of us.

He stood there watching me, like he was waiting for some sort of reaction.

"Great!" I smiled enthusiastically.

"You have no idea what a waste pump-out station is, do you?"

"A place where you pump out waste?" I guessed. I mean, it was pretty self-explanatory.

"Yeah. Waste. As in the waste from a boat's head."

This time, I knew what he was talking about. The head. A boat's toilet. Which meant *waste* wasn't the typical garbage I'd been thinking of.

All of ten minutes into my first day on the job was not the time to complain about my assigned tasks. Especially when I didn't have any other options. "Okay. I get it. No problem."

Nolan almost seemed impressed by my non-reaction, which may be why, instead of continuing to try to freak me out, he shrugged. "It's really not that bad, more like the opposite of the fuel pump—instead of putting stuff in a tank, you suck it out."

"Like a big vacuum," I added.

"Yeah, sort of like that. Anyway, it's mostly locals here— guys who like to fish, that sort of thing—so low maintenance," he went on, ending our tour in front of the screen door to the office. "That means getting out on the water early, which is why someone has to be here at seven o'clock every day."

This time, I didn't do a very good job of hiding how I felt about my new job.

"There is an upside, though," Nolan added. "The afternoons are pretty mellow. Are you here for the entire summer?"

"Until mid-August, when I go home and get ready to leave for school."

"Freshman?"

I nodded.

"Me, too, at UMass."

I told him I'd be nearby, a twenty-minute bus ride away.

"We just met and already we can't get rid of each other," he joked. "Follow me, I'll show you where you'll be working."

"I thought I'd be in there." I pointed to the office.

Nolan turned around and walked backward as he talked. "George didn't tell you?"

"Tell me what?"

"You're not in the office. You're out here." He pointed toward the shortest dock—the one where I first spotted George yesterday. "Working the fuel pump."

The fuel pump? What did I know about fueling boats? What did I know about boats, period? I was about to correct Nolan when I realized he was joking with me again. "Funny."

"No. Seriously." He wasn't laughing this time. "George really didn't tell you?"

I couldn't tell if Nolan was screwing with me, or if he was being serious. "The fuel pump? Are you sure?"

"Don't look so horrified. It's not that bad, and it's pretty easy. You'll take the lines, tie the boats to the cleats, and then it's really just like filling up a car. Sometimes people will ask for a bag of ice, some water, or something from the office, but other than that, you basically get to hang out on the dock."

The only cleats I knew of belonged on a soccer field, but he did make it sound relatively uncomplicated. "Okay, I think I can handle that. But first, you'll have to show me what a cleat is."

Nolan shook his head. "You've never been around boats before, have you?"

"Not until today," I admitted. "You obviously have a little more experience."

"I've been helping out here since as long as I can remember." Nolan started walking again. "The only reason George even wanted an extra set of hands is so he can spend more time on the water catching stripers."

"So you grew up here, on the Cape?"

"All eighteen years. Can't wait to leave."

I glanced around at the blue water, its color shifting depending on how the ripples reflected the sunlight, like a mood ring. The surface reflected wide beams of morning sun and the full, green trees bending their tired arms over the dirt parking lot. All around us, birds hopped between gnarly branches as if they couldn't decide exactly where it was they wanted to sit as they sang their songs to one another. I would never consider myself a wannabe sailor, but I couldn't imagine wanting to leave this place for a campus with thousands of strangers. "Really? UMass is going to be completely different."

"I sure hope so. The campus is practically as big as this entire town."

"And that's a good thing?"

"That's a great thing. Aren't you looking forward to going away?"

"Sure, but I'm still going to miss my friends and stuff."

"Well, if you play your cards right this summer, maybe you'll have a friend at UMass who won't mind hanging out with you."

It seemed like a nice offer from somebody who, twenty minutes ago, was a complete stranger describing the process of removing human waste with a hose.

"Well, look at that." Nolan pointed toward a motor boat making its way in our direction, the purring of its engine growing louder as it neared. "Your first customer."

"Really?"

"Tell you what, I'll do this one. You just watch me and ask if they need ice or drinks or anything. George calls it the *upsell*, very important."

We stood on the fuel dock and waited for the boat to make its approach. Finally, the motor slowly subsided and the hull tapped gently against the dock, pressing into the rubber fenders secured to the side by thick black nylon ropes. I watched as the boat's owner handed Nolan another rope, and then as Nolan tied it in some sort of figure eight configuration around the low metal horns screwed into the dock every few feet. I assumed these were the cleats, and that whatever it was that Nolan had done to keep the ropes tight around the cleats would be something I'd execute perfectly by the end of the summer. Once the boat was secured, Nolan removed the nozzle from the fuel pump, and from that point on, it did look just like gassing up a car.

"And we need a few mackerel," the boater told Nolan.

Nolan looked over at me. "Hey, come here. Just make sure the nozzle doesn't move." He pointed to the hose in his hand. "I'll be right back."

103

Nolan disappeared down the dock and into the office, returning with a plastic bag filled with three stiff, frozen fish the size of my foot. He handed them to our customer and then took over the fueling again.

When the pump clicked, I watched Nolan take the guy's credit card and followed him into the office, where he walked me through the steps of ringing it through the register. Nolan carried back the bottled water and ice they ordered, then I helped him untie the ropes and the boat pushed off.

"See? Just like a gas station," Nolan commented once the whirring motor was far enough away that I could hear him. "Same principles apply—mainly, don't get it all over yourself, and don't light a match."

"How'd you make that knot?" I asked. "The one around the cleat?"

"It's called a cleat hitch," he explained, and then pointed toward the water. "Actually, I can show you now. Here comes another one."

As Nolan and I waited for the boat to reach us, I turned to him. "One more thing. What's with the fish in the bag?"

"Yeah, meant to tell you about that. In addition to the ice and soda and snacks, there's the bait. We have frozen mackerel, pogies, herring, squid, sea worms, eels, and chum."

"Chum?"

"Think of chum as a bunch of fish parts. Sort of like the sausage of bait—lots of fish stuff mixed together. It's all in the white cooler inside the freezer beside the refrigerator."

Josie and Lucy weren't even out of bed yet. When they finally did drag their bodies downstairs in about two hours, Mrs. Holden would probably have Fourth of July pancakes waiting for them with blueberries, strawberries, and homemade whipped cream. Maybe they'd even enjoy some fresh squeezed orange juice. And I had fish parts.

I didn't really have any reason to believe Mrs. Holden would whip up a festive holiday breakfast. I didn't know what anyone had for breakfast at the house, because my first two mornings there hadn't been spent lounging in bed until the sun streaming into the room finally made it impossible to avoid opening my eyes. On my first morning, I was already out looking for a new job, and my second was spent here, in a shed that housed a stew of dead sea life in a freezer next to a dock where I was inhaling the fresh summer scent of marine fuel. While Josie and Lucy hung out by the pool all day, I'd be learning to tie cleat hitches like a seven-year-old Cub Scout.

* * *

Nolan had been right, and by twelve o'clock, the marina was practically empty. Most of the boats were gone, and there wasn't much to do except listen to my stomach growl as it reminded me that I'd forgotten to bring a lunch.

"Are you sure you don't want to go out and get something to eat?" Nolan asked, taking another bite of the sandwich he'd pulled out of a brown paper bag in the refrigerator.

We were sitting in the canvas director's chairs George had placed on either side of the shack's back door so we could keep an eye on the docks and still help anyone who showed up at the marina's office.

"You get an hour break for lunch," Nolan reminded me. "Take it."

"I'm fine," I told him, even though the smell of his roast beef sandwich was making my mouth water. I wasn't fine. I was famished. I was also hot and tired, and the last thing I wanted to do was get on my bike and ride into town with the sweltering sun beating down on me so I could buy an overpriced sandwich that would basically wipe out the money I made my first hour here. I'd made it through half the day. I could make it a little longer.

"Okay, whatever you say." Nolan took another bite of his sandwich, and my stomach betrayed me by practically begging for a bite. "Oh, for god's sake."

A bag of potato chips flew through the air and landed in my lap.

"You sure?" I asked him.

"Eat."

"I won't forget my lunch tomorrow." I tore open the bag and savored the crunch of my first chip. "I swear."

I glanced down at my palms and noticed that the sore spots I'd been rubbing with my thumbs had erupted into full-on blisters, thanks to pulling and tying boat lines—Nolan taught me that they weren't called ropes—all morning. I knew better than to pop them. My mom called blisters *nature's Band-Aids* and had taught me at an early age that popping blisters only resulted in tender skin and possible infection (you can find all this in her book *First Aid, Fast Aid: Keeping Cool, Calm, and Collected in Unexpected Situations*).

"They'll get better once you get the hang of things," Nolan pointed out, noticing the red swollen pockets of skin on my palms.

I ate another chip and ignored the salt stinging my chapped hands. I was almost tempted to lick the salt from the potato chips off my fingers, but decided to wipe them on my shorts instead. What was a little salt when I'd already been splashed with fuel, dripped on by waterlogged lines, and even had the new experience of accidentally stepping in the remains of a gutted fish.

In less than two months, it would all be over—my last summer with Josie, Lucy, and Luke before college, maybe even our last summer *together*—and what would I have to show for it? Callouses.

"This isn't exactly how I expected to spend my summer," I told Nolan between chips.

"Why not?" he asked.

"I guess I'd start with the fact that my hands smell like gasoline instead of waffle cones."

Nolan looked confused.

"I was supposed to work at the Scoop Shack," I explained. "My two best friends have jobs there."

"They're lucky, that place always has a ton of job applications for the summer."

"Yeah, well, my friend Josie's dad owns the place."

"And she couldn't get you a job?" Nolan laughed. "That's harsh."

"Long story."

"Well, it's too bad it didn't work out, but this can be way better than working at an ice cream window."

"How's that?"

"For starters, you get to be outside all day, which reminds me, you might want to wear a hat tomorrow. You're looking kind of red."

"So skin cancer, callouses, and the scent of flammable liquids. That's better?"

"You forgot the chum," Nolan added, dusting the crumbs from his lap as he took one last bite of his sandwich.

"Ah, yes. The chum," I repeated, before stuffing the last of my lunch into my mouth. "How lucky can a girl get?"

* * *

"Well, you survived." Nolan pointed to the clock. It was 4:05, but now that I knew the clock in the office was five minutes fast, my brain automatically adjusted. The fuel dock closed for the day at four o'clock. "It's quitting time."

I was sunburned, exhausted, and my deodorant had decided to call it quits about three hours ago.

"So are you coming back?" Nolan asked as I slid my bike helmet out from under the cash register counter.

"Do I have a choice?"

"Three summers ago, George hired a girl and she lasted two days. Barely. She'd hang out on the fuel dock in a bikini top and complain anytime a boat pulled up for service, like they were interrupting her tanning schedule. Not that I have anything against bikini tops, but she was a pain. George swore he'd never hire another girl."

"Maybe he decided to forego gender stereotypes when he met me," I reasoned, sounding a little too much like my mother.

"Yeah, I'm sure that was it, and it had nothing to do with the fact that it's July and he's desperate to get more time out on his boat."

Desperation. Like George, I knew how that could drive you to do things you once never imagined.

"I guess I'll see you tomorrow at seven," I told Nolan.

"I don't come in until nine."

"Was that an option?" I asked. "Because had I known . . ."

Nolan smiled and tossed me a bottle of water from the refrigerator. "You're seven to four, I'm nine to six."

I held the cool, sweating bottle to my chest before securing the buckle of my helmet under my chin.

"That's a good look for you," Nolan added.

Even though I probably should have cared that the scent of fish, fuel, and nine hours' worth of July humidity clung to my skin in an invisible cloud of stench, and that I probably looked worse than I smelled, all I wanted to do was go home and collapse. And shower. If my mom saw me right now, she'd probably recommend donning a pair of rubber gloves from now on, which wasn't a bad idea. Only I wasn't sure which I hated more, the smell of fuel embedded under my fingernails or looking like a housewife in a dish detergent commercial.

"Well, then, see you at nine," I muttered, using all my strength to push open the screen door to the parking lot. I could barely muster up the energy to walk to my bike, let alone pedal all the way back to Josie's house.

"Don't forget to pack a lunch," Nolan called after me. "I'm not sharing my chips tomorrow!"

I raised my hand into the air without even looking back, resisting the temptation to hold up my middle finger as I departed. Instead, I waved and started my two-mile ride home.

* * *

By the time I pulled into Josie's driveway, I was ready to fall into a lounge chair by the pool, if I even managed to make it that far before my legs buckled beneath me right there in front of the garage.

Fortunately, I managed to put one foot in front of the other long enough to make it inside to the kitchen, where I spotted Lucy and Josie out on the back patio. They didn't see me standing in the shadow behind the sliding screen door, but I could see them perfectly. Lucy was braiding her hair, which I'd learned was something she did every day before leaving for work because Mr. Holden made all the girls wear their hair tied up under their Scoop Shack baseball caps. I guess long strands of hair dotting banana splits were bad for business. Josie sat beside Lucy, her legs crossed like a pretzel as she fiddled with the buttons on the camera her parents gave her for graduation. They had to be at the Shack in half an hour, and then I'd be alone again while Mr. and Mrs. Holden went to a July Fourth barbeque.

"So how was it?" Lucy asked when she heard me slide the door open. "Did you ride through a sprinkler on the way home?"

"It's almost ninety degrees and I just rode a bike two miles." I held my arms out to the side as I walked toward them, a meager attempt to air out my stinking pits. "It's sweat."

Josie wiggled her nose. I watched as a familiar crease formed between her eyebrows, which meant she was trying to figure something out.

"I wouldn't go near an open flame," Josie finally told me. "You smell like gas and a can of tuna fish."

Lucy leaned toward me and sniffed. "She's right. I thought you were working at the snack bar at some yacht club."

"It's not a yacht club, it's a marina. And it turns out the snack bar is the fuel pump, and we sell bait."

"You're all red." Lucy pointed to my cheeks.

"Sunburn," I told her. "I was outside pumping gas and helping boats tie up to the dock."

"That sounds nice." Lucy looked to Josie. "Doesn't it?"

"Sure, it must be pretty by the water all day," she chimed in. "How's your boss?"

"George? He wasn't there. I worked with his nephew."

Josie perked up. "A nephew? Does he have a name? And an age?"

"Nolan. And he's starting UMass in the fall."

"I think we've met him, isn't he a friend of Alyssa's?" Josie asked Lucy, and then turned to me. "He's cute."

"I guess."

"You guess?" Josie repeated. "Come on, Emily, you have a boyfriend, you're not dead."

I tried to picture Nolan away from the dock—what I'd think of him if I ran into him in the halls at school. The only word I could think of when it came to Nolan was *unkempt*. It was a word my mom used to describe people whose hair needed a cut, whose clothes needed a good ironing, and who didn't seem to care much about what she termed *personal appearances*.

Even so, I had to say, the look fit Nolan—the dirty blond hair that seemed to land wherever the breeze pushed it, the wrinkled khaki shorts and thin, faded T-shirt my mom would have removed from his clothing rotation and put into use as a dust rag. I got the feeling Nolan just didn't care about whether his hair was falling into his eyes or his shorts were hanging so low they could have used a belt (my mom believed belt loops existed for a reason). He may be counting the days until he left the Cape for college, but Nolan was exactly what you pictured when you thought of a guy spending his summer by the ocean.

"Sure. I'd say he'd be considered cute," I conceded.

"See, I knew you could do it!" Josie snapped a long lens onto the front of the camera and then smiled at Lucy. "She's not dead after all."

"As long as you have to pump gas, at least you get to look at Nolan while you're doing it," Lucy offered up as a consolation prize before twisting an elastic around the tail of her braid.

"Now it's our turn to work for the man. Off to do the ice cream thing." Josie carefully placed the camera and lens into the padded camera bag on the table and zipped it closed. "You want to come with us? Hang out while we decipher the orders of little kids who can't decide between chocolate dip and chocolate fudge?"

"Yeah," Lucy agreed. "Come with us. You can relax at the picnic tables and talk to us while we work."

Their offer was actually tempting. I was looking at a night alone in a house that, after only two days, didn't feel quite like home. But after spending all day in the sun lugging the fuel hose and pulling boats to the dock, every muscle in my body ached. Even my butt was sore from sitting on the bicycle seat. I couldn't imagine getting up from the patio chair, let alone showering and spending the next five hours sitting on a picnic table bench.

Still, I missed them. And if visiting them at work meant I could at least spend a little time catching up, then it was worth it.

"How about if I come by later?" I offered. "I need to shower and stuff, but I can ride my bike over."

"Okay, but don't forget." Lucy stood up and Josie joined her. "Or fall asleep."

"I won't," I promised, closing my eyes and letting my body sink into the chair.

I was asleep before I even heard them walk away.

chapter eleven

I probably would have slept until morning if the buzzing of my phone on the chair arm hadn't woken me.

"So how was your first day?" the voice asked, and it took me a moment to get my bearings straight and remember where I was.

"It was okay." I sat up and rubbed my eyes, which stung from the salt on my fingers and nine hours of ultraviolet rays reflecting off the water into my corneas. I really had to find a hat. "It's a job."

"I thought you'd call when you were done, maybe catch the ferry over." Luke's voice sounded so hopeful I glanced at my phone screen to check the time.

When I'd told Luke that I talked myself into a job at the marina, his first reaction was, "Really?" His *really* was part disbelief that anyone would hire me to do something I knew nothing about, part surprise that I found a job so quickly, and part letdown. If I had to assign a ratio, I'd say it was 40/50/10. I understood the disbelief and surprise. I mean, I could hardly believe George was willing to even listen to me recite the handful of reasons he should hire someone who didn't know the difference between a mainsail and a garage sale.

It was the ten percent—the inflection in his voice that had punctuated the word with a big question mark—that I didn't get. Sure, Luke was stuck on crutches and relegated to tagging along with Charlie if he wanted to go anywhere, but every day that went by without a job made me one day closer

111

to having to go home. I thought at least Luke would be glad I'd be making money so I could actually afford to visit him when I *wasn't* working, but instead, it was like I'd gone and gotten a job so quickly *on* purpose instead of *for* a purpose.

"I promised Lucy and Josie I'd visit them at work. Besides, it's kinda late to be heading over there. I haven't even showered from work yet," I added, hoping he'd take pity on me without having to actually experience the pungency of the odors that seemed to have settled into my pores.

Luke was quiet. "So no fireworks?"

"You could come here," I suggested, but even as I did, I knew it would never happen. By the time Luke found a ride to the ferry and hobbled his way over, it would practically be time for him to go back.

"Wish I could, but you know I can't."

Now we were both quiet, and I couldn't help but think it was the beginning of many quiet moments between us as we started to grasp the reality of our summer situations—of being separated by all the reasons we couldn't make it work out even if, according to a map, we seemed so close and it appeared so easy.

* * *

"You made it!" Josie yelled when she spotted me walking toward her window at the Scoop Shack.

The kids and parents waiting in line turned to see who she was shouting to over their heads. I waved to Josie and smiled apologetically to the sweaty parents who looked at me like I was single-handedly responsible for the whining kids tugging on their arms while begging for more whipped cream.

Josie waved back, a large vanilla cone with rainbow sprinkles in her hand, and then turned her attention to a little boy who was jumping up and down trying to give Josie his order. I took my place at the end of the line.

There were six take-out windows lined up across the front of what, literally, looked like a barn. Mr. Holden had refurbished the inside of the building, but kept the outside in its original condition, which included rough red wood shingles to match the worn red picnic tables on the grassy patch between the barn and the gravel parking lot.

112

The place was packed, with lines at least eight deep at every window. I didn't see Lucy.

"I swear, it's freaking crazy tonight!" Josie told me when I finally made it to the front of the line after ten minutes. Her Scoop Shack T-shirt was splattered with hot fudge. "I cannot wait to get out of here. You're going to stay until we close, right?"

"Sure," I answered, even though all I really wanted to do was fall into bed and close my eyes. Just standing there talking to her was taking every ounce of energy I could manage.

"Cool. Alyssa—you'll meet her, she's the girl who's two windows down." Josie leaned out her window and pointed. "She told us that a bunch of people are getting together afterwards at the beach. You're coming."

"I am?"

"Yes, you are." Josie frowned at me and I looked away, for the first time noticing Lucy in the back of the barn carrying a tub of maraschino cherries. "She's got FFT duty—fruit, fudge, and toppings," Josie explained.

"I don't know about the beach. I have to be at the marina at seven tomorrow." Just saying the time made me yawn. "Besides, I have my bike."

"You're coming," Josie repeated, and then picked up a pencil and leaned toward me, resting on her elbows. "So what do you want? And please don't say a shake, because I seriously have made at least fifty tonight and I just might slit my wrists with a blender blade if I have to make one more."

I took pity upon Josie and ordered a cup of soft serve instead.

There was no way she'd let me get out of going to the beach with them after work. I kind of felt terrible that I was even thinking of excuses, even though getting up at six a.m. to bike two miles seemed like a pretty valid excuse to me. Josie and Lucy could stay out as late as they wanted, within reason (the Holdens had decided we were old enough to use our own *good judgement* when it came to a curfew, but when they'd strolled in at two a.m., Mr. Holden let them know that *good judgement* meant no later than one thirty). I, on the other hand, would be wearing a plastic helmet strapped to my head and dodging cars before they even rolled over and realized they could sleep another six hours.

"Here you go, chocolate soft serve in a cup, no toppings." Josie handed me my order. "Kinda boring, aren't you?"

For a minute, I thought she knew I was trying to think of ways to get out of going to the beach, and then I realized she was referring to my order.

"There's nothing wrong with sticking to what you love," I told her, reaching for my cup and spoon.

"There's nothing wrong with trying something new, either. Next time, at least taste the cherry dip or cookie dough pieces. Live a little!" She laughed at me.

I took my ice cream, which Josie didn't make me pay for, and went to sit down at one of the picnic tables.

I quickly discovered that an ice cream stand on July Fourth was the ultimate people-watching opportunity. I determined that there were three distinct groups of ice cream goers: kids having meltdowns, parents trying to stop the whining and tears, and people like me, who ate our ice cream thankful that we weren't either one of them.

"Hey, Emily!" I heard my name and looked over at the Shack, expecting to find Lucy or Josie trying to get my attention. But Josie was still helping customers and Lucy wasn't at any of the windows.

"Emily!" I heard again, and this time realized the voice was calling my name from the parking lot.

I spotted Nolan and another guy walking toward me, but before they reached my table, his friend peeled away and headed toward the walk-up windows.

Nolan pointed to my empty ice cream cup. "Celebrating making it through your first day at the marina?"

"Not exactly. My friends are working tonight." I pointed to Josie, who happened to look up at that exact moment and mouthed *get me out of here* before rolling her eyes at a set of twins having tantrums on the ground below her window. "What about you?"

"My buddy's girlfriend works here, so he wanted to come by and see her." I noticed that Nolan's friend was standing at the spot two windows down from Josie, where Alyssa was stationed. "Besides, I'm always up for ice cream, especially when he's buying."

I held up my empty cup. "Free."

"Must be nice to have friends in the right places," Nolan joked.

"It is, and if they're lucky, I'll return the favor with a free bag of chum."

Nolan laughed. "Wow, you're a really good friend."

"The best," I agreed. "They're about to close, so if you want your ice cream, you better get in line."

"Good call. See you tomorrow."

I laid back on the picnic table bench and covered my eyes with my arm. "Bright and early," I reminded him.

After the Shack closed the walk-up windows, and Josie and Lucy finished cleaning up for the night, they found me sitting at the picnic table waiting for them. Lucy sat down on the bench beside me and started counting a handful of dollar bills she'd pulled from her pocket.

"Tips," she told me, and then tugged on her braid, scraping her nails through the strands as she tried to remove the sticky goo still clinging to the ends. "I smell like a jar of caramel sauce exploded in my hair and you're out here meeting guys after one day."

"I'm not meeting guys," I told them.

Lucy sniffed the tail of her braid and made a face. "I thought I saw you talking to yacht club Nolan."

"It's a *marina*," I reminded them. Why did they think I was living large when my job actually sucked?

"We'll meet you there?" Alyssa called out to us as she walked toward a car with her boyfriend and Nolan.

"Yep!" Josie called back.

I felt a vibration in my pocket and wrapped my fingers around the phone, sliding it out to read the screen. *Miss you.* Then another vibration: *Can you talk?*

"You know, I'm really tired and I have to get up insanely early tomorrow." Almost as if on cue, I yawned again. Thinking about your alarm going off at six a.m. will do that to you, I guess.

"No way." Josie looked at the phone in my hand. "You're ditching us for the night?"

"I'm not ditching you. I'll go next time. Promise."

"You just got here and we have a lot of time to make up for," Lucy tried. "Besides, it's dark. You can't ride your bike home."

"It has a blinking reflector, and I'll walk beside it."

Lucy and Josie exchanged a glance. I knew what they were thinking. It was the same thing I was thinking—our first chance to go out and have fun together, and I was choosing a bed, and a vibrating phone, over them.

"Just go. I'll be fine," I assured Lucy, making this about the dangers of riding a bike in the dark instead of the dangers of choosing a boyfriend who was a boat ride away over friends who were standing right in front of me.

"You guys coming?" Alyssa yelled at us. Nolan stopped walking and watched, waiting for our answer.

My phone vibrated again, like a buzzer that sounds when a game show contestant picks the wrong answer.

"I'll text you when I get home so you know I'm not lying dead on the side of the road somewhere," I told them, and then, in an attempt to get them to laugh, added, "And if I *am* lying on the side of the road, you guys can just pick me up on your way home. But don't hurry, I need the sleep."

Lucy almost laughed, but Josie barely cracked a smile.

"We're coming," Josie yelled to Alyssa, and then started walking toward her car.

I watched as Alyssa grabbed her boyfriend's hand and led him in the opposite direction. Nolan paused for a second, as if he was going to say something, but he just waved and turned away.

"Be careful," Lucy reminded me, and then followed Josie.

I stood in the parking lot and watched them until the taillights of Josie's car moved across the gravel and disappeared down the road.

Once they were out of sight, I pressed the first name on my favorites list.

"Hello." Luke's voice was warm and smooth, like the hot fudge I'd seen poured over sundaes.

"Hi." I couldn't help smiling into the darkness. "What's going on?"

"Just missing you," he answered. "What about you?"

"Heading home from visiting Lucy and Josie at the Shack. Keep me company?"

"I think I can manage that," he told me, and I took the handlebars of my bike in each of my hands and started pushing it home.

I had the phone propped between my ear and shoulder, which wasn't exactly comfortable and it sure wasn't optimal if I was going to make it home as fast as possible. Walking a bike home in flip-flops also wasn't ideal—I'd collected enough dirt and sand between my toes to provide the benefits of exfoliation for at least the next year.

Between the crickets clicking in the tall grass growing beside the road, the gulping of frogs in the woods, the occasional whooshing of cars passing me, and a phone that bounced as I guided the bike's tires over the rocky dirt, I could only catch about every third word out of Luke's mouth. What I did hear made the long, dark walk a lot better than if I'd been by myself.

"Shit!" I shrieked as a gust of dusty air and gravel kicked up beside me, each tiny edge flying through the air and slicing into my bare legs like shrapnel.

"What?"

I navigated my bike onto the grassy shoulder. "A freaking car just whizzed by."

"I should let you go. The last thing we need is you ending up on crutches, too."

Luke was right. But crutches weren't the last thing I needed—the last thing I *really* needed was to have to call my mom and tell her I was in the emergency room because, in addition to being fired from my job at the Shack, I was walking down a deserted road in the dark by myself in a strange town where nobody would report my missing body until the morning, when they found seagulls pecking my eyes out. Not that I even knew if seagulls would do that, but given my luck since arriving on the Cape, it seemed like a fitting end to my time here.

Still, I pushed my bike along the uneven patches of dirt and grass without saying good-bye.

The car's taillights grew dimmer in the distance, and the road fell dark again. I was probably less than a quarter mile from the Holdens' and, in the strobe of moonlight overhead, I could see the trees thinning out as they started to give way to the beach.

A stone wall rose up beside me—a jagged border dividing the brittle, dry grass on the shoulder of the road from the long, swaying beach grass on the other side. I could see the white light of the moon reflecting off the rolling surface of the water separating Cape Cod from Martha's Vineyard.

The sound of water slapping against sand grew louder and, if the decibels of the noise around me were any indication, I was in the middle of prime cricket country. I remembered once reading that only male crickets chirp, and they had different songs for different purposes. It was their way of attracting females. Apparently there was a thriving cricket pickup scene in Falmouth.

"Emily?" Luke finally asked. "You still there?"

"I'm here."

"You're awfully quiet. Is everything okay?"

"I was just thinking about crickets. I used to like listening to them when I was little. I imagined all these crickets talking to each other outside, making plans for what they'd do all night while I slept. Now they're just annoying."

Luke laughed at me. "Is that all? Your growing intolerance for crickets?"

"Maybe it's more." I swallowed and realized for the first time how all I'd wanted to do was be with Luke and Josie and Lucy, and instead I was alone. "I miss you."

"Hey, can you stop walking for a minute?"

I laid my bike against the stone wall.

"Where are you?" Luke asked. "Anywhere near the beach?"

"Yeah, I'm almost to Josie's house."

"Okay. Turn and face the water."

I turned to my right. "Now what?"

"Look over toward the island."

"It's dark. I can't see that far."

"I know, just wait a minute. Keep looking."

At that moment, a burst of fireworks lit up the sky over the island, pink and blue and yellow and green streaks scattering across the velvety darkness like a dandelion in the wind.

"See that?" he asked. "That's where I am."

"Wow, they're gorgeous," I breathed, as another explosion of color lit up the horizon.

It was quiet where I sat, but I could hear the pops and sizzles of fireworks coming from Luke's end of the phone. If I closed my eyes, it was almost like I was right there beside him.

"Pretty cool, huh? Why don't you take a seat and watch them with me?"

I kicked off my flip-flops and walked along the wall until I found a level spot to crawl over. I wiped the sand and tiny pieces of splintered shell from the wall before sitting down and letting my bare feet dangle over the edge as I faced Vineyard Sound.

"Okay, I'm sitting," I told him.

"You can't be here, and I can't be there," Luke said. "But that doesn't mean we can't watch the fireworks together."

I laid back on the cool stones, their hard, bumpy surfaces pressing against my back.

A single bright purple streak exploded into what seemed like one million little pink stars in the distance, each one throwing off trails of cotton candy–colored sparkles as they fell toward the island.

"That was awesome." I found myself smiling in Luke's direction and, even though I knew he couldn't see me, I had a feeling he was smiling back.

"When I was a kid, I used to try to pinpoint the exact moment when a single firework fizzled out," Luke told me before a burst of green shattered into emerald comets that sliced through the sky. "It's a lot harder than you think."

Now I tried to do the same thing, fixing my eyes on a spot of green as it lost momentum, the green flare flickering and fading as it gasped for air like a runner reaching the finish line, and then turned and started falling toward the earth. I watched the green dissolve, its spark growing smaller and dimmer, but Luke was right. Even though I could tell the flare was dying out, I couldn't tell exactly when it was gone.

chapter twelve

I often wondered how much Josie's parents knew. In the days following the school assembly, did Mrs. Holden wonder why I wasn't around? Could she hear Lucy and Josie whispering my name behind a closed bedroom door? Did Josie tell her what happened, and did Mrs. Holden tell Josie's dad?

If they knew anything, the Holdens never acted like it. Putting aside the fact that Mr. Holden fired me on the very same day I'd been welcomed into their home for the summer, it was as if nothing had changed. When I was in the kitchen, they asked if I was hungry and told me to help myself to anything in the pantry. Mrs. Holden had shown me how to use the washing machine and even gave me my own laundry basket. And, although he'd taken me off the Scoop Shack payroll a little too easily in my opinion, when I'd returned from my unsuccessful morning of job hunting, I'd found a brand-new bicycle pump in the garage. I knew he was being nice, but I couldn't help wondering if Mr. Holden was also eliminating any excuse I had for not being able to get to my new job.

On my second day, I was better prepared for work, mostly thanks to Mr. and Mrs. Holden. I had my sunglasses on my head, was lathered up in the sunscreen Mrs. Holden left me on the bathroom counter, and had borrowed a baseball hat from Mr. Holden. I even managed to pack a peanut butter and jelly sandwich for lunch and a bag of grapes to snack on, which Mrs. Holden had kept in the freezer so they'd still be cold when it came time to eat them.

I was staring into the refrigerator, trying to decide between raspberry or blueberry yogurt for breakfast before my ride to the marina, when Mrs. Holden came into the kitchen.

"I can pick up more snacks if you write them on the grocery list," she offered. "It's over there on the desk."

I decided on raspberry and closed the refrigerator door. Mrs. Holden handed me a spoon. "How's the new job?"

"Great," I told her, because I knew that was what she hoped I'd say. "I'm learning a lot."

"Good, I'm glad to hear that." She pulled two chairs out from the kitchen table, sat down in one, and waited for me to sit in the other.

I didn't have much time to eat my yogurt if I was going to make it to work by seven, but I accepted her invitation anyway. "Thank you for the frozen grapes, and for having me for the summer."

"It would have been awfully quiet with just Josie around. Besides, with you girls leaving in the fall, Mr. Holden and I were happy to have you all here, even if . . ." Her voice trailed off.

"Even if I screwed up," I finished for her. "I know. I'm really sorry about that."

"Well, it all worked out, right?"

"Right. It's really nice here. I love your house."

She looked around the kitchen, running her gaze over the window and along the exposed wood beams crisscrossing the ceiling. "There's something nice about the history of this place, isn't there?"

"Josie told me that Mr. Holden used to pass by this house when he was a kid."

"He thought it was the greatest home he'd ever seen, which, considering he was about seven years old at the time, means he was probably infatuated with the big tire swing in the side yard. We hadn't even been inside when we made the offer, bought it sight unseen. I think Mr. Holden sort of had a wake-up call when we walked through the front door—the floors were scratched raw from the previous owner's dogs, the walls had twenty-year-old wallpaper, and the plumbing had to be replaced. It needed a lot of work once you got past the blooming hydrangeas out front. His visions of what he thought the house was didn't exactly match the reality."

"You'd never know it now," I told her, scraping one last spoonful of raspberry yogurt from the bottom of the container.

"I thought it would never be finished, there was so much work. It was actually easier to build the other house from the ground up, even though it's three times the size. There's a big difference between trying to fix what's wrong and doing everything right from the beginning."

"But it was worth it," I told her.

"Absolutely," she agreed.

I pushed my chair back and went to the sink to rinse out the yogurt container before dropping it into the recycling can. "I have to go, can't be late!"

"Have fun!" Mrs. Holden called out as I waved good-bye.

"I will!" I called back so convincingly even I almost believed I would.

* * *

When I made it to the marina, George was already in the office getting ready for the day. According to the clock on the wall, I'd arrived with two minutes to spare.

"So you decided to come back?" he joked, his hands clutching clear plastic bags stuffed with freshly caught bait.

"You bet!" I announced, looking past the pink, blood-tinged water and the bulging eyes staring at me from the bags.

"Well, you have good timing." George kicked the base of the freezer. "Can you open the top of this? These just came in, and they need to get on ice."

For the rest of the summer, that's how my mornings would start. Just me and George and whatever poor sea creatures happened to fall prey to a fishing line and a Ziploc bag.

During the next two hours, I shadowed George around the marina taking mental notes of all the morning rituals I'd be undertaking for the rest of the summer—hosing down the docks, counting the cash in the register, listening to the voicemail for messages left over night. We pumped fuel and ran bait out to the boats when they needed it. Even if we were busy, it wasn't difficult stuff, and seeing the water just steps away from the office made doing these simple tasks seem less tedious than they could have been anywhere else. Combine the ocean views with the breeze drifting through the open windows and doors, and it was actually pleasant.

Once the morning tasks were completed, George turned his attention to loading up his boat for the day, and I parked myself in the director's chair on the dock halfway between the office and the fuel pump. Every once in a while, George would call my name and introduce me to his friends and customers, and by the time Nolan arrived for work at nine o'clock, I'd met Dennis, Bobby, and Mr. and Mrs. Martin, who told me to call them Wally and Peg. I quickly learned that there is one question everyone in a marina wants to know: are the fish biting? I made a mental note to ask George the same thing tomorrow morning so I'd have an answer for everyone, instead of doing what I did today, which was turn toward George, whose boat was idling in the slip nearest the office, and let him take over.

The boat was loaded with his fishing rods, fresh bait, and fuel, and George was ready to take off the moment he spotted Nolan's car turning into the parking lot. I was perched in my chair on the dock beside the fuel station when George signaled to me to meet in front of the office's back door.

George went inside and grabbed a water from the refrigerator. "You two are in charge, don't make me regret it."

Nolan walked through the office and joined me on the dock just outside the back door, solemnly holding up three fingers and pledging, "Scout's honor," to George as he passed him.

"That might mean something if you hadn't dropped out of the Boy Scouts."

"I'm sure Emily was a Girl Scout. She can vouch for us." Nolan looked at me and I nodded, holding up my own oath.

That seemed to satisfy George, because he didn't protest and instead just reminded Nolan to lock up when he closed. We both watched as George removed the lines holding his boat to the dock, and then backed out of his slip as easily as if he was reversing out of a lined parking space at a shopping mall.

"Why didn't you come out with us last night?" Nolan asked, flopping down in the director's chair next to me.

I decided I didn't have to be right next to the fuel pump in order to see boats arrive, so I went to get my chair and brought it back, setting it beside the office door and across from Nolan. "I wanted to make sure I wouldn't be late for work, considering it's only my second day."

"George was probably surprised you showed up at all. He owes me ten bucks."

"You bet on me?"

"We did. We make bets on everything, though. Last week, George bet me I couldn't balance a sabiki rod on my chin for more than ten seconds. So don't take it personally."

I didn't. I was just surprised Nolan took my side in the bet. "So who won?"

"George. It was a lot harder than I anticipated." Nolan moved his chair over into the shade under the office's overhang.

"What did you all do when you left the Scoop Shack?" I asked.

"Didn't your friends tell you?"

I never heard Lucy and Josie come home. I'd tried to stay awake, and even alternated closing one eye for a few minutes and then the other in an effort to get some rest without actually passing out, but the last thing I remembered was thinking how grateful I was for my memory foam pillow.

I'd set my phone alarm to vibrate so it wouldn't wake Josie and Lucy when it went off, but I didn't try nearly as hard as I should have to be silent as I fumbled around in the darkened bedroom getting dressed for work. I may have dropped my bottle of suntan lotion on the hardwood floor and been a little louder than necessary as I stomped to the bathroom to brush my teeth. They must have had a really fun night, though, because neither of them moved, and neither one answered when I whispered good-bye.

"I was asleep when they got home, and they were still passed out when I left this morning," I told Nolan. "Our schedules don't exactly match."

"In that case, come with me and I'll fill you in." Nolan jumped up, and I followed him over to the pump-out station.

He checked the level of the holding tank and gave me the highlights of last night, which consisted of Alyssa getting drunk and throwing up all over the passenger window of Tyler's car because she didn't get the window down fast enough, some guy named James losing his keys in the sand for an hour until they found them with a metal detector someone went and got from their garage, and Josie running into the ocean fully dressed on a dare.

I didn't know Alyssa or Tyler or James, but I knew Josie. And there's no way she would take that dare. "She did not."

"She did so," Nolan insisted.

"But Josie hates the water."

"Not anymore," Nolan told me. "Or at least not when eight people are chanting her name."

"And Lucy let her?"

"I think it was Lucy who offered to hold her car keys, otherwise we probably would have been looking for two sets."

A delivery truck with an igloo logo on its side pulled into the parking lot, and I trailed Nolan as he went to meet the driver.

I still couldn't believe it. Josie wouldn't jump into a crystal clear, chlorinated pool in the middle of the day in her own backyard, but she'd run into a black ocean at midnight—by herself?

"What did she get for doing the dare?" I asked as Nolan piled bags of ice onto my outstretched arms.

"Nothing, as far as I know. Basically, she just got to be a badass."

A badass? I had to laugh. If Nolan knew about the six-foot long unicorn float Mr. Holden bought for Josie when he opened the pool this year, he might think twice before calling her a badass. Mr. Holden had told Josie he'd had it with her only venturing in up to her ankles on the pool steps, and if a glitter-infused unicorn with room for two couldn't entice her to finally take the plunge, then he'd give up. Josie loved the unicorn float, with its silver horn and rainbow-colored vinyl mane, but even glitter that shimmered in the sun couldn't get her to take the unicorn for a ride in the deep end.

Apparently, it wasn't mythical creatures or six-foot long floats that Josie needed to take the plunge. It was eight people chanting her name. Seven strangers and one best friend from home. I guess one best friend was enough to get the job done.

I followed Nolan into the office, where we set the bags of ice in the freezer, beside the cooler with the bait.

"They said you have a boyfriend who's on the Vineyard for the summer?" Nolan was making a statement, but he made it sound like a question. It made me wonder who had brought up my relationship status—Lucy and Josie, or Nolan.

"Yeah, he was supposed to work at a lacrosse camp in New Hampshire, but he did something to his knee and now he's on crutches and waiting to find out if he needs surgery."

Nolan placed the last of the bags of ice in the freezer and went over to the counter, where he pulled a filing box out from the shelves under the register and thumbed through the tabs until he found what he was looking for. "That sucks. I needed stitches on my forehead once and I practically passed out. I can't imagine having surgery."

"First he has to do physical therapy. That's why he's staying on the Vineyard—he can't work and his family friends have a house there."

Nolan placed the ice receipt into the folder marked *I* and tucked the file box back into place. "That's convenient."

"It is," I agreed, and then for some reason added, "Or maybe it isn't, I don't know. The family has a daughter, Sam, and she doesn't like me because of something I did months ago."

"Months ago? She sure knows how to hold a grudge."

"It wasn't something I did to her, it was something I did to Luke, my boyfriend."

Nolan paused before asking me the next logical question, almost as if he wasn't sure whether to let the subject drop or get me to spill my guts. "Is this where I ask what you did that was so bad, or should we move on to another topic?"

I weighed my options. On the one hand, Nolan didn't know Luke and he barely knew me, so he would have an objective opinion about Sam's reaction. On the other hand, if Nolan responded like Sam did, I was basically inviting him to think I was a terrible person, too.

I decided to tell him a sanitized version, leaving out the gory details but giving him enough information to form an opinion. I didn't know Nolan well, but so far, he seemed like someone who wouldn't rush to judge me without taking two things into consideration: 1. I'd been a model employee since George hired me, and hadn't complained about any of the tasks to which I'd been assigned, and 2. Someone who was willing to ride a bike four miles each day to vacuum shit out of boats and pump gas in the blistering sun couldn't be all that bad.

"So what do you think?" Once I finished telling Nolan the story, I leaned over, set my elbows on the counter, and waited for him to decide. "Do you think it's weird that she reacted like that?"

"You look like you're waiting for a verdict." Nolan rested against the counter, his arms crossed over his chest. "I'm not sure I have one. I mean, let's face it, all girls are nuts, so I'm not surprised she was a little unhinged, but then again, from what you just told me, it's not like you're the picture of sanity, either."

"Point taken," I admitted, and then added, "At the time, I mean."

"On the other hand, Sam?" He paused, waiting for me to confirm her name, and when I nodded, he continued. "Sam does sound a little overinvested in your boyfriend."

Overinvested? *Protective* I was expecting, maybe even *possessive*. But overinvested? What was I supposed to do with that?

"This is exactly why I don't have a girlfriend," Nolan continued. "You're all nuts."

"Does that mean you had a girlfriend, or that you don't want one?" I asked, trying to better understand his sweeping generalization of my entire gender.

"I had one—she was there last night, actually—but we broke up a few months ago. What about you and your boyfriend? What happens after the summer?"

"His name is Luke," I reminded Nolan. "And he'll be at Tufts, so we won't be too far away from each other. Not even two hours."

"You'll have a car?"

"No. But there are busses." I could tell Nolan was about to challenge my transportation plans, so I pointed to the wall with nails hammered in every few inches and changed the conversation. "What's up with those?"

"They're nautical knots. Like the cleat hitch I showed you? There are about a hundred different boating knots, each with a specific purpose. Like this one." He reached up and removed what looked like a noose from one of the hooks. "This is a bowline. You can use it for a ton of things, like keeping sheets attached to the clew of a headsail or connecting two lines to make one line."

Nolan may as well have been speaking in a foreign language.

"Just looks like a noose to me," I told him.

"Maybe, but the thing about a bowline is that no matter how tight you make it, or how strong the hold, it's crazy easy to undo." Nolan demonstrated by pulling the noose tight into what looked like an impossible knot, and then with one tug on the end of rope, the whole knot fell apart. "All it takes is one pull and it comes undone."

"So all these *lines* are yours?" I asked, making sure to use the correct terminology.

Nolan nodded. "Yep. This is what I do on rainy days to kill time or when it's dead around here."

"Pretty impressive."

"Here." He handed me the untied line. "I'll show you how to make a bowline. George will be blown away if he sees you doing this. The only thing the other girl learned to tie was her phone charger cord around her finger while she took selfies."

I held the two ends of the line, one in each hand, and Nolan guided me through the steps.

"The rabbit comes out of the hole," he began, with the rabbit being the end I had to slip through a loop I formed along the remaining length of the line. "Then the rabbit goes around the tree and then jumps back into the hole."

My bowline didn't look half bad. I pulled on the line and the noose slid closed. "Please tell me you didn't make up the whole rabbit story because you didn't think I'd understand the more technical version."

"Nope, that's the same way I learned it. A rabbit, a hole, and a tree—that's about as technical as I get."

I slipped the line out just like I'd watched Nolan do, and my secure knot easily dissolved.

"See, you're a natural. By the end of the summer, you'll be able to do all of these." He swept his hand toward the wall where his handiwork hung. "I'll teach you everything you need to know—two half hitches, roller knots, a clove hitch—"

"I already did that on the dock, right?"

"That was a cleat hitch. A clove hitch is totally different. Oh, I have so much to teach you." He let out an exhausted sigh, but I could tell he was teasing me. "But first, there's a twenty-foot Boston Whaler pulling up to the fuel dock, and I think it has your name on it."

I jumped to my feet and saluted him. "Aye aye, Captain."

Nolan smiled. "You've come a long way from your Girl Scout days."

"Full disclosure, I was a horrible Girl Scout. Couldn't even make it past Brownies because I literally did not earn a single badge. I think my mom took it harder than I did."

"I didn't figure you for a slacker."

"Did you really quit Boy Scouts?"

"When you're rushed to the hospital for five stitches in your forehead while trying to earn your gardening badge, it's time to give up the dream."

* * *

"Whatcha doing?" Lucy asked as she and Josie flopped down on either side of me.

"Watching an instructional video," I told them, making room on the bed so they could see my laptop screen, where an overweight, white-bearded man narrated step two of a square knot.

"Why is Santa wearing a tank top that says *Don't give up the ship?*" Josie asked.

"That's Boater Bob, and he's teaching me how to tie a square knot."

I thought they'd have more questions, but Josie and Lucy seemed satisfied with my answer, and the three of us finished watching Boater Bob. They probably figured it was part of my job training, but really the only lines I ever had to tie were the ones on the dock, and by the end of day two at the marina, I'd completely mastered a cleat hitch.

When Boater Bob gave us a thumbs up and signed off, I closed my laptop and pushed it toward the end of my bed. "Where were you guys?"

"In town." Lucy handed me a bag. "Peanut butter fudge, want some?"

She didn't have to ask me twice. I reached in and took a square.

"So what's your work schedule?" Josie wanted to know. "It would be nice if we could actually do something together."

"I found out today that I'm off every Wednesday and Thursdays until noon."

"We'll never see you," Lucy complained. "We're off Tuesdays and every other Monday."

"I could ask George to switch my days," I offered. "But I'm not sure it would do any good."

"Well, Boss Man isn't exactly flexible when it comes to our schedules," Josie moaned, as if I needed reminding. "I think he's afraid all the other employees will think he's giving us special treatment."

"If special treatment is getting assigned to garbage duty every night, I could do without it." Lucy took the bag back from me and helped herself to her own square of fudge.

"Are you going to see Luke on your first day off?" Josie asked me.

"Probably. But not until next week, because George thinks I should have a full week of experience before earning any sort of reprieve."

"Sounds like we won't be able to do anything together until, what, next Thursday *morning*?" Josie emphasized the morning part, making it sound even shorter than it was. And earlier. Then she rolled off my bed and stood up. "I'm going to take a shower before work."

I waited for Lucy to say something about my schedule and how I should stay here with them on my first day off instead of going to see Luke.

But Lucy didn't say anything and she didn't move. Neither did I.

When we heard the sound of the shower, Lucy turned on her side to face me. "Remember Eager Beaver?" she asked.

"Of course I do." How could I forget the matted brown stuffed beaver with a velvet quilted paddle tail? I'd always thought it was sort of odd that Lucy didn't have a teddy bear or a stuffed Minnie Mouse from Disney World, like most girls. She had a semiaquatic rodent. A cute, cuddly, friendly rodent, but still a rodent (so is Minnie but for some reason that polka dot bow makes all the difference).

"Well, when I got him, his fur was all plush and thick, and I thought his suede nose felt exactly like a real beaver's nose would feel, except it wasn't wet."

"I didn't know his nose was suede."

"Of course you didn't. It was so soft I used to rub it all the time and eventually it just wore away. Did you know he had two little white felt buck teeth?"

"I always thought it was weird that a beaver had no teeth."

"They fell out after a few years." Lucy paused and ran her finger along her upper lip, like she was trying to remember exactly where Eager Beaver's teeth fell out and if she'd saved them for the Tooth Fairy. "Anyway, you see what I'm saying?"

"Eager Beaver had poor dental hygiene?"

"His teeth fell out because I couldn't stop playing with them. I'd flick them back and forth and curl them up under his lip and rub them between my fingers. But that wasn't the point ... actually, you totally made me forget my point."

I had a hard time seeing how there was even a reason Lucy was telling me this, but I let her retrace her train of thought and waited for her to figure it out.

"Okay! Yeah, my point was something like this—I loved Eager Beaver so much, I basically turned him into a balding, toothless, deflated piece of roadkill."

Now she'd completely lost me. "Are you reminiscing about a stuffed animal, or are you trying to teach me some profound lesson?"

Lucy shook her head. "I have no idea. It sounded right when I started, but now I've totally confused myself. What I was *trying* to say was this: After a few years, Eager Beaver looked nothing like he did when I got him for my birthday, but he was still Eager Beaver. Not exactly as adorable as the day I got him, but still the same to me, even if my mom tried to throw him in the trash because she said he was probably filled with dust mites."

"I bet Patty told her that."

"Probably, but thankfully I won that battle."

I realized I hadn't seen Eager Beaver on Lucy's bookshelf since I moved back to Branford. "Hey, Luce, what happened to Eager Beaver?"

"Let's just focus on the deep and insightful lesson you're taking away from this."

"But I'm still wondering what happened to Eager."

"Fine. My mom finally tossed him in the trash because the doctor said he may be contributing to my allergies." Lucy sat up and crossed her legs. "See how this relates to you and Luke?"

"That's what I'm supposed to be getting from this? If I play with Luke's front teeth too much, they'll fall out?"

Instead of laughing as I'd hoped, Lucy frowned at me. "I think you know what I'm saying."

I knew Lucy thought her point was pretty clear, but I decided there were two ways I could see the Eager Beaver situation. The one I preferred was that, no matter how much someone changes or how circumstances make things different on the outside, inside they're still the same person. I had a feeling, though, that Lucy intended me to take away the other point, which wasn't something I wanted to learn at all: Eventually, no matter how important something is to you, even the things you love the most can end up not being good for you.

Long-Distance Relationship Tip #20:

Communicate regularly and creatively. And by
"creatively" I mean pictures, videos, and the like.
Not mind reading.

---

chapter thirteen

I f there's one thing I know, it's how to be a good house
guest. My mom's book, *Open Invitation: How to Visit When
You Want to Be Invited Back*, was a national best seller, and
I lived through the mania of *Ten Tips for Exceptional Guests*
when it was licensed to a towel company, who embroidered
the tips on towels and sold them in every department store
across the country.

Before leaving for the marina, I always washed my yogurt
spoons or cereal bowl and laid them in the dish rack beside
the sink to dry (at an early age, I learned that Cheerios have
the same adhesion properties as cement if you let them sit
around too long). I made my bed, put in a load of laundry
that I collected from around our room, and closed the front
door so silently when leaving, you would have thought I had
a future in the fine art of home invasion.

It's funny how quickly something new can become routine.
After a few days of waking up at six o'clock, my body stopped
fighting and gave in to crawling out of bed at such an ungodly
hour. I'd whittled my morning activities down to an impressive
fifteen minutes—I could brush my teeth, shower, and dress
without even checking the time, although it helped that *dressing
for work* meant grabbing a pair of shorts and a T-shirt. I could
feel my way around our bedroom in the dark without tripping
over the spot where the edge of the area rug met the hardwood
floor or grabbing the wrong pair of flip-flops, and knew I'd be
downstairs in the kitchen by six fifteen and out the door by

six thirty. It made me wonder if, with enough time, eventually everything loses its novelty, not because it ceases to be new, but because we adjust and it becomes normal. What once seemed inconceivable doesn't just become possible, it becomes acceptable. And I accepted that my days would begin before the average person even rolled over to check the time, that my hands would reek of fuel, and that I'd become immune to the sight of lifeless, pucker-mouthed fish sealed in Ziploc bags.

I didn't complain when George said I shouldn't take my first days off, because it was almost mid-July and I needed the paycheck. But by the time my first Wednesday off finally rolled around, I was ready for a break.

I slept later than I had since I'd moved into the Holdens' house for the summer. For the first time, I was going to catch the ferry from Falmouth directly into Edgartown, which was closer than leaving from Woods Hole, so I could ride my bike and keep it there for my trip back. Unlike the ferry from Woods Hole, the Falmouth ferry only carried passengers, and it ran just a few times a day, leaving every two and a half hours. My morning choices were an eight thirty or an eleven, and even though I couldn't wait to get to the island to see Luke, I decided a few extra hours of sleep were worth getting there a little later.

I slipped out of bed around ten and tiptoed to the bathroom so I wouldn't wake Josie or Lucy. When I returned—showered, teeth brushed, and ready to go as soon as I got dressed—they were both sitting up in their beds waiting for me. For a minute, it occurred to me that this might be some sort of intervention. Maybe they were still going to try to get me to stay.

"It's still early," I whispered, making my way over to my bed, where I'd laid out my possible outfits for the day. I hadn't been able to decide between a sundress or shorts and a tank top, not that it would make a difference to Luke. But it wasn't really Luke I was thinking of as I assessed my two options. It was Sam.

Luke and I hadn't talked about her since my first visit, almost as if we'd mutually decided she was the third rail we should avoid. When we spoke on the phone, Sam's name was almost conspicuously absent as Luke shared stories about his days on the Vineyard. Unless he told me, I didn't know who waited in line with him at Back Door Donuts or how he got

134

there. Without ever saying it out loud, I think we both decided it was easier to pretend Sam had nothing to do with us, that she didn't mean anything, than try to figure out how or why she seemed to mean so much.

Luke had offered to talk to Sam about her sneak attack in the kitchen, and I'd said no—not because their closeness didn't bother me, but because I didn't want Sam to know that it did. Today, it was just going to be me and Luke. I'd planned it that way, and Luke had quickly agreed, even if it meant taking a bus around the island with a bunch of visiting tourists instead of being transported in a car.

"Sorry if I woke you, you can go back to sleep," I told them. They should have turned over and gone back to sleep by now.

Josie stretched her arms high above her head and let out a high-pitched squeal as she arched her back like a cat. "We're not going back to bed."

"We're going with you," Lucy added.

"You're what?" I asked.

"We're going with you!" Lucy threw her covers off and jumped onto my bed. "Surprise!"

"You are? For the whole day?" I pushed my outfits onto the floor and joined Lucy, who was now curled up in a fetal position with her head resting on my pillow. They weren't ambushing me, they were surprising me!

Josie was less of a morning person than Lucy, but she managed to make her way over to my bed and curled up next to us. "Of course for the whole day. We thought it was about time we actually did something fun together."

There was hardly enough room for all three of us on my twin bed, and I was sure if anyone made the slightest move, Josie would be pushed over the slim inch of mattress keeping her from landing on the floor. Still, there was something about all being smooshed together like that, the way we used to crowd into the same bed in middle school on sleepovers. We'd always wake up the next morning with only one of us in the bed, the other two sprawled on the floor among the blankets and pillows we'd set up the night before because, even though none of us had wanted to admit it, at some point we'd give in and find our own space.

135

We were taller and bigger now, so fitting the three of us on a single bed required even more strategic placement of legs and arms. I was sandwiched in the middle and sharing my only pillow with them, which meant Josie's hair tickled my face every time I inhaled.

I blew a piece of Josie's hair away from my nose so I could breathe. "I thought you said your dad wouldn't let you move your schedule."

"He wouldn't, but that doesn't mean we can't swap days with other people if they're willing."

Lucy wiggled her toes, and I wondered if it was because pins and needles were setting in and she was trying to keep them from falling asleep.

"Alyssa and Mariah offered to switch when we told them we wanted to go with you." Josie wedged her knee against mine as she tried to get comfortable.

"I've only been to the Vineyard once, so I can't wait." Lucy started to rotate her left ankle in counterclockwise circles, which made me pretty sure I was right about her foot falling asleep. "Are you surprised?"

"Are you happy?" Josie asked before I could answer Lucy.

"Are you kidding me, of course I am, surprised *and* happy."

If I wasn't acting thrilled, it wasn't for the reason Josie and Lucy probably suspected. It wasn't that I didn't want to spend my day off with them, or that I wanted to keep Luke to myself. The idea of spending the day with all of them was amazing, I just wasn't so sure that Luke would agree.

I was happy and surprised, and also relieved. Until I'd heard that I wouldn't be walking into Melanie's house alone, I hadn't realized how much I dreaded the possibility of running into Sam—of having her look at me like I was not just an unwelcome visitor in her home, but someone who needed to be removed from Luke's life. Suddenly knowing Josie and Lucy would be there made me feel like I had protectors on my side, reinforcements. With Lucy and Josie there, Sam was outnumbered.

Josie stuffed her hand under my pillow and grabbed a fistful of memory foam to keep her balance. "Of course, we'd be lying if we said we weren't curious about meeting Sam."

Lucy smacked Josie's leg with her foot. "Don't say that."

"What? It's true."

"Fine, it's true," Lucy admitted. "But even if Sam wasn't there, we'd still want to go with you."

"Well, you better get ready if we're going to make the eleven o'clock ferry," I told them, and then remembered a huge bonus to having Lucy and Josie go with me. "Does this mean we're taking your car to the ferry?"

"It sure does." Josie began untangling our arms and legs as she slid down the side of the bed. "No bike for you today."

As if it wasn't enough that they'd swapped work schedules to surprise me with our first real day together, or that they'd be there and have my back if I had to come face to face with Sam again, now Josie was going to drive us to the ferry. Today was going to be better than I ever planned.

chapter fourteen

E mily warned me ahead of time, if you call receiving a text fifteen minutes before her ferry arrived a *warning*. She was still coming to the Vineyard, but she wasn't coming alone.

The whole thing was weird, especially considering that Emily had practically planned every minute we would have together while she was here. Emily not only looked up the bus schedule to Aquinnah so we could have lunch at the restaurant on the cliffs next to the lighthouse, but she calculated our trip almost down to the minute so we would arrive after the lunch crowd, with enough time to get back to Edgartown for ice cream at Mad Martha's.

The idea of hobbling onto a bus with my crutches wasn't exactly appealing, but there was one thing I hadn't thought of when I'd decided to stay on the Vineyard with Charlie and Sam for the summer: it's actually really boring. With Sam working and Charlie doing anything *but* working, I'd basically realized that when he was kayaking or playing tennis or biking over to a friend's house, the only thing left to do was torture myself. This typically involved watching game videos of last season's Tufts lacrosse team, checking out the videos being posted by the camp where I should have been coaching, and looking up gnarly images of orthopedic surgeries gone wrong. Not exactly productive activities.

Ever since Emily told me she had Wednesdays off, though, I'd been looking forward to having her here. And while, at home, I was used to the fact that being around Emily usually meant being around Josie and Lucy, too, I had no idea what the four of us would do all day. Together. On an island. Me, my girlfriend, my sort-of-ex-girlfriend, and their best friend. It sounded like a reality TV show.

And since I couldn't exactly tell Emily that I wished she'd asked me first, I did the next best thing I could think of. I recruited Charlie for the day.

At least we didn't have to drive all the way to Vineyard Haven to pick them up, which would have been pretty much impossible, since we couldn't all fit in the Jeep with my leg taking up the whole back seat. Usually, Sam got first dibs on the car, since she was the one who had a paying job to get to, but Charlie convinced Melanie to let him use her SUV for the day so we could get around. I think Charlie was more excited about Emily visiting than I was, if only because he had worked his way through most of the girls on the island already, and Josie and Lucy were two new prospects.

"So Josie's the one you went out with before Emily," Charlie clarified as we waited for the ferry to come into Memorial Wharf, which was right downtown and just a few minutes from Charlie's house.

"Yeah, but it's not like I jumped from one to the other," I told him. "There was a break in between."

"Right, the whole party thing where Josie found you with that girl . . ." Charlie thought the story was infinitely amusing, and no matter how many times I told him it wasn't that interesting, he found a way to get me to retell it all over again.

"Do we really need to rehash the details?"

"I don't think there are many girls who would be so forgiving of you dating their best friend after that."

"Josie and I were never that serious, and besides, like I told you, she helped get me and Emily back together."

"You know what? After everything you've told me, it actually sounds like Josie is the really nice one."

"I never said she wasn't nice. She just isn't for me."

"I get it. Hey, I'm the one who told you not to blow it with Emily by doing something stupid." Charlie shot me a knowing look, which I wanted to ignore but couldn't. "Besides, she can sure as hell play ping pong."

I stared down at the rubber cap on the tip of my crutch.

"You haven't told her, right?" he asked, although it was more of a confirmation than a question.

I shook my head and pushed my crutch through the coating of sand that had blown across the parking lot, marking an X beside my foot and then scrubbing it away.

"Good. Keep it that way." Charlie lowered his voice even though there was no one nearby to hear us. "Trust me."

I wasn't convinced Charlie was right, and not just because he hadn't had a serious girlfriend in his life. But he was the closest I ever came to having a brother, and I realized that, even if he barely knew Emily, he knew how much she meant to me. Still, I couldn't help thinking I should tell her what happened while she was on tour with her mom, even if Charlie thought that was the equivalent of asking her to kick me in the balls.

"So you're cool if Josie and I hit it off? Or the other one?" Charlie didn't have a type, which meant he usually cast a wide net, but since Lucy had just broken up with Owen, I was pretty sure she wouldn't be all that excited to have Charlie all over her as soon as her feet hit dry land.

"The other one is Lucy," I told him. "And yeah, I'm good. But don't get your hopes up."

"Duly noted," Charlie assured me. "You want to wait here or walk over to the railing where they come in?"

"I think I'm going to sit down over there," I told him, pointing my crutch at the low brick wall surrounding a life-sized sculpture of a finback whale's smooth black tail diving into the green grass like a question mark, creating the illusion that its massive body was submerged underground. "You can meet them on the wharf if you want, though."

"Make a good impression." Charlie considered my suggestion. "Not a bad idea. I'll bring them over."

By the time I made it to the wall and sat down, the passenger ferry from Falmouth was nudging itself alongside the wharf, where Charlie was waiting to greet the girls as soon as they stepped off the boat.

I expected to see Emily at the head of the line, anxious to jump onto the wharf and find me. But Josie led the passengers off, her camera in one hand as she pointed things out to Lucy with the other—the small Chappy Ferry carrying a few cars and standing passengers across the narrow inlet to the harbor, the pristine white homes lining the edge of the water, even me.

Josie was pointing at me.

I stood up, but Josie started waving for me to move aside and held up her camera, as if I should have known it wasn't me she was interested in, it was the photo op behind me—which was a good thing.

It wasn't that Josie scared me, at least not in the same way as a two-hundred-pound defenseman attacking me at full sprint did. It was just that I still didn't know exactly how to act around her—whether she was really okay with me now that Emily and I were back together, or if it was just a matter of time before she decided she'd made a mistake when she arranged for me and Emily to meet and work things out. No matter what happened, she was still Emily's best friend, and that meant I couldn't piss her off without serious fallout.

I caught so much shit from my friends for even agreeing to meet Josie when she texted me about Emily right after the time capsule assembly. After all, she'd been the one to fish the guide out of the trash and give it me. "I think you should see this," Josie had told me before handing over a notebook with Emily's familiar bubbly handwriting across the front. At first, I'd thought she was giving me notes for a class, but then I saw my name, thumbed through the pages, and realized I was reading words and details from my conversations with Emily. And then there were the tips. Emily had reduced our relationship to a neatly numbered list of dos and don'ts, cataloging our progress with the detached, objective observations of a scientist recording the results of an experiment. I didn't even know what I was reading. It made no sense. The person dissecting every word I spoke, every move I made, sounded nothing like the Emily I'd spent weeks getting to know. It even occurred to me that Josie could've made it all up, that she was still angry at me. But that would've been a lot of trouble to go to just to get back at me, and there was no mistaking that every page was written in the careful penmanship of a girl who grew up writing thank-you letters after every holiday.

Every midfielder on the lacrosse team told me how brilliant it was to turn the tables on Emily and show everyone what she was really like. Our goalie was convinced that moving away had caused Emily to have some sort of mental break, like one of those girls you see on a true crime show, who seem totally normal on the outside, until they snap and you realize what you thought was a sweet smile was hiding the psycho with a knife behind her back. All my friends on the team—even the guys on the bench, sophomores and freshmen who didn't know Emily before she moved away—had an opinion of her now, and it could be summed up in two words: *stay away.*

What she did to you. That's how they referred to it. Why would you want to talk to her *after what she did to you*? How could you even consider giving her a second chance *after what she did to you*? You must really hate her *after what she did to you.*

When Josie had first texted and asked to meet me to talk about what happened, I didn't even reply. I ignored her and barely resisted the urge to tell her to fuck off. But she was unrelenting—a quality that had contributed to our own breakup, but that finally wore me down when it came to Emily. I agreed to meet after school, if only to have her stop blowing up my phone. We met and I listened, *barely*. I'd had no intention of doing anything Josie asked, least of all forgiving Emily. I hardly even looked at Josie when she told me why they hatched their plan, and how Emily had thrown the notebook in the garbage can before the assembly because she'd decided she couldn't go through with placing it in the time capsule. Fine. Whatever. So Emily had finally grown a conscience at the last minute; that didn't absolve her of the lies she'd told me for three months.

When Josie finished pleading Emily's case, I asked if she was done and she nodded.

I'd started to walk away, leaving Josie in the parking lot with her excuses and explanations that didn't make a bit of difference to me.

"So it doesn't matter? Nothing I said changed your mind?" Josie had asked.

I'd kept my back to her and continued walking.

"You know, she didn't have to tell us how she felt about you. She could've just said she lost the notebook or dropped it in the toilet or whatever, but she didn't." Josie wasn't letting up. "She didn't want to go through with it anymore. She was done pretending you didn't matter, even if it meant losing her best friends."

I didn't turn around, and Josie gave up trying to stop me. Even though I didn't have practice that day, I went to the field and tried not to think about what Josie had said, but no matter how many plays I ran or drills I practiced, I couldn't get one thing out of my head. Not the excuses or attempts to defend Emily, but how Emily didn't want to pretend anymore. I was pissed, that was real. I was also confused and about a million other things I didn't understand. But I'd be lying if I said I wasn't also pretending. Because I was pretending that I'd stopped caring about Emily.

Everyone assumed we were over, which is what happens when your breakup plays out in a gym filled with every student, teacher, and administrator in the school watching as you call out your girlfriend for being a liar. No one expected me to do anything other than treat Emily how she'd treated me, only they didn't know what *wasn't* on the pages of the notebook, and I did. Emily may have been pretending to be my girlfriend, but I knew she wasn't faking how she felt. And neither was I.

Then, out of the blue, Josie texted me two words: *Friendly's now.*

And I went. Even though Owen told me I was crazy and grabbed the car keys from my hand so I couldn't drive.

It would have been easier to hate Emily than try to understand how she could do that to me. I didn't hate her, though. I hated what she did, but I couldn't believe that it had all been an act. There was no way she was that good of an actress. And our last day together, when she came over to my house . . . afterwards, I'd accused her of sleeping with me as some sort of final act she needed to complete before finishing The Book of Luke. I didn't want it to be true. I wanted to believe it meant more to her than a concluding paragraph in her notebook before writing *The End.*

What I didn't know, though, was if the pain she'd inflicted was a bruise that would fade with time, or a permanent scar I couldn't ignore. Maybe that's why I'd finally let my friends get to me; why, with Emily across the country with her mom, I'd decided to shut everyone up for good by proving what I could do to her.

Josie pointed her camera lens at the whale tail sculpture to my right and got all serious, like she does when she's in photographer mode.

That's when I saw Emily step out from behind Josie, and she saw me.

Emily's pace picked up and she practically speed walked over, her hands swinging by her sides, just short of running.

"We made it!" Emily announced, throwing her arms out like exclamation marks.

"You sure did." I laughed and nodded toward Charlie, who was having an animated conversation with Lucy over by the car, his hands grazing her shoulders and arms as he emphasized every other word by touching her bare skin. "I don't know who's happier, me or him."

"I sure hope it's you." Emily stepped closer and sat down on the brick wall next to me. "Otherwise I spent six hours of my pay on a round trip ferry ride for nothing."

"Not nothing," I assured her, laying my hand on her knee, which was damp and splotchy with sunburn. I bent my head down and rested her pink nose against mine. "You need sunblock."

"Hey, stay there." Josie held her camera up, squinting the eye that wasn't pressed against the viewfinder. She waved her hand frantically, directing me and Emily to sit closer together.

"Is this what it's been like all summer?" I asked Emily, pulling her against my side as Josie turned the camera in different angles, rotating it to the right and then the left, as if that made a difference in what she was seeing.

"Lucy says she mostly shoots at the beach—shells, waves, seagulls, that sort of thing," Emily told me, although she seemed almost perplexed by Josie's chosen subject matter. "She's suddenly embraced the ocean and everything in it."

"She does know this whale isn't real, right?"

Emily looked over her shoulder at the tail and then whipped around to face me. "What?" Her mouth fell open, as if I'd just told her there's no such thing as Santa Claus. "It's not?"

For one click of Josie's camera, I thought Emily was serious. Then she broke out into a grin that lit up her entire face like the sun shimmering on the surface of the harbor, and we collapsed against each other, our laughter tumbling between us as Emily's hair blew in the breeze and obscured our faces.

"I was worried for a minute. I thought you were serious."

"I may not be a marine biologist, but I think I can tell a live mammal from a sculpture—especially when it's diving into a patch of grass behind a white picket fence."

"Hey!" Charlie yelled across the wharf parking lot, trying to get our attentions. "Lucy wants to head to the beach."

Josie suddenly found something more interesting than the man-made whale tail. "Me too!" she chimed in.

"What about you?" I asked Emily.

"Can you really go?" She touched the crutch being held up by the brick wall. "There's no way you can get around on sand, can you?"

"I haven't tried yet," I admitted. "But I can if you want."

"Let me go talk to them." Emily jumped up and headed toward Josie, grabbing her hand and leading her over to Lucy and Charlie.

Honestly, I was hoping Emily didn't decide we should go, but it wasn't just because there was no way in hell I could use my crutches on South Beach. Sam was working today, and, even though Emily hadn't brought her up since the last visit, I knew the best thing to do was to keep them apart. If not to avoid another run-in between them, then at least to keep today from going off the rails.

Emily came running back to me, her face flushed, which made her eyes seem even greener in contrast. "Okay!" she started, all breathy and excited, although I wasn't quite sure why. "Here's the deal. They're going to go to the beach for a little bit and meet us back home. Are you okay with that? Charlie said they could drop us off at the house on their way, but I thought it would be fun if we hung around here in town, and you could show me around."

"And you're okay not going with them?"

"It was my idea, actually, but I made you—or *your knee*—the bad guy here," she confided, like she'd pulled off the greatest coup ever. "If you tell them, though, I'll deny it."

"So this giddy Emily I'm seeing here is actually brilliantly sly Emily, who managed to get us alone for at least the next couple of hours with her friends being none the wiser?"

"One and the same," she declared.

Man, I loved this girl.

* * *

"It looks like you're an old pro on those things." Emily was surprised by my ability to keep up as we walked along the uneven brick sidewalks leading back to Melanie's house. "Way better than the last time I saw you."

I'd taken Emily around downtown Edgartown—slowly, but thankfully the town is basically four streets, so Emily still got to see all the shops where I'd spent the last few weeks. She'd kept saying how *adorable* it was, how *sweet* all the small shops were with their flower baskets and windows dressed in bright greens and pinks. But when she'd commented about how *quiet* it was just one street over from the main street, I knew what she was really saying: *boring*.

In true Emily style, though, she didn't want to focus on the negative, and by the time we reached Melanie's house, she'd almost convinced me that quiet was the greatest thing in the world.

"I'm glad we did that," she told me as we walked through the side yard on our way to the boathouse. "Now I can picture you here and imagine what you're doing without me."

"Well, tomorrow you can picture me at physical therapy," I said.

"That's a good thing, right?" Emily's voice was more optimistic than mine.

As we passed the back patio, I glanced through the screen door into the kitchen to see if anyone was home, but the glare from the sun made it impossible to see inside. We kept walking. "Sure, but only if PT works."

When we reached the boathouse, Emily went inside first and I followed. I'd been hoping we'd have at least another hour alone before Charlie brought the girls back. The last time Emily was here, there was all the stuff with Sam, and then Emily was insisting she had to catch the ferry back; by the time we got past all the distractions and I convinced her to stay, it was like we had to reset our entire day and start over. I didn't want that to happen again by letting all this talk about my knee put my head in a place that was anywhere but with Emily.

"How often will you go to PT?" Emily asked, taking a seat next to me on the sofa.

"Two times a week to start. I'm going on Sam's days off so she can drive me." Her name came out before I could stop it, and I waited for Emily's reaction.

"Well, the sooner you start, the sooner you can get better, right?" Emily didn't flinch or even blink at the mention of Sam, which I took as a good sign that she'd decided to forget about the kitchen incident.

I could have gone on—told Emily that Melanie had asked Sam to take me because Charlie already had one traffic ticket for blowing through the stop sign on Cooke Street, and she was threatening to make Charlie pay for his own car insurance. I'm not quite sure how he'd do that considering he'd earned all of twenty bucks all summer by walking their neighbor's dog for a weekend, but Melanie had pretty much banned Charlie from taking the car more than a mile from the house. I knew the only reason Charlie even had the keys to the SUV today was Emily. Melanie had no problem punishing Charlie for a $155 ticket, but she didn't want to make me suffer, too.

But I stopped short of telling Emily why Sam had been assigned to chauffeur me to physical therapy sessions, because even though she didn't act like it bothered her, I knew that the less we talked about Sam, the better.

Emily reached for my legs and swung them over her knees, laying them across her lap. She ran her hand along my brace, tracing each screw and hinge with her fingers. "This thing is pretty serious."

"It's all mine for the next six weeks." I knocked my knuckles against the brace, the aluminum absorbing the sound with a dull thud.

"You sound so bummed." Emily slowly moved her hand up the length of the brace and over my shorts, until it rested under my T-shirt, against my waistband. "What can I do to make you smile?"

I knew she was trying to help, but she didn't get it, not really. Emily saw what everyone else saw. At Heywood, I was the lacrosse guy, the one everyone expected to play in college. They didn't know that when it came time to decide where to go to school, I'd had two choices—a Division I school or a Division III. An athletic scholarship where I'd be lucky to play a few minutes of a game, if at all, or financial aid loans and a shot at a starting position. I'd made the choice that would let me play, even if it meant being in debt. By jumping off that bridge, I'd not only screwed up my knee; I may have also screwed up the next four years.

But I hadn't told Emily any of this because she had her own stuff to deal with after Mr. Holden fired her. She was so worried her parents would find out and make her go back home, which I knew was why she'd accepted the first job offer she got, even though she should have waited a week to see if anything better came along. And then there was the whole incident with Sam, which was ridiculous.

As soon as Melanie and I got home from dropping Emily off at the ferry that night, I'd found Sam and told her exactly that—if I was over it, I sure didn't need Sam stirring things up with Emily. Especially since I was the one who had to deal with being in the middle of the two of them all summer. Sam had listened and nodded like she understood, but that was as far as she went. There was no apology or promise to be nicer the next time Emily came over for a visit. I didn't want to make an even bigger deal about it, so I let the subject drop.

"It's hard to explain," I told Emily.

"Try me," she urged, moving her hand back to my knee.

"It could all be over, just like that." I snapped my fingers. "Then what? What happens if I can't play?"

"There's still a chance everything will be fine. And if not, well, you can deal with that when the time comes."

I knew she was just trying to help, to get me to stop spiraling down, each thought cascading into the next until the only conclusion I could come to was that my lacrosse days were over. I'd spent every summer running suicide sprints, covered in mud, just trying to improve my speed. I'd played through sprained ankles, shin splints, and a concussion. I'd tiptoed through ladders, ran patterns around cones, and spent hours alone doing wall ball drills. The games were what everyone watched, but they had no idea what went on before I even stepped onto the field. Emily didn't know that I could barely remember a time when I wasn't cradling a ball in the net of my stick—the physical and mental commitment to a sport that was as much who I was as what I played.

She had no idea what came before her, how it was just as important to me as what came after.

"It was, I don't know . . . it made me *me*." I tried to put into words what I was thinking. "And now what?"

"You aren't just lacrosse, Luke. That's crazy."

I shook my head and avoided Emily by looking over at the dart board. There wasn't anything Emily, or anyone else, could do or say that would make a difference. At this point, the only opinion that mattered was the doctor's.

Emily nudged herself between me and the back cushion, creating enough room to lay her head on my shoulder. Maybe she finally understood what I meant, or maybe she realized there was nothing she could say that would make my situation better. Either way, just feeling the weight of her body calmed me down and brought me back to what was happening now instead of what might happen in six weeks. She didn't have any magic words to fix everything, and she couldn't predict the future, but just getting the thoughts out of my head made me feel less wound up, if not exactly better.

"It just sucks." I sighed.

"That seems to be this summer's theme," Emily agreed, and this time, it was her turn to sigh.

"You're not having a good time with Lucy and Josie?"

"We hardly see each other. It's just nothing like we planned."

"I sure didn't plan this. I jumped off a bridge with five-year-old kids doing back flips, and I end up spending my summer on crutches. I was talking to Sam about it—" The moment I said her name, I wished I could take it back.

Now, instead of ignoring it, Emily's body stiffened and she sat up. "You talked to Sam about it?"

"Well, yeah. I mean, she's here every day, and it's not like I have anyone else to talk to."

"I'm here," Emily reminded me, and then added, "I mean, I may not be *here* here, but I'm always here for you if you want to talk."

"I can't call you every time I think of something to say. That's impossible, Em, and besides, you're working all day."

"So I shouldn't get a job so I can wait around in case you call me?" Emily asked, but it wasn't a question at all, and I knew it.

"That's not what I meant," I tried again. "I was just saying that even if I wanted to talk to you, it's not like I can just call anytime I want."

Emily's phone vibrated and she glanced down at the screen. "They're on their way home from the beach."

Emily tapped back a reply.

Shit, not again. This was turning out to be just like Emily's last visit, although this time we'd managed to get to a bad place all by ourselves. "I thought we'd have a little longer before they got back."

"They just wanted to see what the beach here was like," Emily said, as if it was a completely logical explanation for a beach visit that barely lasted two hours.

"It's not that different from Falmouth," I pointed out.

She shrugged halfheartedly, like it didn't matter. "Well, maybe the beach over here is more interesting."

"Because?" I asked.

"Because it has different lifeguards?" She tossed it out there like a vague suggestion, but I'd have to be completely oblivious to not get that it was an obvious reference to Sam.

"They came here to check out Sam?"

Emily moved my legs off her knees and slid over so we weren't sharing the same cushion any longer. "No, they just wanted the three of us to spend the day together."

I was beginning to feel like this entire visit had been a setup. "And yet they were unfazed when you told them to go to South Beach without us?"

"We should just drop this." Each time Emily answered a question, she seemed to move farther away from me until, finally, she was at the opposite end, right up against the armrest.

"Drop it? Is that why you're here?" I wanted to know. "So your friends can check out Sam?"

"You know it's not, Luke, but even Nolan thinks she's overinvested in you."

Nolan? The guy she works with? Emily made a big deal about me telling Sam about how we got together, and here she was telling some guy she just met about Sam? And who the hell says overinvested?

"Why were you telling him about Sam?" I asked.

"I told him about your knee and why you were here this summer instead of working at camp."

"And Sam just happened to come up?"

"I also told him who you were living with." Emily tossed her head back and stared at the ceiling. "Can we just forget about this?"

I wanted to. This was not the day I was expecting, and it definitely wasn't how I wanted to spend my time with Emily. Forgetting about this would be nice, I just wasn't sure it was as easy as that.

Emily turned her head to me. "Why is everything so complicated?"

"I don't think it has to be," I told her. "Not if you don't want it to be."

She chewed on her lip as she considered my answer. "What do you want, Luke?"

"What do I want? Jesus, Emily, I want my knee to be healthy. I want to be able to practice with the team and have a shot at being a starter in the spring. I want to stop all this bullshit with you and just have things be normal again. I mean, what else is there?"

"I don't know." She shook her head as she said it, which made me think she did know. She knew exactly what she wanted me to say, and I wasn't getting it right.

"Here you are." Charlie let the boathouse door slam against the wall as he swung it open. "We're not interrupting anything, are we?"

"You're fine," I told him, even though Emily and I weren't. Josie and Lucy followed Charlie inside.

"The beach is gorgeous!" Lucy set a pile of shells down on the corner of the ping pong table.

Josie picked up a pool cue and spun it in the palm of her hand. "You play?" she asked Charlie.

Charlie eyed Josie, trying to size her up. "Can she play pool like you play ping pong?" he asked Emily.

For the first time in what seemed like a while, Emily's face softened and she smiled. "I think you'll have to play her to find out."

"You rack," Josie told Charlie, and as I watched him collect the balls from each of the pockets, I had a feeling he was in for another beating.

As Josie called solids after the break and the game began, I felt a tentative hand gently land on my thigh. I kept my eyes on the table as Josie missed her first shot and Charlie took his turn, sinking the fourteen ball in the corner pocket. Still, Emily kept her hand on my leg, the warmth of her palm against my shorts. When Charlie missed his next shot, and Josie called the seven ball in the side pocket, I finally looked over at Emily. She was still sitting against the armrest, but she was watching me, her outstretched arm bridging the gap between us as she waited for me to decide what happened next.

I wanted to do what she said: forget about it. I laid my hand over Emily's and kept it there, my fingers resting in the spaces between hers. She waited before reacting, almost like she wasn't sure if I was going to change my mind, and then she slid over toward me until, like before, our bodies were so close it was hard to tell where I ended and she began.

I leaned in close to Emily's ear and whispered, "Can she really play?"

Emily turned her face to me and whispered back, "I don't think so, but it doesn't look like Charlie can, either."

Lucy, Emily, and I watched two of the worst pool players I'd ever seen take almost forty minutes to finish a game. Finally, after Josie scratched on the eight ball, Charlie declared victory, even if it was an ugly one.

"Winner gets the loser a drink, come on," Charlie told Josie, who wasn't as sore a loser as I'd thought she'd be.

"Bring us some!" I told Charlie as he pulled Josie out the door by the arm and they headed to the house.

"Ping pong?" Emily asked Lucy, who was quick to accept her invitation.

"She's really good," I told Lucy, but she waved me away and didn't seem worried.

She took a paddle from Emily and walked around the table to the opposite side. "I play soccer, how different can it be?"

A paddle? A table? A ball about a hundred times smaller than the one Lucy was used to kicking with her feet? I didn't say any of this, though. I just sat back and prepared to watch Emily win.

Three games later (when Emily won the first game, Lucy had insisted on best out of three), Charlie and Josie returned without any drinks. I was about to remind them that they'd forgotten to bring ours when Josie announced they had to leave.

She picked up her camera bag and slung it over her shoulder. "Last ferry is in thirty minutes."

"We're only ten minutes from the wharf," Emily reminded her, but Josie shot her a serious look and Emily didn't argue. I guess after what had happened the last time she was supposed to catch a ferry, Emily didn't want to get into it with Josie.

Right away, I knew Charlie had done something. Josie was way too anxious to leave, and it wasn't because she didn't want to miss the last boat back to Falmouth.

"You don't have to walk," I told Josie, trying to step in and play the good guy so she didn't take whatever happened with Charlie out on Emily. "We'll drive you."

Josie gave me a look of pure disdain, as if I was personally responsible for Charlie and whatever it was he did that pissed her off. "Lucy and Em, I'll meet you at the car."

I caught Charlie's eye, and he shrugged at me as if he had no idea why Josie couldn't get away fast enough.

Even with five of us in the SUV, the ride to the wharf was awkwardly silent thanks to Charlie. It made me wonder if Emily was right to think that everything, no matter how simple it should be, became complicated.

The ferry was already at the dock waiting for passengers when we arrived, and Josie didn't waste any time boarding with Lucy close behind her, completely confused by the turn of events. Charlie decided to stay in the car, which didn't surprise me.

"I should go be with them," Emily told me as we stood in the parking lot facing the wharf. It was late enough that all the commercial fishermen's trucks were gone for the day, replaced by tourists milling around taking photos of the boats in the harbor.

"Do you know what happened?" I asked her, and she shook her head.

"Nope. But I think we both have the same idea." She looked over at the car and then to the ferry. "Hey, I'm sorry about before."

I laid my arms over her shoulders and turned her toward me. "I know. Me, too."

"Maybe one of these trips we'll get it right," Emily joked, but she seemed almost sad as she forced a laugh.

"Next time no friends," I told her.

"And no Charlie," she quickly replied.

"Deal," I agreed.

Emily wrapped her arms around my waist and held me tight, her breath rising and falling as it almost mimicked the sound of the harbor water beating against the wharf.

"I should go." She pulled away and kissed me one last time. "Do you remember the first time you kissed me?" she asked, walking backward toward the ferry so she could face me.

"I remember the first time I *tried* to kiss you," I answered. "You were babysitting and when I showed up, you acted like I was—"

"I told you not to come over," she reminded me, not letting me finish. She continued walking backwards. "And you scared me to death, lurking outside the front door."

"I wasn't lurking, I rang the doorbell. You told me to leave. And then when you decided to let me stay, you gave me a Sprite in a My Little Pony cup with a pink straw shaped like a horse head."

"I remember that." Emily smiled at the memory and then looked over her shoulder at the ferry, holding her finger up for Josie and Lucy to see, motioning to them that she'd be there in a minute. "I couldn't believe you didn't ask for another cup. You actually looked really cute drinking out of it."

"So you kissed me."

She stopped walking. "No, that's not what happened. You were leaving, and before I could close the door, you grabbed my hand and pulled me toward you."

"And then you kissed me," I finished for her, ending the story.

"We kissed each other."

"Okay, I can live with that."

Emily paused, and I got the feeling she was considering whether or not she should let me believe this version of our history. "You're sort of right, but not exactly."

"Sort of?"

She resumed walking backward across the parking lot, her voice growing louder so I could still hear her even as she got farther away. "Our first kiss was about two minutes before that. And it was me who grabbed you, right before you walked out the door. And I missed your mouth, so it was sort of off center, and I thought I might have given you a fat lip because it was more like bumping faces than kissing." She stopped to breathe and then glanced over her shoulder to make sure the ferry was still waiting. "It wasn't exactly as perfect as you remember, but that was our first kiss."

"Believe me, when someone comes in that hard and fast, you don't forget. But I still like to think of the other one as our first kiss."

"Why?" she wanted to know.

I shrugged as if I didn't have an answer, but I did. It was because, right after the second kiss, Emily had felt her lips with her finger, like she was trying to trace exactly where we'd touched. It was because, when I got in my car, I saw that she was still standing in the doorway exactly where I'd left her, like she didn't want to move until I was gone.

"Because instead of pulling me by the collar and accosting me like you had a job to do, that time *I* surprised *you*. And you just stood there looking stunned while you watched me leave."

"Oh my god, I can't believe you remember all that."

She was almost to the ferry, but I didn't let it end there. "Or maybe it's just because that first kiss was really, really bad, and I want to block it from my memory."

"Not funny," she yelled, but she was laughing. "Just so we're on the same page, let's go with your first kiss."

"That works," I yelled back, because it did, and because Josie and Lucy were pulling her onto the boat and we'd run out of time.

chapter fifteen

'd dropped Nolan's name on purpose. As soon as I did it, I'd wanted to take it back—inhale the word and keep it from escaping. But I couldn't do that, and even if my initial reaction to hearing that Luke had confided in Sam about his knee was to dangle Nolan in front of him and see if he took the bait, I instantly regretted it. When he'd mentioned that Sam was driving him to physical therapy, I didn't react, but when he brought up talking to her, it was different. That time, Sam wasn't just solving a logistical issue; she was stepping into a role I was supposed to play.

I'd wanted to level the playing field. He had Sam, and I wanted him to know that I had Nolan. But instead of feeling better by making Luke experience how I felt when Sam's name was mentioned in conversation as naturally as he'd talk about Owen or any of his friends, I felt like a jerk, which was why I'd immediately tried to play it off like the conversation hadn't been about Sam at all. I'd pretended she was just a sidenote.

Was it jealousy? Partly, yes, but it was also something more. When Luke talked about Sam, he made me feel *less.* Less important. Less special. I knew Luke hadn't done that purposely, but that almost made it worse, as if his relationship with Sam was second nature, as instinctive as breathing, a pairing that was uncomplicated and easy.

I don't know why I asked Luke if he remembered our first kiss. It wasn't something I'd planned, but as I was leaving for

156

the ferry, I suddenly wanted to find out if we saw us the same way. Funny, we'd both been there that night I was babysitting for the Brocks and yet we chose to remember it differently, which made me wonder if he'd look back at today and only recall how we'd laughed about the whale tail while Josie took our picture, our walk through town, the way I'd rubbed his knee on my lap while he explained how afraid he was that he'd never play again.

I knew what Luke was really saying when he told me lacrosse made him *him*. What he meant was that lacrosse made him feel special. It made him feel like he mattered, it was something that gave him a place that felt right. I understood because, when I thought about what made me feel special, what made me feel like I was in the right place, that I was exactly where I *belonged*, the answer was unmistakable: with Luke.

Josie and Lucy chose seats on the top deck of the ferry, which meant the sun beat down on our backs as the boat made its way toward Falmouth. None of us tried to have a conversation, and I think we all wanted to pretend it was the churning of the ferry's engine that kept us from talking. It was a convenient excuse, though, to give us time to figure out how to bring up the two topics that had started and ended our trip.

"So how was the beach?" I finally asked when I realized neither Josie nor Lucy was going to bring it up.

"We met her," Lucy said.

"I figured that. Did you get to talk to her?"

"Yeah, her and her lifeguard friend Becca."

I waited for Josie to say something—to chime in with her impressions of Sam, of which I was sure she had plenty. Josie reached into her bag and pulled out her camera as if Lucy and I weren't even there.

"Do you think they clone lifeguards?" Lucy asked. "Sam's friend Becca looks exactly like her. Same blonde beachy hair, same sunglasses. They even sat the same way up in their lifeguard chair, with one foot tucked under them and the other one on the platform, waiting to run into the waves and save lives."

"I doubt scientific advancements in cloning would start with lifeguards. What did you think?" I turned toward Josie, who had the camera's lens pointed at the waves fluttering out behind the boat.

She moved the camera down onto her lap and started clicking through the photos she'd taken, each one appearing on the small digital color screen for a few seconds before she moved onto the next. "She was fine."

"Fine? That's all I get?"

Josie stopped clicking and looked up at us. "We only talked to her for a few minutes, but she seemed normal enough."

Normal. Josie had swapped work shifts, paid for a ferry ride to Martha's Vineyard, and finally got to meet Sam, and her reaction was *normal*?

No. There was nothing normal about this at all.

"Okay, what happened? You were totally fine until you went into the house with Charlie."

Now even Lucy was watching Josie for an answer. Whatever had happened, Josie hadn't let Lucy in on it, either.

"Did you and Charlie . . ." Lucy didn't finish her question, but we all knew what she was asking. Did Josie do something with Charlie.

"God no," Josie burst out, seeming like herself again.

"You were gone a long time, and then you came back and suddenly we had to leave."

"I wasn't about to take any chances we'd miss the last ferry," Josie explained, matter of fact. "And no, I did not do anything with Charlie. Believe me."

I looked over Josie's shoulder at the photos she was once again viewing in reverse order. I recognized a few shots of Melanie's chicken coop and the exterior of the boathouse, and then imagined their time on South Beach as Josie clicked through images of little kids building sand castles with bright pink and yellow plastic pails.

"Wait, stop there," I told her and held out my hand. "Can I see those?"

She hesitated, which I didn't take personally, because asking to hold Josie's camera was like asking a mother to hand her newborn to a hyena.

"I'll be careful," I promised.

Josie reluctantly gave me the camera, and I clicked through the photos she'd taken in front of the whale tail.

"Can I have this one?" I asked, showing her the last photo in the sequence, where Luke and I were laughing, our heads bent together with my hair swirling around us in the wind.

We weren't looking at Josie or the camera, and it was as if she'd caught us frozen in a moment of time.

"Really? You like that one?" Josie frowned at me and took the camera back.

"I love it. You're amazing. Can you print it out for me?" Josie didn't have a dark room at the Cape house, but she did have a new mega-pixel color printer designed especially for photographs.

"I'm not sure I have any photo paper left." She pressed a button and the digital screen went dark.

"Regular paper is fine."

"Sure, if that's what you want," she agreed, and placed the camera back in its bag.

Josie really was an amazing photographer, the way she made my hair look like delicate strands of spun sugar frozen around us, creating a cocoon that hid our faces except for our mouths, which were open and so animated you could almost hear us laughing. That's what I wanted to remember about today. That moment when it still felt possible to have a perfect day together.

"I'm going to head down and get a seat out of the sun, you want to come?" Josie stood up.

"No," Lucy said, tipping her head back and closing her eyes. "I'm enjoying the cool breeze up here."

I had been about to go with Josie, but decided to stay with Lucy instead. Once Josie was down the stairs, I took out my phone and typed some words into Google.

"What do you think really happened when Josie went in the house with Charlie?" Lucy asked me, her eyes still closed and her head resting against the seat back.

"You don't believe her?"

"Part of me does, but she was being really weird, and Charlie was definitely acting like he wanted something to happen. I mean, that pool match was painful—I can't imagine anyone doing that unless he thought he had a shot. Maybe she doesn't want us to know because Charlie's still in high school."

It was possible Josie was just embarrassed. Lucy had spent more time with her this summer than I had, but even I had a hard time believing Josie would be all that excited to admit she got together with a guy who was still in high school, especially when that guy was a friend of Luke's.

I continued to search on my phone, scanning articles that seemed to have the information I was looking for until I found what I needed. I tapped Lucy on the shoulder.

"Hey, Luce, can I ask you something?" She opened her eyes but kept her head tipped back, so she was almost looking down at me. "What would happen if you couldn't play soccer at Duke?"

Now she sat up. "I guess I'd be going somewhere else. It was basically all about the best offer. If another school offered a better scholarship, I'd have gone there."

"I meant what if you couldn't play. Period. Anywhere."

"If I couldn't play at all? Anywhere?" she repeated, like the thought had never even occurred to her.

"Yeah."

"I don't know. I'd probably feel like it was all a big waste of time."

"What was?" I said.

"Twelve years of practicing, giving up my weekends for tournaments, staying in on Friday nights during the season so I wasn't too tired to play the next day, summers spent doing three-a-days, shin splints, a dislocated finger, and a broken nose."

"You broke your nose?"

"Yeah, junior year in a game against St. Mike's, their player's head collided with my face."

I squinted, trying to see if Lucy's nose looked any different than I remembered from freshman year. "It looks the same."

Lucy pinched her nose and ran her fingers along the bridge, from the tip to between her eyes. "Maybe not *exactly* the same, but it's fine."

"Luke is really worried he won't be able to play this season."

"I don't blame him."

"I Googled MCL tears, and there's a really good possibility that Luke will be fine after his physical therapy." I may have spent more time trying to understand *abnormal valgus laxity* than I'd intended, but that's what I'd concluded.

Lucy smirked, tipped her head back again and closed her eyes. "Well, as long as you *Googled it*, I'm sure he'll be fine."

"I know, I'm not a doctor, but neither is he."

"True, but it's his knee."

"Meaning?"

"Meaning . . . remember how you felt when you didn't get into Brown after you had your heart set on it for, like, years?"

How could I forget? I could still picture the director of admissions, Ronald Parker, with his name badge and his gold wire-rim glasses. "Yeah."

Lucy sat up and turned to face me. She propped her knee up on the seat between us and hugged it. "But it was out of your hands, right? You took your SATs, wrote your essays, did your interview, sent in your application, and the rest was up to them." Lucy ticked off each of these steps on her fingers, then took the first finger and bent it down again into her palm "Now what if you'd messed up? What if you overslept the morning of your SATs, what if you couldn't figure out what to write and your essay sucked, or what if, during the interview, you let it slip that you only got an A in chemistry because you cheated off the guy who sat in the seat one row ahead of you."

"I wouldn't do that!"

"I know, but if you had, if you'd been responsible for ruining your one shot at something you'd worked your ass off for, how would that make you feel?" At this point, her fingers were all bent over and she held up a fist.

"Like shit."

"Yep. So it isn't just about whether or not Luke's knee gets better or he needs surgery or he has to take a season on the bench. It's that he's the one who jumped from that bridge, and he has no one to blame but himself." And on that note, Lucy simulated the sound of an explosion as she blew up her fist. "Is that what you guys were talking about in the boathouse when we showed up? You seemed kind of intense."

"Sort of."

Lucy could tell my *sort of* meant *not really.* "Is everything okay with you two?"

"I think so."

"You think so? That's not exactly a resounding endorsement for a guy you once told us you were totally in love with."

I hadn't actually told them that. Months ago, Josie had asked me if I really liked Luke, and I'd admitted I liked him, *a lot.* But I couldn't quite bring myself to tell my best friends what I'd realized myself. Even though I didn't say it, they knew what I meant.

"I thought it would be better with him being nearby, but it's actually harder in some ways."

"You knew it would only get harder after graduation," Lucy reminded me. "If you think about it, it's not going to get any easier."

"I wasn't expecting easier, I just . . . I don't know. I didn't think it would be so complicated." Although I didn't say it, I thought that, we'd figure it out, not because we were afraid of breaking up, but because we wanted to stay together.

When I'd left Chicago, when Sean was breaking up with me, I still thought I loved him. I'd *told* Sean I loved him, but looking back I know I didn't. I think I *wanted* to, which isn't the same thing. There are several definitions of love in the dictionary—I knew this because I looked it up when trying to figure out how I felt about Sean. I'd learned that the word originates from the Old English *lufu*, is of Germanic origin, and also comes from an Indo-European root shared by Sanskrit and Latin for *desire*. What I didn't know? That the Latin root for love is also shared by the word *leave*.

According to Merriam-Webster's Dictionary, when Sean and I were together I could answer yes to several definitions of love: *A deep romantic or sexual attachment to someone.* (Yes! Even if the sexual attachment hadn't yet occurred, but had been planned for in my head a million times.) *An intense feeling of deep affection.* (Bingo!) *A great interest and pleasure in something.* (Absolutely! At least most of the time, if not when he was telling me our long-distance relationship was over before it even had a chance to begin.)

After four months together, I'd wanted to believe we were *more*—that we were on some sort of trajectory leading somewhere that didn't end with him breaking up with me on the front walk of my now-former house in Chicago, as snowflakes fell onto the jacket I'd given him for Christmas and my family waited for me in an idling cab parked in our driveway. But he was right; there was no way we could have stayed together after I moved back to Branford. I can admit that now, even if I'd wanted to stab him with an icicle at the time. It wasn't love, it was familiar, a sense of security, a way to have something and someone to hold onto when it felt like I was being forced to give up everything that mattered to me.

Maybe I was going about this all wrong. Maybe the real test of a relationship isn't how hard you try to stay together, but how you stay together even when you aren't trying really hard.

chapter sixteen

"Want to earn some overtime?" George asked me two days later.

I was helping him scrub out the freezer, which he'd defrosted the night before. The freezer had a partition down the middle to keep the bags of ice separate from the cooler with the frozen bait, and, needless to say, George chose to scrub the side for the ice. I had the pleasure of scraping away the frozen, crusted fish juice that had leaked from the cooler into the bottom corners of the freezer.

"I'd love to," I told him as I bent over at the waist, the upper half of my body submerged in the freezer. I shook a trail of baking soda out of the box with one hand while I ran a damp sponge over the white powder with the other. It was my idea, the baking soda. George had wanted me to use liquid dish soap, but I'd suggested that, while that may get the freezer clean, it wouldn't remove the lingering fishy odor. When George gave me a skeptical look, I'd told him my mom did this sort of thing for a living and he could trust me. Already, I could tell my half of the freezer was smelling a lot better.

"I was hoping you'd say that. There's a bluefish tournament, and a few of my buddies asked me to join them." George patted a wad of dry paper towels inside his half of the freezer before starting to load the new bags of ice that had just been delivered. "It's next Wednesday and Thursday."

I stopped scrubbing. "My days off?"

"I'd pay you time and a half," he reminded me.

The summer was slipping away and I needed the money. My parents were expecting me to come home with at least a thousand dollars saved, and at this rate, I wouldn't come near that.

"Okay, deal," I agreed, rinsing my sponge out in the pail of clean water beside us before taking another dive into the freezer.

I probably wouldn't have agreed so easily if I hadn't just returned from my second lousy visit with Luke. Even though Lucy and Josie had changed all the plans I'd had for our day together, I'd still thought it would be better than my first visit. At least I'd known I wouldn't be blindsided by Sam, and that Luke had been looking forward to getting out of the house and going places, even if it meant taking the bus.

But so far, my track record for trips to the Vineyard wasn't so great. Even though, when it came time for me to leave, we'd managed to make everything seem like it was back to normal again, our good-byes felt like a consolation prize—not exactly what you wanted, but at least you got to walk away with something to hold on to.

I didn't know why our days together seemed to be like an amusement park ride. One minute, we were gliding along effortlessly, and the next, we were careening off track with no idea how to right ourselves. Roller coasters made my stomach turn inside out and I always avoided them in favor of the rides that spun you around so fast you could barely walk a straight line when you got out of the car (or, in the case of Disney World, the teacup). My last two trips to see Luke not only felt like an out of control roller coaster plummeting so fast I couldn't stop it from crashing, they also left me feeling like I'd stepped off a spinning ride that left me so dizzy I couldn't figure out which step to take next.

Last time, it was Luke who'd attempted to smooth things out by asking me to stay longer. This time, I was the one to reach out for him, and while laying my hand on his leg wasn't exactly an apology, it was as close to one as I could get in a boathouse filled with our friends.

George's offer would make it easier for me to put off my next trip to the Vineyard. I knew Lucy and Josie wouldn't be joining me, and Sam would hopefully be at work, but I wasn't sure I wanted to risk a third strike so soon.

"Hey, what are you doing here?" George exclaimed.

I poked my head out of the freezer and saw Nolan coming through the front door.

"Picking up my paycheck," he said, which explained why he'd be at the marina on his day off.

"It's over there." George pointed to the drawer under the cash register. "Don't spend it all in one place."

"There's only one place I'm going."

George picked up the damp paper towels, crumpled them in his hand, and tossed them toward the trash can in the corner of the office. "Let me guess. Nobby Farm."

Nolan rubbed his stomach.

"You must really like vegetables," I said. "I've never seen anyone look so excited to visit a farm."

"Nobby isn't just any old farm." George hoisted the final bag of ice off the floor and placed it atop the pile he'd made in his side of the freezer.

"They grow chili peppers." Nolan grabbed his paycheck from the drawer and slipped his finger under the flap so he could peer inside the envelope. "Fifty different kinds."

I took one last sniff of the freezer and, satisfied, dropped the sponge to the bucket. "I can't eat spicy foods."

Nolan rolled his eyes at me, as if I'd just said the most ridiculous thing he'd ever heard. "There's no such thing as *can't*. There's only *unwilling*."

"How about, I *can't* so I'm *unwilling*?" I offered as a compromise.

Nolan and George exchanged a look that made me think they had some secret, silent language.

"Fine. Take her." Whatever it was they were communicating to one another, Nolan had managed to convince George to say yes.

"What am I missing?" I asked them.

"You need to go." Nolan folded his paycheck and pushed it down into the side pocket of his shorts. "Nobby Farm is a one of a kind experience that is not to be missed."

"I hate to say it, but he's right." George surveyed the contents of the freezer one last time, bending over to sniff my side to make sure I hadn't skimped on the baking soda.

He closed the top and leaned down on his elbows to seal it tight. "You have to experience it once. You can take her next Wednesday morning, first thing."

"But you have your bluefish tournament," I reminded George, although I wasn't as concerned about his competition as I was about my bank account balance. "I was going to get time and a half that day."

"We're not leaving until eleven o'clock, so I want you both here by ten or else."

Nolan laughed. "Or else what?"

"Or else I'll be late, my buddies will be pissed, and you'll wish the only pain you felt was the sting of Nobby's hot peppers."

"Works for me," Nolan said, even though I still hadn't agreed to miss a morning of overtime to visit a farm that sold something I didn't even like.

"I can pick you up at Josie's if you want. Then you don't have to ride your bike here," Nolan offered, as if he knew he had to sweeten the deal to get me to say yes.

When I didn't instantly agree, he added, "Nobby's also sells handmade chocolate."

An air-conditioned car and chocolate. It sounded like, next Wednesday morning, I'd be starting my day at a pepper farm.

* * *

It was a short ride to Woods Hole, and Nolan kept the air conditioning blasting the entire time.

"Thanks for the muffin," I said, wiping my blueberry-stained fingers on the napkin at the bottom of the brown paper bag I'd found on the passenger seat when Nolan picked me up.

Woods Hole was smaller than Falmouth. The downtown was basically a single street running parallel to the Steamship Authority terminal, where most cars took a left-hand turn instead of continuing down the hill toward the shops and restaurants. Instead of following the cars turning onto the road to the terminal parking lot, Nolan hung a right down a residential street.

"How big is this place?" I asked.

"It's a farm. I don't know, a few acres? The store is basically the old house that was on the land."

As Nolan drove, the street grew narrower until it turned into a one-lane road, and a yellow DEAD END AHEAD sign announced we were about to go as far as we could.

"Are you sure you know where you're going?" I asked, and Nolan pointed ahead to the cul-de-sac where we could turn around.

Strung between two tall wooden posts flanking a dirt driveway, a sign declared *Nobby Farm*. As we got closer, I noticed that the posts were carved with peppers, their stems painted a dark green.

Nolan slowed down and drove under the sign onto the dirt driveway. "There it is."

In a clearing ahead of us, a small, red farmhouse with a wraparound porch was surrounded by gardens with red, yellow, orange, and green peppers growing on vines that crawled up stick keeping them from flopping over onto the ground.

"It sure is colorful," I said as Nolan put the car into park and a cloud of brown dust settled around us.

"You think this is cool, wait until you see inside."

The wooden porch was part of the store, and when we walked up the steps, we were greeted by tables piled with peppers of every size and color. They were organized like a rainbow, their shiny skins blending from the darkest scarlet to the palest buttercup yellow.

Inside, it was more like a general store—if the general store only sold pepper-related products. Shelves of salsas and jellies and marinades in mason jars lined the walls, while the center tables were stacked with bottles of hot sauce and tins of chili rub.

"Pretty cool, huh?" Nolan was acting like this was a candy store, not a farmhouse filled with potential instruments of torture.

As I passed the first table, I picked up a box of Hell on Earth chocolate and turned it over to read the description on the package—Belgian chocolate with dried mangos, toasted pumpkin seeds, and chili essence.

"That sounds weird, but it's good," Nolan said, giving the chocolate his seal of approval.

Nine dollars for a small box with eight pieces. I wasn't so sure spicy chocolate was my thing, but I decided to buy it anyway. Luke always went for the spiciest salsa on the table, so I thought he might like to try it. Nine dollars was pricey, but it felt like a trade-off. Giving up my days off meant I wouldn't see Luke, but I was being paid time and a half, so I could afford to splurge on a present for him.

"See this?" Nolan pointed to a jar of ghost pepper jelly. "Everyone used to think the ghost pepper was the hottest pepper in the world, until . . ." He reached over to a table and picked up a bottle of hot sauce. "The Carolina Reaper."

"The Carolina Reaper?" I repeated. "Sounds like they're overhyping that one."

"Hardly. Even I tear up with this stuff."

I walked around what I assumed was once the house's living room, reading labels and trying to figure out how someone could justify charging ten dollars for a jar of salsa. Although the price was insane, I decided to buy a jar for the Holdens anyway. It was my small, spicy way of showing them that, even if I'd been fired, I appreciated them letting me stay for the summer.

I met Nolan at the register, where he had three jars of salsa, a bottle of hot sauce, and a tin of Satan's Favorite chili powder.

"Want one?" he asked, pointing to the plate on the counter. There were quarter-sized cardboard cups filled with salsa and a bowl of tortilla chips. *Samples* was handwritten on a folded index card.

I picked up the jar of salsa beside the plate and read the name on the label. Seven Circles of Hell. "No way."

"Come on, I'll show you. It's not that bad." Nolan took a tortilla chip and poured the contents of one of the cardboard cups onto it before popping it into his mouth.

His eyes welled up and he clenched his jaw like he was trying not to scream. "It hurts so good."

"Why would you want to do that to yourself?" I asked, watching him pant like a dog.

"If it didn't hurt, it wouldn't be the hottest chili pepper known to man, right?"

"Whatever you say." I put the box of chocolate and my jar of Hot as Hades salsa on the counter, and the sales girl rang me up.

There was a bottle of Gatorade waiting for Nolan in the car, and as soon as he opened the door, he reached for it.

"I come prepared," he told me, downing almost all of the fluorescent orange liquid before he even put the key in the ignition.

Nolan glanced at the Nobby Farm bag I'd set at my feet. "I'm glad you got something, even if it isn't the Carolina Reaper."

"The salsa's for the Holdens," I told him.

"Are you actually going to try the chocolate?"

"It's for Luke."

"He has a higher tolerance than you do? Or he's just more adventurous?"

"Probably both," I admitted.

"Did you tell him you were coming here today?" Nolan asked. "With me?"

Last night when we were talking, I didn't mention my early morning field trip or Nolan. I'd let Luke believe I was heading straight to work in the morning. When I told Luke that George offered me overtime if I worked on my days off I didn't have to point out the obvious. Luke knew that meant we would go one more week without seeing each other. I was prepared for his disappointment and another reminder of how my job was messing things up, so I was relieved when Luke didn't try to convince me to tell George no. But it also surprised me when he said *okay* so quickly. He said he understood, and it was exactly how I'd wanted him to respond, because the last thing I wanted was to get into it about my job. But when he didn't resist, I suddenly wanted him to. I wanted more—a reaction that made me feel like it had some effect on him.

I think that's why I didn't tell him about going to Nobby Farm with Nolan. Withholding it gave me a sense of keeping something for myself, of knowing something that Luke didn't. There was a certain power in that, and even if Luke didn't know that, I did. For some reason, it took some of the sting out of Luke's reaction to losing a day with me.

Instead of answering Nolan's question, I reached down for the box of chocolates and tore off the cellophane wrapper. "I think I'll try some."

I removed the lid, pinched a small, round dollop of chocolate between my fingers, and placed it softly on my tongue while anticipating the worst. As the creamy chocolate started to melt it tasted sweet, but then a slow stinging sensation crawled through my mouth like a rash. I wanted to spit the chocolate out, but just imagining the horror on my mom's face was enough to keep the blazing mush in my mouth. I considered gargling with the Gatorade left in Nolan's bottle, but instead, I let the flavor scald my taste buds like a chocolate-flavored blow torch until it finally slid down my throat.

Nolan glanced over at me as I swallowed. "Maybe you should just give Luke the rest of the box."

I put the lid back on the box and placed it into the bag on the floormat, right beside the jar of salsa.

"Yeah, I'll do that," I told Nolan, but I knew I wouldn't. Like discarded evidence, the chocolates were going in the trash.

We made it to the marina by ten, and George left for his bluefish tournament on time. Over lunch, Nolan taught me to make a Spanish bowline, and when he went out to the docks to help an incoming boat unload gear and the day's catch, I took the box of chocolate and shoved it to the bottom of the trash can by the pump-out station. When Nolan drove me home after work, I hoped he couldn't tell that the box was missing from my Nobby Farm bag. If he did, he never asked why.

* * *

I found Lucy and Josie upstairs in our bedroom, but as soon as I walked in, I could tell something was wrong. Josie was sitting on the floor beside Lucy's bed with three unzipped Duke duffel bags lined up beside her. Lucy was stacking piles of clothes haphazardly on her bed, although they looked more like mounds of laundry than any semblance of an organized wardrobe.

"What's going on?" I asked.

"She's packing," Josie told me, holding open one of the bags as Lucy stuffed pairs of shorts between the teeth of the zipper.

"My grandmother fell and broke her hip. She's in the hospital." Lucy grabbed a stack of tank tops, rolled them into one big ball, and shoved them into her bag. "My mom's heading down to Georgia to take care of her for a couple of weeks."

"And Lucy's going, too," Josie added, struggling to pull the sides of a duffel bag together so Lucy could zip it closed.

"What? You can't leave," I told Lucy, then joined Josie on the floor. "We need you here. With us."

Finally, Josie was able to get the canvas sides close enough together for Lucy to tug the zipper into place.

"I have to be at school in three weeks anyway for pre-season." Lucy sat back on her heels and sighed as she looked at the remaining clothes on her bed. "We're driving down to see my grandma, and then my mom is going to drop me off at school on the way back home."

"So, like, that's it? You have to leave now?"

"In the morning. My mom's coming to get me."

Josie pushed aside the full bag with her bare feet. "And she won't be alone."

Lucy stood up and flopped down on her bed, which made the remaining piles fall over. "Your mom is coming, too."

"My mom is coming *here?*"

"Yep. They ran into each other at the grocery store, and my mom told her it looked like she'd be picking me up early. Your mom offered to come for the ride and visit. They're going to take us out for breakfast."

"This is not good," I told them, and collapsed down next to Lucy.

"Tomorrow's Thursday. You don't have to be at work until noon," Josie said.

"I told George I'd work overtime, but that's not my biggest problem. My mom doesn't know I was fired," I admitted.

Josie looked at me like she couldn't believe I thought I'd ever get away with my mom not finding out. "You never told her?"

"Are you kidding me? You're talking about a woman who made me follow her around the country so I'd have something to put on my resume in four years. She would've killed me if she heard I couldn't even hold down a job at an ice cream stand, or worse, she could've tried to make it a *teaching moment* and made me go home."

Lucy and Josie sat silently watching me as I played out the options in my head. But no matter what I came up with, there was no way around it. Either my mom would find out from the Holdens, which would be even worse, or she'd find out from me. I'd have to come clean.

"Well, I guess I have to finish packing." Lucy finally broke the silence, but instead of collecting the remaining clothes on the bed, she just sat there. "I'm sorry I have to leave you guys."

That's when it hit me. My mom would come, and I'd bite the bullet and tell her about getting fired, but after that, she'd leave and my summer would go on. Only it wouldn't be the same, because Lucy would be gone.

Everything was changing. Again.

"It's your grandma, Luce, we understand," Josie told her. "I hope she's okay."

"Me, too. But we still have one more night together," I reminded them. "What are we going to do?"

"We rally," Josie announced, and for the first time since they told me the horrible news, she smiled. "And we rally big."

I wasn't sure what that meant, but I was in.

* * *

Lucy still had one last shift at the Scoop Shack, which meant we couldn't put our final night plan into action until the Shack closed. Josie texted to tell me she and Lucy would swing by to get me after work. Apparently, rallying meant having everyone over to Alyssa's house because her parents were in Boston for the night.

Everyone from the Shack and a few other people I hadn't met were already outside on the deck when we arrived. Lucy was swarmed with people telling her how much she'd be missed. The names and faces I recognized said hi to me, but then quickly turned back to their conversations and games of cornhole. Rather than try to fit in, I trailed Josie into the kitchen like a puppy dog.

"You want one?" She held up a Twisted Tea bottle. Before I could answer, she bumped the refrigerator door closed with her hip and handed it to me.

"I still can't believe Lucy's already leaving." I pictured the calendar Mrs. Holden had hung above the desk in the kitchen—how every morning she'd cross off one more day in a countdown to the end of the summer. The next time we'd all be together, we'd be wearing sweaters and getting ready to put up the Christmas tree, which my family did every year on the Friday after Thanksgiving.

Josie opened and closed three cabinet doors before finding the one with the trash can. She tossed her Twisted Tea cap in, and then held out her hand for mine. "Well, at least I have some good news. I talked to my dad. You don't have to tell your mom you were fired."

I don't know which made me choke on my drink, that Mr. Holden was willing to let my mom believe I was a model employee, or that Josie had asked him to do me a huge favor. Josie patted me on the back until I stopped coughing. "He's going to lie for me?"

"No. I convinced him to let you take Lucy's spot at the Shack."

I did not see that coming, not only because Mr. Holden was a one and done type of boss, but also because something had changed between Josie and me since we all went to the Vineyard. I couldn't put my finger on what was different, exactly. She was almost gentle, like I'd become something delicate she had to handle carefully. Maybe Josie felt bad because she didn't think Sam was as terrible as I wanted her to be. Maybe something really did happen between Josie and Charlie, and she didn't want to tell me because, after everything we went through with Luke, she was afraid it would make things weird between us again. Whatever it was, asking her dad to give me Lucy's job at the Shack totally blew me away.

"I can't believe you did that for me."

"Of course I did. He was going to rearrange everyone's schedules to cover Lucy's hours until he found someone to replace her, but this way, we'll get to work together and you can finally have your days free."

I had to admit, that sounded nice. "I don't know what to say."

"Say yes!" she exclaimed, like it was a total no-brainer. Obviously I should say yes!

I wanted to, I really did. So why wasn't I jumping at the offer? It wasn't just that I'd have to learn a whole new job, because ice cream wasn't exactly foreign to me. It was more that I'd be starting over again, just when I'd finally settled into what my summer had become. Besides, everyone at the Shack already had their place, their rhythm, and I'd be trying to catch up. Sure, I knew Josie's work friends, but they were her friends, not mine. At least at the marina I had Nolan, who

I'd actually spent more time with this summer than anyone else. But how could I explain that to Josie? How was it possible that I felt so far away from my best friend when we slept in the same room every night?

"Yes!" I told her, because I knew that's what she wanted to hear, and it's how I wanted to feel.

"Good, now let's go find Lucy and make sure we give her something to remember on the long ride to Georgia." Josie reached for my hand to lead me outside, and as she did, my phone vibrated.

I moved my hand away and reached into my pocket to silence it. I saw Luke's name and the photo of us in front of the whale tail. At least I knew he'd be happy I was leaving my day job behind.

"I'll be right there." I held up my phone so she could see the call coming in, but also so she could see that I loved her photo so much I put it on my phone.

Josie paused, deciding whether she should stay and wait for me or leave. She opened the back door, filling the kitchen with music and the thud of beanbags, and then held up her Twisted Tea in a sort of farewell toast.

I walked down the hall until I found an empty bedroom and stepped inside where it was quieter.

"Hi." I smiled as I answered.

Luke didn't respond.

"Hello?" I tried again, moving over to the window for better reception. "Luke?"

Still nothing. I put my hand over my other ear and listened, trying to decide if we had a lousy connection or my volume was just too low. "Can you hear me?"

Luke didn't respond, but I could hear his muffled voice, which sounded far away and like he was talking to me from across a crowded room. That's when I realized he wasn't talking to *me*. He was having a conversation with someone else. And she was laughing.

"Luke?" I tried one more time, my voice louder, but now he was laughing at something the girl had said. I heard the distinctive *crack* of pool balls smacking together.

Luke wasn't calling to talk, or to tell me he missed me and just wanted to hear my voice. He'd pocket dialed me by mistake.

I should have hung up and texted him to let him know. But I didn't.

I continued listening, trying as hard as I could to decipher the words being spoken on the other end. The phone was muffled, though, and I couldn't make out any words—just the inflection in their voices as one person took over for the other. I squeezed my eyes closed and attempted to recognize the voice. It had to be Sam.

I was eavesdropping. I felt like a party crasher who discovers her invitation wasn't lost in the mail. I'd never been invited in the first place. The only thing you can do in that situation is pretend you were never there to begin with.

I pressed end, and the sound of Luke's laughter abruptly stopped as the line went dead.

I dialed Luke's number and waited for him to pick up. Instead, his phone went straight to voicemail.

"Hey." Nolan peered into the bedroom from the hallway, and I wondered how long he'd been standing there.

"When'd you arrive?" I asked, the phone still in my hand.

"Right after Lucy started dominating cornhole." Nolan moved into the doorway. "Everything okay?"

"Yeah. Fine." I slipped my phone back into my pocket.

"I was just looking for the bathroom," Nolan said.

"I think it's back there." I pointed down the hall.

"Thanks." He started in that direction, and then popped his head back in the room. "You sure you're okay? Want me to get Josie or Lucy or something?"

I walked to the door. "No."

Nolan hesitated, shrugged slightly, then started toward the bathroom again.

I could hear everyone gathered around the fire pit in Alyssa's backyard, their voices carrying down the hall from the kitchen. Lucy and Josie were probably wondering what was taking me so long, and assuming I was huddled in a quiet corner lost in conversation with Luke. If I told them about the pocket dial, how my call went straight to voicemail, I knew they'd step into their roles as best friends and rally to my side. But this felt different from telling them about Sam, or how I would report back to them about Luke while we were putting together the guide. Those were just facts, like a broadcaster delivering news or the weather—*today, it will be seventy-eight and partly cloudy with a chance of showers.* I'd *expected* a certain response and knew what they would say, because the answers were easy, black and white. They'd tell me what I wanted to hear because it would make me feel better.

In the past, the first thing I would have done was find Josie and Lucy and tell them about the muffled voices on the other end of the phone. And I would have expected them to tell me it was nothing, hand me another Twisted Tea, and ask me to replay, in detail, every indecipherable syllable I'd heard, until they reassured me my only concern should be the unreliable buttons on Luke's crappy phone.

But now things were different. Maybe, instead, Lucy would look down at the ground before reminding me that tonight wasn't about Luke; she was leaving tomorrow morning and we wouldn't see each other for months. Maybe Josie and Lucy would be too busy with their summer friends to notice me waiting off to the side while they recounted stories of crazy parents and their high maintenance kids. It was possible Josie would turn away and wave off the wafting smoke of the fire pit before softly telling me that perhaps Luke had pressed *ignore* because, at that moment, he wanted to continue talking to someone else instead of me. Maybe things were changing so much that telling someone what they wanted to hear wasn't going to work anymore.

And that's why, instead of rushing out of the room to find Lucy and Josie, I called after Nolan. "Hey, Nolan? What would happen if I quit my job at the marina?"

He stopped and turned around to face me, his mouth open in disbelief. "You're going to quit?"

"I was just wondering, before I came along, what were you and George going to do all summer without the extra help?"

Nolan seemed leery of my question, like he didn't trust that, no matter what answer he gave, I was just stalling before telling him I was leaving the marina. "I have no idea. But I do know George is way happier now that he can go fishing most days and not worry that the place will fall apart without him."

It made me feel good to hear Nolan say that, even if I doubted my presence was really that reassuring to George. "What about you?"

"Oh, it's way better for me, too." Nolan seemed to relax a little as he held up his hands and showed me his knuckles.

"No more cracked, dry hands from constantly washing the fuel off?"

"Not since you shared your secret recipe of honey, olive oil, and lemon juice."

"You can thank Polite Patty for that," I told him. "She wrote an entire chapter in one of her books on handshake etiquette, and rule number one was healthy, supple skin."

Nolan laughed. "Half the time, I don't know if you're serious about your mom or making this stuff up. Anyway, it's just nice to have someone to talk to. It makes it less like work and more like we're just hanging around at the docks all day and, every once in a while, we have to pump a few gallons of fuel and deliver a few bags of ice." Nolan leaned against the hall wall and crossed his arms. "So, why are you asking if you aren't planning to quit?"

"Forget it, I was just curious," I told him, ready to find Lucy and Josie and join them. "One more thing: I know George will be at the tournament, but is it okay if I come in a little later tomorrow? My mom is coming down for a visit and I have to talk to her about something before I head to work."

"The woman responsible for these is coming here?" Nolan held his hands up, turning them over so I could admire each side. "How could I possibly say no?"

He couldn't. And I couldn't say no when Josie offered me Lucy's job at the Scoop Shack.

For the first time ever, I wished my mom had a piece of advice I could use in this situation. Unfortunately, in this case, healthy, supple skin wouldn't solve my problem.

chapter seventeen

We were all up early the next morning, or at least early for Josie and Lucy, because Mrs. Denton wanted to be on the road back home no later than nine thirty. My mom would be at the Holdens' in less than an hour, and Josie had fixed it so I wouldn't have to tell her about getting fired, which meant I shouldn't have been dreading the conversation I was about to have, or procrastinating by helping Lucy finish packing up her side of the room. There wasn't much left at this point, just the little things that made Lucy's small area her own—the pink plush bunny slippers with white ears sprouting up from the tops of Lucy's feet, a Heywood Academy Varsity Soccer sweatshirt hanging from the bed's footboard, and a collection of seashells she'd piled up on the windowsill beside her headboard.

She'd offered me her bed so Josie and I would be closer together, and I told her I'd think about it, but I knew I wouldn't take her up on the idea. It wasn't just that I'd have to move all my stuff, because, let's face it, it wasn't like I'd collected more than a few boat lines on my side. It was more the idea of filling in the void left by Lucy, somehow erasing the fact that she'd been here with us instead of being reminded of her every time I looked across the room and saw her perfectly made, empty bed. I liked the idea of feeling her absence if I couldn't feel her presence.

Lucy kneeled down on the floor and bent over, lifting up the bed skirt for one last check under her bed before sitting back on her heels. "Remember when you came back to Heywood?" she asked me, pulling out a lone tennis ball, which was completely odd because none of us had played tennis all summer.

"Of course I do," I told her, wondering where the tennis ball came from.

"We didn't know what to expect when we found out you were moving back." Lucy moved her legs out from under her and sat cross-legged, tossing the tennis ball from one hand to the other. "Josie and I played out all these scenarios and what we'd do if it turned out we didn't like you anymore."

"Well, you sure did a good job of hiding it if you didn't." I thought about that first day we'd seen each other—how they ran up to me and wrapped their arms around my shoulders, squeezing me tight while peppering me with questions.

I sat down on the floor across from Lucy, suddenly curious what I'd find if I looked under my own bed.

"Yeah, you turned out to be okay." Lucy grinned and tossed me the tennis ball. "I'm going to miss you guys, but I'm almost ready to leave. You know what I mean?"

I shook my head no.

"It's like I'm ready to find out what comes next." Lucy looked down at her hands as she twisted a thread from the edge of the comforter around her thumb.

"I'm not sure I am," I said, although a part of me could see why, after living in Branford her whole life, Lucy was ready to experience somewhere new. Lucy hadn't moved away from everything and everyone she'd grown up with. She didn't have to make new friends and figure out a new school in Chicago, and then find out that, once she finally felt like it was home, she had to leave again. It wasn't like I wanted to stay in Branford forever, either, but I could have used a little more time with the people I'd just returned to.

I tossed the ball back to Lucy, and she caught it with one hand. "Is it the Luke thing?"

I shook my head. "That's not all of it. There's you and Josie, too, you know."

"We're not going anywhere," she assured me. "Well, I mean, we are *going* somewhere, but we'll always be here. We've put up with each other this long—what's a few hundred miles going to change, right?"

I might have agreed if I didn't already know how hard it would be. I'd thought the same thing about Jackie and Lauren, but I'd hardly spoken to my two best friends in Chicago since graduation. No matter how many times I sent them pictures or texted to say hi and let them know what I was up to, it wasn't the same as being there. Even if I could picture where they lived and the people they were hanging out with, my life back in Branford was nothing more than an idea to them, with people and places they'd never know or experience. After a while, it just gets harder and harder to find things you share because you aren't actually sharing anything at all.

Thinking about Jackie and Lauren reminded me of the surprise going away party Lucy and Josie had for me before I moved to Chicago. They'd planned the whole thing themselves, down to the cake, which they baked from scratch. I didn't know it at the time, but they'd read my mom's latest book, *Wediquette for Brides and Grooms*, from beginning to end as they prepared to host the perfect send-off. When Josie and Lucy read that saving a piece of cake to eat again on the couple's anniversary was good luck, they'd decided to save a piece of my cake in Lucy's freezer until I came back to visit. Of course, they completely forgot about it, and two years later, Mrs. Denton found a frostbitten, freezer burned piece of chocolate cake stuffed behind a box of frozen lasagna.

"Emily? I know things with Luke are weird right now, but maybe they'll never be perfect, or at least not as perfect as you want them to be. I'm not saying you two won't figure it all out, but it won't kill you if you don't."

I hadn't told anyone about Luke's pocket dial. Not Lucy, not Josie, and definitely not Luke. Now I wondered what Lucy would say if she knew about it.

"I know. And do you have to make me sound so melodramatic?"

"Not melodramatic, just maybe . . . I feel like sometimes you believe if you try hard enough, you can make something what you *think* it should be instead of letting it be what it's *meant* to be." Lucy reached under her bed again and pulled out a lone white sock, three empty Tic Tac dispensers, and Josie's missing sunglasses case, which she placed on the nightstand between their beds.

I didn't want to believe that Lucy was right, but if she was, I knew what I had to do. And not just about the situation between me and Luke.

The Tic Tacs, sunglasses case, and sock made sense, but the tennis ball? "Why is there a tennis ball under your bed?"

"I roll on it to help my back after shifts at the Shack. It's something the team trainer showed me."

"How come I've never seen you do it?"

"I do it in the morning when you're already at work, but I can show you if you think you're missing something really exciting," she offered, rolling the ball toward me with her foot.

"That's okay, I trust you. Are you all packed?"

Lucy surveyed the room. "Just about."

I stood up and took one last look at Lucy's side of the room. It was almost as if she'd never been there. "I'll be right back to help you bring your bags down. I just need to go find Josie."

After searching every room in the house, I found Josie in the backyard by the garden scrutinizing her camera's digital display screen as she crouched down close to the ground.

"Hey, check this out," Josie called to me when she heard the sliding door open. She waited until I reached her before handing the camera over to me so I could see the digital display for myself. "Pretty cool, huh?"

I expected to find some artistic rendering of the red tomatoes clinging to a vine, or green speckled squash splayed out in a bed of leaves.

"It's a slug?" I guessed, cradling the camera in my hand and amazed that Josie had handed it over so easily.

"I know it's a slug, but when you shoot it up close like this, it looks like an entirely different thing, all shiny, and those points coming out of its head make it look like it's wearing a crown."

I wondered if she'd feel the same way about her photography subject if I told her the shine was created by mucous glands and the crown was actually tentacles. I really didn't see anything cool about it. It just looked like a slug to me, but I didn't have Josie's eye for composition.

"What is it you like so much about photography?" I asked.

"There's something cool about capturing a moment in time, something that will never be the same again." Josie stared at the small digital screen as she tried to explain. "It's always about the past. The moment a picture is taken, it's behind us. Like this slug—it'll never look exactly like this again. Even if it's in the same spot and the same light, it's different."

I thought about the photo she'd taken of me and Luke on the wharf, my hair tossed around by the wind, our expressions both animated and frozen at the same time. I'd never seen us look like that before, and I wondered if it was possible to be like that again, or if Josie was right.

I handed the camera back to her. "Can I talk to you for a sec?"

"Sure, what's up?" She turned a dial on the camera, pushed a few buttons, and squatted back down on the ground to get closer to her subject.

"I really appreciate what you did with your dad and all, I do, but I can't quit my job at the marina."

Josie looked up at me. "Why not?"

"Because they need me."

Josie's face changed, and now she was watching me with an expression I imagined looked a lot like mine when I first saw the image of the snail. "So it was okay to bail on your first night at the Shack, but you can't stop working for some guy you just met?"

"I didn't bail that night, Josie. I made a mistake. And I don't want to make another one."

"So what are you going to tell your mom?"

"I guess I have to tell her what happened. At least now she can't make me go home. That's the only reason I took the job at the marina in the first place. I wanted to stay here with you guys."

Josie turned her attention back to the garden.

"I'm sorry, Josie. I'll tell your dad if you want me to."

"No, that's okay. I'll tell him." Josie pointed the lens at a cucumber vine and focused back on the camera's screen.

I knew my mom would never make a scene in front of the Holdens and Lucy's mom, but I figured I'd give her the rest of the car ride to get it out of her system, just to be safe. "I better call my mom and warn her."

183

"Are you sure that's why you took the job at the marina? To stay here with us?" Josie asked, her finger pressing a button that released the rapid clicking of the shutter.

"Of course it is. Why else would I be getting up at six o'clock in the morning and riding a bike two miles?"

Josie didn't answer.

"Seriously, Josie, why would I do that if I didn't want to stay?"

She looked over her shoulder at me, the camera still poised in her hands. "I know you wanted to stay, Emily. I'm just not sure we were the reason."

"Then why?" As soon as the words were out, I knew. "I didn't stay because of Luke."

"Are you sure? I'd really like to believe you're here because we all wanted to spend our summer together, but sometimes it feels like we're just your backup plan."

"What's that mean?"

Josie placed the camera on the grass and stood up to face me. "I mean when you can't see Luke, it's great to hang out with us. But if you had to choose? I don't think we'd be the winners."

"That's not true."

"And now Lucy's leaving and you'll be at the marina all day, and it sucks even more because at least before I knew that *one* of my best friends wanted to be with me."

"That's what you think? That I don't really want to be here?"

Josie shrugged.

"I wanted to be here with you. I wanted to have the summer we talked about and planned. Besides, if staying was supposed to make everything great between Luke and me, it definitely hasn't worked out that way."

"Why? What's wrong?" Josie suddenly looked concerned.

"Nothing. I don't know. I just feel like something isn't right."

"Do you know what it is?"

"It's nothing. Look, I want us to have fun, even with Lucy leaving. I just don't want to screw over George. I've had enough plans fall apart this summer, the least I can do is stick this one out."

I expected Josie to continue protesting, but instead she surprised me by backing down. "Okay."

"Really?"

Josie opened her mouth as if she was about to say something, then thought better of it. "Really."

"Thanks for understanding." I squatted down on the lawn and bent over the garden to get a better view of Josie's subject. "That really is a pretty cool slug."

Josie frowned at me. "Now you're just trying too hard."

Maybe Lucy was right. Maybe it was something I had to work on.

chapter eighteen

My mom wasn't happy when I told her Mr. Holden fired me, but by the time she and Mrs. Denton arrived at the house, she'd decided a pleasant visit was more important than ripping her daughter a new one in front of everyone. It also meant she couldn't make me stay when I had a job waiting to pay me time and a half for working overtime on my morning off. For the first time all summer, something worked out okay.

It wasn't *all* fine, though, because Lucy was gone. According to her texts, she and her mom had just passed over the state line into Georgia and they'd be at her grandmother's in a few hours. Just like that, from one place to another. Her timing couldn't have been more perfect. For the first time in weeks, we woke up to rain splattering against our bedroom windows. Even Josie couldn't sleep though the sound of gushing water overflowing from the gutters on the corner of the roof.

I kept hoping the rain would stop, but it continued to fall despite my attempts to bargain with Mother Nature. By quarter to seven, I had to accept the fact that I'd be riding my bike in the rain. I'd never been late for work before, but since I didn't have a raincoat or any other jacket that would keep me dry, I'd probably arrive looking like a drowned rat. I hoped George would be sympathetic and give me a break.

I was on the verge of cutting armholes in a kitchen garbage bag for protection when Josie turned over and found me

186

staring out our bedroom window at the puddles spreading across the driveway.

"You know what's weird? You'd think people would avoid ice cream on a day like today, but after being locked inside playing board games for hours on end, it's like families make a mad dash to the Shack before they all kill each other."

Josie got out of bed and stood next to me. Together, we listened to the tin sound of raindrops on the gutters outside.

"Did you bring a raincoat?" she asked.

"Nope. I wasn't exactly anticipating riding a bike in the rain when I packed."

"I can give you a ride if you want," Josie offered. "I can't pick you up, because we're all taking on extra hours with Lucy gone, but if you can find a way home, I'll drop you off."

"Deal," I quickly agreed.

"She forgot these." Josie picked up a white scalloped shell from the pile on the windowsill and traced the smooth, raised lines with her finger. "Should we bring them back for her?"

I removed a small, creamy yellow shell from the ledge and held it in my palm. "I'm sure if she wanted to take them, she would have."

We both stood there holding our shells, and I wondered if Josie was thinking the same thing as me—that Lucy had left them for us as a reminder that, even if she wasn't coming back, a part of her was still here.

"We should probably go," Josie announced, placing her shell back on the windowsill with the others. "Let me change and I'll meet you downstairs."

* * *

"You want to come in and see the place?" I asked when we pulled into the marina.

Lucy and Josie had never visited me at the marina, although I'd been to the Scoop Shack a few times. I knew that the lines on the far ends of the barn typically moved the fastest, and that the tip cups were stuffed with a few dollar bills at the start of a shift to encourage customers to contribute more than the meager change left over from their orders. Each white Styrofoam cup was individually decorated by the server, the names of their colleges or reasons for working drawn on in colored marker. Lucy had drawn a soccer ball, her jersey number from Heywood, and *Duke Blue Devils* in blue on her tip cup. Josie's had *Skidmore College* scrawled around the rim and random flowers in bright colors. They each came home with at least thirty dollars in tips after every shift. I didn't earn tips, unless you counted how George taught me to remove the bait bags from the freezer without getting my hands covered in frozen fish blood.

"Wow, it really *isn't* a yacht club." Josie genuinely seemed surprised.

"I told you that a million times."

"I thought you were exaggerating so we'd feel bad for you. It's just a small wooden shed."

"Small being the operative word."

The parking lot was deserted, which meant we could avoid the muddy puddles running into one another from either end of the lot. It also meant we could park in the spot closest to the marina office. We both covered our heads with our hands and raced through the rain to the front door.

"This is it!" I announced, stomping my soggy flip-flops on the wood floor to squish out all the water.

"You weren't kidding." Josie ran her hands down her arms like squeegees, wiping away the raindrops. "It's tiny."

"But we call it home." Nolan had moved the director's chairs inside and was leaning his against the wall, his feet propped up on the freezer while he flipped through one of George's fishing magazines.

"What are you doing here?" I asked.

"George called and asked if I could open. He seems to have lost all desire to work now that you've given him a taste of the good life. Did you come to keep us company today?" Nolan asked Josie. "This place is dead."

"I'm going home and crawling into bed until I have to chain myself to the take-out window for a double shift before dealing with all the families who've been cooped up together inside all day." Josie walked over to the wall and took a reef knot off a hook. She rolled it around in hand like she was trying to figure out which came first, the left-handed overhand knot or the right-handed overhand knot. "They typically reach their maximum board game threshold by three o'clock. Work will be crazy."

"Better you than me," Nolan said.

"At least I get a break in between shifts." Josie gave up on the knot and set it back on its hook. "I plan on going home and passing out in the hammock for an hour before the insanity starts all over again."

"Well, tell Alyssa I said hi, if she's working," Nolan told Josie. "And take this."

He tossed the fishing magazine to Josie, who turned it over and read the cover. "*It's Tuna Time?* Not exactly my first choice in reading material."

"Don't read it. Put it over your head so you don't get wet."

"Brilliant." Josie opened the magazine and held it like a hat. "See you after quitting time, Em!"

Nolan and I watched as she splashed her way through puddles before ducking into her car.

"George won't miss his magazine?" I asked.

"Have you seen the pile of magazines in his boat? He won't even know it's missing."

"So what's today's knot?" I asked Nolan, settling into the director's chair beside his. In the weeks since I'd started at the marina, he'd taught me more than fifteen different knots, which now hung on the wall along with the ones he'd completed before I arrived.

"I was thinking a Zeppelin bend."

"That sounds quite advanced for a beginner like me."

"It's like the alpine butterfly bend we did last week," he explained, handing me two red nylon braided lines. "Basically, we're going to interlock overhand knots with the ends threaded through the middle."

"This isn't so bad," I told him, following his instructions.

"It's crazy strong—that's why it's called a Zeppelin bend. Supposedly, it could hold down an airship and keep it from flying away." Nolan took another set of lines and started on his own knot. "Did you tell your mom how much more useful these skills are than pouring butterscotch on a sundae?"

"I didn't get that far. It was weird, actually. I mean, obviously, on the one hand, she was pissed I didn't tell her when it happened, but on the other hand, she almost seemed impressed."

"Impressed?"

"Yeah, like I'd shown how resourceful I could be or something. Don't get me wrong, the *pissed* definitely won out, but in the end, she didn't threaten to take me home with her as punishment or anything, so I considered it a win." After three attempts, I held up my knot for Nolan to see.

"Are you sure you haven't been practicing? We're running out of knots for me to teach you."

"I thought you told me there were hundreds of knots." There was still a row and a half of hooks left to fill, which would just about take us up to my last day at work. We'd already completed four rows, starting with my first basic bowline.

"There are, but even I don't know how to make every one. I'm lucky you're leaving soon, before you tap me out."

"I don't even want to think about leaving. It feels like I just got here."

"George is already dreading your last day. He says it's been the best summer he's had in years."

Years? George and I had our routine pretty nailed down by now, and he was always nice to me, but even I knew he could have done better. He finally got so sick of me asking which fish were biting he started writing it down for me and posting it on the bulletin board every day. "I never knew he enjoyed our mornings together that much."

"Yes, *of course* that's the reason. It has nothing to do with the fact that he likes fishing every day instead of working." Nolan's smile faded. "He's even considering selling the place."

"What? No way."

"He already has a buyer who's interested. They're trying to see if the town will let them expand the slips and build a bigger office, maybe put in a restaurant."

"They can't do that! This place is perfect the way it is."

"I hate to break it to you, Emily, but this is about as no-frills as it gets when it comes to marinas. George will be able to sell this place and never work again. He says it's time to let someone else deal with the headaches."

I couldn't imagine the marina changing. The big, white freezer chest and the cardboard boxes displaying candy bars. The refrigerator that hummed all day. Even the faded canvas director's chairs that we moved inside and out depending on the weather. It would all be gone, replaced by a real office that didn't have uneven wood plank flooring or rows of hooks on the wall where colorful lines could be hung as part of a summer-long lesson in knot tying.

"Is it wrong to wish that everything would stay the same?" I asked Nolan.

He laughed at me. "No, it's not wrong. It's just not terribly realistic."

"Not even a little?"

"Not even a little," he told me. "Besides, what fun would that be? If you'd taken a job at the Shack you wouldn't know how to use a pump-out station while holding your nose."

"True," I conceded, unaware that Nolan had caught me pinching my nose with one hand while holding the pump-out hose with the other. I thought I'd hidden it pretty well by turning my back away from the office.

"When you started here, you could only tie your shoelaces, and now look at you." He pointed to the wall. "After today, you'll even be able to keep a blimp on the ground if you want to. Did you ever think you'd be able to do that?"

"I'm not sure I ever thought I'd need to, but it's nice to know I have the skills in my back pocket."

"You even tried a piece of Hell on Earth chocolate."

A wave of thunder rolled overhead, its low growl muffling everything around us, even the humming of the refrigerator.

"It was horrible." My throat almost closed up just remembering it.

"Is that why you threw them out?" Nolan put my Zeppelin bend on the empty hook beside the pile hitch I'd learned a few days ago. "I found it when I was emptying the garbage."

All I had to do was tell Nolan I didn't want to subject anyone to the vile aftertaste I'd had to live with for almost twenty-four hours. Instead, I told him the truth. "Luke didn't know we went to Nobby Farm."

"Would he have a problem with it?"

I shrugged. "I don't know. He wasn't really thrilled that I told you about Sam."

"It was no big deal, Emily. We went to a farm. You watched me cry, and I witnessed you permanently damaging your taste buds. All in a day's work, right?" Nolan was making fun of our time together and I appreciated it. It made the situation seem so ordinary, even when there was nothing normal about eating a ghost pepper.

I started rearranging the candy bars into even rows. "I can't say anything about it now, because then he'll wonder why I didn't tell him in the first place."

"Is he really that jealous?" Nolan asked.

"Actually, he's not." I caught myself almost sounding disappointed.

"Then you should've just told him before we went. Instead, now you have to pretend you didn't experience one of the greatest pepper farms in the world, and there's nine dollars' worth of chocolate in the dumpster."

I didn't really have any reason to think Luke would fly off in a jealous rage at the thought of me going to the farm with Nolan. Would he have wondered why I was doing it on a morning when I'd told George I'd work overtime? Maybe. Probably. But I can't imagine Luke thinking it was that big of a deal. If I was honest, part of me knew that all along. If I really thought about it, I didn't keep it from Luke because I was afraid of his reaction. I kept it from him because I didn't want to share the only thing I'd done all summer that didn't include Luke or Lucy or Josie. I wanted to keep something for myself, the way he got to keep what he did on the Vineyard without me. Driving to Woods Hole to buy salsa and hot sauce before work wasn't exactly a romantic date, but it was the first time in months I did something without worrying about what anyone else would think.

Looking back, I wished I'd told Luke, even if I did save him from an experience that could have turned him off of chocolate for the rest of his life. Now it felt like keeping it from him made it more important than it should have been, like a secret. And we'd sworn, no secrets.

* * *

For the next two hours Nolan and I read George's fishing magazines and waited for someone, anyone, to show up and take a boat out. Nobody did.

I tried not to count the minutes, but it was hard when the second had on the clock over the door ticked in the background. At this rate I'd read a year's worth of fishing knowledge and still never have baited a hook.

Nolan glanced at the clock. 9:05, which meant is was really 9:00. "You can take off if you want," he offered. "Nobody's going out on a day like today."

The rain was still filling the puddles outside the front door, where my bike would normally have been parked. "I don't have my bike."

"I can drive you home, if you want. George won't care. It's not like we're going to sell anything here."

I took out my phone and tapped a quick text message. Josie was already back in bed, but I thought there might be a chance Luke was up.

"Actually, can you drop me off at the Falmouth ferry?"

"You know it's pouring out, right?"

"Yeah." I glanced around the office, but didn't find what I was looking for. "Anything that could help with that?"

Nolan raked his fingers through his hair and sighed. "There is something, but you have to promise me you'll bring it back in perfect condition, or George would kill me. And don't tell him I let you use it."

Obviously, Nolan was not giving me a fishing magazine.

"Promise." I held up two fingers. "Scout's honor."

Nolan shook his head and grinned. "You can't fool me. I know you were never a model Girl Scout."

I replaced my two fingers with a pinky. "Pinky swear. I'll return whatever it is you're about to give me in perfect condition. He'll never know."

Nolan slapped a baseball hat on his head and stood up. "That will have to do. I'll be right back."

That was one pretty powerful pinky.

chapter nineteen

I texted Emily that I'd meet her at the wharf, but she replied that she'd walk to the house instead. I hoped the rain would stop by the time she arrived, or at least let up long enough so she wouldn't have to stomp through the streets of Edgartown in ankle-deep puddles. The rain had turned to a drizzle, but the sky was so dark it looked like it was about to crack open any minute and downpour.

Hopefully this visit would go better than the last two, even if I had a physical therapy session this afternoon, so we wouldn't have a lot of time together. When I told Emily, though, she didn't seem to mind, and it made me think maybe that's been the problem this summer—all the planning and anticipation leading up to her visits put too much pressure on us. Our expectations were so high, there was no way the reality could live up to the hype. There was something to be said for unexpected, spur-of-the-moment decisions. The good ones, I mean, and Emily's was a good one.

They say the third time's the charm, and I sure hoped that was true, because the last two times Emily came to the island were weird to say the least. The whole thing with Sam, and then having her friends here and the bizarre situation with Charlie and Josie. After they left, I'd asked Charlie what happened to freak Josie out, but he insisted he didn't do anything. According to Charlie, one minute they were in the kitchen with their hands stuffed into a bag of Goldfish, and the next Josie was looking at her phone saying it was time to go. Even I couldn't imagine Charlie doing anything stupid like making a move on Josie while she was eating a snack food made for four-year-olds, but then again, it was Charlie.

Obviously, Josie got over whatever happened, because Emily never mentioned it again, which was good. The last thing we needed was another reason for us to get sideways.

When it was time for Emily's ferry to arrive, I went out to the porch to wait for her. It was Sam's day off, so she was sleeping in, and Charlie usually didn't roll out of bed until Melanie was pounding on his bedroom door and threatening to physically remove him with a shovel. I figured I had the rain on my side, and if I played my cards right, we could avoid both of them until Emily had to go back.

The wicker chairs on the porch were protected from the drops sliding off the roof, but I could see the rain dimpling the puddles on the front walk as it continued to fall. I sure hoped Emily had an umbrella.

The tapping of the rain as it landed on the roof was the only sound on the entire street. No birds in the trees, no lawn mowers in the neighbors' yards, and no kids riding their bikes down the sidewalk. When I'd decided to stay on the Vineyard, I knew it would be different than home, but I didn't think it would be so *calm*. That was the only word I could come up with to describe the quiet—the lack of activity anywhere but in the heart of downtown. It's why I seriously considered leaving weeks ago, and even talked to Charlie about it. He listed a ton of reasons I should stay, but all he rattled off were things he was doing. Not things I could do with a busted knee. There were plenty of places I could do my physical therapy at home, and my therapist said he would pass my records along if I decided to leave. There was really nothing keeping me here. Just someone.

I couldn't drive a car with my brace, and Emily didn't have a car on the Cape. If I went home, we wouldn't see each other at all. I considered bringing it up to Emily to see what she thought, but then I talked to Sam about it, and she offered to include me when she went out with her friends. I decided to not tell Emily I was thinking of leaving and hoped Sam meant what she said. She did, which was why I spent most of my time hanging out with lifeguards when I hadn't even touched sand since Sam dragged me out of the water at Jaws bridge.

I spotted a bright yellow dot turn the corner and start down the street in my direction. As it grew closer, I heard whistling and then singing, and, finally, under the saucer-like brim of a school bus yellow rain hat with a chin strap, I saw Emily's face.

"What are you wearing?" I asked as Emily pirouetted up the walkway and a gigantic yellow raincoat billowed out around her. It was twice as big as she was and fell well below her knees, which was almost good, because the only part of her that could possibly get wet were her shins. And her feet, which might as well have been bare, because her flip-flops weren't exactly keeping them dry.

"You like it? The latest in foul weather gear for hardcore fishermen." Emily struck a pose. "We have welded seams for waterproof protection, flap pockets"—she swept her hand along the front of the jacket, directing my attention to the appropriate spots—"and silver reflective tape so you can't miss me in the dark."

"Nice hat," I observed, and Emily smiled.

"This is actually cool, check it out." She turned around. "The rim is lower in the back, so rain doesn't get down your neck. Brilliant, right?"

"Brilliant," I agreed. "But none of it fits you."

Emily came up onto the porch and stood in front of me. "Yeah, it's George's."

"He didn't have an umbrella?"

She shook her head, and water sprayed out of the waterlogged clumps of hair sagging against her shoulders. "Apparently umbrellas are not seaworthy."

"Let's hang all that in the mudroom so it can dry."

"Sounds good, but first things first." Emily bent down and wrapped two yellow, waterproof arms around me. Even though I wasn't wearing foul weather gear, and the rain on her hat's brim ran down my neck, I held her tight.

We hung George's jacket and hat on hooks in the mudroom off the kitchen, and then I led Emily upstairs to my room. "Everyone's still sleeping," I whispered as we passed the closed doors leading to Charlie and Sam's rooms.

"Maybe we should go to the boathouse so we don't wake anyone," Emily quietly suggested. I couldn't help wondering if she was trying to be considerate or if she didn't want to be in the house when Sam and Charlie woke up.

"We can do that," I told her and turned around. "Melanie keeps umbrellas in the mudroom. No foul weather gear required."

Obviously I couldn't keep us dry and use my crutches at the same time, so Emily held the umbrella over our heads on our way to the boathouse. It was still drizzling out, but I could see patches of blue fighting their way out between the ragged edges of the clouds. The day wasn't going to be so bad after all. Maybe we could go into town before I had to head to PT. Even Emily seemed happier than she had the last time she was here. I didn't know what had changed, but it felt like the Emily I remembered was back.

"Been playing a lot of pool?" Emily asked, nodding toward the chalkboard on the wall where we kept score.

"It's not like I have much else to do." I set my crutches next to the door and limped over to the couch.

Emily stared at the chalkboard a little longer, probably trying to add up the number of games I'd won. Beside my initials, we'd scrawled seventeen hatch marks. Beside Sam's initials, S.N., there were eleven. Charlie had three. "You think PT is helping?"

"I don't want to get ahead of myself, but yeah, I do."

Emily came over and sank down on the cushion next to me. "Josie convinced Mr. Holden to give me back my job at the Shack now that Lucy's gone."

I hadn't even considered that working at the Scoop Shack was still an option. Even with PT two afternoons a week, Emily and I would be able to see each other more often. We wouldn't have to plan weeks in advance or put so much pressure on making every single minute some earth-shattering experience.

"That's awesome, and actually really nice of her," I added, because Josie did deserve some props for that. "Makes me glad I decided not to go home."

"You were thinking of leaving?" Emily was surprised.

"I thought about it. I mean, once you had to take the job at the marina, it wasn't like I had much reason to stay."

Emily shifted uncomfortably, even though the sofa was so old, it was like sitting on a marshmallow. "So what happens when I tell you I didn't take Mr. Holden up on his offer?"

"You didn't take it? Why?"

"I've gotten the hang of things at the marina."

"But you could work with Josie. And have all day free so you could come over here more."

"I was talking to Nolan about it, and—"

"Nolan? What's he have to do with this?"

"Nothing, I was just trying to figure out what I wanted to do."

"And he convinced you to stay?" This didn't make any sense. I knew Emily felt bad for me when I'd told her about my knee, but she didn't do a very good job of hiding the fact that she was glad I'd be staying on the Vineyard. She'd kept telling me how lucky it was that she only had to work nights. There's no way she would've taken a job at the marina if it wasn't her only hope of staying on the Cape, so why was she suddenly so hell-bent on keeping a job she didn't want in the first place?

"He didn't have anything to do with my decision," she insisted. "It just didn't feel right, leaving George stuck when the summer is almost over and it would be too late for him to replace me."

"Let me get this straight," I told her, trying to be as logical as possible even though the whole thing seemed completely illogical to me. "The job you wanted in the first place because you could work with your friends and have your days free to do whatever you want—including hanging out with yours truly—is offered to you, and you turn it down?"

"You're making it sound like I'm doing something wrong, but it's different now. Even my mom and Mr. Holden think it's the right thing to do."

"Well, as long as you've consulted everyone who matters." I knew I sounded like a dick, but I couldn't help it.

Emily's face crumpled for a second, and I felt bad about giving her such a hard time. I was being a little harsh, but compared to all the shit I put up with this summer—my knee, living on an island without any way to get around, going to physical therapy instead of working to make some money before I headed to school—the least she could do was take the job she was *supposed* to have and make our last few weeks good ones.

"Is that what you were doing when Josie and I went out with Lucy for her last night? Thinking about how much I mattered?" Emily asked, her eyes cast down as if she was studying her hands and seeing them for the first time. She kept her voice low and level, choosing each word carefully. "You pocket dialed me and I could hear you talking to someone. When I called back, it went straight to voicemail."

How was this conversation turning on me now? I hadn't done anything wrong. "I have no idea what night you're talking about or who I was talking to, Emily."

"Do you remember when we promised no more secrets?" she asked, looking up at me. Her eyes were wide and hopeful as she waited for my answer. "Did you mean it?"

I took a deep breath. "I did."

"So did I, which is why I want to tell you that yesterday morning, I didn't go to work early. I went to a pepper farm with Nolan. And then I went to work."

A pepper farm? "Are you talking about vegetables?"

"Yeah, but they're crazy hot peppers."

This conversation had taken a strange turn. How did we go from Emily telling me she wasn't going to take the job at the Holdens' ice cream stand to talking about peppers? "You don't even like spicy food."

"I know. But George and Nolan said I just had to experience it. I should have told you and I didn't, but I am now." Emily propped her foot up on the cushion and hugged her leg tight to her chest. She rested her chin on her knee and turned to face me. "Is there anything you want to tell me about the night I heard you on the phone?"

If I was in court and had sworn to tell the truth and nothing but the truth, my answer would've been just that. The truth. I wasn't hiding anything about the night I accidently pocket dialed her. But even though Emily phrased her question that way, I didn't think that was what she was asking. What she really wanted to know was, had I been keeping any secrets.

I shook my head and Emily's body relaxed.

"I would never do anything to hurt you on purpose," I told her, which was the truth.

She sat up and let her knee flop over on top of mine. "Do you remember when—"

"Why do you do that?" I interrupted, not letting her finish. "Do what?"

"Ask if I remember things that happened between us. If I was there, Em, why wouldn't I remember?"

Emily shrugged and chewed at her fingernail. "I guess I'm afraid you don't. Or, if you do, it's different from how I remember things."

"So it's not a test?" I clarified, trying to understand.

She shook her head and gave me a weak smile. "I'm sorry I didn't tell you about the pepper farm. And I hope you understand why I can't quit on George with just a few weeks to go."

I could handle Emily going to a pepper farm with Nolan, partly because I knew it wasn't her idea and partly because it didn't exactly seem like something you'd ask a girl to do if you were trying to win her over—least of all Emily. While I wasn't a fan of her decision to stay at the marina, I did get it. And I wasn't surprised her mother thought she was doing the right thing. She probably wrote a book on the topic and knew all the dos and don'ts of accepting and declining offers of employment. "I get it. In a few weeks, we'll be back home anyway."

Emily brightened up. "Josie keeps talking about this end of summer bash we're going to. It's my last night on the Cape before I leave."

I'd heard Charlie and a few of Sam's lifeguard friends talking about it. "It's supposed to be a big deal."

"If you ask Josie, it's going to be the most amazing going away party I could ever ask for, even if I won't know most of the people there." Emily shifted onto her hip and rested her elbow against my thigh. "I'm really glad I came over today."

Now she was smiling for real, and that made me grin. If there was one thing I wasn't immune to, it was Emily's infectious enthusiasm. "Me, too. You should surprise me more often."

"What time is your PT?" she asked.

"Two o'clock," I told her.

"So we have a few hours." Emily tapped her finger playfully against her chin and stared at the ceiling as if she was trying very hard to think of something. "Let's see, what can we do?"

"Darts? Pool?" I knew better than to suggest a game of ping pong. "Whatever you want."

"You know what I want? For you and me to stay just like this."

"On a sagging couch with an obnoxious flower pattern?" I asked, and she laughed, just like I hoped she would.

"No." Emily moved her arm and laid her head down on me. "I meant happy."

```
┌─────────────────────────────────────────────┐
│                                               │
│   Long-Distance Relationship Tip #38:         │
│                                               │
│   Be like a proton.                           │
│                                               │
│   Stay positive.                              │
│                                               │
└─────────────────────────────────────────────┘
```

chapter twenty

Shit.

I frantically turned the raincoat over and patted down the pockets, shaking it out and hoping the hat would fall onto the deck of the ferry.

Shit!

The hat was missing, and I knew it had to be hanging on the hook in Melanie's mudroom. The rain had stopped by the time I left, so I'd just grabbed the jacket and draped it over my arms on my walk back to the ferry. I didn't even notice the hat wasn't tucked inside the coat. Nolan was going to kill me.

I tried to think of my options, none of which were very good and all of which involved either having to tell George or having to tell Nolan.

Left the hat at Luke's, my bad, I texted to Nolan, cringing as I waited. The message's status went from delivered to read. Immediately, Nolan's name flashed onto my screen. I dreaded the lecture I was about to get, but I answered anyway.

"You're lucky," he told me before I could even say hello.

"I'm not feeling so lucky." I held my other hand over my ear so I could hear him above the groan of the ferry's engine.

"The Vineyard Shipyard called. They need a boat part today, and apparently we're the only ones who have it."

I guessed that was good news, but I didn't see how it would keep George from going ballistic on me when he found out his hat wasn't in his boat. "And that helps me how?"

"I'm taking George's boat and heading over there to drop it off," Nolan explained. "Have Luke bring it to the shipyard. Where are you?"

"On the ferry back. We should be docking in ten minutes." Luke could probably ask Sam for a ride to the shipyard, but I had a better idea. "Why don't I go with you and I'll run and get the hat."

"Fine. Stay there when you get in, and I'll pick you up in the boat."

Two surprises in one day.

"Deal."

* * *

By the time we got back to Edgartown, the skies were a smooth, cool blue without a single cloud spoiling the sun as it prepared to go down for the day. Nolan told me I had to be back at the boat in thirty minutes so we could make it across Vineyard Sound before it was too dark. The one benefit of riding my bike to work was that I could actually run a good distance before I had to stop to catch my breath. As soon as Nolan docked the boat, I left him to his delivery and sprinted toward Melanie's house, avoiding the random puddles that still hadn't dried.

Even in my flip-flops, I managed to make it to Melanie's in decent time.

The door behind the front screen was closed, but I noticed that, even though the SUV was gone, the Jeep was parked in the driveway.

I knocked on the doorframe and hoped Luke would answer so I could see the look on his face when he realized it was me. If he wanted surprises, you couldn't get any more unexpected than this.

I rapped my knuckles on the door one more time and put my ear up against it to listen for footsteps. When I didn't hear any, I decided to go around back to see if I'd have better luck.

The back door was open, and I jiggled the screen door handle to see if it was locked. It wasn't.

"Hello?" I cupped my hands around my eyes and peered through the screen into the kitchen. I could see two glasses on the kitchen table, each one half full.

"Anyone home?" I tried again, but there was no response.

I guess that's one of the downsides of surprising someone—they don't know you're doing it. Luke probably went somewhere with Charlie or Melanie after he got home from his PT appointment. Even if I wouldn't get to see him, I still needed to find that hat.

I decided to let myself in and take a quick look in the mudroom.

It wasn't hanging on the hook, which would explain why I forgot it in the first place, and also why my heart was pounding. My mom would assume my rising blood pressure was a result of breaking and entering a house when no one was home, which was not only illegal, but incredibly rude. Actually, it was the thought of having to tell George that I'd not only worn his foul weather gear without asking, but I also lost it. I was about to give up when I spotted a yellow strap poking out from under a pile of beach towels on the bench under the coat hooks.

I grabbed it and a yellow, brimmed hat followed. Bingo!

Now it was time to hightail it back to Nolan before Melanie came home and found me rummaging around her mudroom like a burglar. I placed the towels exactly as I found them and backed out of the mudroom, making sure it didn't look like someone had ransacked the room. As I closed the kitchen door behind me, I heard noises coming from the direction of the boathouse. It had to be Luke.

Nolan was expecting me back on the boat in fifteen minutes, so I had to make it quick if I was going to surprise Luke and still make it back in time. He'd seemed to appreciate my ridiculous hat when I was skipping up the walkway in the rain, so I put it on and quietly walked toward the boathouse, crouching down as I snuck up to the side window so I could pop up and yell, *Surprise!*

Through the sheer, checkered curtains in the window, I could see two people inside—two bodies bent over the pool table, one of them in a bright red tank top that had a big, white plus sign on the front, announcing that whoever was wearing it could swim three hundred yards and perform CPR.

The gauzy checkered curtains let me see just enough to recognize Luke, but I couldn't see the other face. Luke stood behind her, his body shadowing her silhouette as their arms overlapped and his hands rested on top of hers. He shifted their arms as he helped her align the single pool cue resting between their fingers. "One, two," Luke counted, sliding the cue between their hands, strands of curly blond hair falling on the green felt as they rocked back and forth together.

I watched through the curtains and held my breath. You would have thought I'd be prepared for this. I'd certainly thought about it enough. Imagined how I'd react, what I'd do. By now, I should have been throwing open the door, yelling, screaming, cursing at Luke.

Instead, I couldn't move.

It was really happening.

"Three," Luke called out, but instead of hearing the crack of the cue ball scattering stripes and solids over the table, I saw a headful of blond curls turn toward my boyfriend and kiss him.

I clutched my stomach and doubled over and my hat fell into the grass beside my feet.

I had no words. There was no air in my lungs, and no sound in my throat. There was only the urgent need to run away.

I scooped up the hat and ran across the backyard, away from the boathouse, away from Luke and the fuzzy image of Sam turning to kiss him. I ran faster, as fast as I could until my legs couldn't carry me any farther, and then I collapsed on the ground beside a row of hedges lining the sidewalk, droplets of this afternoon's rain still clinging to its shiny green leaves. Then, for the first time, I looked back.

I didn't expect Luke to run after me; he hadn't even known I was there. Even if he did, he could hardly walk, let alone take off after me. He couldn't catch me even if he wanted to.

I kneeled next to the hedge and clutched the hat hard against my chest, my stomach rising and falling in shallow, convulsive pulses. I shouldn't have been shocked, really. I knew this would happen. I'd practically predicted it.

I felt the bile rising in my throat, warm and sour. Tears blurred my vision until there was no way to keep them from springing loose, and as they tumbled down my cheek, I threw up into a row of Edgartown's most perfectly manicured hedges.

I had two choices: I could continue running away, or I could return, open the boathouse door, and face Luke, even if it meant facing the fact that we had come to an end.

For the first time, I realized, *truly realized*, what it felt like to believe you knew someone and then discover you were wrong. I knew what it felt like to be Luke when he found out about the guide. I knew what it was like to be Josie and Lucy when they found out I hadn't been honest about my feelings for Luke. I wasn't angry, although I knew that would come later. I was empty.

I stood up straight, wiped my mouth with the back of my arm, and inhaled the sweet Vineyard air one last time. I knew I wouldn't be coming back.

chapter twenty-one

"**S**hit." I dragged the back of my hand across my lips, as much an attempt to keep Becca from trying to kiss me again as to try to wipe away what just happened.

"Shit?" Becca backed away from me until she bumped against the pool table. She steadied herself on the edge. "That's not exactly the reaction I was expecting."

The pool cue was still in my other hand, and I kept it there between us, like a line she shouldn't cross.

One minute, I was showing Becca how to bank a shot into the corner pocket without sinking the eight ball, and the next thing I knew, she was trying to kiss me. Well, not exactly trying—she was actually doing it. "Look, I don't know what to say."

"I guess I thought . . ." Becca bit her lip and looked toward the door, like she wished she could make a quick escape. Instead, she moved over to the sofa and dropped down onto the furthest cushion. The entire time she covered her mouth with her hands, the same way girls do in horror movies when they realize they shouldn't have opened the basement door to find out where the creepy noise was coming from.

"That was really dumb. I don't know what I was thinking." She talked into her hands, but I could still understand what she said, and what she really meant—she wanted to forget this ever happened.

Now I felt horrible. I mean, it was barely a kiss. It couldn't have been a few seconds before I pushed her away. No harm, no foul.

I laid the cue stick down on the felt.

"It's not that I don't think you're great and all. I just wasn't expecting that." I didn't want her to think I meant she should try again, now that I would be expecting it, so I added, "You know about Emily, right?"

"Yeah, but . . . I'm sorry. This is mortifying." This time, Becca hung her head in her hands and I felt even worse.

"Hey, what's going on?" Sam stood in the doorway watching us.

Becca looked up at me, and we exchanged a look that we both quickly understood.

"Nothing," we answered in unison.

Sam cocked her head to the side like she knew we weren't telling her the truth. But instead of continuing to grill us, she must have decided it wasn't worth figuring out what it was, because she handed Becca a bottled water.

"Here." She held the other bottle in my direction, but when I reached for it, she pulled it back. "Nothing, huh?"

I shook my head. "Nope. My water?"

Sam put the bottle in my outstretched hand. "Whatever you say. I just think it's odd that I head into the house to go to the bathroom and get us some water, and when I come out, I see Emily sprinting through the backyard."

"What? Emily was here?" There was no way. Why would Emily be here? "Are you sure it was her?"

"I think I know what Emily looks like. She took off up the side yard, toward the street. And she was carrying some crazy yellow hat."

"She never said she was coming back," I started, and then realized the least of my problems was figuring out why Emily didn't tell me she was returning. It was what Emily thought she caught me doing with Becca.

"Do you think she saw us?" Becca asked me, but I couldn't even answer, because my brain was already trying to figure out what to do next. I obviously couldn't go running after her with my crutches, and I wasn't even sure where she was headed if I could.

"Saw what?" Sam looked from Becca to me and back to Becca. "What's going on? And don't tell me nothing."

"I did something dumb," Becca started, her eyes pleading with Sam to help her explain what had happened. "I mean, I thought you said . . ."

Becca didn't finish explaining, but suddenly I got it. I couldn't believe Sam would do something like this. "You told her it was okay?"

Sam stepped back against the wall, as if I'd offended her or something, like she was the victim here. "Wait, how am I to blame?"

Becca saw an opportunity to not be the bad guy and she took it. "I thought you said they weren't really together."

I guess Sam *would* do something like this. "You told her that?"

Still, Sam wasn't backing down. "That's not what I meant. I meant Emily was there and you were here, and who knows?"

"Jesus, Sam." My hands flew to my head and I grabbed fistfuls of hair as I tried to make sense of what the heck was going on. "What the hell were you thinking?"

Becca sat there, her eyes bouncing back and forth between me and Sam, like she was a spectator waiting to see who would make the winning shot of a tennis match.

"I didn't mean she should make a move on you," Sam told me, and then turned to Becca. "I didn't tell you to make a move on him, did I?"

"Well, no . . ." Becca looked pained and like she wished she was anywhere in the world except in the middle of this situation.

I actually felt bad for her. This wasn't her problem. It was mine. And Sam's. "You know what, Becca, this isn't your fault. Maybe you should go."

Becca didn't try to convince us she should stay—or waste any time on her getaway. "Okay, sorry, I hope everything works out."

As soon as we saw Becca pass by the window, Sam started to argue her case. "I swear, I didn't tell her to try anything with you. She was asking me about you and if you had a girlfriend, and I told you were apart for the summer."

"That's bullshit, Sam, and you know it." I wasn't going to let Sam get away with acting like it was no big deal or not her fault. It was a big deal. And her fault.

"I didn't know what she was going to do." Sam placed her hand on my shoulder, and I shook it off.

That was the thing about knowing someone almost your entire life. You knew when they were full of shit. "You may not have known what she would do, Sam, but you knew what she *might* do."

Sam exhaled loudly, like she was getting ready to admit defeat. "Hey, I'm sorry, really. Maybe I shouldn't have said what I said."

"Maybe? How about *definitely*."

She reached for the unopened bottle of water Becca had left on the edge of the pool table and unscrewed the cap. "I don't get how you can just forget about what she did to you. It was way worse than what just happened here."

"You don't have to get it And I don't have to convince you of anything. What I have to do is talk to Emily. And you're going to help me explain what happened with Becca." I took out my phone and called Emily. I was sent straight to voicemail. "Shit."

Sam took a long drink of water and watched me knock my crutch against the wall as I tried to think of what to do next.

"Give me your phone." I held out my hand and Sam put her phone in it. I dialed Emily's number and hoped she'd answer an unrecognized call from New York. It rang and rang without Emily picking up. "Fuck."

"Text her," Sam suggested, and that's what I did.

I watched as my message changed from delivered to read.

Sam came over and peered over my shoulder as we waited for the response.

Call me, I typed. *I need to talk to you, it wasn't what you think.*
We both watched my screen and waited for a reply.
There was none.

"Maybe she's already blocked you." Sam left my shoulder and went over to the dart board, where she removed three darts and brought them over to me.

"What the fuck? It's not bad enough I have to deal with this knee shit, now this?"

"Here."

"What am I supposed to do with those?" I asked.

"Throw them? It might help."

I took the darts from Sam and aimed one at the board, where it didn't land anywhere near the bullseye. And it didn't help at all.

I held the other two darts, digging the plastic fins into the palm of my hand as I squeezed them tight.

This was exactly what I'd been trying to avoid, only this time, I didn't actually do anything wrong. Even if Emily was willing to talk to me, even if she listened and understood what really happened with Becca, there'd still be the last time. The time I *did* do something wrong. It wasn't just what I'd done that night, but what I'd continued to do every day since—let Emily believe she was the only one who'd made a huge mistake.

chapter twenty-two

For three days, I ignored every unrecognized or unknown number that showed up on my phone. I blocked Luke's number because I didn't want to hear his explanations or excuses for what I saw in the boathouse. I didn't want to read his texts, or even worse, hear his voice, listen to the person I thought I knew break my heart over and over again.

He did have a secret, and I knew what I'd found. Luke and Sam. Together.

I hadn't said much on the boat back to the marina, and Nolan must have realized I'd meant it when I'd said I didn't want to talk about what happened, because he hadn't asked any questions.

When we got back to the marina, Nolan drove me to the Holdens, where I found Josie on the hammock in the backyard. All she'd had to do was look at me, and the tears I'd been holding in for hours had erupted like a dam bursting under pressure. She'd pulled me down onto the hammock and rocked us with one foot dragging along the grass. Sometime later, I wasn't even sure how long, Josie had gotten up and gone inside the house. When she'd returned, she'd joined me again and we'd stayed like that until the sky had started to lose its color, like a lamp on a dimmer, slowly darkening until the only light we could see above us had been the white twinkling of stars through the tree branches.

As far as I knew, that as the only night Josie had ever asked her dad for special treatment, and the only night she hadn't shown up at the Scoop Shack for her shift.

"Do you really want to get over Luke?" Josie had asked.

A breeze had ruffled the leaves overhead, and I'd rubbed the goose bumps on my arms. "Yes, more than anything."

"I'm going to tell you something, Emily, but I want you to be really, really sure that you're ready to hear it."

Her words had scared me, but not as much as the look on her face. I hadn't answered, hoping Josie would take my silence as an invitation to continue. At least then I wouldn't have had a choice; she'd have just said it, whatever it was. Still, she'd waited for me to speak before continuing, wanting my permission to do something she really hadn't wanted to do.

"Tell me."

Josie had inhaled deeply and then let out a long, smooth breath, like the wind clearing away debris left behind by a storm. "Luke cheated on you."

"I know, Josie. I was there. I saw it."

"No, Emily. Before that. When you were away with your mom on the publicity tour. Charlie told me." Josie had waited for me to begin connecting the dots.

"That day on the Vineyard, when you went into the house together," I had started, beginning to draw the lines. The way she'd abruptly suggested we leave the island. Her hesitation when I'd asked for a copy of the picture she took of me and Luke. It was why she'd asked if something had happened when I'd told her things were weird between us. Josie knew.

"I don't think Charlie planned to tell me, not that it matters. He was saying how Luke was like a big brother to him and then he started telling me how close they were and how they told each other everything."

When I met Charlie, he knew. When he challenged me to a game of ping pong, he didn't just see Luke's girlfriend—he saw the girl Luke had cheated on. It had made me wonder who else knew. Did Luke confide in Sam, too? Was I the only one who didn't know?

"Twice," I'd told Josie. "I can't believe he did this to me twice."

No more secrets, he'd promised. I guess that's the thing about cheating boyfriends, though. You can't believe anything they say.

* * *

"I can't believe this is it." Our feet sank into the damp sand as we walked along the edge of the water. I turned around to study the footprints we'd left in our wake, walking backward so I could face Josie. "The summer is really over."

We'd decided to take a walk on the beach across the street from the Holdens' house, a sort of last stroll down memory lane, if memory lane was littered with the hollow shells of horseshoe crabs and dry, twisted strands of seaweed.

When I got home from the marina a couple hours ago, bringing an end to my bike riding days, I'd washed the bike with the hose on the side of the Holdens' house and filled the tires with air one last time. Then I'd set the bike back in the garage where I'd found it my first morning on the Cape. Was greasing the chain and shining the tires with Armor All overkill? Probably, but it was impossible to avoid my mom's voice in my head as I heard her recite one of her favorite golden rules: Leave things better than you found them.

"Can we just decide right now that we'll be together next summer?" I asked Josie, tossing out an idea I'd been thinking about all day "I'm sure Lucy would be up for it."

"I don't know. There may be a soccer team thing Lucy has to do, or maybe I'll apply to the summer photography program I found in New York." Josie stepped around a deserted sand castle that was slowly disintegrating on the beach, its pail-shaped turrets already almost completely crumbled. "And as much fun as it's been swirling ice cream cones all summer, I don't think this is something I plan to do again. Ever."

"So what happens? Lucy's on her way to Duke, I'll leave the Cape, and then you'll be at school in a few weeks. That's it?"

Josie walked over the piles of dried seaweed that had washed onto the beach. "You make it sound so shitty. Of course that's not what I want to happen."

"Well, me neither."

"But that doesn't mean we need to plan what we'll be doing a year from now."

"But if we don't, then what?"

"What if we do? Will it really make a difference?" Josie bent down and picked up a flat beach stone, cocked her arm back, and tossed it across the surface, where it skipped four times before sinking. "You know, I once had this best friend. She was great and we hung out all the time, and then she moved away and I thought we'd probably never see each other again. But then she moved back, and it was like she never left, and we had this great idea for our senior time capsule. Any guess what that was?"

I stopped walking and sat down on the sand. "Let's say it involved writing a guide that would help teach guys how to treat girls."

"Yes, let's say that." Josie grinned and sat down next to me. "Only when it was time to test that guide on the worst guy around—who was my ex-boyfriend, I might add—things didn't go according to plan. Instead of dumping him when the experiment was over, she realized she was in love with him."

I cringed, remembering what happened next.

"And she kept it from me, and from Lucy, and I thought, that's it. There's no way we can be friends again. But you know what happened?"

"She begged for your forgiveness? Groveled at your feet and promised you her firstborn child?"

This time, Josie laughed. "Well, yeah. But I was going to say that I realized there was something worse than having your best friend make a choice that hurts you. And it's making the choice to not forgive that friend, and not having her in your life at all."

"So what's going to happen next year? What happens when we don't see each other every day and we make new friends, and then we get together over Christmas break and have nothing to talk about?"

"I don't know," Josie answered, picking up a twig and dragging it in the sand to write out her initials. "I mean, I barely know what's going to happen in four weeks, let alone four months. The only thing I know for sure is that tonight is going to be amazing."

I sure hoped tonight's end of summer bash lived up to all the hype, not because I really needed a big, memorable send-off, but because I wanted one for Josie.

* * *

Mrs. Holden did a double take when we came downstairs, eyeing Josie's halter top as if she was deciding whether or not to comment. "You girls look nice," she said, probably deciding it wasn't a battle she'd win.

Mr. Holden had just finished up dinner and was about to head back to the Shack. He'd agreed to let all of the senior staff have the night off for the party, leaving the Scoop Shack in the questionably capable hands of the youngest employees. He wasn't excited about it, but Josie had finally convinced him that the staff deserved to celebrate together one last time before everyone scattered in different directions. What had put him over the edge, though, was when the senior staff cleaned out the storage room without being asked. Mr. Holden said, after that, there was no way he could say no.

"Don't stay out too late." He handed Josie her car keys.

"We won't," Josie promised, but I knew she had no intention of adhering to our curfew tonight. As far as Josie was concerned, the entire summer had led up to this party, and she was going to enjoy every single minute of it, even if that meant paying the price tomorrow.

When we got in Josie's car, she sat in the driver's seat but didn't start the ignition. "What do you think, are we going to be too early?"

I buckled my seat belt. "You said everyone was going to start showing up at eight."

"But there is such a thing as fashionably late, right?"

"Not according to Polite Patty. Late is never good. Early isn't great, either, but it's better."

Josie nodded and started the car.

I'd said good-bye to George and Nolan a few hours earlier, bringing an end to my bike riding days. I'd said good-bye to all the boat owners and, when George handed over my final paycheck, it had included a gift card to Bath & Body Works, which was not just unexpected, but also completely unnecessary. When I'd told him that, he said I'd earned it—that without me around to help out, he never would have realized it was time to sell the marina.

"I hope you mean that in a good way," I'd teased, and George had said he meant it in the best way.

I wouldn't miss getting up at six o'clock every morning, but I would miss spending my days by the water. I didn't have to say good-bye to Nolan until tonight, though, because he was planning to be at the party, too. I'd promised him I'd text him when we left Josie's house, but I forgot.

I patted my pocket and realized it was empty. "I forgot my phone at the house," I told Josie.

"We are not going back."

I made a face.

"Seriously? I'm here. Lucy's probably sitting in a roadside Denny's with her mom somewhere between Georgia and North Carolina. Who else would you really want to talk to?"

Who else. There was nobody, really. Not anymore.

"Okay," I conceded.

Josie seemed surprised that I'd given in so easily. "So we're not turning around and you're good with that?"

I nodded. "But you're wrong."

"I am?"

"Lucy hates Denny's."

* * *

There were already at least thirty people on the beach by the time we got there. Most of them were circling the coolers that were lined up far enough away from the water so they wouldn't get wet when the tide came in. A few were already surrounding the bonfire that was just starting to flicker higher than the rocks surrounding it. A speaker was propped up on a stack of rocks, and Josie told me that Alyssa had created a mix of the summer's most popular songs—a sort of audio memory book that would forever remind us of the strange in-between feeling we had our last summer before college.

Josie and I made our way over to the coolers, and Josie expertly extracted two cans from the ice.

She tossed me one and pressed her wet hand against the bare skin of her chest. "Damn, it's still hot, even without the sun."

I pulled the tab on my can and took a long sip.

Josie wasn't kidding. And not only was it still pretty sweltering out, but without the sun, we had the added bonus of beach gnats. I slapped at my ankle.

"Is that Nolan?" Josie pointed down toward the water's edge, where I could see someone who looked like Nolan wading in up to his knees.

"I think so." I slapped my arm. "I'm going to say hi."

I was hoping that once I was away from all the drunk, sweaty bodies, the gnats would give up and pursue easier prey.

Nolan dipped his hands in the water and patted down his arms.

"Hot?" I asked.

Nolan looked up and rolled his eyes at me. "I can handle heat. It's the no-see-ums that are driving me nuts. I think they like my deodorant." He finished rinsing off his arm and waded through the water back to the beach. "How's your going away party?" he joked.

I glanced back at the bonfire, where at least twenty people were now either standing or sitting on the makeshift driftwood seats surrounding it. Josie and the Scoop Shack crew were loitering around the coolers. "I didn't know I was this popular."

"I've been coming to this thing since ninth grade, and I've never seen this many people." Nolan dried his hands on his shorts and sat down on the sand, where his red Solo cup was waiting for him.

"Sorry I didn't text," I apologized. "I forgot my phone at the house."

"No big deal. I just bet you're glad you won't be waking up and heading to the marina tomorrow."

At first, I thought he was referring to the half-empty can in my hand, which, after a few more, wouldn't be conducive to waking up early and biking two miles. But then I realized he wasn't implying I'd be hung over.

I brushed the mound of sand beside Nolan until it was flat and sat down. "Would you believe me if I said I was actually going to miss it?"

"It's been a good summer, don't you think?" He tipped back his cup and swallowed the last of his drink.

A good summer. If I looked at all of it, I wasn't sure I'd agree. But if I considered the days, the moments, there were a few that weren't so bad.

"I don't know that I'd say it was good, but it wasn't all bad," I admitted, looking across Vineyard Sound to the island in the distance. White points of light twinkled like stars, moving with the breeze sweeping across the water.

I inhaled deeply and downed what was left in my can.

Somewhere over on the island was the summer I'd thought I was going to have. The summer I did have was sitting next to me. The damp skin of Nolan's arm pressed against mine and I could feel the gritty gains of sand leftover from the water. I could sense his body as he breathed, each inhale and exhale a beat behind me until, a few minutes later, our breaths were synchronized.

I could do it. I could do exactly what Luke did, do what I knew would hurt him just like he hurt me.

"George is really going to miss you," Nolan mused, almost as if he felt bad for him.

I leaned in toward Nolan, the shadow of his face dimming the lights in the distance until I almost couldn't see them at all. "Are you?"

For a moment I was afraid he'd kiss me. Then I was afraid he wouldn't.

Before he could answer, I laid my hand on his shoulder, pulled him toward me, and squeezed my eyes shut, blocking out the lights altogether before feeling the uncertainty of strange lips press against mine.

"Emily?" I recognized her voice before I even looked over my shoulder to find her standing there.

Sam. Even in the dark, her shiny blond hair reflected the light of the moon as she stood between Charlie and another girl who looked like her.

"Emily, is that you?" Sam repeated, squinting as she searched the dark beach for an answer.

On either side of her, Charlie and the other girl were quiet as they waited for me to reply.

And I couldn't. The words wouldn't form in my mouth. All I could do was watch Sam watching me.

Nolan sat back, creating space between us. He seemed as confused as Sam—why didn't I just answer her?

"Yeah, it's her." Someone else stepped out from behind Charlie. Someone taller and darker. Someone who could tell it was me, even if the only thing he had to illuminate the beach on a summer night was the yellow moon overhead.

Luke.

"Emily?" Nolan said my name, the horror on my face registering with him for the first time. "What's going on?"

But I couldn't think about Nolan or Sam or Charlie. Everyone, *everything*, receded into the background as Luke and I locked eyes, the flickering of the fire in the distance reflected in his glare. And then, without saying another word, he blinked and the flames disappeared, replaced by the back of Luke's head as he turned away from me and walked into the darkness.

I stumbled to my feet and started after him, but Sam took a step forward, blocking me. "Don't."

"Please move," I told her.

Sam didn't budge. I stepped to the right, then to the left, but she wouldn't give me any room to pass.

"Get out of my way!" I practically screamed. "What is your problem?"

"My problem?" she shouted back at me. "He came here to find you, Emily. You wouldn't return his calls, and he hauled our asses all the way here hoping he'd have a chance to talk to you and explain."

"Explain?" It was no use trying to get by her. Sam wasn't budging, and Luke was gone. "What is there to explain? I know what I saw, Sam."

"He came here to tell you what you really saw, Emily. He wanted me to come with him because, for some reason, he thought hearing it from me would make a difference."

"Hear what from you? What could you possibly say that would make a difference?"

"It's not what you think."

"What I think is that I found Luke kissing you."

"What you saw was Becca kissing Luke." Sam nudged the girl standing uncomfortably behind her kicking sand with her bare feet.

Even if it wasn't Sam, did it really matter who it was?

"He wasn't exactly struggling to get away from her, Sam."

"There was nothing going on with them—*nothing*. They were just friends, and she thought she could get him to change his mind, but all he wanted was you."

220

Charlie stepped forward. "He tried to tell you he was coming over, which you'd know if you hadn't blocked him."

Who was Charlie to act like this was my fault?

"This isn't the first time, is it Charlie?" I turned to face Sam's brother—someone I'd once thought was on my side, but who now stood there like I was the one who'd wrecked everything. "He did this once before, didn't he?"

Charlie's face froze as we locked eyes and I dared him to deny it. "Who told you that?" he wanted to know.

"What difference does that make?"

"Whoever decided to tell you obviously left out the part about how bad Luke felt. They left out how he wanted to tell you, and I convinced him not to because he already knew he made a huge mistake and telling you wouldn't change that."

"Luke wanted to come over to try and fix things with you," Sam reminded me.

"He's been lying to me all summer," I shouted, thinking it was my turn to remind *them* what Luke had done. "Every time we talked, every time I left my friends to visit him, he was lying."

"You think that's what he's been doing? Really, Emily?" Sam raised her voice so it met mine, completely unafraid and not backing down no matter how many times I laid it out for them—Luke cheated on me, not once, but twice. "Let me tell you what he's really been doing. First of all, he's been missing you. It's all we have to listen to, how he can't be with you, how he wishes he could go to Falmouth to see you instead of always making you go to him. And you know what else? There was the small matter of his knee, the possibility that he wouldn't be able to play lacrosse, that he'd need surgery, that everything he ever looked forward to was over. So trying to repair his knee and thinking about you. *That's* what he's been doing, Emily."

"Wait." Something Sam said stopped me, and I realized that Luke hadn't hobbled away from me. He'd walked. "When did he stop using his crutches?"

"Two days ago. You'd know that if you would have talked to him."

Nothing was making sense. Sam and Charlie had an answer for everything, a reason, an explanation that didn't line up with the stories I'd heard or what I'd seen through the boathouse window.

I was done talking to Sam and Charlie. I needed to hear it from Luke.

I started to push past Sam, but she reached for my arm and held it, her fingers tight against my skin. "Don't, Emily."

I shook her hand free, but then Charlie stepped in front of me, blocking my path. "He's really pissed, Emily. I think you should just let him go."

For a second, I thought he was talking about now—that I should let Luke go away and cool off before trying to talk to him. But then I realized he meant more than that. Charlie was telling me to let Luke go for good. There was no repairing the damage this time.

"I told him you'd do this, when I found out about that notebook you kept and what you did to him last time. I said you'd do it again." Sam shook her head at me. "And you know what he said? He told me you wouldn't."

"You don't know me, Sam, and you sure as hell don't know me and Luke."

"What I know, Emily, is that you just blew it." Sam spun around, turning her back to me as she walked up the beach to the party, Charlie and Becca following close behind.

"Let me guess," Nolan said, stepping next to me as we watched them all fade into the crowd. "That was Luke."

I sank down into the cool, damp sand and wrapped my arms around my knees, holding them tight against my chest as I rocked back and forth. I squeezed my eyes shut and let the sound of the rolling waves wash over me—push me away and then pull me toward the water's edge, again and again, drowning out the voices from the party and dulling the steely edge in Sam's voice before she'd turned her back on me.

It wasn't the words, or who spoke them. It wasn't what I'd heard that I couldn't shake as I curled into myself like a shell, trying to blend in with the sand and disappear. It was what I'd seen—what I couldn't forget no matter how hard I tried to remove myself from what had just happened.

Even the lull of the waves crawling toward me couldn't quiet the image of Luke, the look of confusion and disbelief as he tried to make sense of me, of what I was doing on the beach with Nolan. And then I'd seen it, the almost imperceptible stiffening of his shoulders, a stillness in his expression that, although at first it had appeared reluctant, could only mean one thing.

It wasn't anger or hate, or even hurt. No, what I glimpsed was worse. Something that, in all of our time together, I'd never experienced, even after he found out about the guide: acceptance. Acknowledgment. And a recognition that, this time, the only thing left for him to do was walk away for good.

chapter twenty-three

I didn't cry. My mind didn't race through best-case scenarios
and play out what could happen next. There was no next.
There was a party raging behind me. A guy sitting next
to me who looked like he wished he could disappear into
thin air. And somewhere out in the night, four people who'd
traveled all the way from Martha's Vineyard had all their worst
thoughts about me confirmed. One of them actually mattered.

Luke cheated on me, maybe not when I thought he did,
but he did. What made it worse was that he kept it from me,
and yet all I could think of was how I'd done the very same
thing. I lied for months to keep him from finding out the
truth about me, about the notebook, about our plans for
the time capsule. When I realized he was more than just an
experiment, I could have told him. I should have destroyed
the notebook weeks, even months, before I did, and instead I
lied every time we were together. Every time I let him believe
we were more than a set-up. Because I was afraid of what he'd
think of me, but also because I was scared of losing him if he
discovered the truth.

"Is there anything I can do?" Nolan ventured. Given
he'd been dropped in the middle of my mess, it was nice of
him to offer, especially since, a few minutes ago, I'd had my
tongue in his mouth.

"About what just happened between you and me," I started,
but Nolan held his hand up to stop me from continuing.

"Look, I don't know if I did something to make you think *that* should happen." Nolan spoke slowly as he struggled to just come out and say what he meant. "I'm sorry if I did, but I don't—"

"Just stop," I told him. "Please stop. I'm sorry. I shouldn't have kissed you. It was totally fucked up. *I'm* fucked up."

It was a perfect opportunity for Nolan to say, no, I wasn't fucked up at all.

He didn't.

"Am I?" I asked weakly.

Nolan seemed to be contemplating how to answer.

"The truth," I insisted, even if it wasn't lost on me that I'd once promised the same thing to Luke. No secrets. To be honest, no matter how hard that was.

"A little?" Nolan leaned away from me, as if he wanted to be able to quickly escape if I didn't like his answer.

With the fire lighting her shadow, I could see Josie stomping toward us, zigzagging back and forth as she tried to avoid stepping on the mounds of dried seaweed in her path. "What's going on?"

Nolan looked at me and then up at Josie, silently asking my permission to tell her. "Luke was here."

"I thought that looked like him, but he wasn't on crutches. What was he doing here?"

Nolan stood up and held his hand out to me, waiting for me to take it. "Come on, I'll take you home."

Josie kneeled down beside me and gently squeezed my shoulder. "It's okay, I got it," she said, because even though she didn't know exactly what just happened, she knew this was when best friends stepped in to take over.

"Is it okay if I head back to the party?" Nolan asked me, and when I nodded, he turned to Josie. "Let me know if I can help."

Nolan left us alone, just me and Josie suspended in some weird middle ground between bursts of laughter and the pops of the crackling bonfire, and the lazy, rhythmic rolling of the waves as they slithered toward us and then backed away.

I didn't know if Sam and Charlie and Becca were still at the party, but I was pretty sure Luke was gone.

"Are you going to be okay?" Josie finally asked.

I started to say yes, but a question came out instead. "Why'd you tell me that Luke cheated on me when I was on tour with my mom?"

"I didn't at first." Josie's hand slid off my shoulder and landed in the sand between us. She raked her fingers through the grains, front to back, creating rows that went deeper and deeper as she spoke. "I knew, but I didn't say anything, and then you caught him again and I hated seeing you feel like that. I mean, it was the second time he cheated on you, Emily."

"He didn't," I corrected her.

Josie stopped raking, but she'd already dug a small moat between us, the kind I used to build around sandcastles when I was younger—a protective barrier from the waves that never actually saved my hours of work, because it was just sand and, no matter how hard I tried, a single wave was all it took to destroy it.

"But you said you saw him," she reminded me. "You were there."

"No." My voice was steady as I watched the waves crawling closer to our feet, almost touching them before retreating. "What I saw was Luke and a girl I thought was Sam, but I didn't know what was really going on. Sam told me that Luke didn't do anything."

"And you believe her?"

"I do," I told Josie, and then I almost laughed. I believed Sam, of all people. "What I don't get is why you finally told me."

Josie jumped, startled by the water that tumbled over her bare feet. "Because you're my best friend and he hurt you. You said you were done with him."

"Is that all Charlie told you? That Luke kissed someone else? Or did he tell you more?" I asked.

"What do you mean?"

"Did he also tell you that Luke regretted doing it and felt terrible? Did you know that Luke wanted to tell me, but Charlie convinced him not to?"

Josie shrugged. "Yes? So?"

"You left that part out, and I guess I'm wondering why,"

"Because you'd just caught your boyfriend kissing some girl and you felt horrible, and I wanted to help."

I wanted to believe her, I really did. But there was something I couldn't shake, a feeling that the residual effects of what happened months before continued to linger—a barely perceptible film of doubt that had coated our relationship ever since that day I'd admitted to Josie and Lucy that Luke was more than just an experiment. Josie had felt betrayed by me, by the way I'd kept my feelings for Luke a secret from her and Lucy. But now I wondered if what really bothered her was that she'd had him first. Even though she'd told me it didn't matter, that our friendship was more important than some guy she'd dated for a few weeks. Luke had broken up with Josie and ended up with me, even if the way we got there wasn't as simple as that. What was starting to feel simple, though, was the explanation for Josie's decision to tell me. The way she glanced at Lucy when I'd leave to go visit Luke, the slight shaking of her head when she knew I was talking to him on the phone—it all added up to one answer.

"You know what it feels like?" I asked Josie, not even waiting for her to answer before rushing on. "It feels like you wanted us to break up. Like you've wanted that for a long time now, and the only reason I can come up with is that you still hate that I ended up with Luke and you didn't."

I waited for Josie to defend herself, to lash out at me and tell me I was crazy. But instead, I watched as my words diluted her, like milk swirling in a cup of coffee until it transforms the dark, stormy color into something paler and less potent. "Seriously? That's what you think of me?"

"I don't know what I think anymore, Josie."

"You still don't get it, do you?" She cast her eyes down at the sand as if she couldn't even look at me anymore—like she was looking for something she dropped and knew how slim the chances were that she'd ever find it.

"Get what?"

Josie shook her head at me, like she couldn't believe I didn't see something that was so obvious. "It's never been about *you* taking *Luke* away from me. It was about *Luke* taking *you* away from me."

I let her words sink in as a wave slipped over my feet and covered my ankles.

"You moved away, and when you came back, Lucy and I had our best friend again, only it's always about Luke—first

227

with the guide, and then because you two were together, even this summer."

"But I'm here. I came here to be with you."

Josie frowned. "You arrived four weeks after Lucy and I got here, and you didn't even bother showing up for your first night of work. You should have been there—*not* because you were afraid of getting fired, but because we were waiting for you. Then you get a job that doesn't even let you be with us, and finally, when you're free, you just want to be with Luke."

"That's not fair," I told her.

"You know what's not fair? That Lucy and I were nothing more than your fallback position—your safety net if things didn't work out with Luke. Besides, if I wanted to break you and Luke up, then I could've told you weeks ago, when Charlie first told me." She paused, letting that fact sink in. "I don't know if I ever would've told you if you hadn't found him in the boathouse. I didn't share everything Charlie told me because I didn't want Luke to get another chance to screw you over again. Maybe I was wrong. Maybe you're right, and a part of me wanted to spend our last weeks of summer together without having to share you with him. But I'm not the one who cheated on you, Emily. Luke is."

Boom.

If Josie had a microphone, she could have dropped it right then and walked away.

No matter how many explanations Sam and Charlie offered, Josie was right. That's all she could see—what Luke had done to me, how he'd hurt me. And that's all I'd seen, too, but I wasn't sure I only wanted to see it that way anymore. I just didn't know how not to.

"You're right," I told her. "I know you are, and I'm sorry."

"For what? For thinking I went out of my way to screw you over, or for being a shitty friend?"

I couldn't help thinking that they were one and the same. "Both?"

Josie almost cracked a smile.

"Both," I repeated. "I'm sorry I'm such a freaking mess."

She picked up a shell and turned it over and over in her hand, alternating between rubbing the pearly smooth inside and the ribbed outside. "You're not a mess." This time, she did smile when I rolled my eyes at her. "Okay, maybe a little, but mostly you're just *in* a mess right now."

"So what can I do?" I asked, hoping she knew how to fix things.

"About you and Luke?" she asked.

"About *you* and *me*," I answered. "I want to make things right with us."

"We're best friends, Em. That doesn't change just because you—or even *I*—screw up every once in a while."

"I'm still waiting for you to screw up. Maybe then I'll feel better."

Josie laughed.

"I'm really going to miss you." I reached for her hand and we held the shell pressed between our palms. "Who else am I going to find to put up with my crazy?"

"Probably nobody," she teased, and then turned serious again. "Seriously, though. What about what Sam told you? What about Luke?"

"He cheated on me. Even if he didn't do it this time, he *did* do it."

"You made him the test subject for a guide to change shitty guys—and lied about it for months while pretending to be his girlfriend." She managed to summarize our relationship's less than optimal beginning into a single sentence. "It's not like you didn't make any mistakes you wish you hadn't."

I dropped my head back and looked at the sky, hoping there would be an answer written up there, a sign telling me what to do. Maybe there was a constellation exactly for this situation, something the ancient Greeks had discovered and named *the answer* because that's what it provided to the confused people looking for it.

It was hard to even believe that this was the same sky Luke and I had shared weeks ago, when fireworks lit up the space between us.

But this time, there were no eruptions of color, no flares lighting up the sky with trails we could follow to one another. I couldn't even make out the big or little dipper. All I saw was a haphazard smattering of random white spots.

"Luke knows he made a mistake, and he regrets it," she reminded me. "And he would've been brave enough to tell you about it if Charlie hadn't convinced him not to." I listened to Josie tick off three reasons why I should be able to move past Luke's mistake. "I'd never tell you it was no big deal, but is it bigger than how you felt about each other?"

Felt. It was as if a jellyfish landed on my chest, the use of the past tense stinging me as I realized that was the only thing Luke and I might share ever again—a past.

After everything we went through to be together, I never would've thought I'd have to choose which was more important to me—feeling hurt and angry, or being with someone who could make me feel that way but make me feel a million amazing, wonderful ways, as well. I wasn't sure I knew how to come to terms with the coexistence of those feelings, or whether I could accept that if it was either/or, all or nothing, I'd probably end up with nothing.

"I don't know how to answer that," I admitted.

"Maybe you should just talk with him. Give yourselves a chance to figure it out before you decide how you want to answer."

"I think it's probably too late for that."

Josie swiped her phone and the screen lit up. "Maybe, maybe not. The last ferry out of Woods Hole is at nine forty-five. You have twenty-five minutes."

"What if he's already on the boat?"

"And what if he's eating a stale pretzel at the Steamship Authority while he waits for the nine forty-five back?"

"You'll drive me?" I asked, hopeful. I'd never make it if I had to go back to the house and get my bike.

Josie stood up and dug her hand into her pocket. "Take my phone. Alyssa's number is in there—call if you need me. And here." She tossed her car keys in the air, and I grabbed them before they landed on the sand. "You can drive yourself. I think it's time you earned four wheels."

chapter twenty-four

B arely ten minutes later, I arrived in Woods Hole and turned left into the Steamship Authority. The last time I was in Woods Hole, I'd been on my way to Nobby Farm with Nolan. The town had been filled with visitors waiting for the ferry, killing time by walking the streets and milling around the entrances to stores. Tonight, though, it felt different, almost deserted, like one of those towns in a movie where something ominous had sent people dashing inside for safety. The white lines dividing the loading area into car lanes were still there, but there were barely half the number of cars idling. A few rows were completely empty.

I guess the last ferry back during the week is only for two kinds of people—the ones who missed the earlier ferry and anxious ex-girlfriends hoping they didn't miss their last chance.

As I drove toward the back of the lot, I searched the passenger area for Luke, but even the disks of light shining from the lampposts didn't help me spot him in the dark.

I parked Josie's car and methodically scanned left to right for Luke, stopping only when a lane was directed to load and the cars started crawling toward the ramp leading to the boat.

Finally I saw him, standing next to one of the pylons by the passenger ramp, his white ferry ticket in one hand, and the other resting on the railing.

"Luke?" I called his name and he looked over.

When he saw me walking toward him, he shook his head at the ground and inhaled deeply and slowly. "Emily."

He didn't look up as he muttered my name.

"Emily," he said again, this time meeting my eyes.

I stood close enough to see the expression on Luke's face, but far enough away that I wouldn't be tempted to reach out and touch him. "I know that you didn't do anything with Becca. And I know you cheated on me when I was on tour with my mom."

"So why are you here? Just so you can tell me what an asshole I am? That I'm exactly the guy you thought I was when you started writing the guide?"

Until he said it, I hadn't even realized that was true. On paper Luke was a boyfriend who cheated on his girlfriend. An asshole. But that wasn't who I saw standing in front of me. I saw Luke, who was completely *unlike* the guy I expected to find when I started writing the guide. He was the person who forgave me after I made a huge mistake. He trusted me again after learning that I'd lied. Luke was the guy who loved me even after I gave him reasons not to.

"This isn't working anymore. This—" He waved his hand between us, gesturing toward my chest and then his, as if there was some invisible force field between us he was referring to. "You and me."

I wondered if the growing lump in my throat was visible under the lights, or if my eyes shone brighter as a wall of tears slowly built up behind every blink of my lashes. "So after everything, now you're really giving up on us?"

Luke looked up at the ferry behind him, his eyes sweeping along the deck as if searching for someone who was no longer there. Then he looked back at me. "No, Emily, I'm giving in."

"You're giving in? What does that even mean?"

"It means I'm throwing in the towel. You win."

The pebble in my throat was growing into a stone that had lodged itself so deep, I wasn't sure any words could make their way around it when I opened my mouth. "I don't call this winning, Luke."

"I'm sorry, Em. I really am. When you were away with your mom I did something shitty and the reason I did it is even shittier. But I kept thinking about what Charlie said—telling you wouldn't change anything and all I'd do is hurt you. And you know what? That was the last thing I wanted to do.."

Luke didn't want to hurt me, but that's exactly what he was doing right now.

"It's just too hard. Maybe you were right. Maybe . . ." Luke's voice trailed off before finishing.

"Maybe what?" I asked.

He looked down at the ground, avoiding my eyes. I recognized his expression. Defeat. I'd seen it after a few of his games, and even though his face wasn't coated in mud and dried blood wasn't caked on his lips, I could tell he'd given up. Defeat was like a sponge that absorbed every other feeling until it left nothing behind but an acceptance that the battle was over. "I don't know."

He said he didn't know, but he did. He was just afraid to say it. "Well, I guess we're even now."

Luke looked up. "Even?"

"I screwed you over with the guide, and then you screwed me over by cheating when I was away with my mom." I swallowed hard. "Like I said, we're even."

The ferry's horn punctuated the silence between us, a period at the end of the story of Emily and Luke.

Luke glanced up the passenger ramp, where the ticket taker stood waiting for him. He started to walk up the ramp and then stopped and turned to me.

"Well, if that's what you think of me, then I guess you don't really know me at all." Luke walked up the ramp and handed over his ticket. The final parting sound wasn't Luke's words hanging in the air, but the thud of the ferry door closing behind him.

It was really ending. Even through all the hurt and anger of the past few weeks, there was always a part of me that didn't really believe we were over for good. How could we be? Luke and I had been through too much together, and we'd survived. There was so much good that I'd still thought, somehow, we'd make it work out. In a way, I'd almost believed that the pain we'd inflicted upon each other this summer would let us be brand new again, like fresh snow after a storm. Only now I realized that maybe, even after everything we'd gone through to be together, we couldn't weather the secrets and insecurities and bad choices that had started to fill in the space between us. Instead of renewing us, we'd let the storm destroy what mattered the most. And now the damage couldn't be undone.

This wasn't like the last time. There was no public humiliation, no guide being held up in front of the entire school. This was different. Even though there were families on the deck of the ferry, and people with official Steamship Authority shirts walking around getting ready to close down for the night, nobody was watching us, waiting to see what happened next.

I should have gone back to the car. I should have driven away and never looked back to see if Luke was standing outside on the ferry's deck watching me. But I didn't. I couldn't. My feet wouldn't move and the ache deep inside wouldn't let me. I stood at the railing by the passenger ramp and listened to the chaos of the engines as they churned through the water, and then faded as the ferry glided farther and farther away from me, leaving behind a wake that eventually dissolved as if it had never been there at all.

"You okay?" A guy was cranking the steel ramp back into place, probably getting it ready for tomorrow morning, when new passengers arrived and his routine started all over again.

I shook my head.

"You forget something? Leave it on the ferry?"

The answer was no, but I found myself nodding.

"Well, it's too late. You can't go back now."

Even if a ferry could take me back to him, the distance between us had grown so vast I wasn't sure we could ever find our way to one another again. But I wished we could. I wanted to more than anything in the world.

I kept my eyes fixed on the ferry, its lights growing smaller and dimmer as it traveled toward the island, taking a part of me with it.

When it finally disappeared, there was nothing left to do but to go back to Josie's house.

I held my phone curled in my fingers as I walked to the car. When it vibrated, the movement cracked open something inside me, like a dam bursting open. Through my tears, I stared at the blurry screen, taking a deep breath, relieved, sorry, grateful that Luke hadn't turned his back on me for good.

Only when I glanced at the screen, I realized it wasn't my phone, it was Josie's. And it wasn't a text or a call from Luke. The tremble was nothing more than a calendar reminder. Tomorrow, I was leaving.

Summer was over.

chapter twenty-five

The bluish-white strobe of headlights illuminated the empty Steamship Authority parking lot, and I stepped aside to let the car pass. Instead, it slowed down and came to a stop.

"You're going to get killed," Josie scolded through the open passenger window of Mrs. Holden's car. "What are you still doing here? This place is deserted."

"He's gone," I told her.

"You didn't get here in time?"

I shook my head. That wasn't what I meant, but Josie didn't know that. All she knew was that she'd found me standing alone in the ferry parking lot.

"He was here, but he left."

"Leave my car. We can come back and get it in the morning," she told me. "I'll take you home."

"I can drive," I started to protest, but Josie reached over and opened the passenger door.

"I know you *can* drive, but you're not going to. Just get in."

I followed her directions and slid into the seat beside her, the leather cool against my thighs.

I expected Josie to pepper me with questions, but instead, she headed toward home, mouthing the lyrics to the songs streaming through the speakers instead of trying to have a conversation. Finally, when we were almost home, she reached over and turned down the volume.

"Are you okay?" she asked—the one question I wasn't expecting.

I shrugged. "It was bound to happen, right? Better now than later."

"Sure," she agreed, but I could tell she was just going along with me because she knew that I wanted to drop the subject.

"Thanks for coming to find me," I said. "And I'm sorry you had to leave the best party of the summer."

"Are you kidding me? I couldn't let you go home alone. I think that's number one in Polite Patty's *Top Ten Rules for Best Friends*."

I smiled into the dark and turned to look at Josie. "That's a great book title."

Only her profile was visible in the shadow of the lights rising from the dashboard, but I could see her smile back at me. "Yeah, I've been working on it all summer."

* * *

When I opened my eyes the next day, it felt like every other morning since I'd arrived. I'd grown so used to waking up early for the marina that my body didn't know that today I could sleep in, because today I was going home. My parents told me to expect them around noon, which meant I only had a few hours left. I could spend them in bed, or I could take care of one last thing before I left the Cape.

"What are you doing up?" Josie rubbed her eyes.

"I'm going to take one last bike ride," I told her, slipping on shorts and grabbing my flip-flops from beside my bed. "I'll pick up your car on the way home and put my bike in the trunk. Go back to sleep."

"You sure? I could take you," she offered, but she pulled the covers up around her chin and rolled over.

"I'm sure. I won't be too long."

The house was still quiet. Mr. and Mrs. Holden weren't even up yet. I walked my bike from the garage and pedaled across the crushed-shell driveway for the last time. Before I got Josie's car from the ferry terminal, I had one last thing I had to do, even if it meant biking an extra two miles to do it.

the next chapter of luke

The marina was in full swing, and as I walked around the office to the docks, I waved hello to the regulars I'd come to know by name.

"What are you doing here?" George practically ran into me as he swung around the corner of the office with five boxes of candy bars stacked in his arms. "Aren't you supposed to be going home today?"

"Let me help," I told him, and took the boxes from him, placing a few under one arm and the rest under the other.

I followed George inside and put them all down before tearing open the tops and setting them on display. "Who's that?"

George followed my gaze over to the docks, where Nolan was talking to someone I'd never seen before. The man was kneeling down on the dock, his ear pressed against the planks as he knocked them with his knuckles and listened.

"That, Emily, is the proud new owner of the Edgewater Marina."

"You did it? You sold the marina?"

"I did." George had a huge grin on his face, but I couldn't tell if it was the result of a savvy real estate deal, or if he was already imagining next summer out on his fishing boat.

"Good for you." I tried to sound enthusiastic, but my attempt came out halfhearted at best.

"What? You were hoping for a job again next year?" George tried to get me to smile.

"Not a chance," I replied. "It's just hard to imagine someone else owning this place."

"Time marches on, and thankfully for me, it's marching in a hot real estate market." The marina's buyer looked up. When he saw George, he waved him over. "The papers are signed, but let's hope he didn't just discover the pylons are sinking."

George went out to the docks, passing Nolan as he headed in the opposite direction.

I waited for Nolan in the office, a summer's worth of nautical knots hanging from nails on the wall, our handwritten labels taped beside them. Slip knot, halter hitch, rolling hitch—there had to be twenty knots of mine on the wall.

"Hey, are you okay?" Nolan stood in the doorway. "Josie was really worried when you didn't come back last night."

I scanned his face for any signs that this was going to be awkward, but he seemed just like regular Nolan. "She found me. I'm fine."

He didn't believe me. "You don't look so fine."

"Just what a girl wants to hear, thanks." I grabbed a Kit Kat from the box and laid a dollar bill down on the counter.

Nolan rang up my candy bar and placed the money in the register. "You know what I mean."

I was afraid it might be awkward to see Nolan after what had happened last night, but I also knew I couldn't leave without saying good-bye. I would have had a completely different summer without him, and not just because he taught me how to use a pump-out station. There were ups and downs with Josie and Lucy—and, obviously, Luke—but Nolan was the one person I hadn't worried about disappointing. Maybe in the beginning, it was because I didn't care what he thought about me as much as what he thought about my ability to pump gas and run ice out to the boats. But in the end, it was because he became a new type of friend—the kind that starts from scratch, without the weight of a past. There was something freeing about that, even if a few months ago, all I'd wanted was for everything to stay exactly as it was.

"How about, I'll *be* fine," I offered instead.

"Did you and Luke work it out?" Nolan asked.

I shook my head and took a bite of my Kit Kat.

"What about us, are we good?" Nolan wanted to know. "I know I said some stuff that maybe wasn't what you were expecting."

"Apparently, I'm not that good at knowing what to expect, so don't take it personally," I told him, and remembered when he'd said the same thing to me so many weeks ago, when I'd first started work. "You and George still betting?"

"No, he was out fishing too much this season, which sucks for me, because I usually end up on the winning side."

"Except when it comes to balancing sabiki rods on your chin," I reminded him.

"Well, there's that. I did try to get him to take a bet back in July, but he wouldn't take me up on it."

"What was it?" I asked, licking the melting chocolate from my fingers.

Nolan reached for the paper towel roll and tossed it to me. "On your first day off, I tried to bet George twenty bucks that you'd stay the rest of the summer, but he said no. When I asked why, he told me that any girl willing to figure out how to tie a bowline was definitely capable of working here for the summer."

I went over and removed the bowline from its hook, turning it over in my hand as I remembered the day I first learned to tie it. I replaced it and took the Zeppelin down.

"You can take it with you if you want," Nolan offered. "In case you have any airships to grounded."

"Thanks." I wrapped the ends of the lines around each other, so it would fit in the small nylon pouch Velcroed to my bike's seat.

"What time are you leaving today?" Nolan asked. "Maybe we could have lunch?"

"Wish I could, but my parents are probably already on their way down here."

"Then I guess this is it. I meant it when I said we should hang out at school."

"I'd like that."

"So let me know when you're settled in and all."

"I will." I pointed to the wall. "Thanks for teaching me how to make knots."

"Oh! That reminds me." Nolan bent down and disappeared behind the counter. I could hear him shuffling the stacks of folders and muttering to himself before he stood up again and triumphantly slipped something behind his back. "You still have a lot to learn, and I thought this might help."

He removed the blue hardback book he'd been hiding and handed it to me.

"Is that a giant double figure eight knot on the cover?" I asked, taking the book from him and reading the title, *The Big Book of Knots*. "I can't even do a constrictor knot, and you expect me to do a double figure eight knot?"

Nolan laughed. "There are more than three hundred knots in there. You can start with something simpler."

"Thanks, it's awesome." I held the book to my chest, its flat cover pressed against me. For once, someone had given me a useful how-to book—something with step-by-step directions that were guaranteed to work. "Hey, Nolan, I'm really sorry about last night. I didn't mean to get you mixed up in my mess. I really hope we can stay friends."

"Count on it, Emily."

I glanced at the clock and subtracted five minutes. "I should go. I still have to pick up Josie's car in Woods Hole."

I took a final look around the office and turned to leave one last time. "You know, I never thought I'd be sad to say good-bye to this place, or you," I added. "But I am."

"Consider yourself lucky," Nolan said. "Would you rather you just left and were glad it's over?"

He was right. I was glad it was hard. It should be. Otherwise, how would I know that it was special? "Not at all."

My bike waited for me outside, like it always did, but so much was different now. In a couple weeks, I'd be sharing my room with Kaitlin Fleur, my new roommate. I'd start filling up my phone with new names and numbers, just like I'd done with Nolan. And a few months from now, the marina would have a new owner and maybe a new name. The boats would be gone, the trees would be bare, and the Scoop Shack would be sealed up for the season.

I'd had it all wrong. Changing wasn't hard. *Not changing* was.

chapter twenty-six

M y roommate was a mermaid in her previous life.
I learned this fascinating little fact as I slipped the elastic corners of my brand new cushioned mattress pad onto the barren twin bed against the wall. The fresh bedding still smelled like fabric softener. My mother believed that everything was better with fabric softener, as if the scent of *cotton meadow* was a magic elixir against the unpleasantness of everyday life. Her next book was going to contain an entire chapter on scent etiquette—*What Your Nose Knows.*

The only thing my nose knew right then was that, if the musty, stagnant aroma of my new dorm room was any indication, the college facilities manager could benefit from the olfactory etiquette tips in the next installment of my mother's bestselling series of books.

The girl who I would spend the next nine months waking up to had already unpacked and was in the process of decorating the opposite side of the room. Her mother obviously subscribed to the motto *fend for yourself,* because while I stretched my freshly laundered, meadow-scented linens across my bed, my new roommate pounded nails into the wall with an improvised hammer—the heel of a faded black combat boot.

My mom could have suggested a less destructive hanging method, as well as the correct tools and ergonomic technique. But my parents were already on the highway heading home, and in an hour and forty minutes, they'd walk into our house and probably find TJ had already turned my old bedroom into a man cave for his friends.

"Why don't you try something in here?" I offered, handing my roommate a small box of various supplies my mom had packed for me. "I think there are tacks or hooks or something that might be easier."

Kaitlin took the box and started rummaging through the various sheets of Sticky Tack and plastic hooks with easy to remove, non-damaging adhesive backing.

"What do you think you were?" my new roommate asked after selecting the plastic-coated pushpins.

"When?" I asked, focused more on making my bed than the voice coming from across the room, which, thankfully, was no longer punctuated by the sound of crumbling plaster.

"In your previous life," she explained. "My boyfriend, Mark, was a dolphin."

My mermaid roommate was dating a dolphin. How perfect.

"I'm not sure I ever thought about reincarnation before," I told Kaitlin, although I *was* sure that I had started to think, in this life, my roommate might be a wack job. She looked pretty normal—no fish scales or tail hidden in her jeans as far as I could tell. With her long, dark cornrows gathered into a high ponytail and smoky, almond-shaped eyes, she was almost exotic looking, and nothing like the pale redhead I'd come to think of as the quintessential mermaid, thanks to Disney.

When I'd found out my roommate would be Kaitlin Fleur from New Jersey, there was no mention of her previous aquatic existence, or that of her marine mammal boyfriend. Still, Kaitlin brought a refrigerator stocked with snacks and cans of Starbucks Doubleshot energy drinks, which she offered to share with me without hesitating or asking if I drank coffee (I don't). In the thirty-seven minutes we'd lived together, she seemed nice enough, which was more than I could say for Josie's roommate at Skidmore, a militant vegan who wore *Lobsters Have Feelings Too* and *Cows Love Vegans* T-shirts and attempted to *vegucate* Josie on the finer points of slaughterhouse injustices. I gave their living situation no more than a month before they each requested a new roommate.

The pushpins must have worked because, when I turned around, Kaitlin's entire wall was covered with purple, turquoise, and gold jewel-toned tapestries. They looked like they belonged in a subtitled movie with belly dancers and snake charmers coaxing pythons out of wicker baskets, not a dorm room in Western Massachusetts. Kaitlin stood back and admired her handiwork before turning to me.

"Want to see him?" She reached for a silver filigreed picture frame that had been propped on the nightstand she'd constructed from a stack of plastic milk crates. "This is Mark."

She came over to my side of the room and held out the photograph of Kaitlin and her boyfriend sitting on a beach, her head resting on his shoulder.

I stared longer than I should have.

"We were at St. Germain's together," she told me, although I already knew she'd gone to boarding school; it was one of the first things she'd told me when we were texting. "He's a year younger, so he's a senior now."

"He's really cute," I offered, because he was, and because I figured if I kept the conversation on Mark, she wouldn't ask why my voice suddenly sounded funny.

"Yeah, he is." Kaitlin ran a finger slowly across the frame's glass, as if attempting to brush away the sand in the photo. "We were on the Jersey Shore, in Stone Harbor. Ever been there?" she asked.

I shook my head, not trusting myself to speak. I'd had my own photograph. My own summer day melting around me and my boyfriend. Only instead of resting my head on the shoulder beside me, I was laughing in front of a man-made whale tail.

I looked away. "A dolphin, huh?"

"Yeah, what about you? Is there a guy? Or girl?" she added.

I slipped my pillow into the crisp, cotton case my mom had neatly folded around a lavender-scented sachet—a little aromatherapy to help me relax and sleep soundly in my new bed.

I shook my head. "My fish got away."

Kaitlin shrugged and gave me a wide smile. "That's okay."

"There's more fish in the sea?" My attempt to make her laugh only made the smile fade and be replaced by what looked like genuine concern.

Kaitlin set the picture frame down on the milk crate nightstand and angled it toward her bed. "Look, Emily, I have

Mark, but I need to focus on classes if I'm going to get into a top grad school program. We don't need guys, but if you want them, there are a *billion* out there when you're ready." She emphasized the *B* in billion, as if I'd be disappointed by mere millions. "There are four other colleges within fifteen square miles of us, and they're all a twenty-minute bus ride away. And the bus is free!" Kaitlin continued, reciting our college's website with startling accuracy.

I didn't know what freaked me out more—Kaitlin's ability to see right through my attempt to make light of my situation, or the fact that I was about four years behind Kaitlin in planning for post-college life. I mean, it was our first day. Our first *hour.* And here I was already lagging in just about everything, from room décor to future career plans.

"It's not a big deal, really," I assured Kaitlin. "A guy is the last thing I need right now."

Kaitlin nodded her agreement and then changed the subject. "Do you know what classes you're going to take?"

There had to be at least two hundred different courses listed in the catalog. How could I possibly pick four? Unlike those people who knew *exactly* what they wanted to study and *precisely* what they'd do the day they graduated, I was a classic *undecided.* As well as a procrastinator. At least that's what I'd been telling myself, because I figured procrastinating was acceptable for a first-year college student. What wasn't acceptable? Trying to figure out what was going on in your ex-boyfriend's head every time you read the course description for Psychology 101.

"I haven't narrowed it down yet," I told Kaitlin, and then, in an attempt to once again divert my thoughts to a totally innocuous topic, added, "What about you?"

I figured someone who believed she'd spent her previous life with a single finned tail instead of two human legs would be into studio art or philosophy. Maybe even dance (she had to be almost six feet tall and was definitely thin enough to be mistaken for a ballerina, although after our brief conversation, I could already tell she was more likely an improvised dance kind of girl).

"Here's what I was thinking." Kaitlin showed me a page she'd obviously printed from a spreadsheet. It turned out my mermaid roommate was an engineering major. And she had already planned out her entire course load for the next four years—computer science and math classes, with East Asian Languages and Literature thrown in for good measure. She may have been a mermaid, but Kaitlin was also organized. And obviously brilliant. Despite the lack of a portable toolkit with an assortment of tapestry-hanging accessories, my mom would love her.

"I'm going to head over to the campus center, I'm starving." Kaitlin set the page down on her desk. "Want to come?"

Her side of the room looked like she'd already been there for days, but my side remained pretty bleak, more *prison cell chic* than dorm hangout. My duffel bags still sat in lumps on the floor, their seams bulging as they waited for me to pull the zippers and let them spew my clothes out in a pile of wrinkles. Kaitlin had already put her personal touch on her half of our room décor and plotted out her college career in neat, evenly spaced spreadsheet cells that probably had some sort of sophisticated algorithm behind them to ensure her classes didn't conflict with visits from her dolphin boyfriend. I was way behind the curve.

"I think I'm going to finish unpacking."

"Okay, be back soon!" Kaitlin grabbed a ten dollar bill from the top of her dresser and stuffed it into her jeans pocket before heading out the door and leaving me in our new room.

I was alone for the first time all day. Just me, a tired and scuffed hardwood floor that had already impaled a splinter into my big toe (lesson learned, socks from now on), a blank wall pleading with me to do something as cool as Kaitlin's exotic tapestries and stale dorm air that was starting to make me feel claustrophobic.

I went over to Kaitlin's side of the room to open the window, but paused when I reached the silver frame on her nightstand Mark *was* really cute. I could see why she didn't care if he was still a senior in high school.

Still, Kaitlin was obviously smart. She had to know that the odds of the mermaid and the dolphin living happily ever after were about a million to one. If they were even that high. My mother would tell me not to be such a cynic, but after this summer, I felt like I'd earned the right to crap on the fairy-tale garbage I'd been delusional enough to believe. Absence *did not* make the heart grow fonder. Sometimes it just made everything harder.

Kaitlin and Mark probably had another three months, tops, before their long-distance relationship hit the skids. Everything would change now that Kaitlin was away at college. High school was a lifetime ago. Even the summer already felt long gone.

I squeezed my eyes shut and shook my head, erasing the mental image of a calendar with that day circled in red, a vivid reminder of what had happened. That night. The image of Luke's shadowy figure as he turned his back to me and left me standing alone on the ferry dock.

The picture of us on Martha's Vineyard was still in one of my duffel bags, I knew that. It was facedown at the bottom, beneath my socks and sweatpants and all the new underwear my mom insisted on buying me, because who starts college with the same underwear they wore in high school? Not the daughter of an etiquette guru, apparently.

My breath caught in my throat, and as much as I wanted to believe the lack of a well-oxygenated environment was to blame, I knew that wasn't true.

That photograph in my bag—I didn't know why I even brought it to school with me. I should have left it at home with everything else I'd decided to leave behind. That had been my plan. But this morning, I was finally leaving for good, and my mom and dad were downstairs yelling to me that it was time to go. I'd glanced around my bedroom one last time to make sure I wasn't forgetting anything important, and I'd spotted it. A blue, glossy triangle of color poking out from beneath my desk lamp. A corner of the ocean. I couldn't see us—the rest of the photograph was hidden under the lamp base—but I knew we were there. Me and Luke. I'd grabbed the photo and stuffed it into the bottom of my bag before flipping off the light switch and heading downstairs.

I shouldn't have taken the picture with me, but I couldn't leave it behind. And the reason made my eyes sting and my chest constrict, like my heart was breaking open inside me and every muscle, every bone, was trying to keep it from shattering into a million pieces.

Breathe, I reminded myself. *Just keep breathing.*

I reached over and cracked open the window to let in fresh air. Already the breeze was different, more unsympathetic. Summer was definitely over.

And so were me and Luke.

* * *

The reincarnation theory notwithstanding, Kaitlin did turn out to be normal.

We'd been roommates for five weeks, and, so far, we actually got along. (As predicted, Josie and her vegan roommate, who preferred to go by the name Fern even though her real name was Doreen, lasted ten days before requesting that the director of housing step in and remove one of them. Josie threatened to hurl a vegan-friendly imitation leather boot at Fern's head if she forced her to listen to one more grotesque fact about the exploitation at factory farms.) Lucy had texted that her triple at Duke was huge and her roommates seemed fine, except for the fact that they were twins and Lucy could never tell them apart. (Apparently, one of them had a distinctive birthmark on her left butt cheek, but Lucy was willing to guess at who was who without asking for dermatologic verification.)

As far as roommates went, I felt pretty lucky. Kaitlin's nightly phone calls from Mark, who wasn't supposed to be on the phone after eleven because St. Germain's had a strict policy, were tolerable for the most part. Sometimes, when the calls were winding down, her voice would get all low and soft, and I'd conveniently find a reason to go to the bathroom or down the hall to the kitchenette. Listening to all the *miss you's* was bad enough, but hearing Kaitlin profess her undying love was downright unbearable when the only *I love you's* I was getting came from my mom, and were accompanied by reminders to separate my white and colored laundry before washing.

I tried not to think about Luke, but there were times, mostly at night, when I was laying on my bed studying, and something I'd read would trigger a memory or a thought, and suddenly it was as if I'd stumbled down a path and couldn't find a way to turn around. My mind started backing up, like those scenes in movies where the film seems to run in reverse, the characters walking backward as dry, brown leaves lift from the ground until they're pinned back to their branches and brilliantly green. Going back in time. Here I was, reading Plato's *Republic* for my Government 100 class, and instead of taking notes on the historical influence of its Socratic dialogue, I kept imaging what Socrates would have to say about the *justice* of what had happened between me and Luke. The whole concept of people not being able to tell the difference between what's real and what isn't—how two people can think they're seeing the same thing, only to discover that, in reality, it's completely different.

I started to think that maybe Plato was on to something, and, as one of the most pivotal philosophers in history, probably had it all figured out. Until I got to the big takeaway and realized even Plato didn't have the answer, which meant I could have saved myself three hours of reading by just ordering Chinese food and reading the little slip of paper inside the fortune cookie. The big reveal from ancient Greece's esteemed philosopher and the founder of the first institution of higher learning? We're all human.

Modern day translation? We all fuck up.

In the days that followed that night on the ferry dock, I'd kept waiting for my phone to ring—to see Luke's name appear on my screen. So many times, I wanted to pick up the phone and call him, ask if we could just forget what happened, forget who did what and who was wrong. But I couldn't. It wasn't that simple, untangling the snarled ball of missed expectations that had become us, unfurling the knots created by our mistakes. Because as much as I wanted to do that, I couldn't help toying with those knots, running my fingers over them again and again, until they became so tight I didn't know how to begin prying them loose.

I could have told Kaitlin the gory details about me and Luke from the start and avoided the seemingly innocuous questions that she'd pepper me with out of the blue—questions that only made me remember what I was trying so hard to forget: What was his last name? (Preston, Luke Preston.) What color eyes did he have? (A soft, gooey brown, like the caramel you pour on a sundae.) How'd you meet? (Umm . . .) Did your friends like him? (Double umm . . .)

But I didn't tell Kaitlin any more than I had to. I'd barely told Josie and Lucy exactly what had happened that last night.

With all the pre-college preparation, my meager explanation had been good enough for them. They were willing to accept my answers at face value. As long as I was okay, the details didn't matter, they'd told me. Who said what, who was right or wrong—the answers didn't change the outcome. Unlike Plato, my friends weren't interested in theoretical conversations when the answer was so very clear: everyone else was ready to close the book on the story of Emily and Luke, and begin the next chapter of their lives. It was time I did the same.

Instead of getting an exhaustive review of the facts, over the first few weeks of school, Kaitlin just learned the basics—Luke and I started going out the second half of our senior year, we made it through June and July, but by the time August rolled around, we were over. I had a boyfriend for a little while, and then I didn't. Not exactly a novel story, nothing unusual about it.

But for all of her proficiency with scientific equations and the indisputable answers they produced, Kaitlin was still a sucker for the unpredictable formula for love. It was already October, and our conversations had gone from comparing professors and reading requirements to normal life stuff—toss me a pen, can I borrow a tampon, want to order a pizza for dinner instead of eating in the dining hall? I guessed it was only a matter of time before she wanted to scratch the surface and uncover what was really underneath my seemingly easy answers to her questions about Luke.

"Seriously, what really happened?" Kaitlin finally wanted to know. "There has to be more to it," she insisted.

Kaitlin and I were lying on our beds attempting to study. It was a Friday night, and we probably should have been looking for a party or hanging out downstairs in the lounge, but it was the first night of our four-day October break weekend, and we'd decided that what we really wanted to do was stay in and enjoy our little vacation. Kaitlin was waiting for Mark's nightly phone call, and I was trying to get a jump-start on my upcoming geology paper. (I'd thought a class about rocks and crystals would be fun and interesting, but I had quickly discovered I was not a budding geoscientist).

"What do you mean, what *really* happened?" My mom had instilled in me that repeating a question that someone had just asked showed that you were listening. In this case, however, I was just buying myself time to think of an answer.

"There had to be something. A fight?" Kaitlin stared up at the glow-in-the-dark stars she'd stuck to the ceiling over her bed. I'd thought that an engineering major would make sure the stars accurately reflected actual constellations, but instead, the pale yellow bursts haphazardly dotted the ceiling in no particular formation. "Did he lie to you about something huge? Did you get pissed at something he did?"

"It doesn't matter anymore."

Kaitlin turned onto her side to face me. "But we learn from our experiences. I mean, what's the point of coming back if we can't take the lessons from our past lives with us?"

A few weeks ago, I would have thought she was nuts, but Kaitlin wasn't kidding. She really believed all this past life stuff. I'd learned to actually kind of appreciate her offbeat take on life (or afterlife), even if I still couldn't figure out the mermaid thing. I mean, mermaids don't actually exist outside of books and Disney movies. So her past life seemed a little convenient and also a little wishful—who wouldn't want to be a mermaid? They always had great boobs, fabulous hair, and even though they spent ninety-nine percent of their time underwater, their skin never shriveled up.

"Not everything can have a lesson, Kaitlin. Sometimes shit just happens." I sounded like a bumper sticker.

"Nothing *just happens*. I'll help you figure out what you were supposed to learn. Then at least you won't make the same mistake again in the future."

When I thought about me and Luke, about how we'd started and where we'd ended, I couldn't pinpoint just *one* mistake—a single incident or event that eventually made it impossible for us to stay together. Instead, I remembered moments where each of us had made a choice. And, finally, those choices had led to a moment where one final choice was made, and Luke made it. In the end, I wasn't given a choice at all.

"See these?" I held up two of the textbooks scattered around me on my bed. "I have enough learning to do this semester."

Kaitlin shook her head at me. I could practically hear her *tsk tsking*. I had a feeling she was beginning to think I was a lost cause. "Then you'll be destined to repeat the same mistakes, over and over and over again."

What did I learn from my experience? When you throw a notebook in the trash, make sure the subject of said notebook doesn't get his hands on it. In other words, learn how to use a shredder.

Maybe lesson number two was *don't attend all-school assemblies.*

"Just tell me," Kaitlin insisted. "You'll feel better, I promise."

I seriously doubted that reliving that night in August would make me feel anything but completely and totally crappy.

Kaitlin sat up and leaned against the wall beside her bed. She pulled her knees into her chest and hugged them. Now I had her complete attention. "I don't believe you."

"What don't you believe?"

"That it's history, that it's old news." Kaitlin frowned at me. "I think you're still in love with him. Why else haven't you gone to see that guy you know over at UMass? Nolan? He's twenty minutes away. I know he's texted you."

"You do?"

Kaitlin rolled her eyes at me. "Just admit it, you're not over Luke."

"Talking about it won't change anything."

"But it matters, Emily," she insisted.

"Why?"

"Because maybe he's your dolphin." Kaitlin didn't even crack a smile when she said this. She was totally serious.

She was crazy, but she was also brilliant, and I loved her and her bizarre beliefs that she never gave up on, no matter how ridiculous they made her look. I wished I had that ability.

You know what else I wished? That Luke could hear this conversation. That he could meet my wacky roommate and see the wild tapestries on her walls. That we could exchange a look and both know that, even if Kaitlin's ideas were completely out there and totally nuts coming from someone who could also explain continuous dynamical systems and discrete geometry, she was pretty awesome. And so were we. And that made me miss him even more.

"Did you ever think that maybe it's not really over?" Kaitlin continued, and when I didn't answer, she made one final attempt. "But we won't know until I hear the whole story, right? Start to finish. So start."

"I wouldn't even know where to begin." I snapped the cap onto my yellow Highlighter. It wasn't like I was making a tremendous amount of progress on the mineralogic problems associated with crystallography anyway.

"Begin at the beginning," Kaitlin instructed me.

So that's what I did. I started with my move back to Boston my senior year, and stopped where most stories stop—the happy ending, when Josie arranged for Luke and me to work things out.

"And then everything was great," I concluded, much like a librarian closing the last page of a children's book before looking up at her class of adoring, satisfied listeners. "We were happy."

"Obviously there's more," Kaitlin pointed out. "What's the rest of the story?"

I sucked in my breath and rolled over onto my stomach, hoping a change of position would keep me from dissolving as I thought back to graduation—to when I'd thought we really would have a happy ending, even if the nagging uncertainty of our situation had started to worm its way into my head. Back to when I didn't know that when you decided to let yourself love someone, it meant you were also setting yourself up to have someone to lose.

"You want the whole story or the abridged version," I asked. It was almost two o'clock in the morning.

"The whole story," she told me. "Chapter by chapter."

I inhaled deeply, like someone about to be submerged underwater for a very long time, and prepared to tell Kaitlin the whole story in painstaking detail. "We graduated a month later."

"And . . ." she wanted to know.

I fixed my eyes on the covers of my geology textbooks, the vivid images of purple prismed crystals, craggly silver speckled rocks, and golden molten lava blurring together into a kaleidoscope of indecipherable smudges. I forced myself to blink, bringing my eyes back into focus.

"And then it was summer," I said. "The beginning of the end."

I took her through the ups and downs of our summer, until I got to the night I found Luke at the ferry.

"And?" Kaitlin inched forward, her arms wrapped around her knees as she pulled them in tight to her chest. "Then what?"

I swallowed the lump in my throat and shrugged. "And then he decided to give up on us."

"Wow." Kaitlin sat back against the wall and shook her head. "Just wow. So that's it? You haven't talked to him since?"

"Nope."

"I can't believe it." Kaitlin rolled over onto her back and stared at the stars on the ceiling. "After all that," she mused.

"Yep, after all that." I closed my eyes and lay there silently, wrung out from retelling the story of our breakup. It had exhausted me, remembering the details, the sequence of events that added up to the end of me and Luke. "We never even said good-bye."

"What do you mean?" Kaitlin asked.

"I mean, that was it. He just walked away from me. There was never even a good-bye."

For some reason, that made a difference to me, as if without the finality of a good-bye, there was still a chance—a door that remained open with enough light finding its way through the crack to give me hope.

"Oh, Emily."

"The thing is, I feel like I didn't have a choice."

"Sure you did. You could have run after him. You could have called him the next day. Or the next. Shit, you could call him right now."

"I think the statute of limitations on that ship has sailed," I told her, mixing my metaphors. It was too late and I was too tired to care. She got the point. "Besides, he wouldn't have talked to me. You have no idea how he looked when he turned away. He was done. He was so done with us, with me, all of it. He'd had enough."

"So if you had a choice now, what would you do?"

"I'd go back to when everything was easy."

"But that's not even a choice, Emily. There's no option to press rewind. The way I see it, you basically have two options. You can either get over it and move on. Or you can do whatever it takes to try to fix it."

"Both of those sound pretty unpleasant."

"I didn't say it wouldn't be hard. I just said you have options. Whether you pick one is up to you. But don't complain that you never had one."

"Here's my pick; I'm going to close my eyes and sleep for the next twelve hours."

Kaitlin sat up and grabbed my arm, squeezing over and over again, as if she was trying to pump the energy back into me. "There's no way you're going to sleep."

"Are you kidding me? We've been up all night. I just want to pass out."

"No!" she insisted. "That can't be the end. I mean, he's your dolphin!"

I frowned. Was she going to pull out the mermaid/dolphin card now? "Seriously?"

"I don't mean he's actually your *dolphin*. I don't know what he was *before*." She paused, realizing that this line of rationale would not win me over. "I just mean you have to go."

"Go where?"

"To meet him. Tomorrow—it's when you both promised. So go!"

"I am not going to meet him in a parking lot. Not that he'd even be there, which means I'm not going to go to a parking lot and stand there by myself looking like an idiot, waiting for someone who will never show up."

"But you both promised, doesn't that mean anything?" For someone who had stayed up all night, Kaitlin sure was wide awake.

"That was before everything happened, Kaitlin. I don't think our promise applies anymore."

"Don't you want to know for sure?"

"Oh, I know. Believe me, he made everything perfectly clear."

"Go. He'll be there, I just know it. Wouldn't you hate yourself if he went and you didn't?"

I'd spent weeks hating myself, being sorry, wishing I could change everything. I was already well acquainted to the feeling.

"He won't show up."

"But you don't know that for sure. Besides, if you get there and he isn't waiting for you, then you know it's really over. For good. You'll have closure."

As much as I didn't want to admit it, Kaitlin was right. There was a part of me—a stupid, ridiculous, delusional part of me—that still hoped.

"That's what you want, right?" she asked. "At least then you can move on, Emily. Because right now, from what I've seen, you haven't gotten past it."

I shrugged.

"You really have nothing to lose," she reminded me, as if that would help, pointing out that I'd already lost everything that I used to think mattered so much. It didn't exactly make me want to go through it all again.

"Come on." Kaitlin nudged me. "Go."

"I've been up all night. I probably look like shit." I sat up and glanced across the room at the mirror on the wall above Kaitlin's dresser. "No, I *do* look like shit. Besides, how would I even get there?" I asked.

She handed me her phone, which was open to a page with the Peter Pan Bus Lines schedule. "Look, there's a bus leaving for Boston in forty-five minutes. Take a quick shower, get dressed, throw on some makeup, and go."

"You think so?" I asked, actually warming up to the idea. What if Luke went, if for no other reason than because he'd promised he would. "But it will cost me, like, forty dollars to get from the bus station to Friendly's."

"Call your brother."

Really, I was going to put my future in the hands of TJ?

"Get in the shower. I'll text TJ for you." Kaitlin held out her hand and waited for me to give her my phone.

"Make him promise not to tell my parents. I don't want them to know I'm going home," I told her as I typed in my password and handed the phone over. "And don't make me sound desperate, or TJ will never let me live this down."

chapter twenty-seven

I t was nuts. And, contrary to what Kaitlin said, forty-five minutes was *not* enough time to shower, put on makeup, and still make it down the hill to the bus terminal. Which was why Kaitlin had tossed all of my makeup into my backpack, and I was now trying to apply mascara while balancing a handheld mirror on my lap as the bus careened down the Mass Pike toward Boston. What should be a two hour trip by car was going to take almost three hours on the bus, which was plenty of time to put on make-up, but too much time to think about what might happen when I arrived.

Kaitlin had convinced me that I needed closure, but it wouldn't come cheap. After spending forty-six dollars on a round trip bus ticket, and handing over another twenty to TJ (Kaitlin couldn't convince him to pick me up at the bus station for any less than that), I was going to be out over sixty dollars. And there was no guarantee Luke would even be waiting for me.

"I'm not even going to ask," TJ said when I opened the car door and slid into the passenger seat. "Just put the money in the console and we'll be on our way."

TJ wasn't kidding. He didn't ask a single question—not why my roommate was the one asking for the favor, or why it was so important that I get to Friendly's by two o'clock. For all he knew, I was just having a really bad craving for a strawberry Fribble.

257

"You didn't tell mom or dad you were picking me up, did you?" I asked him.

He shook his head. "Nope. Leave another twenty and I'll even pretend I don't know who you are."

"You wiped me out. I only have ten bucks left."

We drove along in silence, although I had a feeling TJ was trying to figure out how to get the last of my cash.

TJ pulled the car into the Friendly's parking lot five minutes ahead of schedule. I scanned the spots for Luke's car. Even though I'd spent the entire bus ride preparing for this moment, my throat started to ache. His car wasn't there.

"Look at that," TJ pointed out. "We made it with five minutes to spare. That's probably deserving of a tip, right?"

I ignored his effort to bilk me out of more money, and instead reached for the door handle to let myself out. "Unless I text something different, meet me back here in an hour."

"Wait a minute. Your roommate never said anything about taking you back to the bus. This was strictly a drop-off. I have places to go, people to see."

"Give me a break, TJ, you do not."

"Do so. I'm meeting my friends in exactly fifteen minutes, and if you don't get out of the car, I'll be late."

"So how am I supposed to get back to the bus station?"

TJ shrugged. "I don't know. You'll figure it out, I'm sure. You are the brains in the family, right?"

He didn't wait for my answer. He barely waited for me to close the door before taking off and leaving me in the parking lot.

* * *

I waited. For thirty minutes, I stood in the Friendly's parking lot listening to the traffic on Route 9 go by. I watched the leaves on the trees in the parking lot prepare to turn colors, a few of them tearing off in the wind and blowing away while I shifted from foot to foot and wished for a bench to sit on. And eventually, I had to admit that he wasn't coming, no matter how *official* our promise had been. Luke didn't need closure. He just needed to be done with me. For good.

I said it in my head, and I repeated it aloud to the bushes lining the sidewalk to the front door.

Luke isn't coming.

After everything we'd been through, he'd decided *we* weren't worth it.

When the tears started, I couldn't stop them. They came, one after another, in a stream that ran down my cheeks so fast I didn't even bother trying to wipe them away.

Loving someone isn't enough. Love isn't a wave you ride. It's diving into the ocean. It's the unpredictable currents and ebbs and flows that take you in different directions or pull you down until you can't breathe. If you're lucky, you learn to swim. And if you can't, you drown.

And that's how I felt. Like I was drowning. Like I'd finally given up and accepted that, as much as I thought I could fight to get us back, I wasn't strong enough.

We'd said things to one another, made promises we'd meant to keep, had feelings we'd believed would last, and it didn't matter. We made mistakes and we hurt one another, and we couldn't find our way past the mistakes and pain. We were like any other couple—we dated and we broke up. We weren't special at all.

And that realization, that *special* doesn't last, or that maybe it's not even possible—that's what was the most painful. To think that what I'd thought was the most real thing I'd ever known had been a temporary figment of my imagination.

I didn't know Luke at all. The Luke I'd thought I knew, the person I had loved, would be here right now.

My eyes were finally dry, but my cheeks were still stained with tears when I approached the hostess at the podium. "Table for one?" she asked, removing a single menu from the wooden holder between us.

I nodded and followed her.

There were at least six open booths where she could have sat me, but she selected the exact one where Luke had been waiting for me the day he decided to forgive me for writing The Book of Luke.

"Can I take your order?" the waitress asked as she placed a fork and knife down on the tabletop.

"I won't be needing those," I told her. "Just a straw, please. And a strawberry Fribble."

Twenty minutes later, the waitress was circling me, probably hoping I'd either order more food or free up the table for better tipping customers.

"Anything else?" she asked for the fourth time.

I decided to put us both out of our misery. "No thanks, just the check."

My sorrows had been drowned in a strawberry Fribble, but I still had no idea how I was going to get back to school. I could call my parents, but then I'd have to explain everything, and they'd no doubt want me to spend the night at home. I just couldn't deal with licking my wounds in my old bedroom. If I wasn't willing to call my parents, I only had one other choice. Kaitlin's parents had given her a credit card to use only in the case of an emergency. I could call her and ask if she'd pre-pay my ride back to the bus station.

As I walked out to the parking lot to call her, I was already figuring out how many hours I'd need to babysit for my History professor's toddler in order to pay Kaitlin back.

My head was down as I dialed her number, which was why I didn't see the car at first. The honking horn finally made me look up, just in time to keep from walking into the passenger door, where the window was going down.

"You're here?"

"Yeah, I'm here," TJ answered. "Get in. I'll take you back to the bus station."

I hesitated only a moment before opening the door and letting myself sink into the empty passenger seat. As we drove away, I looked straight ahead, the parking lot fading in the side view mirror.

It was over. Really over. There was only one thing to do now.

"Thank you," I told TJ. "Thanks for coming back to get me."

He just shrugged and kept driving.

We were almost to the bus station when TJ finally broke the silence. "Okay, I have to ask. What are you doing here?"

I didn't want to tell him, but it wasn't because I was afraid he'd make fun of me. I mean, I was used to that. It was for a different reason. I was afraid that saying the words out loud—*I was keeping my promise to Luke*—would force me to admit the truth. Because I didn't keep my promise to Luke.

I wasn't honest with him about feeling scared. I didn't give him an opportunity to explain. I thought being with Nolan would make me feel better, but it only made me feel worse..

"I was hoping Luke would be there."

TJ frowned. "Why would Luke be there? Isn't he at school?"

I didn't answer.

"Besides, didn't you two break up?"

I stared through the windshield and nodded.

I waited for TJ to make some snarky comment, but instead, he just let the words fill the car, my lack of an explanation expanding around me. I could've left it at that. But there was more to the story, and even if it didn't matter to TJ, it suddenly mattered to me.

"Aren't you wondering why?"

"Let me guess. It involved a notebook?" TJ glanced over at me and smiled, trying to get me to do the same. "It's probably for the best, right? I mean, you're both at school now, it was inevitable."

I still couldn't bring myself to believe that, even if it was true.

TJ navigated across two lanes and brought the car to a stop in the drop-off lane of the bus station. "You okay?"

"I'm all set," I told him. "Thanks again. I know you didn't have to come back and get me."

"Yeah, well, I couldn't leave you stranded with nothing but Fribbles and french fries. I'm not that cruel." He laughed at his own joke, and I managed a smile. "Good luck."

Luck. I wasn't sure that was what I needed at this point, but I'd take it.

"Bye, TJ." I opened my door and stepped out into the exhaust of the idling busses, searching for the one that would take me back to school.

I tried to sleep on the bus ride, even though the only thing I had to rest my head against was the metal frame of a window so cold, it had ice crystals that stuck to my hair. I'd been up for more than twenty-four hours, and I doubted I'd be able to stop thinking about what had just happened long enough to actually doze off. I closed my eyes anyway and hoped I'd wake up a new person—the type of person who could view standing alone in a Friendly's parking lot as a new beginning.

Long-Distance Relationship Tip #62:

If you're lucky, time apart will make your relationship stronger. So, before you jump into anything you should really ask yourself, *am I feeling lucky?*

---

chapter twenty-eight

Being awake for thirty-two hours straight has a way of making even the most uncomfortable sleeping position seem downright cushy. When I opened my eyes, we had already exited the highway and were minutes from the bus station. I hadn't called Kaitlin to let her know I was heading back to school. She probably thought my reunion with Luke had gone exactly as planned. As I walked toward campus from the bus station, it was almost dark, and what felt like the longest day of my life was almost over.

When I walked into our room, Kaitlin was video chatting with the dolphin. As soon as she saw me, she blew him a kiss and said good-bye.

"Well?" she asked, sitting up on her bed.

"No luck." I shrugged before flopping down on mine, which I hoped made me look way less disappointed than I felt. "He wasn't there."

Kaitlin sucked in a mouthful of air and then slowly let it escape. "Wow. Wasn't expecting that."

As much as I'd prepared myself, as hard as I'd tried to steel myself against the likely probability that Luke wouldn't show up, a small part of me had believed he might.

"I'm sorry. I didn't mean to get your hopes up." Kaitlin came over and laid down next to me.

"It's fine," I lied.

Kaitlin rested her head on my shoulder and started twirling my hair between her fingers. "If it's any consolation, if the story you told me about you guys is true, I bet he's miserable, too."

I doubted it. "It's easier to be the one who leaves than the one who's left behind," I told her.

Kaitlin pondered this for a minute. "I never thought of it like that."

"Has anyone ever broken your heart?" I asked, and she shook her head no. "That's why."

"Okay, totally random thought here, but you know what they say about getting back up on the horse?" Kaitlin turned on her side and propped herself up on her elbow. "Why don't you give Nolan a call?"

I actually laughed. "Um, that'd be a big, fat no."

"I'm not saying you become his girlfriend or anything. It just might be nice to hang out with a guy who doesn't make you feel crappy."

Kaitlin was trying, and I really appreciated that she wanted to help. Still, I'd learned my lesson the first time I turned to Nolan to make myself feel better about Luke.

"I can't use Nolan like that," I told her, not that Nolan had any interest what so ever in taking me up on my offer the second time.

"Then what about using me?" Kaitlin twisted around onto her back and lay across my stomach, her arms sprawled out as if she'd been shot. I had all six feet of her dead weight pressed into my diaphragm, making it difficult to catch my breath long enough to tell her to get up. "Dinner! A movie! Use me, I'm all yours!"

Kaitlin was having way too much fun at my expense, but it was working.

"I can't breathe," I gasped, rolling out from under her.

She flipped over onto her stomach. "But I made you smile, didn't I?"

"Maybe," I admitted, smiling.

"Seriously, let's go get something to eat. Are you hungry? My treat."

I curled onto my side and buried my head into my pillow. It was way better than the metal window frame on the bus. "I'm exhausted. I just want to pass out."

Kaitlin started to object, and then stopped. "Fine. I'll bring you home something, though, okay?"

I may have lost Luke, but I had a roommate and a new best friend who was pretty awesome.

She wasn't so bad, for a mermaid.

* * *

Kaitlin was gone when I finally opened my eyes thirteen hours later. Her bed was perfectly made, and a takeout container sat on top of her milk crate nightstand with a fluorescent Post-it note stuck to the side. *Breakfast for a brand new day!* was written in her handwriting. I got up and went over to see what she'd saved for me and found four slices of cold cheese pizza with the crusts stuck together. It was the perfect way to start to a brand new day.

It was a beginning, not an ending. The start, not the finish, even if it felt unfinished, with words unsaid and questions unanswered. I think that's why I'd gone to meet Luke. It wasn't that I'd expected to find him in the parking lot waiting to pick up where we left off. That wasn't possible. He wasn't a boomerang who would come back every time I sent him away. It would have been nice, but there was no tidy bow that could wrap us up neatly and make our relationship look pretty again. In the end, it hadn't been pretty or neat, but unruly and cruel and complicated.

I used to think we were like the double fisherman's knot that Nolan had showed me—two knots that neatly slid together and sealed themselves tighter over time. There was no easy way to separate them, no effortless undoing. There was just cutting the knots out for good, and that meant neither end would ever be the same after they were apart. Or at least my end wouldn't. But, really, we were like the bowline knot, two different people joined together, only to be easily slipped apart when it no longer served its purpose.

Even if Luke *had* been there, even if he was willing to pretend we were fine and forget what we did to one another, I knew we couldn't. The cut that severed us had been blunt and final, but it had left me frayed, and I knew it wasn't as easy as just putting us back together again.

And I didn't want to anymore. I just wanted to say what I should have said that night at the ferry. I just wanted to close this chapter and begin a new one.

Luke was nothing more to me than a memory now, and I couldn't undo that. All I could do was hold that memory close and be thankful that no one, and no length of time, could ever take that away from me. It was mine. I hoped that, in some way, the memory of me was also a part of him.

I reached for my phone and dialed the number I knew by heart, even if I'd deleted it from my contacts months ago. His phone rang twice before going to voicemail. Should I leave a message? Did my name still appear on his phone screen when I called, and had he decided not to answer? It didn't matter. I left a message and let Luke choose whether he listened to it or not.

"Hi, Luke, it's me," I started, and then realized how long it had been since he'd heard my voice. As much as I hoped Luke remembered what I sounded like, what it once felt like to hear me say his name, I added, "Emily." I spoke tentatively, as if already anticipating that Luke would have his finger on the end button. I rushed on, hoping he'd listen long enough to let me finish what I had to say.

"You're probably busy so I'll keep it short. I just wanted to say that I hope your knee is all better and that school's good and you're having fun." I tried to sound like I meant it, because I knew that's what I should be hoping for someone I'd once loved so much.

"Actually . . . I just wanted you to know that I'm sorry, which is weird because you're the one who cheated on me, right?" I laughed as if I was making a joke, even though Luke knew me well enough to tell that it wasn't real. "I'm sorry that I didn't give you a chance to explain what happened with Becca. But even more than that, I'm sorry you couldn't tell me what happened while I was gone. You were willing to listen and try to understand when I screwed up, and I wished I had the opportunity to do the same for you. I'm not saying I wouldn't have been angry and hurt, but I'd like to think I would've listened and realized we can both make mistakes that we regret. And it doesn't mean we're bad people or that we'd do it again if we had the chance, it just means we made a couple of awful choices. I don't know why it matters that

I'm telling you this, but it does. To me, at least. So, that's all. I'm sorry everything got screwed up. And don't hate me too much. That's it. Well, that and goo . . ." Before I could finish saying good-bye, a beep cut me off. I'd used up all my time.

I really didn't know if Luke would bother listening or if he'd delete my message without even taking the time to hear what I had to say. I wished it didn't matter. I wished that just telling him how I felt would somehow free me—untangle the knots that still tied my thoughts to him, still bound up my heart.

Deep breaths, I told myself, holding the quiet phone against my chest as I slowly inhaled and exhaled.

The phone suddenly vibrated and I looked down at the screen, half expecting to see Luke's number. But it was Kaitlin—*My ID on my dresser?*

I went over to check and texted—*Found it.*

Bring to campus center? she texted back.

Give me 10, taking shower.

Maybe Kaitlin was right. Not about calling Nolan to help me get over Luke, I wasn't going to do that. I would touch base with him, but not because I needed Nolan to make myself feel better. It would just be nice to have a friend nearby who was starting over, just like me.

No, Kaitlin was right but about doing something to move on.

My mom always said there's not much a hot shower and clean hair can't help, and as much as I thought her theories always conveniently involved better hygiene, I had to admit I was glad she'd sent me to school with four different body washes to choose from.

I wanted to stay under the spray of hot water as long as possible, but I didn't want to leave Kaitlin hanging. I quickly washed my hair, foregoing the conditioner, rinsed myself down with just enough Summer Breeze body wash to remove the lingering effects of six hours on a bus, and ran back to my room to get dressed.

After jumping into a pair of sweats and a T-shirt, I grabbed Kaitlin's ID and threw open the door, where I ran right into the body standing in the hallway.

"Here it is!" I thrust the ID at Kaitlin and hoped she wouldn't kill me for taking too long.

Only it wasn't Kaitlin.

"Hi."

Luke. He was standing in front of my doorway, his hands stuffed into the pockets of his jeans.

"Hi," I practically whispered back. It was all I could to stop myself from reaching out to touch him even though it was instinctual, innate, a sensation so deeply woven into me that I didn't know how to stop it.

But Luke hung back in the hall, keeping a safe distance between us.

"I got your message," he told me.

My chest contracted, as if the air in my lungs refused to move until it heard what he would say next.

"It was nice to hear your voice," he added, and I could swear I saw a brief smile settle across his lips before it dissolved.

I breathed in deeply, forcing the invisible weight off my chest. This wasn't making any sense. Why was he here?

"But I just called, like, ten minutes ago."

"I listened to it in the street. Downstairs."

It took me a moment to understand what he meant, but then I got it. He was here. Even before I called and rambled on thinking I'd never hear from him again, Luke was here.

He was so close and yet those few feet between us seemed like a chasm that was almost impossible to cross.

"Do you want to come in?" I asked, but I didn't move aside to make room for him. All I wanted to do was stand there with him, recognizing all the details that I still knew by heart.

Luke didn't answer, and I actually believed he might walk away—that he'd come here, but now that we were face to face, he didn't want to get any closer. "Why don't we go for a walk instead?" he suggested.

I couldn't answer as I swallowed the idea that he didn't want to move toward me.

With my back turned to him so he couldn't see my face, I finally said, "Sure, just give me a minute."

Luke didn't follow me into my room, where I took a book from the bottom of my nightstand drawer and placed it on her bed with Kaitlin's ID. Then I texted her *Luke's here.* I knew she'd understand.

Back in the hallway, I closed the door behind me and followed Luke down the hallway toward the stairs. He never turned around to look at me, and he didn't speak.

When we passed through the lobby, I moved next to Luke and led him along the sidewalk, not knowing where I was taking him until I realized we were heading toward the pond. It was early and campus was so quiet. We hadn't been together since that hot, humid night at the ferry, which felt so far removed from the crisp morning air and crimson leaves now littering the sidewalk. The trees overhead formed a canopy of autumn colors, so different from the lush emerald green trees in the marina's parking lot but no less beautiful.

"You were there yesterday," Luke said.

I nodded. "How'd you know?"

Luke took out his phone and showed me a text. It was a photo of an almost-empty Friendly's parking lot, and below it were the words *She waited*. I glanced at the top of the screen and saw the sender's name. TJ. He must have driven by the parking lot on his way home and taken the picture.

"I didn't ask him to send that," I told Luke.

He put the phone back into his pocket. "I was pretty sure you didn't."

"But you came here anyway?"

"I gave a guy on the lacrosse team twenty bucks to let me take his car and promised I'd return it full of gas."

"I could help you pump that, if you'd like," I joked, and he gave me a brief, polite smile.

"I thought about turning around. I had no idea what I was going to say to you when I got here. I sat in the car for an hour. I can't tell you how many times I put the key in the ignition and almost took off."

"I'm glad you didn't." I watched Luke's face to see if he was glad, too, but I couldn't tell.

"I was just about to leave, and then I got your voicemail."

"Why didn't you answer when I called?"

"Like I said, I didn't know what I wanted to say to you."

"And now you do?"

Luke let out a small laugh. "No, not really."

"Then maybe I should start."

Luke stopped walking and sat down on a wrought iron bench overlooking the pond.

268

I took the seat beside him. I left enough space between us so that our legs didn't touch but I could still smell the scent of coconut from his shampoo. "I'm sorry. I made a mistake."

"You made a choice, Emily." Luke was quick to respond, almost as if he'd prepared for this exact conversation.

"Maybe sometimes they're the same thing," I suggested.

Luke reached down and picked up a parched leaf, its edges curling up into themselves. He twirled the long stem between his fingers as he spoke. "You wanted to hurt me with Nolan. You didn't know I'd see you do it, but I know you, Emily. You went *out of your way* to hurt me. *On purpose.*"

"It was stupid. I thought if I did something to hurt you back, then we'd be even, that what you did wouldn't hurt so badly."

"See, that's the thing, Emily. This wasn't some game where we keep score."

"I know that now, but at the time, I just wanted know I could make you feel as horrible as I felt."

"Well, I guess you succeeded."

"I wish I hadn't."

Luke nodded at the ground. "Me, too."

Maybe how a relationship starts, in some way, also destines how it ends. Maybe the way Luke and I began—with agendas and rules and motives and untruths—meant we could never end up any other way.

As much as I wished we could magically erase everything that had happened over the summer, I knew it wasn't that easy.

Luke was here, but I think we both knew that this was the end. We had nowhere to go, nothing to salvage from who Emily and Luke were before. There was so much between us, and yet the complexity of our relationship was what kept us together and then drove us apart. This was the period at the end of our story. The end.

The end used to scare me. The finality of it, how you could never go back to what you knew, what made you feel safe. It wasn't just scary, it was sad. It was like watching the people and places you love in a rearview mirror as you pull away, the memories of everything you shared diminishing the further away you get, growing smaller and blurrier until you're so far away they fade completely.

But endings also made room for beginnings. And that was when you got to start over.

I held out my hand to Luke. "Hi, I'm Emily. I'm not perfect, and I probably won't ever be, but I'm trying to learn from my mistakes."

Luke hesitated, and my outstretched hand lingered, alone, in the space between us.

Instead of pulling it back, I went on.

"I can tie twenty different types of nautical knots, my quads are looking pretty good from biking more than two hundred fifty miles this summer, and sometimes I try too hard to make things exactly like I think they should be because I'm scared of what will happen if they aren't."

Still, Luke avoided my hand.

I thought I saw a small smile beginning to make its way across Luke's lips, which made me charge on even though all I wanted to do was move my hand closer to him and lay it on his chest to feel his heart beating—let it travel up to his neck until I could feel the two days' worth of stubble on his cheeks.

"I can be silly and serious, quiet and loud, confused and still absolutely one hundred percent sure of myself even when I shouldn't be. Also, I can get a five on an AP English exam, but I really shouldn't attempt to write my own how-to books. Ever."

This time, he really did smile. "Is that everything I need to know?"

"There's one more thing," I told him. "I think I've finally figured out that I can't keep trying to change how something started, but I'm hoping I can start over and change how something ends."

Luke set the leaf down on the bench and reached for my hand, his palm warm against mine as he shook it. "Well, it's nice to meet you, Emily. I'm Luke. I'm the guy who thinks you're nuts. And I'm also the guy who thinks he still loves you."

I drew my hand away his Luke's and touched my fingers to my lips, feeling the heat of heat of his skin, warm like our first kiss. "I can't believe you're really here."

Luke nodded. "I'm really here."

"What now?" I asked.

"Well, I don't normally do this with someone I've just met, but how about we—"

"I think I'd like that." I grabbed Luke's hand and stood up. It didn't matter what he was about to suggest, my answer was yes.

Instead of standing, Luke sat back on the bench and looked at me. "You know, for two people who just met, it feels like we've known each other forever."

"Funny how that can happen."

The thing is, he was right. We knew the best and worst of one another, and yet we didn't know anything. There were new things I wanted to tell him, about my classes, about TJ appearing in the parking lot after Luke didn't show, and about Kaitlin, who was going to come back from the campus center looking for her ID and find a leather-bound journal on her bed with a bunch of blank pages waiting for her tips on long-distance relationships. She was way better at it than I was.

But I was in no rush. We weren't on a clock. We could take our time, without any guarantees or promises that we might not be able to keep, because we weren't the people we were when we first met, or the people we were when we first ended. Every day we were together or apart, we'd change a little—morph into new people who could be different and yet still feel the same about each other.

It's not easy, and there are no assurances that it will work out. When you're in a relationship, sometimes cracks appear, and, instead of working together to fix them, we begin to fill them with words and actions that push us further apart. So many things can go wrong, so many things can change, but at the end of the day, we love who we love. As long as that didn't change, maybe Luke and I had a chance.

Read on for a sneak peek at
When We Were Summer, Jenny O'Connell's first book in the
Island Summer Series!

Available now in bookstores everywhere.

chapter one

I closed my eyes and inhaled just long enough to recognize the first sign of summer. Luckily, I opened them again in time to see the four-way stop ahead. But as I pressed my foot on the brake and came to a stop at the intersection, I inhaled again, leaning my head out the open window. I knew that scent even before I could see where it was coming from. The smell of summer. Skunk.

I glanced at the clock on the dashboard: 8:49. Mona's ferry would be arriving in eleven minutes. Almost ten months of waiting and I had just eleven minutes to go.

After looking both ways, I dropped my foot on the gas pedal and headed toward the ferry. Even without spotting the skunk, the slight burning in my nose told me I was getting closer, until there it was, pushed just off the road toward the bike path. Mona always complained when I lowered the car window at the first whiff of skunk. She'd crinkle up her nose and then pinch it shut, her index finger self-consciously rubbing the bridge of her nose and the invisible bump that wasn't noticed by anyone but her. Still, I always kept the window down and breathed deep, even knowing how much it bugged her, because eventually she'd always end up laughing, a nasally laugh that turned into a snort when she finally unpinched her nose.

But now, I avoided looking at the black-and-white mound next to the bike path and instead looked straight ahead at the sign announcing I'd entered Vineyard Haven.

It was near the end of June, and a Sunday, which meant there would be two types of cars at the ferry—the tourists leaving the island after a week's vacation, and the tourists arriving. The thing is, if it weren't for the fact that they were facing different directions, you probably wouldn't be able to tell which was which. But as someone who has lived on the island her entire life, I could tell. It wasn't the stuff they packed in their cars, because coming or going, the SUVs and sedans were layered to the roof with duffel bags, pillows, beach chairs, and boogie boards. If they were really ambitious, and unwilling to trade their expensive ten-speeds with cushy leather seats and spindly rearview mirrors for an on-island rental, there were always the bike racks hanging off the backs of trunks, wheel spokes slowly turning as they caught the breeze off the harbor. And it wasn't their license plates, because just about every other car was clearly labeled "tourist"—Connecticut, New York, New Jersey, and even a few Pennsylvanias tossed in for good measure. No, it was the difference between the shiny, sparkling cars with their polished hubcaps, and the cars coated with dirt and sand, their once gleaming exteriors dusted on-island like powdered donuts.

I made the left onto Water Street, following a BMW with WASH ME handwritten in block letters in the layer of dirt on the bumper. I patiently waited for the cars ahead of me to pull into the Steamship Authority parking lot and line up single file between the painted rows so they could board the ferry. Then I veered left and pulled Lexi's car into the row of spaces for people like me.

My sister knew I'd wanted to meet Mona at the ferry, and since she was planning to be at the deli early to let in the last of the contractors, she'd offered me her car. Even though July Fourth was almost two weeks away, which meant the worst of the summer traffic hadn't even started, I left the house early. Not as early as my parents and Lexi and Bart, who just *had* to be at the deli by seven, but early by a seventeen-year-old's standards, and *especially* early for someone whose last day it was to sleep late.

Mona's ferry wasn't in sight yet, so I walked to the edge of the water, where waiting families shared overpriced muffins from the Black Dog. They were all there, the Vineyard vacationers you saw in travel brochures and websites. There was the little boy who'd undoubtedly whined until his mom purchased the stuffed black lab puppy now clutched under his arm. His brother with the shark-tooth necklace. The girl with the rope bracelet. A mom in Lily Pulitzer Capri pants.

They might as well have been wearing the same T-shirts—I WENT TO MARTHA'S VINEYARD AND ALL I GOT WAS EVERYTHING I ASKED FOR.

"Kendra!"

I turned toward the voice calling my name and recognized Ryan Patten down by the gazebo. He waved and started walking toward me. When you lived on the island, you didn't really expect to see people you knew at the ferry this time of year. Maybe in November when you were heading off-island to Target, or in March when everyone was going stir-crazy from the long, gray winter, but for three months during the summer the ferry was for strangers.

"What are you doing here?" Ryan asked, pulling a leash, and a very large dog, behind him.

"Mona's on the nine o'clock." I pointed to the golden retriever sniffing the grass and flicking his tail against Ryan's leg. "Who's that?"

"Dutch. He's along for the ride. My cousins and aunt and uncle are coming for a visit. You know how it is."

I nodded as if I did, but I didn't. Nobody in my family ever moved off the island. "So, what are you doing this summer?"

"Renting bikes at Island Wheels. What about you?" Dutch pulled at his leash and I followed along as Ryan let him continue sniffing the trail of whatever he thought he'd found.

"Working at the Willow Inn. We start tomorrow."

"We?"

"Me and Mona," I told Ryan, lowering my voice as if there was any chance she could hear me from the ferry.

I hadn't told her yet. The job was my surprise. We'd always talked about working at one of the inns for a summer. It met all three of our criteria. One, no lines. The idea of scooping ice cream while a line of exhausted parents and their demanding kids impatiently shouted out orders for Oreo cookie frappés wasn't exactly appealing, no matter how much free ice cream you could eat. Two, no retail (see number one, but replace pissy parents and their whiny kids with pissy women who don't understand why there are no more size 6 Bermuda shorts on the rack). And three, no nights. Serving breakfast at the Willow Inn was perfect. Technically, there could be times when people would be anxiously waiting for their morning coffees, but with only nineteen rooms, it wasn't like there'd be a line for the blueberry muffins. Besides, we'd always figured people were still optimistic that early in the morning, and therefore nicer to be around. By the end of the day they'd be sunburned, cranky from spending twenty minutes in traffic on Main Street, and downright rude after driving around for an hour, looking for a parking space, only to discover a ticket on their windshield when they returned. The Willow didn't serve dinner, just breakfast and picnic lunches for guests. Spend three minutes with a hostess trying to placate families who have been waiting over an hour for a dinner table, and you'd understand why.

Luckily, the guy who sold Lexi the cash register for the deli knew someone who knew the new owner of the Willow, and two weeks after Lexi placed an order for the Sam4s register with integrated credit card capabilities, I had secured jobs for Mona and me.

"Does Kevin know she's coming back?" Ryan asked.

I shrugged. "I don't know. She e-mailed me with her ferry time and that was it."

Mona hadn't seen Kevin since she left, that I did know. She only came back to the island once after she moved, last October for her grandfather's funeral, and I'm sure I would have known if Kevin had gone to Boston to visit her. Kevin went out with Melissa Madsen for a few months this winter, but I was still sort of hoping they'd get back together when Mona returned, and then everything would be just like it was before she left. At least for the summer.

"It's here." Ryan pointed past the houses hugging the shores of the harbor and I could see the ferry come into view, white peaks of water cresting on either side of the bow as it made its way toward us.

"Hungry?" Ryan asked, and then pointed to the hand I had clutched against my stomach.

What could I say? That seeing the ferry coming toward us, the ferry with my best friend on it, had turned my stomach upside down? That all of a sudden the idea of seeing Mona again made me nervous because I didn't know what to expect?

"Yeah," I lied, and rubbed my stomach as if all I needed was a good bowl of cereal. "Starving."

We started walking toward the dock. "Where are you meeting your cousins?" I asked.

"Where they walk off. They got to Woods Hole late and missed their ferry, again. Couldn't get another reservation for the car until Monday, so they'll have to go over tomorrow and pick it up."

Ryan began telling me how his cousins missed their ferry every year, but even though I nodded in all the right places as if I was listening, all I really heard was the ferry engine revving loudly as it slid into place against the dock.

"You know what I mean?" Ryan finished. He looked to me for a response.

"Exactly," I answered, even though I had no idea what I was agreeing to.

We stood there with Dutch and watched as the front door to the boat's belly opened up to expose rows of idling cars. Once the guys working the controls for the ramp gave them the go-ahead, the cars slowly moved across the steel incline, forming a steady, orderly procession as they took turns driving off the boat and past the ferry building before accelerating in the direction of their rental house or relative's house or, in Mona's case, their new stepfather's summer estate.

I stood on my tiptoes trying to see if I could spot Malcolm's black Range Rover inside. Last summer, when Malcolm married Izzy in the backyard of his house overlooking South Beach, Mona and I wrote "Just Married" along the side of the car with a bar of Ivory soap. The soap was from Mona's grandfather's house. We couldn't find a bar in Malcolm's six-bedroom summer "cottage," where every bathroom had a bottle of L'Occitane almond shea soap on the sink and a matching bottle of body wash in the shower but not a bar of

Ivory soap in the whole place. L'Occitane seemed to be the soap of choice in Malcolm's house, and it smelled amazing. It was actually the second thing I noticed the first time I went to Malcolm's house with Mona. The smell. It wasn't sweet like the air fresheners my mother seemed to have inserted into every electrical outlet in our house. And it wasn't comforting, like the lavender sachets the Willow Inn placed on the guests' pillows every night. The only way I could describe it was manly, like a combination of fresh-cut grass, seawater, and limes. Even though Malcolm had hired an interior designer from Vineyard Haven to decorate his summer home, it was definitely a house that had been occupied by a man. Malcolm didn't have any kids, even though Izzy told Mona he was married briefly to his college sweetheart. By the time Malcolm met Izzy, he'd been divorced for way longer than he was married, which is why the *first* thing I noticed about Malcolm's house was that it was way too big for a single guy with no kids.

"There are my cousins." Ryan nudged me and waved to a family walking toward us. "I guess this is it. Tell Henry I said hi and have fun with Mona."

"I will," I told him, realizing I'd almost forgotten about Mona's twin brother.

And that's when I saw it, the shiny black hood making its way out of the ferry doors and down the ramp. The back passenger window was open and I waited for Mona to poke her head out and scream my name. Instead I watched as Henry waved in my direction.

I waved back and walked toward the car, now pulling up against the curb to let the cars behind it pass by.

"Kendra!" Mona jumped out and ran toward me, her arms outstretched like in those slow-motion sequences in the movies. When she reached me, the force of her hug knocked me backward, quite a feat for someone who was at least four inches shorter, and fifteen pounds lighter, than me.

"You look so great," she told me, giving me one last squeeze before taking my hand and pulling me toward the car. "Mom, look at her, she looks exactly the same!"

Well, not exactly the same—my hair was longer and not as blonde as when Mona left the island last summer, but I didn't point that out. Instead I let her tow me toward the Land Rover.

"Kennie!" Izzy reached through the open passenger-side window and held her arms out.

I leaned in and let her hug me. "Hi, Malcolm," I said over Izzy's shoulder.

Malcolm smiled at me. "Hello, Kennie."

"I know you girls have a lot of catching up to do. So don't let us stop you. Are you going with Kennie?" Izzy asked Mona.

"Yeah," I answered before Mona could even get a word out. "I can take you to the house, Lexi let me borrow her car."

"Great." Mona reached into the backseat and grabbed her purse with one hand and my elbow with the other. "Let's go."